What Reviewer's Say About J

The Celaeno Series

"...captivating, well-written stories in the fantasy genre that are built around women's struggles against themselves, one another, society, and nature." – *WomanSpace Magazine*

"In *Rangers at Roadsend* Fletcher not only gives us powerful characters, but she surprises us with an unexpected ending to the murder conspiracy plot, pushing the story in one direction only to have that direction reversed more than once. This is one thrill ride the reader will not want to get off." – *Independent Gay Writer*

"…compelling narrative, plot twists, intense action sequences, vivid scenery…" – *Midwest Book Review*

"*The Walls of Westernfort* is not only a highly engaging and fast-paced adventure novel, it provides the reader with an interesting framework for examining the same questions of loyalty, faith, family and love." – *Midwest Book Review*

"*The Walls of Westernfort* is…a true delight. Bold, well-developed characters hold your interest from the beginning and keep you turning the pages. The main plot twists and turns until the very end. The sub-plot involves likeable women who seem destined not to be together." – *MegaScene*

The Lyremouth Chronicles

"*The Exile and the Sorcerer* is a mesmerizing read, a tour-de-force packed with adventure, ordeals, complex twists and turns, and the internal introspection of appealing characters. The author writes effortlessly, handling the size and scope of the book with ease. Not since the fantasy works of Elizabeth Moon and Lynn Flewelling have I been so thoroughly engrossed in a tale. This is knockout fiction, tantalizingly told, and beautifully packaged." – *Midwest Book Review*

Shadow of the Knife

by

Jane Fletcher

BOLD STROKES BOOKS

2008

SHADOW OF THE KNIFE

ISBN10: 1-60282-008-2
ISBN13: 978-1-60282-008-1

This Trade Paperback Is Published By
Bold Strokes Books, Inc.,
New York, USA

First Edition, March 2008

Credits
Editors: Cindy Cresap and Stacia Seaman
Production Design: J. B. Greystone
Cover Image: Tobias Brenner (http://www.tobiasbrenner.de/)
Cover Design: J. B. Greystone

By the Author

The Celaeno Series

The Walls of Westernfort

Rangers at Roadsend

The Temple at Landfall

Dynasty of Rogues

The Lyremouth Chronicles

The Exile and the Sorcerer Book One

The Traitor and the Chalice Book Two

The Empress and the Acolyte Book Three

Acknowledgments

This is the place where authors traditionally include lots of thank you's, in an attempt to give the impression that they are not sad, antisocial individuals who spend all their time alone, hunched over a keyboard and never going out, but that the author does, in fact, have many friends. So, in keeping with this tradition, I would like to thank (in alphabetical order):

Aries for help with the policing;
Cindy for help in hiding my perversions;
Connie for sorting out my liaisons;
Jac for help with the sheep;
Jo for help with the sex;
Joanie for asking some good questions;
Julie for laying me out;
Mary for help with the horses;
Paula for the rugby (nothing to do with the book, but still very much appreciated);
Stacia for knowing where to put the commas;
the Thudders for some useful words (mostly clean ones);
Tobi for the cover;
Ze for giving my end the thumbs up;
and finally Rad for everything else.

DEDICATION

To my mother

Joan Millicent Fletcher

12/Dec/1925 - 24/Feb/2007

a thoroughly pleasant woman

Author's Note On Timekeeping

Days on this planet are approximately 25.3 Earth hours in length. The original colonists, in the words of Peter McKay, followed "the standard UNSA practice of botching a compromise between decimalization and divisions that feels right. There will be 20 hours in a day, 100 minutes in an hour, and 50 seconds in a minute."

Therefore:

1 planetary hour = 1.265 Earth hours
1 planetary minute = 0.759 Earth minutes
1 planetary second = 0.911 Earth seconds

Although nobody now on the planet has a watch accurate enough to measure seconds, and even *minute* is a fairly loosely used term.

Midday is at 10 o'clock, and midnight is 20 o'clock. In July, when this story starts, sunrise is shortly before 4 o'clock, and sunset just after 16 o'clock.

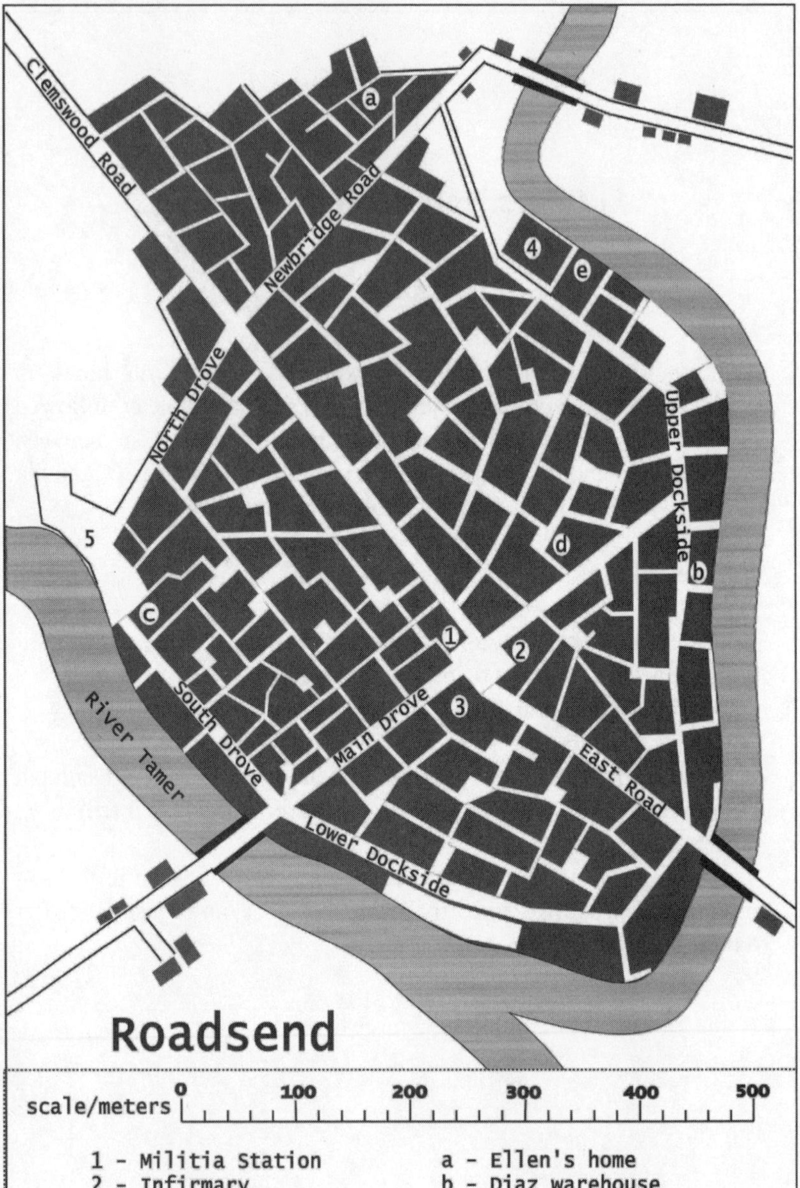
Roadsend
Clemswood Road
Newbridge Road
North Drove
Upper Dockside
South Drove
Main Drove
East Road
Lower Dockside
River Tamer
a
b
c
d
e
1
2
3
4
5
scale/meters
0
100
200
300
400
500
1 - Militia Station
2 - Infirmary
3 - Town Hall
4 - Ranger Barracks
5 - Sheep Docks
a - Ellen's home
b - Diaz warehouse
c - the Twisted Crook
d - the Three Barrels
e - the White Swan

Part One

Robbery With Violence

9 July 519

Chapter One—Black and White

The crew of the *Alisha-Marie* cast off its moorings and the barge moved away from the quay, slowly picking up speed as the current took it downriver, bound for the city of Landfall. As it drifted into the dusk, the skipper's shouted commands carried softly on the warm evening air, a counterpart to the bleating of sheep from the surrounding hills. Eventually the shouts faded in the distance, leaving only the sheep.

In her black Militia uniform, Rookie Ellen Mittal rested her forearms on a rail, listening to the familiar sounds of her birth-town. The working day was coming to a close and the pens were empty. Around her, activity on the sheep docks was quieting, while that in the nearby Twisted Crook Tavern was rising. The voices from its taproom were the softest rumble, though it would be a rare night in Roadsend if they stayed that way.

"Having a nice time, are you? Gawking at nothing. How many sheep have to get stolen before you clowns stop farting around and put some effort into catching the scum who took them?"

The harsh voice jolted Ellen back to her surroundings. Jean Tulagi, owner of South Hollow Ranch, was glaring down at her from horseback.

"We've done everything we can."

"Well, since you've done squat, I guess it proves the Militia are even more frigging useless than they say." Tulagi urged her horse an intimidating step closer. "And supposing they do it again this year? How long do you think we can take these losses?"

"Lieutenant Cohen says it won't be—"

"Your lieutenant has her head so far up her own ass she can't tell whether it's day or night. I wouldn't trust her to—"

A new voice cut in. "If you have any concerns about Lieutenant Cohen's competence, it would be more productive to make a formal complaint to a higher officer, rather than bitching about it in the street to a rookie."

Ellen looked over her shoulder with gratitude. Sergeant Christine Sanchez had joined them and had clearly decided to take charge. Tulagi glared at the new arrival for a few seconds before steering her horse away without another word.

"Thanks, Sarge."

Sanchez merely pursed her lips as she watched the farmer ride off, and then shifted her gaze to Ellen. "Come on. There doesn't look to be too much illegal activity going on here. Let's carry on with the patrol."

Sanchez left the dockside, heading down a dogleg alley squeezed between the backs of warehouses. Her footsteps slipped into the firm, unhurried pace of Militiawomen pounding the beat, the rhythm unbroken even when she "shook hands" with the doors she passed, checking that none had been left unlocked.

Ellen fell in beside her. "Tulagi seemed pretty angry."

"Wouldn't you be, in her place?"

"Farmers always blame the Militia for their problems."

"Doesn't mean it's always unjustified."

Ellen frowned. Even though the sergeant had backed her up on the docks, it sounded as if Sanchez had more sympathy with Tulagi. Ellen tried to take an unbiased view. "I know we didn't get her sheep back for her."

"And we didn't catch whoever did it."

"You think we ought to have done better?"

"Could we have done any worse?"

Ellen thought about the question. "Probably not, Sarge."

"And everyone knows we've given up on it."

"But no new sheep have gone missing for months."

"So that's supposed to be an end to it?"

"Well, Tulagi was worried the thieves will strike again this year."

"She's not the only one."

"Lieutenant Cohen is sure the gang have moved on."

Sanchez stopped and swung to face Ellen. "And what do you think?"

In the fading light, Sanchez's face was twisted in a taunting pout that might have masked either irritation or humor, or maybe a combination of the two. She was in her late twenties, shrewd, firm, and capable. Everyone knew that she was the one who organized the day-to-day running of the Roadsend Militia, as well as making all operational decisions, except for occasions when Lieutenant Cohen wanted to make a show of being in command.

The series of thefts the previous autumn had been one of those occasions. Lieutenant Cohen had stepped in and taken over, issuing a series of orders that had made progressively less sense to Ellen. Yet it was hardly appropriate for a rookie to criticize a senior officer.

"I'm sure the lieutenant has her reasons for thinking what she does."

"I'm sure she does too. Everyone always has her reasons. It's a question of whether those reasons make sense to anyone else."

"You think Lieutenant Cohen is wrong?"

"I didn't say that."

Ellen chewed her lip. Maybe Sanchez had not said it in so many words, but the implication was there. "Lieutenant Cohen is the one with all the information. Maybe she knows things we don't, and that's why she set our priorities like she did."

"And that's what you honestly think?"

"Does it matter what I think, Sarge? Our duty is to obey orders."

"Like it says in the rule book, where it's all written down in black and white?" Sanchez shook her head ruefully. "How about our oath to uphold the law?"

"But isn't upholding the law all about obeying rules? I'm sure Lieutenant Cohen has it covered."

"Oh to be seventeen again and untouched by cynicism!"

"I'm nearly eighteen."

Sanchez threw back her head and laughed, then patted Ellen's shoulder. "It's okay. I used to be as naïve as you once. But take it from me, life can't be reduced to simple black and white." She resumed walking.

Ellen followed, feeling that she was neither as green nor as foolish as Sanchez had implied. Of course she knew the situation was not right, but what could she do other than hope for the best and follow her commanding officer's orders to the letter?

At the end of the alley, they emerged onto Catsfield Road and turned toward the center of town. The streets were almost deserted and the few folk on view were all behaving in an exemplary law-abiding fashion.

"So what do you think about the stolen sheep, Sarge?" Ellen had spent the previous three minutes wondering if it was a breach of protocol to ask, but her curiosity had won out.

"What do I think?" Sanchez pursed her lips. "I think even if you allow for exaggeration and farmers making use of the fuss to swipe a few sheep from their neighbors, it's still over five hundred gone missing. We've never had anything close to that number of thefts before. And stealing five hundred sheep is one thing, being able to unload so many for a profit is quite another. But I can't see a gang going to the bother of stealing all those sheep just to let most wander off into the Wildlands."

"You think there's some other explanation? They weren't stolen at all?"

"No. I think they were stolen by someone who works on a different scale to what we're used to. Someone with a whole organization to call on. When I add it all up, I'm worried the trouble in Eastford has spread out here."

"Oh."

Over the previous months, the same idea had niggled at Ellen, but she had fought to dismiss her fears, telling herself that she did not know enough to understand what was really going on. Surely if there were reasonable grounds to think the Eastford gang might be involved, Lieutenant Cohen would have notified central command at once and asked for extra resources, rather than downplaying the thefts as she had. Cohen had decades more experience than any rookie. Yet now Sergeant Sanchez was also suggesting it as a real possibility. Ellen walked on in silence, mulling over the implications. It could not be true—could it?

They crossed a side street. The slow, deliberate pace gave Ellen plenty of time to look down it, but her thoughts were preoccupied and they had walked on another ten meters before she registered the face she had seen. Ellen came to an uncertain halt.

"Er...Sarge."

Sanchez looked back. "Yes?"

"You know you were saying about trouble from Eastford?"

"And?"

"I think some of it's here already. Except it was ours to start with."

"What?"

"Down that last street, I think I saw Ade Eriksen."

"Damn. Too much to hope that we'd heard the last of our little Adeola." Sanchez sucked a sharp breath between her teeth. "What was she doing?"

"Just standing there."

"Loitering?"

"Sort of."

"Well, let's go and say hello, and make sure she knows we remember her."

They backtracked to the junction. Ade was in the same spot as before, leaning against a wall with her arms crossed. An alleyway opened directly behind her. Her pose was casual, as if she was just passing the time of day by propping up the wall, but at the sight of the advancing black uniforms, her manner changed. She pushed away from the brickwork and took a cautious backward step, retreating. Then she spun and dived into the alleyway, disappearing from view.

"She's keeping lookout for someone." Sanchez was slipping her heavy wooden baton free from her belt even as she started in pursuit.

Ellen chased after. It was a sure bet that whoever Adeola Eriksen was keeping lookout for was engaged in something illegal. Ellen had lived in Roadsend all her life and knew every pathway. The alley Ade had fled down was a dozen meters long, leading to a small courtyard where carts were unloaded. This section of town was mainly commercial, and a warehouse robbery the most likely crime. However, as soon as she left the main street, Ellen heard groans and the thud of blows echoing from up ahead, and then Ade shouted out, "Blackshirts."

As they raced along the alley, the sound of Militia boots ricocheted off the brick walls like whip cracks. Ellen burst into the open a step behind Sanchez. In the center of the courtyard stood a small intertwined knot of figures—three women, assaulting a fourth. Ade skidded to a stop beside them.

At the arrival of the Militiawomen, the three attackers released their grip on the victim, who staggered away, bent double and whimpering. One of the hoodlums turned and fled, heading for an exit on the opposite side of the courtyard. Ellen expected the others to follow, but instead with Ade, they stood their ground, clearly ready to fight.

If the resolute response caught Sanchez by surprise, she reacted quickly, swinging her baton at the nearest woman, forcing the thug to duck. Before she had time to think, Ellen found herself face-to-face with another. The stocky woman was in her thirties, with a scar running down her chin and a nose that looked as if it had been broken on more than one occasion. Ellen was sure she was not a resident of Roadsend. The face was not one that could easily be forgotten.

The last of the daylight caught the gray sheen of metal across the woman's knuckles as her fist swung for Ellen's jaw. Ellen brought her baton across defensively. The crack of wood on bone drew a yelp of pain. The baton had made sharp contact with the woman's wrist, knocking her arm aside. Ellen followed up with a solid backswing into her opponent's stomach. The thug grunted as the air was thumped from her lungs and she curled forward, falling. Ellen completed the job by taking her feet from under her with a kick. The woman landed on the ground hard and made no immediate attempt to get up.

Ellen glanced across the courtyard, hesitating between securing the prisoner and going to help Sanchez. Despite being outnumbered two to one, the experienced sergeant had Ade in retreat. Ade's accomplice also looked to be withdrawing from the fight, but then shifted to the side and slipped swiftly through the shadows to a position behind Sanchez. The woman darted forward and a knife flashed out, thrusting for Sanchez's back. The attack took only an instant, giving no time for Ellen to shout a warning. The blade plunged into the black Militia jerkin.

Sanchez spun around, wrenching the hilt from the woman's hand. She lifted her baton and then froze. Her expression was a surprised frown. Clearly she realized that something significant had happened, but she looked more confused than alarmed. Then her right knee buckled, sending her staggering sideways. The thug moved forward, fists raised, for another attack.

Ellen charged across the courtyard, hoisting her baton. The sound of footsteps must have alerted the woman, because she ducked aside at the last moment. Yet she was too slow to avoid the blow completely. Ellen's heavy baton connected with the woman's collarbone to the unmistakable sound of cracking.

Ellen's momentum carried her on. Her shoulder drove into her target's back, catapulting the woman off her feet. She crashed to the ground and rolled over, squealing while trying to protect her broken shoulder, clearly no longer a threat. Ellen looked around. Ade and the other hoodlum had gone.

Nearby, Sanchez was on all fours, head sagging. As Ellen watched, the sergeant's arms gave way and she slumped to the ground. Ellen dropped to her knees beside her. Rivulets of blood were trickling between the cobblestones. Ellen stripped off her own jacket to press around the protruding knife hilt and stanch the flow.

The sound of movement made Ellen look up. Ade had returned, but only to help away her accomplice with the broken collarbone. The fight was over. In a dim corner of the courtyard, the initial assault victim had recovered sufficiently to stand upright, but was swaying like someone drunk. Dark blood stained the front of her clothes. More was smeared across her face. Despite the gloom and the blood, Ellen recognized her: Sally Husmann, the owner of a warehouse on Lower Dockside.

"Get help," Ellen shouted.

Husmann took a step backward. She did not look in Ellen's direction, showing no awareness that the Militiawomen were even there.

"The sergeant needs help. She's losing blood."

Again there was no answer. Sally Husmann's eyes were fixed on the departing hoodlums. She retreated another step and then turned as if about to flee in the opposite direction.

"Husmann, listen to me!"

The name drew a response. Husmann glanced back at Ellen, and then to the exit her assailants had left by, although they were no longer in sight. Her eyes returned to the blood-covered officer on the ground and she froze as if noticing Sanchez's condition for the first time. For the space of five heartbeats she simply stared, wide-eyed.

"Don't just stand there. Go and get help." Ellen heard her voice breaking in panic.

Husmann's expression cleared and she nodded. "I'll be back. I promise, I'll get someone." She turned and stumbled away.

Ellen heard Husmann's uneven footsteps fade down the passageway. The light in the courtyard was going, thickening the shadows. Something wet soaked into the knees of Ellen's trousers and she knew it was blood. Sanchez's eyes were open and her lips moved, trying to speak.

"Knew it...the Mad Butcher...you've—" Then all movement ceased except for a trickle of blood from Sanchez's mouth.

Tears of desperation stung Ellen's eyes. She felt so useless. Anger flared, aimed at herself and her complete lack of the healer sense. Tests during childhood had shown that she was as devoid of the psychic ability as it was possible for any woman to be.

She pressed around the knife hilt, trying to block the outpouring of life. Her hands were sticky with congealing blood. Was she helping? Ellen did not know what else she could do. She was alone and out of her depth. Sanchez's face was drained white against the black of her uniform. Black and white—and it was not simple at all.

"Hang on, Sarge. Just hang on."

❖

The main room of the Roadsend infirmary was silent. Ellen stood with her back braced against the wall, staring rigidly at the ceiling. She dared not lower her eyes. There were too many things in the room she did not want to look at. In the corner, one of the healers was tending to Sally Husmann. Not only would it be rude to watch, but the raging purple bruises and raw cuts on Husmann's body were appalling. Ellen felt nauseous enough without unsettling her stomach further.

The door straight ahead was another thing Ellen did not want to stare at. On the other side was the room where Sanchez was lying. She had still been breathing when Ellen had helped carry her in, but would she keep doing it for much longer?

Dr. Miller was the most senior healer in Roadsend, responsible not only for running the infirmary, but also for overseeing all the healers and medics in town. That she had elected to treat Sanchez personally ought to have been reassuring—the town Doctor was blessed with the psychic healer sense to a high degree and very experienced in its use. However, it implied that Dr. Miller thought the injury beyond her assistants' abilities. When she had seen the stab wound and the blood bubbling between Sanchez's lips, her face had set in a grim expression that gave little grounds for confidence.

Most of all, Ellen did not want to look at her own hands. She had rinsed them, but she knew blood was still encrusted under her nails. She felt as if it had sunk into her skin, marking her like a tattoo, a visible sign of her shortcoming. What should she have done? If she had been less inexperienced and more alert, reacted faster, moved quicker—would she have been able to prevent the knife attack?

The sound of the street door made Ellen flinch. Corporal Terrie Rasheed and Patrolwoman Jude McCray bustled in and then stopped uncertainly, peering around until their eyes fixed on Ellen. They hurried over. Both were officially off duty and in civilian clothes.

"We heard Chris has been hurt. Where is she?" Corporal Rasheed asked.

Ellen pointed to the door. "In there."

"Is she going to be okay?"

"I don't know. It was bad. Dr. Miller didn't say anything, but..." Ellen bit her lip. "We've just got to pray."

"What happened?"

"We were on patrol. We came across a gang beating up Sally Husmann. I thought they'd run when they saw us, but they didn't. We ended up in a fight and one of them stabbed Sarge."

This was the point that Ellen could not come to terms with, making her doubt her own memory. Criminals ran from the Militia. It was the way things were. In order for a law-breaker to fight back, she had to be blind drunk, or panicked, or out of her head in some way—but not with this gang. They had coolly and purposefully taken on the Militia, and had been ready to kill. The thrust of the knife might not have been entirely in cold blood, but the initial decision to fight had been.

"Who were they?"

"Don't know. I've never seen them before, except for Ade Eriksen, who was with them, acting as lookout."

"Eriksen? I thought she'd gone to Eastford."

"She's come back."

Jude McCray sighed. "That's all we need."

"How about Sally Husmann? Does she know who they were?" Rasheed continued her questions.

"We haven't had a chance to talk to her yet." Ellen nodded toward the corner where Husmann was being treated. "Lieutenant Cohen was here a few minutes ago. She's in the Militia station now, but she left me to escort Husmann over as soon as the healers let her go."

Again the street door opened. The new arrival was yet another distressing sight. Sanchez's partner, Rhonda Tomczyk, slipped in and stood defensively, as if expecting bad news to fly at her in a physical attack. Her face was twisted in dread and confusion. She showed no sign of recognizing anyone until Corporal Rasheed scuttled to her side and put a hand on her arm.

Tomczyk turned to Rasheed. "Is Chris…" Her words ended in tears.

Rasheed shifted her hand to put a supportive arm around Tomczyk and started speaking in a voice too low for Ellen to make out. Jude McCray shuffled over, clearly ready to also offer what comfort she could. The three huddled in a knot, heads together.

Ellen rubbed her palms on her legs. Both her hands and the black trousers were stained. She felt awkward. Should she go over? Would Rhonda Tomczyk want to talk to her? Would the sight of Sanchez's blood be unbearably distressing? Ellen clenched her jaw. And was her dithering due to a fear that Tomczyk would hold her responsible? Yet Ellen knew she had to say something. She was present at the attack and the last person to talk with Sanchez. She was not the one in the most pain, either physical or emotional. Hanging back was pure cowardice on her part.

However, before Ellen could summon her resolve, another sound claimed her attention. In the corner, Sally Husmann had stood, all her clothing back in place and a trace of normal color to her cheeks. She was exchanging a few words with the healer, but then glanced nervously in Ellen's direction. Her expression wavered and her eyes flitted between the three Militiawomen present, as if she were estimating her chances of running away. Yet even had Ellen been alone, fleeing would be pointless. They all knew where she lived, as well as her place of business.

Husmann plodded across to Ellen. "Lieutenant Cohen wants to talk to me?"

"Yes. I'll escort you."

"There's no point. I don't know anything."

"You still know more than us. She wants to talk to you."

Husmann's expression crumpled in panic. Clearly she did know something. Had it been a random attack or robbery there would be no reason for her reaction or her unwillingness to talk to the Militia. Ellen took a firm grip on Husmann's arm and coaxed her forward.

As they passed the huddle at the door, Ellen was caught by the anguish in Rhonda Tomczyk's eyes, and her footsteps faltered. She could not walk by without speaking.

"I'm really sorry. I did what I could. It was all so quick, but I'm sure Sarge is going to be fine. She's in—" Ellen bit back the words that were perilously close to lying. She was not sure at all, and she knew it showed on her face. Ellen turned to Corporal Rasheed. "As soon as you hear anything, can you send a message over to the station?"

Rasheed nodded sharply.

Outside, night had fallen. The stars over Roadsend were in the same constellations as ever, but Ellen could not get over the feeling that the world they shone down on had changed.

The Militia station was only a few dozen meters away, on the opposite side of the main town square from the infirmary. Word had gone out and the remaining three patrolwomen of the Roadsend Militia were gathered in the briefing room. The faces turned anxiously to Ellen when she entered, although nobody spoke. Voicing the question aloud was unnecessary.

Ellen shook her head. "Dr. Miller is still tending to her." She indicated the door of the lieutenant's office. "Is Cohen in there?"

"Yup," Penny Rambaldi answered. She raised her hand over her shoulder and rapped her knuckles on the door behind her. "Ma'am. Mittal is here with Husmann."

"Send them in."

Lieutenant Cohen was seated at her desk in the small office. The leader of the Roadsend Militia was in her mid fifties, fit and strong for her age, with a decisive manner. During her first year in the Militia, Ellen had respected Cohen and been pleased to serve under such an experienced officer. However, as the months passed, Ellen had come to realize that although Cohen's manner might appear decisive, it was due solely to her habit of barking orders, regardless of her mood. Decisions were not something that came easily to her, and once she had set her mind, changing it was impossible, regardless of what fresh information might turn up.

Cohen waved Husmann to the seat opposite. Ellen took up position in the corner. Cohen had not told her to go and she wanted to hear what Husmann had to say.

The lieutenant pushed aside the papers on her desk and then looked up. "Thank you for coming. Do you feel all right?"

Husmann gave a sharp nod in reply.

"I won't keep you long." Cohen leaned forward, resting her elbows on her desk. "Do you know the women who attacked you?"

"No."

"They hadn't been hanging around your warehouse?"

"No."

"So you'd never seen any of them before?"

"No."

Clearly Husmann was going to deny knowledge of everything, and Cohen was showing no sign of challenging her. Ellen knew she ought to keep quiet. The lieutenant was the one conducting the interview, and a rookie should not butt in without invitation, but after the trauma of the evening, she could not stop herself.

"You must have recognized Ade Eriksen."

Husmann swiveled in her chair and looked back, eyes wide in alarm. "Well, yes, her of course, but none of the rest."

Cohen glared at Ellen and raised her voice a notch. "But as I understand it, she was just keeping watch and wasn't one of the people who assaulted you."

Husmann turned back to the desk. "No...no, she wasn't. That's why I didn't mention her before."

Ellen tried to conceal her frustration. Husmann was lying, but rather than exploit her lapse to get to the truth, Cohen was giving her a hand in covering up.

The lieutenant continued. "So, can you tell us what happened?"

"I was on my way home, and I was going through the courtyard when they jumped me."

"Did they say anything?"

"No."

"Did they try to steal anything?"

"No...I don't think so."

"They were waiting for you in the courtyard?"

"Pardon?"

"I mean, they hadn't followed you?"

"Oh, no." Husmann's voice was firmer. It was, Ellen judged, the first totally honest answer she had given.

"Is there anything else you can tell us?"

"No."

Ellen could keep silent no longer. "You said you were on your way home."

Again Husmann glanced around. "Yes."

"Surely it's off your route."

"I was...ah...on my way to buy something,"

"What?"

Cohen slapped her hand angrily on her desk, reclaiming Husmann's attention. "That is hardly important. I don't think—" A knock on the door interrupted her. "What is it?"

"Ma'am, there's a messenger from the infirmary," Penny Rambaldi called from the briefing room.

"I'll see her in a second." Cohen looked at Husmann. "You can go. If you think of anything else, let us know."

Husmann scooted from her seat and was through the door almost before the lieutenant had finished speaking. Ellen was about to follow, but Cohen called her back.

"Mittal."

Ellen shut the door and stood at attention. The lieutenant's tone had been decidedly officious. "Ma'am."

"When I am interviewing someone, I do not appreciate interruptions."

"I'm sorry, ma'am. But Husmann was lying."

"In your opinion." Cohen's tone made her words a challenge and a criticism.

"Ma'am, every trader in town knows all about Adeola Eriksen—she's stolen from half of them. If Husmann was genuinely trying to help us, she'd have volunteered her name straight off. She wouldn't have needed me to prompt her for it."

Cohen looked unconvinced. "You seriously think that Husmann is trying to protect the people who attacked her?"

"I think she's so frightened of them, she won't risk upsetting them more." Ellen took a deep breath. "Before she passed out, the last thing Sergeant Sanchez said was that she thinks it's the big Eastford gang, spreading into our area. I've heard they—"

"No!" Once more, Cohen slammed her fist on her desk. "That's ridiculous. And I don't want you spreading those sort of wild rumors."

"But—"

"No buts. It's an order. You're not to say anything like that again." Cohen sucked in a deep breath through flared nostrils. "Okay. Maybe Husmann is lying. In that case, I can tell you what the truth is. Husmann is in on some illegal deal. She tried to out-cheat her associates and they took their revenge. That's why she's covering. She's as guilty as they are."

Ellen stared at Cohen in bewilderment. Husmann was an established merchant, with no criminal record, and the scenario painted did not begin to explain the hoodlums' willingness to fight and their ready use of lethal weapons. Yet a rookie could not argue with a lieutenant.

"Yes, ma'am."

"Send in Dr. Miller's messenger." Cohen nodded. "And I mean it about spreading rumors. At times like this, we need to keep calm heads."

"Yes, ma'am."

Ellen slipped from the room. One of the healers was waiting to go in. At the sight of her, any concerns over Husmann and the Eastford gang were blown away. Ellen felt her stomach knot. What did the messenger have to report? The healer's face was professionally somber, but an instant later, the smiles from the others in the briefing room registered. Clearly, they had already heard the news, and it was good.

Ellen waited until the door had shut and then turned to a beaming Penny Rambaldi. "Sarge is going to be okay?"

"Yes. Dr. Miller is sure she's going to be fine."

Ellen found herself laughing in relief. The agony of the previous hour dispersed, like mist burned off by the rising sun.

Terrie Rasheed and Jude McCray arrived soon after to join the happy gathering and give a fuller report. Sanchez's injuries included a collapsed lung. She would not be back on duty that month, but a complete recovery was promised. Ellen was called on to describe the incident again and then the informal meeting broke up.

The healer was still in with Cohen, and Ellen did not want to interrupt them, especially after already angering the lieutenant that evening. She sidled over to Corporal Rasheed. "What should I do now? There's still half an hour of my shift to go."

Rasheed ran her hands through her hair, looking unsure, but then sighed. "There ain't much patrolling going to get done tonight, and you've had a tough time too. Go on. Clear off early. If your parents have heard the news, they'll be worrying about you."

"Thanks."

Ellen stopped by her locker to drop in her equipment belt with its baton and whistle, and also her heavy leather jerkin. She paused a moment over this last item. The leather was thick, intended to offer protection in a fight. A normal penknife would not have pierced it. The hoodlum's blade must have been heavy and sharp. A weapon, not a tool—as if any more proof were needed that the gang had set out prepared and ready to commit murder.

Ellen pushed the thought away and glanced at Penny Rambaldi, who was standing nearby, also sorting through her belongings. "Corporal Rasheed told me I can go home early."

"Now there's a surprise."

The dry, sarcastic tone surprised Ellen. "Why?"

"Because you can't send a rookie out on her own. Terrie would have had to give up her own free time to puppy walk you."

"Oh." That had not occurred to Ellen, but regardless of Rasheed's reason, she was not about to complain.

The town square was now in darkness, except for moonlight splashed across the cobbles and strips of thin yellow lamplight escaping between window shutters. Ellen's family lived on the north end of town, on the far side of Newbridge Road—the wrong side of Newbridge Road in the eyes of many. Ellen had grown up with the disdain, and daydreamed of the day when promotion would give her the salary to move her family to a better part of town. For now, though, it was home, and she set off eagerly.

However, before she had gone a dozen steps, a whisper hailed her from a darkened alleyway. "Officer."

She stopped. "Who's there?"

Sally Husmann stepped from the shadows. "It's me."

"What do you want?"

"How is Sergeant Sanchez?"

"She's going to be okay."

"Oh, that's good. I'm so pleased."

Ellen folded her arms and considered the warehouse owner. "You weren't telling the whole truth to the lieutenant, were you?"

"I...it's not easy. I don't mean to...it..." Husmann's voice drifted into incoherence as her eyes sank.

"It's the Eastford Butcher and her gang, isn't it?"

Husmann's head jerked up. "I can't...they'll—" She broke off, panting in fear. "You don't understand."

"We won't understand unless you tell us. We need to know what's going on."

"I'm sorry."

"That's it?"

"I wish I could help, but I—" Husmann stopped. "Here. Take this."

Ellen held out her hand, wondering what sort of clue Husmann would pass over. Instead, several coins landed in her palm.

"Can you see that gets to Sanchez? I'm sure she can use it, what with the new baby and all. And tell her I'm sorry."

Husmann backed off into the darkness and fled, leaving Ellen alone in the town square, holding a fistful of coins.

Chapter Two—Talking to Rangers

Ellen was surprised to see a lamp still burning when she opened the door of her home. Both of her mothers were sitting in its light. Mama Roz, her birth mother, was on her feet before the door closed.

"Ellen, are you all right?"

Mama Becky also struggled up, leaning heavily on her walking stick. "We heard...we were..."

Ellen hurried forward and gathered them both in a hug. "I'm fine, Moms. Not a scratch. It was Sarge who got hurt."

She helped Mama Becky back to her seat and then knelt beside her. In the dim light of the flickering oil lamp she could see tears glinting in her gene mother's eyes. Mama Becky was always the more emotionally demonstrative of her parents. Ellen knew she had her gene mother's features, the same oval face, full lips, and firm jaw, but nothing else. Even the facial similarity was no longer easy to see. Years as an invalid had put weight on Mama Becky, blurring her cheekbones. Pain had etched deep lines around her mouth and white had replaced the last of her dark brown hair.

In build and personality, Ellen was much closer to her birth mother. Levelheaded and cautious, she had Mama Roz's height, square shoulders, and athletic build. She was fast on her feet, as many fleeing criminals had found out.

Ellen planted a kiss on Mama Becky's cheek. "You didn't need to worry. You'd have been told if I'd been injured."

"That's what I said. But you know how your Mama Becky gets." Mama Roz had also settled in her chair. She reached over to hold her partner's hand, an affectionate smile on her face. "I heard about Chris Sanchez as I was finishing work. I said that if you'd been hurt as well, the station would have sent a messenger here."

Mama Becky rubbed her free hand on Ellen's head. "I can't help it. I worry about you."

"So what happened?" Mama Roz asked.

The conversation continued for a short while as Ellen yet again told the story and repeated her reassurances that she was fine, but they could not stay up late. Mama Becky's health would not allow it, and Mama Roz had to be at work by dawn. Ellen watched her parents go to their bed in the curtained-off section of the cottage, then blew out the lamp and climbed the ladder to her own bed—a simple stuffed straw mattress—on the platform under the eaves.

Ellen's clothes felt rough and stiff with dried blood. Fortunately, the summer night meant she did not need to keep them on for warmth. She stripped off her outer clothing and slid under the blanket. The station duty roster did not have her on until late the next morning. She would have time to wash her uniform and then go to the town baths and get really clean. She hoped the black material would not be stained badly. But if it was, would Lieutenant Cohen deduct the cost of a replacement from her pay? Or would it count as unavoidable damage in the course of her duties?

Ellen stretched out on her back. From below, her parents murmured quietly for a while and then there was silence. Ellen stared into the darkness, waiting for sleep to come. If she raised her hand, she would be able to touch the sloping roof of the cottage. She was lying in her own bed, in her own home. Even though it was too dark to see anything, she knew the position of every knot on every rafter. Everything was so familiar, yet she could not shake the feeling that the world had shifted out of alignment, and nothing was going to be the same again.

❖

Mama Becky was sitting outside the door of their cottage, sewing in the last of the daylight when Ellen returned the following evening. As she covered the last few meters of rutted, unpaved road, Ellen felt a soft smile spread over her face. The same sight had welcomed her home ever since she was old enough to be allowed to wander off alone.

At the sound of footsteps, Mama Becky looked up. A fleeting

expression of relief was quickly swallowed by a smile. "Ellen. How did things go today?"

"Fine, Mom. Everyone in town is so upset about Sarge that they have all been extra well behaved." Ellen rested her hand on her gene mother's shoulder. "Come on. It's getting too dark to sew."

Ellen leaned an arm to help Mama Becky stand and then carried her chair into the cottage. "How's your day been?"

"Oh, you know. Nothing ever happens here." Mama Becky settled back in her chair with a sigh. "Mandy called around to ask after you. She wanted to be sure you were all right."

Ellen fought to keep her expression neutral. "That was good of her."

"You could go and see her."

"I...don't think so."

"She's a nice girl."

"Yes. She is."

"So why don't you want to see her?"

"Because I don't."

"Oh." Mama Becky sank in her chair, looking deflated. "You used to get on so well."

"Not always."

"But—"

Ellen interrupted. The merits of her ex-girlfriend was not a conversation she wanted to go through again. "Anyone else call by?"

"Valerie Bergstrom." The change in Mama Becky's manner was conspicuous. Ellen knew it was not due to any personal dislike, but purely the possibility that Valerie represented.

"What did she say?"

Mama Becky frowned but could not refuse to pass on the message. "She wanted the latest news on Chris Sanchez. She said she's going to be in the White Swan tonight, with her patrol buddies."

"Okay."

"Will you go to see her?"

"Er...yes."

"But not Mandy?"

Ellen sighed and leaned over to kiss Mama Becky's forehead. "Valerie worked with Sarge for two years. She's going to want to know about what happened."

"She could ask at the station or the infirmary, like anyone else."

"It's all right, Mom. I just want to chat with her. I won't be signing up for the Rangers today."

The words had been intended as a joke, but were far too close to home to raise a smile. Mama Becky immediately dropped her head, staring down at her clasped hands, knotted in her lap.

Ellen looked at her guiltily. "Are you all right, Mom? Is there anything you need before I go?"

"No. Your mother will be home soon. I'll be fine until she gets in."

Ellen clambered up to her sleeping platform. She stripped off the black Militia shirt, then pulled on the lighter of her two civilian shirts. The uniform trousers she kept on. Ellen owned a thick blue woolen pair, but these were too warm for mid-July. The beige shirt would be enough to mark her as off duty. Ellen studied her knees for bloodstains, but the darkness inside the cottage was too thick to tell anything. However, nobody had remarked on them during the day, so presumably she would not need to buy a new uniform. The condition of the trousers was certainly acceptable for a visit to a pub.

The tormented sigh from the floor of the cottage was soft but unmistakable. Mama Becky was still upset. Ellen glanced down at where she sat before the cold fireplace. The flippant remark about joining the Rangers had not been well judged. Ellen knew that neither of her parents wanted her to apply, although Mama Roz hid her fears better. Ellen's eighteenth birthday was under a month away. The month after that she would complete her two-year probation period. If she stayed in the Militia, she would get the rank of patrolwoman and a corresponding pay rise. Or she could apply to join the Rangers, the elite force who guarded the borders of the civilized world.

Everyone admired the Rangers. Like all children, Ellen had dreamed of killing bandits and snow lions and swaggering around town in a green and gray uniform. The Rangers were exciting. However, the squadrons rotated around the border garrison towns, and although Roadsend was one of these, if Ellen joined she could expect to spend the overwhelming majority of her time elsewhere, coming home only for brief periods. Even though she could have most of her salary sent back, the whole burden of caring for Mama Becky would fall on her birth mother, and Mama Roz was no longer a young woman.

Ellen caught her lower lip in her teeth, restraining a groan. She was an only child, born late. Small wonder her parents were so worried about losing her. They needed her and she had no wish to abandon them.

Of course, there was no saying that if she applied to the Rangers, she would be successful. Barely a quarter of applicants passed the rigorous entrance tests. Ellen shook her head. In truth, her chances of passing the tests were a secondary consideration. The first question was, did she want to join?

Ellen wished she could work out what she wanted to do. Which of the doubts were truly hers, and which were she taking on from her parents? How far was she being manipulated? Her mothers did not put direct pressure on her, but each new girlfriend had been welcomed with increasingly disproportionate enthusiasm. Her mothers' motives were blatantly transparent. They hoped she would find the right woman and want to settle down with her. The thought of someday providing them with grandchildren was an added bonus.

Ellen sighed and stepped onto the ladder. "See you later, Mom. I won't be too late back." She headed for the door.

"Have a nice time."

"I will."

"And be careful. I want you back safe." Mama Becky's voice betrayed a waver.

Ellen stopped and returned to kneel at the side of the chair. She rested her forehead against her gene mother's shoulder and squeezed her hand, trying to express her love and concern. Whatever decisions she made in the months ahead, she loved her parents. If they only knew it, that love, not some infatuation with a new girlfriend, would be what held her in Roadsend.

❖

The sweet smell of beer, a riot of voices, and smoke from cheap oil lamps assailed Ellen when she stepped into the taproom of the White Swan. The tavern was on the north side of town, close to the Rangers' barracks. It backed on to the eastern branch of the River Tamer. On any night, the clientele could be counted upon to include barge crews,

Rangers, and women who liked Rangers. The atmosphere was generally rowdy, but trouble free.

Despite the throng, Ellen did not take long to pick out Valerie Bergstrom at a table to the side, sitting with a small group of Rangers. Unlike the black of the Militia, the green and gray uniforms were far too prestigious to be put aside.

Valerie spotted Ellen at the same time and left the table to wrap her in a friendly hug of greeting. "Hey. It's been a long time. What do you want to drink?"

"The usual, thanks."

While standing at the counter, waiting to get the attention of the bar staff, Ellen considered her friend. Valerie was looking appreciably thinner and fitter than the last time Ellen had seen her. Valerie also exuded the air of confident bravado one associated with Rangers. Who knew—perhaps their basic training gave lessons in deportment.

Valerie was a year older than Ellen. Up until ten months ago, she had also been a rookie in the Roadsend Militia. But then Valerie had completed her probation and immediately applied to join the Rangers. Ellen had not seen her since she headed off to take the entrance tests. Valerie had passed and been assigned to the 12th squadron. By a stroke of luck, the Rangers' rotation of duty had brought the squadron to Roadsend five days before, but this was the first time they had managed to coordinate a meeting.

Once they had been served, Ellen accompanied Valerie back to her table. Three other Rangers were there, one carrying the twin bars of a corporal on her shoulder badge. Valerie started the introductions with this woman.

"This is Gill Adebeyo. She's my Patrol Corporal. The other two are Mel Ellis and Jay Takeda." The Rangers nodded in acknowledgement of their names. Valerie gestured to Ellen. "This is Ellen Mittal. She was in the Militia here with me."

"And you're still in the Militia?" Mel Ellis's tone was condescending.

Valerie cut in before Ellen had a chance. "She's only a rookie."

The answer clearly sufficed and Mel's expression warmed a tad. She was a short, square-framed woman in her mid twenties, with the uncompromising body language of somebody who enjoyed an argument. Jay Takeda was about the same age, taller, leaner, and with an easy-going smile that was all the more welcoming by contrast with her companion.

As soon as they were seated, Valerie leaned across to Ellen. "So what happened with Chris Sanchez?"

"Her and me were on patrol. We'd just left the sheep docks." Ellen took a sip of her beer. "Do you remember Sally Husmann?"

Valerie frowned in thought. "Owns a warehouse on Lower Dockside?"

"That's her. We came across a gang of thugs beating her up. We rushed up with our batons out. I thought they'd leg it. But they came for us. Even so, we had them on the run, until one pulled a knife and stabbed Sarge in the back."

"Didn't she give any sort of warning first? Was she drunk?"

"No warning, and she certainly didn't seem drunk."

Valerie leaned back, shaking her head. "Himoti's tits!"

"I know. You don't expect it. The last Militiawoman hurt on duty was Jude McCray, and that was the accident with the runaway cart."

Mel Ellis gave a snort of laughter. "It's a dangerous life in the Militia."

Ellen broke off and looked down at her hands on the tabletop, working at controlling her expression. It was no secret that the Rangers disdained the Militia, even though it was the place where everyone started. The last branch of the military, the Temple Guard, was equally unpopular. The three-way, mutual antagonism was long established. Generally it went no further than bantering jibes, but Mel was clearly the type of Ranger who held the Militia in out-and-out contempt.

To Ellen's surprise, it was Jay who came to her defense. "Chris Sanchez is a good woman. I did some work with her last time we were in Roadsend."

"So what's she doing in the Militia?" Mel asked, her scorn clear.

"Raising a family."

Mel pulled a face, as if such an activity was a strange affectation, but said nothing more.

"Does Husmann know anything about the gang who attacked her?" Valerie asked.

Ellen shot an uncertain glance at Mel, but then shook her head. "She claims not to."

"Claims?"

"There's something funny going on."

Valerie looked confused, but did not push further. "I heard that Chris is going to be okay."

"Yes. She had a collapsed lung, but Dr. Miller was able to fix it."

"Will she be out for long?"

"A month."

"Have they got a replacement for me yet?"

"No."

"You're going to be shorthanded."

Ellen grimaced. "Tell me about it."

The three older Rangers smiled but then turned to what was clearly an ongoing conversation about an incident at the barracks. Ellen listened, although the story was not easy to follow without knowing the people involved.

Valerie leaned across the table and tapped Ellen's hand to get her attention. "How are things with you? Are you still going out with Jackie?"

"No. We split up ages ago. I was dating Mandy Colman for a while, but we've finished too." Ellen smiled to show that she was not upset about it. "How about you?"

"The way the squadrons get shunted around there's no chance to get serious over anyone. But you know they say lots of women are desperate to examine the contents of a Ranger's uniform?" Valerie grinned. "It's true."

"You've got no regrets about joining the Rangers?"

"None. Are you tempted?"

"I don't know."

Valerie nodded thoughtfully. "How are your parents?"

"Much the same as ever. Mama Roz still works longer hours than me."

"And how about my family?" For the first time, Valerie seemed tentative. "Mom's written a few times, but she's not said much. Has Fran been in a lot of trouble while I've been away?"

"Surprisingly, no. She's still hanging out with Trish Eriksen, but since Ade went to Eastford, it's all been fairly juvenile stuff."

Valerie's sister, sixteen-year-old Fran, was at heart not a bad kid, although hopelessly overindulged by their mother. Unfortunately, Fran had become friends with the Eriksen sisters. At seventeen, Patricia would count as a bad influence, but not a catastrophic one. The same charitable description could not be given to her older sister. Adeola had been serious trouble since the day she learned how to walk.

Valerie nodded, looking relieved. "Let's hope Ade stays in Eastford."

"She hasn't."

"What?

"Ade was standing lookout for the gang that attacked Husmann."

"Shit. You've got problems there."

Ellen hesitated. Despite Lieutenant Cohen's order not to spread rumors, she desperately wanted to talk things over with someone. Valerie knew the situation in Roadsend, and as a Ranger ought to be able to assess things calmly. Maybe she could even come up with a better explanation and put Ellen's mind at rest.

"Um...actually, we've been having quite a few problems since you left. Last autumn, after the cloning, we had a lot of sheep stolen from the hills."

"How many?"

"Over five hundred."

"What!" Valerie's exclamation drew startled looks from the other Rangers, who broke off their own conversation.

"I know, it's..." Ellen made a vague gesture of uncertainty. Sheep were prone to theft. For most of the year they were left to wander free on open ground, with only minimal checks made on them by the shepherds. A few went missing every year. It was the scale of the thefts that was unprecedented.

"Have you caught the thieves?"

"No."

"So how many sheep are still missing?"

"All of them."

"Five hundred, that's..." Valerie's expression of stunned disbelief matched Ellen's own feelings on the matter.

"When did it happen?" Gill joined the conversation.

"We got the first reports when the shepherds went to bring the sheep in for the winter. Didn't think too much of it at the start." Ellen shrugged. "We all know sometimes farmers round up a few sheep that don't belong to them."

It was a matter of folk-law among farmers that sheep would keel over and die just to spite them, especially in the late autumn, when the ewes were pregnant with their cloned offspring. If someone had lost more animals than expected, the temptation was to make up the numbers from another flock, keep the ewes out of sight, tattoo the lambs with their own stamp when they were born in spring and then let the mothers go again.

Jay Takeda laughed. "The old six blank-eared sheep premise."

"What?" Mel's face screwed into a frown.

"It's an old joke. They say there ought to be a half dozen sheep with no number tattooed on their ears and each year a different farm gets to have them. The net result would be the same as all the petty pilfering, but it would be far less fuss and bother all around."

"Where did you hear that?"

"Last time I was in Roadsend I spent a couple of evenings with a shepherd."

"And you talked about sheep all night?"

"No. Not all night." Jay gave a cheery grin that drew laughter from her friends.

When the table had quieted, Gill looked back at Ellen. Clearly she was concerned and not ready to let the matter drop. "But we're not talking about a half dozen sheep, are we? What did your Lieutenant Cohen have to say about it all?"

"Well, I'm just a rookie, so I don't always get to hear what's..." Ellen ducked her head uncomfortably.

"What did she have you do?"

"We went around to all the farms, adding up how many were missing, and where they'd gone from. But five hundred…" Ellen shrugged. "That's enough for a small farm. Even a big farm wouldn't have room to keep so many extra sheep on pasture over winter. We explored the regions where most had vanished, looking for signs of flash floods and things."

"Was there heavy rainfall here last autumn?"

"Not really."

"So what, then?"

"That was it. We went back to our normal routine."

The silence was broken only by "Fucking useless Militia," muttered under her breath by Mel.

Ellen felt her face burn, but she had to concede some truth to the statement.

Gill looked thoughtful. "How about your Sergeant Sanchez? Did she have anything to say?"

Ellen drew a deep breath—this was it. Was she really breaking orders? But how could she not answer? "Um…we were talking about it just before we ran into the fight. Have you heard about the trouble in Eastford—the Mad Butcher's gang? They call themselves the Knives."

"I'd heard there was a bit of fuss there a while back."

"The gang murdered some Militiawomen."

Gill frowned. "I knew a few had died. But I thought it was all due to coincidence and a run of bad luck, rather than a single gang."

Ellen shook her head. "Maybe officially, but that's not what we heard on the Militia grapevine."

"It's all been quiet recently. Isn't the trouble over?"

"No. The reason it's gone quiet is because the Butcher and her Knives have scared everyone into shutting up. If people don't do what the Butcher says, they get a beating, or their house burned down. Anyone who informs to the Militia is dead. But the rumor is that the Butcher's got every thief and thug in Eastford working for her. And she owns shops and warehouses. Pays people to run them for her. She's treating crime like it's a business."

"Sanchez thought she's behind the thefts here?"

Ellen ducked her head. "After Sarge got stabbed, it was the last thing she said before she passed out. But who else could deal with so many stolen sheep? And there isn't any other gang that would be so quick to pull a knife on a Militiawoman. Sally Husmann knew more than she was saying. She's an honest trader, so someone's frightened her into keeping quiet."

"And Lieutenant Cohen is doing nothing?"

"Well...I don't know. I mean, she might be...or..."

Gill leaned on the table and rubbed her face thoughtfully. "I think this is something our Captain Aitkin needs to hear about."

❖

The bleating of sheep below deck was deafening. Ellen picked six at random and checked their ear tattoos. The dim light meant she had to peer closely, to be confident that all matched the number on the sales docket.

The ear tattoos were the main guard against theft. Getting a sheep to stand still long enough to tattoo by hand was not feasible, so it was done using a metal stamp, with dozens of needles set in a pattern that included the farm's identification number. Making the stamp required specialized equipment and the talents of a skilled craftsman. Possessing one without proper authorization was a crime. The tattoos did not stop the occasional sheep from being stolen and eaten, but up until now it had prevented wholesale theft.

Ellen let the last sheep go and looked at the remaining seventy-four in the hold. She considered grabbing a couple more, but the rules did not require that more than six be checked and the barge skipper was a familiar face—someone who had been working on the river since before Ellen was born—and had the reputation of being trustworthy.

Ellen climbed up through the hatch onto the deck of the *Elsie-Shadha*. Noonday sun bathed the scene. The sheep pens were full and three other barges were alongside. In the company of the skipper, Ellen stepped down the gangplank and went into the dockside office. She filed away the dockets detailing the number of sheep, the farms they were from, and the name of the barge. Then she poured wax on the bottom of the transport authorization, stamped it, and handed it over to the barge skipper. It was all very tedious and, as the thefts had shown, completely pointless.

"Safe journey."

"Thanks." The skipper marched up the gangplank, calling to her crew.

Ellen stood outside the office and watched the *Elsie-Shadha* move away from the quay. The *Ronnie-Belle* was also ready to depart, but this barge had taken on its cargo in Roadsend, so the sheep had already been checked in the pens and the paperwork completed.

Ellen frowned pensively. Most sheep were loaded at the upriver wharfs, which was why they had to be checked after they were on the barge. For the thieves, herding their stolen sheep through town in broad daylight would surely be far too risky, so the upriver sheep, like those on the *Elsie-Shadha*, were the ones to hone in on.

Why had Cohen not ordered extra checks? Ellen chewed her lip. One way or another, the stolen sheep had to be coming through the Roadsend docks. Water was the only practical way to transport the sheep to a market where they could be sold. Yet immediately downstream of Roadsend the landscape changed and went from rugged sandstone hills to low-lying wetland. Within a kilometer, the River Tamer was surrounded on both sides by an expanse of marsh. By the time it was again possible to herd sheep close to a deep water channel, the river was flowing through densely populated farmland. Hundreds of stolen sheep could not slip through the countryside without being noticed.

"Hey, Ellen." Jude McCray jogged up.

"What is it?"

"Cohen wants to see you right away, in the station. I'm taking over here."

A nasty cold feeling rippled in Ellen's gut, suspecting the reason for the summons. Her guess was confirmed when she entered Cohen's office and saw Captain Aitkin of the Rangers. Both Aitkin and Cohen appeared angry, and in the case of the latter, a fair bit of that anger was instantly directed at Ellen.

"What is this nonsense you've been spreading?"

"Ma'am?"

"I told you not to—"

Captain Aitkin interrupted. "The report I heard did not sound like nonsense. Over five hundred sheep stolen."

"That is not the point."

"That is totally the point." Aitkin addressed Ellen. "Do you confirm Sergeant Sanchez also thought the big Eastford gang was behind it all?"

"Um..." Ellen felt her throat tighten. What should she say?

"Come on, yes or no?"

"She thought it might be, ma'am."

"The thugs you confronted, they resorted to deadly force without hesitation?"

"Yes, ma'am."

"And the businesswoman they were attacking was too frightened to say what she knew?"

"I think so, ma'am."

Aitkin returned to Cohen. "All of which ties in with what we know of this gang's tactics."

"But what can we do?"

"For starters, get off your frigging ass."

Cohen flinched at the heated tone. Her eyes flitted around the room before fixing on Ellen. "Wait outside."

From the briefing room, Ellen heard the angry voices rising and falling. She could make out enough of what was said to know that Aitkin was pulling rank. Admittedly, the Militia and the Rangers had separate chains of command, but the threat of referring the issue to Militia HQ was enough to intimidate Cohen. After an extended period of shouting, Aitkin left, looking satisfied rather than happy.

"Mittal!" Cohen yelled from her office.

Ellen returned to the room with her heart pounding.

"I thought I ordered you to keep these ludicrous ideas to yourself. Do you know what you've done?"

Ellen clenched her jaw. There was really nothing she could say. For the next ten minutes, Cohen proceeded to harangue Ellen on her stupidity, her disloyalty, her immaturity, and her arrogance.

"I don't expect my officers to go running to the Rangers behind my back, questioning my decisions and trying to stir up trouble. I'm sure it made you feel very important, but believe me, you'll regret it. Don't you ever dare do anything like this again. Do I make myself clear?"

"Yes, ma'am."

Cohen pressed her knuckles on her desk and leaned forward, looking as if she was considering going through it all again, but then she scowled and barked, "Dismissed."

Ellen turned to the door, but before she got there, Cohen spoke again, "And Mittal, your uniform is in an appalling condition. I can see the stains on your knees from here. You will need to get a new set. Order it from central stores and I'll deduct the cost from your next month's pay."

"Yes, ma'am."

Ellen escaped and stood in the briefing room, recovering her composure. She remembered Mel Ellis from the night before. If Mel had met many officers like Cohen, it would go a long way to justifying her contempt for the Militia. But even as the idea drifted through Ellen's head, she froze, shocked at herself for daring think it. Then she considered the cost of a new uniform.

Ellen turned and stared at the door to Cohen's office. To her surprise, she realized that she did not respect her lieutenant at all.

Chapter Three—Broken Hills Ranch

Most of the Militia were already assembled in the station when Ellen sidled in through the street door. She ducked across the room and squeezed herself into a gap between the lockers and the unlit iron stove, trying to be inconspicuous, although with little success. The station briefing room was not large enough to provide a suitable hiding spot, just five meters long by four wide. The door to the lieutenant's office was directly opposite the entrance. On a side wall were further doors to the storeroom and the lockup—the latter obvious from its iron reinforcement and prominent lock. In a corner was the exit to the yard. Apart from the lockers against one wall and the stove, the only furniture was a long table, with a bench on either side.

Lieutenant Cohen stood facing the street door, arms folded and chin jutting out. Her temper had clearly not improved during the afternoon. From beneath brows so knotted that they almost touched, her hostile eyes tracked Ellen across the room.

The briefing was to be informal. Zar Thorensen and Penny Rambaldi sat together on a bench, both in an identical pose with elbow on the table and chin cupped in their right hand. Another patrolwoman, Della Murango, had her hip hitched onto a corner of the table. Corporal Rasheed was leaning against the wall just to the right of the street door—the spot Sanchez normally stood in. The sight made Ellen frown. Until the sergeant returned to duty, everyone knew that Rasheed would be second in command to Cohen. Underlining the point in such a trivial way was insensitive and unnecessary.

Rasheed was in her late thirties, a full decade older than Sanchez, and it was no secret that she had resented the younger woman being promoted over her. However, Rasheed lacked Sanchez's intelligence and as her flabby build testified, she also lacked the drive to exert herself.

Lieutenant Cohen kept glowering in Ellen's direction until the street door opened again, diverting her attention. The last member of the Roadsend Militia, Jude McCray, arrived. Cohen waited for everyone to settle, and then sent one last bitter glare Ellen's way before starting to speak.

"It's bad news, I'm afraid. *Somebody* has been stirring up trouble and has got the Rangers to stick their damned noses in. We're going to have to waste yet more time hunting for the missing sheep, for what chance there is of them showing up now. We're going to visit every damned farm in the district and recheck their paperwork."

Groans sounded around the room.

Cohen continued. "I know. It's the last thing we need when we're shorthanded. But *somebody* wasn't thinking about that. Until we've finished the rounds, all off-duty periods are cancelled. I'm also canceling all daytime patrols. I've started to draw up a roster. You'll be in pairs. I want you to check every cloning certificate, every sales log, and every farm stamp. Make sure they have every scrap of paper in order."

"What good's it going to do, ma'am?" Penny Rambaldi piped up.

"It'll exercise the horses, and maybe it will teach *somebody* to think before she opens her mouth in the future."

Ellen was aware of unfriendly looks coming her way from those who had taken the hint from Cohen's scowls and worked out who the *somebody* was.

"Ain't there something else we can do?"

"If you want, you can have a look at any sheep they have on pasture. If they've got five hundred of the buggers that don't belong to them, it shouldn't be hard to spot." Cohen glared around the room. "Any more questions? Suggestions?"

There were none. Any comments were restrained to low muttering.

"Okay. I've given Terrie the schedule for the next few days. She'll let you know where you're supposed to be."

Cohen stomped back into her room and slammed the door. Corporal Rasheed pushed away from the wall and pulled a wad of paper from her pocket. The four patrolwomen gathered around. Nobody looked in Ellen's direction as she tagged on at the back of the group. She could imagine the waves of resentment flowing in her direction, but then Penny Rambaldi glanced back at her and winked.

Ellen tried to mask her surprise. Presumably, Penny was not holding her solely responsible for the extra workload. Now that Ellen thought about it, Penny had often been less than flattering about their leader.

Soon the four patrolwomen had received their assignments and left, ready to make an early start the next day.

Rasheed pouted at Ellen. "I've got to be your puppy walker. We're taking the farms to the south. I want you here at dawn tomorrow."

"Yes, ma'am."

"And we'll see what all this frigging running around achieves, 'cause I don't know what you think we're going to find."

"It wasn't my idea."

"Whose fault is it, then? The lieutenant's told me all about you going behind her back to the Rangers."

"I was just chatting in the pub with Valerie Bergstrom. I didn't suggest we..."

Ellen's voice died. Maybe she had not directly proposed anything, but she had been hoping for some new initiative to hunt down the thieves. Yet the response was not the one she had envisaged. The Roadsend Militia were responsible for an area covering thousands of square kilometers and upward of two hundred and fifty farms. Visiting every one was going to take the better part of a month. It was a massive amount of work for everyone, and certain to be a waste of time. No thief would be stupid enough to hang on to a forged receipt, detailing the sale of her neighbors' sheep, let alone pass it over to any Militiawomen who came calling.

In early autumn, the sheep were rounded up and brought in to the home pastures. Teams of cloners traveled from farm to farm, using their skill with the psychic healer sense to induce pregnancies. Their work was sanctified by the Sisterhood, and copies of the cloning certificates were held in the Temple. Rather than running around checking the paperwork on farms, it would be far quicker and more productive to crosscheck the Sisters' figures against the records in the docks, to see if any farmers had sold more lambs than they should.

Best of all would be to spend more time in town, talking to the traders and businesswomen, and see if any could be persuaded to break the conspiracy of silence. Something unprecedented was going on, and the Militia needed information. However, Cohen was still refusing to accept that this was not like any other theft. Ellen noted that the briefing had contained no mention of the Eastford Butcher and her Knives. Surely the patrolwomen should have been alerted to this possibility. Why had nothing been said? Ellen stared at the floor, unhappy at the direction her thoughts were taking her. She wished she could put more faith in Cohen.

Seeing that Ellen was going to offer nothing more in her own defense, Rasheed snorted dismissively and wrenched open the street door. "See you here tomorrow, first thing. And don't you dare be late." The words were thrown over her shoulder as she left.

Ellen caught the door before it closed, but waited for a few seconds before heading out, taking a deep breath and composing her face. When had she ever been late for duty? More than that, Rasheed's own timekeeping was decidedly slack. The admonishment was both patronizing and irritating.

However, rookies had to be accompanied by the most senior active Militiawoman available—a practice known informally as puppy walking. Until Sanchez returned to duty, Ellen knew she was going to be spending most of her time with the corporal.

Ellen sighed and stepped out into the street. She hoped Rasheed would not take too long to get over her resentment, because in her current crabby mood, she was not going to be pleasant company.

❖

After twelve days, Ellen knew her hopes were not going to be fully realized. Admittedly, Rasheed no longer kept harping on about Ellen's role in involving the Rangers, or repeatedly taunting her over the whole pointless waste of time. However, a crabby mood was Rasheed's normal frame of mind and her idea of puppy walking consisted of exerting herself as little as possible while getting Ellen to run around performing every menial task that cropped up.

Even when they were riding along amicably, Rasheed's conversation could hardly be described as sparkling.

"My sister's got a nerve. I told her I wasn't having none of it. But she won't let it drop. She said she's coming over tomorrow night. So I told her tough, I ain't going to be in. And she said if I was going to be like that, then she wasn't going to give me my coat back. She's a frigging bitch. I mean, what's my damned coat got to do with it?"

Ellen made a sympathetic noise.

"She thinks the whole world revolves around her. She needs to grow up, or get a fucking good kick up the ass."

Ellen nodded and made more noises.

They were sixteen kilometers south of Roadsend, close by the Upper Tamer River, and approaching the fourth of the farms on their route for that day. The afternoon sun was beating down from a cloudless sky. The air was thick with dust and pollen that clogged in the throat. Ellen was happy not to be required to speak, especially since she was running low on water. She supposed she should be grateful that Rasheed was not expecting her to join in, but she would have been even happier with silence.

The saga of Rasheed's troubles with her sister had been going on for the last five kilometers. In format, it was much like her troubles with the rest of her family and neighbors. Judging by the experience of previous days, the recounting had at least another hour to go. Then Rasheed would go back to the beginning and start repeating some of the highlights. Fortunately the next farm, Broken Hills Ranch, was less than a kilometer away. Examining the paperwork would provide an enjoyable break.

Rasheed's monologue continued unabated as they rode the last few hundred meters to the farmstead. However, the tale held even less of Ellen's attention than normal. Changes had happened at Broken Hills Ranch since the last time she had been there.

The farm was owned by Cassie Drennen, who was elderly, infirm, and eccentric. It had been going downhill for years, as Drennen's ability to manage the workload had failed. From memory, Ellen thought the farm had fewer than four hundred sheep, and that nobody apart from the owner worked there. Yet the shearing shed had a new roof and the main house showed signs of recent repair work. The dry stone walls on either side of the road leading to the farmhouse had been patched up and the surrounding paddocks held at least two hundred half-grown sheep—double the number Ellen would have expected. By July, under a third of that spring's lambs would normally still be in the home pastures, unsold.

Ellen was familiar with the yearly farm cycle. Once winter started to bite, the pregnant ewes were brought in from the open hills. When the lambs were a few weeks old, their ears were tattooed using the farmer's stamp and sufficient numbers to maintain the stock were sent to roam the hills with their mothers. The rest were kept at the farm, to be fattened and sold over the following months and shipped downriver to the butchers in Eastford and Landfall.

Clearly someone new had taken over at Broken Hills Ranch and was expanding the flock. Ellen felt a ripple of excitement. Would the new owner be able to produce the evidence that all the extra sheep had been paid for? And just who had taken over? Ellen had heard no news of the farm being sold, or about anything happening to Cassie Drennen.

Corporal Rasheed finally fell silent as they reached the yard in front of the farmhouse. A woman Ellen did not recognize was at work there, replacing the boarding on a cart. Was this the new owner? The woman straightened at the sight of the black-clad Militiawomen and put down her adze. Two dogs dozed in the shade beside her. They scrambled up and advanced, snarling, until the woman called them back. Once they had lain down again, she gave them a quick pat and walked over, brushing dirt and wood chips from her hands.

Ellen judged that the woman was middle aged, though she looked older due to her skin being weathered by a life spent outdoors. Her clothes were typical for the farms, a loose shirt and well-patched trousers, in neutral colors, protected by a thick leather apron while she worked. A wide-brimmed hat shielded her eyes from the sun. She pushed it back on her head to look up at the mounted Militiawomen.

"Can I help you?"

"We'd like to speak to Cassie Drennen," Rasheed answered.

The woman gave a rueful pout. "It won't do you much good, I'm afraid. I'll get her niece. She's running the place now. She'll explain."

The farm hand strolled off and slipped through the half-open door of the nearby hay barn. Ellen and Rasheed dismounted and tied their horses' reins to a post. One of the dogs stood and shook itself. It padded over cautiously, head down, but not snarling now that the visitors had been accepted by someone it knew. Ellen crouched and held out her fingers for the dog to sniff.

In a short while, the farm hand returned, in the company of another stranger. This woman was younger, no more than in her mid-twenties, dressed in a similar fashion to the farm hand, although minus the leather apron. Her height was within a centimeter of Ellen's. She moved with a loose-limbed nonchalance that did not quite match the sharp expression in her eyes, evaluating the two Militiawomen. Yet something about her manner made Ellen think this was somebody who took very little in life seriously. She stopped less than a meter away and gave a broad smile, revealing even, white teeth.

"I'm the owner's niece—well, great-niece actually—Ahalya Drennen, though I usually answer to Hal. I'm helping out here, sort of as forewoman. Jo tells me you want to speak with my aunt. I'll take you to see her, but..." She tilted her head in a lopsided shrug.

Rasheed rubbed her face, uncertainly. "I'm Corporal Rasheed from Roadsend. We've got some questions, but it sounds like your aunt might not be the best person to answer them."

"Ah, whatever. I'll take you to her anyway."

Hal Drennen started to walk toward the farmhouse. Both dogs lurched to their feet and tagged on, until ordered to "stay." They collapsed dolefully, chins on paws, looking hard done by.

Rasheed and Ellen followed the forewoman around the side of the building to the covered porch at the rear. Cassie Drennen sat on an old chair in the shade, staring out at nothing. Her jaw moved as if chewing, although she appeared to be doing nothing other than sucking noisily on her few remaining teeth.

"Aunt Cassie. You've got visitors."

The old woman glanced briefly toward the new arrivals, but showed no trace of welcome or interest. Her eyes drifted back to the horizon.

"We've come to check up on your sheep, ma'am." Rasheed spoke louder and more slowly than normal, although without effect. Cassie Drennen did not turn her head again. The only sound she made was to continue sucking her teeth.

"She doesn't talk much anymore, I'm afraid. It's old age," Hal Drennen said in a low voice. She sounded genuinely pained by her aunt's condition. "Sometimes she has a good day. But this isn't one of them."

Ellen moved closer. She caught a whiff of stale urine, but Cassie Drennen appeared otherwise well cared for. Her hands on the arms of the chair were trembling and her eyes were watery, but this was no great change from the last time Ellen had seen her. Cassie Drennen had long had the reputation for poor health and failing wits.

Ellen looked back at the other two women. "I didn't know she had any relatives. Nobody's ever mentioned them."

The niece's smile held a shade of regret. "Aunt Cassie and my grandma had a bit of a falling out, decades ago. So she moved up here, away from the rest of the family. But when grandma heard about the state she was in...well...let bygones be bygones. You've got to take care of your family. And this farm." A sweep of her arm took in the surroundings. "It makes no sense to let it go to ruin."

Corporal Rasheed adopted a more official bearing. "Right. Obviously your aunt isn't the person we need to deal with. We're here to inspect your sales log for the last year. We also want to see your last cloning certificate and your authorized ear stamp."

"Can I ask why?"

"We're trying to find some stolen sheep."

"Stolen? Don't tell me more have gone missing?"

"No. We're still hunting for those that got taken last year."

"But isn't it a bit late to..." Hal Drennen's eyes shifted between them in confusion. Then she shrugged. "Whatever. I guess you know your job. Come on. It's all in here." She shoved the rear door of the house open with her shoulder.

The farmhouse kitchen spanned the width of the building. It was sparsely furnished, with a large table in the middle and a dresser against the wall. The plaster and woodwork were chipped and stained from years of neglect, but there also were signs of repair. The flagstone floor was even, with clean new mortar in the joins.

Hal Drennen pulled open a drawer on the dresser and took out a thick bundle of papers, bound together with string. She dropped them on the table and grinned. "There you go."

Rasheed slid onto a bench and untied the knot. Ellen waited to one side, but when Rasheed did not indicate for her also to sit and to join in, she moved away to the window at the front of the building. Shiny new nail heads on the hinges of the open shutters revealed that they had been recently rehung.

The sight of the lambs in the paddock prompted Ellen to ask, "Am I right you're expanding the flock?"

Drennen joined her at the window. "Oh yes. There's enough pasture here to winter a thousand sheep easily, but Aunt Cassie had been letting the numbers drop. She was down to three hundred and seventy-two. I've bought a hundred more this year and hope to do the same again next."

"We'll need to see the sales receipts for the new sheep, then. Do you have them?"

"Ah...yeah. I'm sure they're in the bundle somewhere."

Ellen returned to the table. Rasheed had separated the papers into piles and was starting to go through the nearest. Ellen picked up one pile but she had barely the chance to read the top line of the first page.

"Leave that alone." Rasheed snarled the order.

"I was just going to—"

"I don't need you to mess things up. I've got it all sorted the way I want."

Ellen clenched her jaw. Rasheed was acting as if she were a naughty two-year-old toddler, grabbing things just for the fun of it. "The new sheep in the flock. We should check the purchase record."

Rasheed glared up angrily. "I don't need you to tell me how to do my job. I was a Militiawoman while you were running around in diapers. I'll see to the sales receipts. You go outside and check the sheep. And anything else that takes your fancy."

"Yes, ma'am."

"Is that…" Hal Drennen also appeared surprised at Rasheed's manner, but then settled for a bemused shrug.

Ellen turned away and marched outside. She stood in the farmyard, glaring at the scenery. Rasheed could be unbearably patronizing sometimes.

The farm hand was back at her woodworking on the cart. The dogs' ears perked up at sight of Ellen, but they did not leave the shade. Ellen guessed that she might as well check the sheep. The last thing she wanted was for Rasheed to have grounds to accuse her of slacking. Ellen crossed the farmyard, pausing only to take a drink at the well. The cold water tasted sweet and washed the dust from her throat. Feeling somewhat better, Ellen refilled the flask on her saddle-pack, then left the yard and entered the first paddock.

The half-grown sheep drifted slowly away from her, but did not cease their grazing. Ellen would need to get close to read the numbers on their ears. However, the sheep became appreciably more fleet-footed whenever Ellen got within arm's reach, trotting off across the grass. Eventually she managed to corner one and pin it down long enough to read the tattoo. Inside the scrolled border was 681—the number allocated to Drennen's farm. This was no surprise. Even if the mothers were the sheep stolen the previous autumn, the lambs would have been tattooed with the farm stamp when they were born.

"If you find any with 189 on their ears, it means you're holding the sheep upside down."

The voice made Ellen jump. Hal Drennen was leaning over the low stone wall, grinning at her. Ellen stood and let the sheep escape. It scrambled away, back legs shunting in frantic tandem.

"Thanks for the tip, but I think I might have noticed." Ellen wandered over to the wall.

"Just trying to assist the Militia."

"You didn't want to stay and assist Corporal Rasheed?"

"I thought about it. She could probably use the help, but then I thought if she needed to count over ten, she was going to have to take her shoes and socks off, and I didn't want to hang around for that. She's not the brightest star in the sky, is she?"

Ellen ducked her head, trying not to smile, which would be completely improper. But after the way Rasheed had been acting, it felt good to hear somebody else voice the thoughts she wanted to say herself.

"Corporal Rasheed is an experienced officer. I...er...don't—"

A soft laugh interrupted her. "It's okay. I wasn't expecting you to answer the question."

Ellen looked up and met Hal Drennen's eyes. The farmer's gaze held her in a candid appraisal that was level and unwavering, intensifying as the seconds passed. Ellen felt her heart jump a beat, causing a surge to ripple through her stomach. Hal Drennen's face was narrow, seeming slightly too small for her mouth, so that a hollow formed on either side, although the overall effect in accentuating her cheekbones was far from unattractive. Her hair was cropped short, the dark brown speckled by a layer of hay dust, golden in the bright sunlight. Her expression was open and relaxed, but the depth in her eyes was serious and very meaningful.

Ellen tore her gaze away and stared across the field, while trying to concentrate on the job in hand. “If you’re here to help, I have some questions for you.”

“Go ahead.”

“How long have you been working on your aunt’s farm, Ms. Drennen?”

“Oh please, drop the Ms. Drennen bit. Call me Hal.” After a short pause she prompted. “Your colleague didn’t give your name.”

“Mittal. Rookie Ellen Mittal.”

“Rookie? So you haven’t been in the Militia for long?”

“Almost two years. Another month and I’ll have finished my probation.”

“So you must be what, eighteen?”

“Nearly.”

“That’s a relief.”

“Wha...” In confusion, Ellen looked back at Hal, who was still grinning at her. “Why?”

“You had me worried. You know what they say, the first sign you’re getting old is when the Militiawomen start to look young.” Hal paused and then added, “I wonder what it means when you start to think the Militiawomen look hot? And I’m not talking about Rasheed. She doesn’t look young to me either.”

The first flare of surprise was lost when the ripples in Ellen’s stomach erupted as fully fledged somersaults. She fought to maintain her composure. She was an officer of the law, investigating a crime. To call Hal’s words inappropriate was an understatement. Ellen knew she ought to take charge of the conversation, but her thoughts had scattered and she could not begin to string words into a sentence. “I…um… don’t…”

Hal had not finished. “What made you join the Militia? Was it just knowing that the uniform would look good on you?” Her eyes very slowly and deliberately traveled the length of Ellen’s body and back to her face, blatantly checking her out.

Ellen felt her face burn.

“A bit more color on your cheeks doesn’t hurt either.” Hal’s laughter ended in an amused sigh. "I'm sorry. I didn't mean to embarrass you. Come on. Do you want me to help you round up some more sheep to check, as per your corporal's instructions? Or shall I show you around the farm?"

Ellen took a deep breath, scrabbling through her head for a coherent answer. "Um...why don't you give me the tour?" She clambered awkwardly over the gate and joined Hal on the road.

The hard-packed earthen yard in front of the main house was now deserted, except for the cart with its conspicuous new boards of clean white wood. The farm hand, Jo, and the dogs were gone. Ellen could hear a shepherd's high-pitched whistles from the fields to the rear.

The farmhouse itself was built in a combination of styles and materials that made it plain that the original one-story stone building had been extensively modified over the years, most notably by the addition of a timber-framed upper floor. Two small windows peered out under the eaves. A short flight of steps led up to the wooden veranda running around the house.

The farm buildings were all positioned off to the right. The largest of these was the hay barn, where Hal started. From there she went on to the stables and the lambing pens, pointing out the hay that was being stockpiled to see the flock through the winter, the work to repair the existing structure, and her plans to expand and improve the farm. They finished in the shearing shed at the back of the farmstead, with a view leading down to the river, some half kilometer distant.

As the tour progressed Ellen's self-possession returned. She kept reminding herself that she was a Militiawoman, on duty, with an important job to do. However, Ellen could not help her attention from drifting away from the farm buildings and onto the farmer, noting the sharp muscle definition on Hal's forearms, the way the material of Hal's shirt stretched across her shoulders as she pointed out a new roof brace and the cheery lilt in her voice.

There had been nothing subtle about the way Hal had been hitting on her in the paddock. Ellen felt her stomach flip again at the memory. She knew the young farmer was someone she could most definitely be interested in—if it were not for the possibility that Hal was tied up in the sheep thefts. Surely this sudden and unadvertised change in Broken Hills Ranch was exactly the sort of thing they should be alert to. Was it just a front for the Butcher's gang? Was Hal one of the Knives, or was she who she claimed to be, a relative helping out her great aunt? Cassie Drennen was clearly in no state to confirm or deny anything.

Ellen looked up at the new roof on the shearing shed. A considerable amount of time and money had been put into the property. "You didn't say how long you've been here." Ellen spoke without looking back at Hal.

"About a year, on and off. I've been here pretty much full time the last eight months."

"And you've done all this work yourself, with just Jo's help?"

Hal laughed. "Hey, I'm not that good. Grandma has been lending me extra hands to help, whenever things are slack on her farm."

"And her farm is...?"

"South. Near Monday Market."

The shearing shed was open on three sides. To her left, Ellen could see through to the back of the farmhouse. Cassie Drennen was still on her chair, staring at nothing. The rear door stood ajar to one side. What had Rasheed found out from the papers? Was Hal on the level? Ellen chewed her lip. How careful should she be? How careful did she need to be?

"So, is there anything else you'd like to see more of?" Hal's tone was provocative.

Ellen glanced over her shoulder. Hal was leaning with her elbow propped against an upright support, legs crossed at the ankle. Her smile was relaxed and confident. Her eyes danced in a way that made it clear her offer was not limited to sheep.

Ellen turned away. In truth, the answer to one of her questions was obvious. She needed to be very careful indeed. She wandered to the side of the shed overlooking the river. At the nearest point, a small wooden jetty poked out into the water. It was still too far away to be sure, but Ellen thought that this also looked to have been repaired.

"Do you use the jetty?"

Hal came to stand at her shoulder. Ellen felt as if sparks were leaping the scant centimeters between them, carrying a charge like summer lightning.

"Sometimes."

"I think I'd like to see it." Ellen needed to put some space between herself and Hal. She started walking.

"Do you have a girlfriend?"

The abrupt question brought Ellen to a dead stop. Her breath caught in a gasp. She turned slowly. Hal had not moved. Ellen's pulse rate surged. Walking down to the dock was no longer a possibility. Her knees were not strong enough. "No. Not at the moment."

Hal closed the distance between them, but made no attempt to touch Ellen. "That's surprising. I'd have thought you'd have a queue lining up halfway to Landfall."

"I broke up with my ex about a month ago." Ellen found that she was again staring deep into Hal's eyes, level with her own. "How about you?"

"I'm completely available."

Hal's hand brushed up Ellen's arm, moving to her shoulder. Abruptly, Ellen's eyes refocused, taking in the new roof. Awareness of the situation returned in a rush; she had to be careful.

Ellen jumped back. "I'm on duty."

"And?"

"I'm not supposed to..." Ellen swallowed.

"Kiss available farmers?"

"No."

Hal gave a broad smile that was pure mischief. "And if you weren't on duty?"

"I might be talked—"

Ellen could not finish. Hal had again moved close, transfixing her with an intense gaze. Hal's hands slipped around Ellen's back, pulling her close. Their lips were centimeters apart.

"Mittal." Rasheed bellowed from the front of the house, her voice so loud it set off startled bleating from nearby sheep.

Ellen broke free of Hal's grip. She backed away and then turned. "I've got to go."

"Just one thing."

Hal's voice again brought Ellen to a halt. She looked back. "What?"

"When are you next off duty?"

"When we've finished checking all the farms."

"And that will be?"

"Another ten days or so."

Hal nodded thoughtfully. "Maybe I should start coming into town more often."

"I'll look out for you." Against all her common sense, Ellen could feel a grin spreading across her face. She hurried away, jogging around the main building.

Rasheed's mood had not improved noticeably. She scowled as she waited for Ellen to untie her reins and hop up into her saddle.

"I checked the papers." Rasheed volunteered the information.

"Was it all okay?"

"Yes. And the purchase receipts for the new stock. Did you spot anything untoward?"

"No, ma'am."

Rasheed urged her horse forward. "Right. Blue Stripe Ranch next."

Ellen fell in beside her. As they passed the gate of the first paddock, Ellen twisted in her saddle to look back. Hal stood at the top of the steps to the veranda, watching them go. Hal waved her hand in a gesture of good-bye that looked suspiciously like blowing a kiss. Ellen felt the smile return to her lips, until Rasheed's voice jolted her.

"If my sister thinks she's hanging on to my coat, she's got another frigging thought coming."

Chapter Four—Breaking the Rules

Sergeant Sanchez lived with her family in a three-story terraced house in a quiet part of town. Ellen knocked on the door and waited, while looking up and down the narrow street. Few people were about. Even though the sun was sinking, the red brick walls on either side still radiated the trapped heat. No breeze stirred the stifling late afternoon air.

The door opened. Rhonda Tomczyk smiled when she saw Ellen on the doorstep. "Hi. Have you come to see Chris?"

"It's just a social call. I heard she's okay to see visitors."

"She has been for a while."

"Yes...well...I wanted to come over before, but we've been really busy." Ellen felt awkward. It sounded like an excuse, even though it was true.

"So I've heard." Sanchez's partner clearly did not feel slighted by the tardiness. She smiled and stood back, holding the door open wide. "Come in, I know Chris will be pleased to see you. She's out the back."

The yard at the rear of the house was no more than six meters wide and twice that in length. Despite its small size, three trees grew there. They were barely half the height of the building, but their knurled branches showed that they were fully mature and had been there a long time.

Sergeant Sanchez was sitting on the grass in the shade, with her back leaning against one trunk. She looked pale and tired, though she smiled in welcome. Her infant daughter was lying asleep on her, sprawled with her baby curls resting on Sanchez's chest.

Rhonda Tomczyk disappeared back into the house. Ellen shuffled across and flopped down onto the grass, feeling a touch self-conscious. She had never made a social call on any of her Militia colleagues before, except for Valerie Bergstrom, which hardly counted since Valerie had also been a rookie at the time.

"Hi, Sarge."

"Hi. It's good to see you."

"Yup. Good to see you too. How're you doing?"

"Fine. Getting to enjoy taking it easy."

Ellen held out the coins. "This is for you. From Sally Husmann. I think she felt guilty that you were hurt, helping her."

"Really?" Sanchez gave a wry smile. "Pass on my thanks if you see her before I do."

"Will do."

"Did she say anything else when she gave you the money?"

"Not really. Just a few hints. I asked about the Butcher but she was too scared to talk."

"When was this?"

"The night you were stabbed." Ellen ducked her head. "I'm sorry I haven't handed the money over sooner, but this is my first free time since you've been out of the infirmary."

"That's okay. I know you've been busy."

Ellen sighed. "Too true."

"Have you finished making the rounds of the farms?"

"Not quite. But Corporal Rasheed and me are on town patrol for the next eight nights, so we stopped early, to give us an hour clear before we start pounding the beat."

Sanchez hesitated for a second, then said, "You do know that, according to the rules, station commanders can only cut back on off duty when it's completely unavoidable?"

Ellen frowned uncertainly. "Well, I wasn't sure, but none of the others objected when Cohen said it. I thought, maybe, the scale of the thefts was important enough to warrant it."

"Importance isn't the issue. She could cut off-duty hours if it was the only way to catch the thieves, but what she's got you doing is…"

"A complete waste of time?"

"Is that a criticism of the lieutenant's orders?" Sanchez's tone held a hint of surprise.

"No, Sarge. I wouldn't—"

Sanchez bowed her head, hiding her face, but her shoulders were clearly shaking with laughter. She brushed the hair from her baby's forehead and then looked up again. "Do you know you're the only person who calls me Sarge?"

"Oh. Sorry."

"I don't mind." Sanchez's expression grew more serious. "But you're allowed to call me by my name. It's Chris. And you can call Corporal Rasheed Terrie. You can even call Lieutenant Cohen Jake, if you're off duty and happen to be feeling well disposed toward her. Alternately, you can call her *that frigging moron*, and I'll quite understand."

"Ah. Um..." Ellen was unsure what to say.

"You're a rookie, but you're not a child anymore. You don't need to be unthinkingly respectful of adults. And you've got a right to your own opinions."

"Right...er...Chris." Ellen chewed her lip and looked down at the grass. She could feel her face burning. "I thought I'm not supposed to do anything that might bring the rule of law into disrespect."

"True. But sitting here, just you and me, I think you're quite safe to say whatever you want. Anyway, Jake is far ahead of you in spreading disrespect for the Militia."

"I must admit that I, um lost…"

"Yes?"

"I lost some respect for her when she made me buy a new uniform, because of the stained knees."

"I heard." Sanchez—Chris sighed and then held out her hand. "Why don't you take these back?"

The coins landed in Ellen's palm. She looked up. "The money was for you."

"It was my blood staining your trousers. It's only fair if I buy you the replacement."

"But the real reason Cohen made me pay was because I'd broken her orders and told the Rangers about the Butcher."

"Yes. And I owe you an apology for that as well."

"Why?"

"Because I should have done something months ago. Somebody was going to have to stick her neck out and it ought to have been me. That's what I get my nice big sergeant's salary for. I shouldn't have left it to a rookie to cover for me." Chris pursed her lips. "Last autumn, I wanted to call in the Rangers. Terrie was dead against it and Jake sided with her. I should have pushed harder. But I let it ride, thinking she'd have to change her mind in the end. By the time I realized she wouldn't, it had gotten too late. But I was all ready for when the thefts start again this year—and they will."

"But Lieutenant Cohen is in charge. You aren't responsible for what she does."

"When you complete your probation, are you going to apply to the Rangers?"

Ellen frowned, confused at the abrupt change in topic. "I don't know. I haven't made my mind up. I'm thinking."

"When I was your age, I thought about it too. But I'd met Rhon, and I knew I'd have to give up a lot of things if I joined the Rangers. I'm not overly ambitious. A good job, Rhonda, and the chance to watch my kids grow up. That's all I want. The Rangers can keep the adventure and the glory. They're welcome to my share of it." Chris smiled down at her sleeping daughter and stroked the baby's palm. Tiny fingers clenched around hers in reflex. "But it's a sad fact that most of the brightest and best get out of the Militia as soon as they can, and some real dregs get left behind. On the plus side, if you stay in the Militia and are halfway competent, you're guaranteed the promotions." Chris looked up, her face serious. "Unfortunately, even some of the dregs get promoted."

"Like Cohen?" Ellen was surprised to hear her own voice say the words aloud.

"She's not the worst. To be fair, she'd be a good enough sergeant or corporal, as long as she wasn't the one who had to make decisions. I'd say she was coming up to retirement, and someone owed her a favor. An old friend pulled strings so Jake got to spend the last few years as a lieutenant. Something she can brag about to her grandchildren, and she'll get a bigger pension. But she's simply not up to doing the job."

"But it's not as if it takes any…" Ellen waved her hands, trying to express the extent of her incomprehension. "The Eastford Butcher and her Knives have to be behind it all. It's the only thing that makes sense. But Cohen has this total block against the idea and she throws a fit if you even suggest it. Why?"

"She really likes the idea that she's in command, but deep inside, I'm sure she knows she's just acting out the role. She can't deal with the Butcher on her own, and she hasn't got enough understanding to realize no other Militia lieutenant could either. So she thinks asking for help will make her failings obvious to everyone. She's blanked out the idea of the Butcher. As if by closing her eyes, she can make it all go away."

"She was angry enough at me for involving the Rangers."

"Because you've made her look even more incompetent than she would have if she'd notified HQ herself. And maybe she's got the same grudge against the Rangers as Terrie."

"I know the cor…Terrie hates the Rangers. Is there a reason behind it?"

"Terrie hates the Rangers because she applied to join them and she failed the entrance tests. It's left her with a chip on her shoulder big enough to make a four-poster bed out of, and still have enough wood left over for a wardrobe. Remember the grief she gave Valerie for daring to apply?"

"I remember what she said when we heard Valerie had passed."

"Quite."

"I can't say I'm surprised Terrie failed the tests."

Chris chuckled. "Can I take it you don't like having her as your puppy walker?"

Ellen grimaced by way of answer.

"Don't worry; I'm sure I won't be the only one to think you were right to tell the Rangers."

"But it hasn't achieved anything worthwhile."

"Don't write the Rangers off so quickly. I'd lay money that Captain Aitkin has sent a report to Fort Krowe. It may take some time for reaction to get back, but things ought to be moving."

Ellen pulled her legs up and rested her chin on her knees, thinking. "Is that why Cohen has got us running the checks? So when HQ starts asking questions she can point to all the work we've done."

"Maybe."

"And she picked the most time-consuming, pointless thing for us to do, so it will prove she was right when she said it was a waste of time looking for the sheep?"

"To be honest, I wouldn't bother spending much time trying to understand her," Chris said, grinning. "Has all the running around turned up nothing at all?"

Ellen raised her head. "Not exactly, but..."

"But?"

"Nothing definite, but there've been changes out at Broken Hills Ranch. Terrie and me were there two days ago."

"What sort of changes?"

"A woman claiming to be Cassie Drennen's niece is in charge. They've expanded the flock."

"Have they now?" Chris sounded interested.

"She said it was by a hundred sheep, but from the number of spring lambs still in the fields, I'd have said it was a lot more than that."

"Was the paperwork straight?"

"Terrie said it was. She checked while I looked outside. The niece showed me around."

After a few seconds of silence, Chris asked, "And why has that got you blushing again?"

"Oh, um..." Ellen felt her face burn even redder. "She was flirting with me."

Chris laughed. "Was she nice?"

"Yes." Ellen knew she had answered the question a tad too quickly, but over the previous few days, Hal had occupied her thoughts a fair bit, along with an awareness of just how nice the young farmer was. "But I didn't trust her. We only had her word she's Cassie Drennen's niece. She could be one of the Knives for all we know. I've never heard of any relatives before."

"Neither have I, but Cassie must have had some once." Chris looked thoughtful. "I remember hearing she'd moved here ages ago from somewhere to the south. I'll ask around."

"How? You're not up to going anywhere."

"I don't need to. Half the population of Roadsend are paying me visits. What did the niece say her name was?"

"Hal. Short for Ahalya Drennen."

"Are you planning on seeing her again?"

"No. I mean it wouldn't be wise, would it?"

Chris smiled. "I don't know, a nice woman flirting with you isn't something that happens every day."

"She might be a Knife."

"And she might not. Either way, it wouldn't be a bad move to keep tabs on her. If she's in with the Butcher, you could learn something. And if she isn't..." Chris's smile broadened. "It would be a shame if you pushed her away."

"I don't know how seriously she meant it. She was kind of joking."

"Joking doesn't mean she wasn't serious. My advice is, if she comes looking for you, don't run. But be careful what you say, and don't risk getting hurt if she turns on you. Just use your head and keep your emotions under control."

Ellen nodded and then looked up at the sky. The sun was dropping toward the rooftops. "I've got to be off. I'm meeting Rash...Terrie at the station in a few minutes." She stood.

"Take care."

"Right."

"I mean it. You're young. You don't trust your own judgment and you want to play things by the rules. But use your head. If you have to choose between the rule book and your common sense, then toss the rule book out. If you have time, you can always come and talk to me. Don't do something stupid just because you're ordered to."

"My duty is—"

"Your duty is to uphold the law, to catch the thieves, and to see that nobody gets murdered along the way. And your own murder would be no more acceptable than for any other citizen."

"I'll try to be careful."

"Being careful isn't the point. That's why I've said all this to you. It wasn't just for the sake of a good gossip. While I'm out of action, you're pretty much on your own. In a crunch, Penny and Della are the best of the bunch, but neither are hot on using their initiative. And I'm thinking some initiative is what's called for—like with you talking to the Rangers. Jake's ordered you not to speak to them again, hasn't she?"

"Yes."

"Ignore that order. Until HQ gets someone qualified out here to take over, the Rangers are your best bet. If you find out something they need to know, then tell them. Jake Cohen is in a blind panic and the worse it gets, the more she's going to have the Militia acting like headless chickens. It isn't going to catch the thieves, and worse than that, it could get somebody killed."

"I don't know..." Ellen stared at the grass, trying to organize her thoughts. She was aware that in part she felt flattered the sergeant trusted her enough to speak so honestly, but in part she also felt out of her depth.

"You know you saved my life?" The quiet intensity in Chris's voice made Ellen look up.

"When?"

"When I was stabbed. You did all the right things, leaving the knife in place while stopping the flow of blood. I very nearly died. It was a desperately close thing. Your actions are why I can sit here now, in my yard, with my daughter." Chris stroked the baby's head. "I don't want to have to go to your funeral someday soon and tell your parents how sorry I am and how they can be proud of your memory, and all the other inane platitudes."

❖

The drunken woman collided heavily with a table, slopping the drinks on it and coming within a wobble of upsetting it completely. She barely managed to keep herself from ending up on the floor. Patrons seated around the table grabbed what remained of their beer and shouted, adding to the chaos in the taproom. The drunk ignored them and lurched toward the bar. "I juss wan—"

Ellen caught the woman's arm and yanked it up behind her, firmly enough to restrain her, but not enough to cause real pain. The woman stumbled back, looking more confused than upset, as if she could not work out why her legs were no longer carrying her where she wanted to go. Her eyes tried to latch onto Ellen's face, but she was clearly having trouble. Possibly she was trying to work out which of the two Ellens she should talk to.

Terrie Rasheed caught the other arm, and between them, the Militiawoman frog-marched the drunk out of the Three Barrels Tavern, into the calm of the square outside.

The woman protested. "I juss wanna nuvver drink. I got money. Tell her she hasta gimme one."

"You've had too many already," Terrie said firmly.

They released the woman, who staggered a few steps, until she found a wall to grab on to. "Juss one—"

"Go home."

"I—"

"You can go home, or you can spend the night in the station lockup. Your choice."

The drunk took a few gulps of air. Maybe it helped to clear her head, because she was able to release her grip on the wall. She scowled unsteadily at Ellen and Terrie, as if finally registering their Militia uniforms.

"Blackshirt bitches." However, the words were only muttered and she was already turning to leave, stumbling toward an alleyway.

Once the drunk had disappeared from view, Ellen let her breath out in a sigh. The small square was deserted in the moonlight. Midnight was little more than two hours away. Things ought to quiet down soon. The working day would be starting in six hours and most folk were already asleep in their beds. However, the Three Barrels Tavern was still doing a brisk trade. Noise from the taproom was rising again, but it was the normal hubbub of conversation. The disturbance was over.

"You stay out here. Make sure she doesn't come back or pull a stupid stunt. I'll go and check that everything inside is okay." Terrie snapped the order and marched back into the Three Barrels.

The door swung shut. Ellen stared cynically at the spot where Terrie had been standing. This was the second night of patrolling with the corporal, and Ellen was getting more than a little fed up at being told to keep watch outside trouble-free taverns, while Terrie spent ten minutes checking out the interior. This had happened four times the previous night, and the only thing to be said for it was that by the time they had finished the patrol, Terrie had been in a conspicuously good mood.

Ellen closed her eyes and flexed her shoulders, trying to dissipate the resentment that could achieve nothing except for making her even less happy with life.

"Can I take it you're still on duty?" An amused voice spoke from the shadows.

Ellen jerked around. "Who's there?"

Hal Drennen emerged into the moonlight. "I said I'd come into town to see what was on offer, and look what I've found."

"You've been watching me?"

"It wasn't deliberate. I was having a quiet drink until the fun started."

"You were in the Three Barrels?"

"Yes. I saw you handle the drunk, and very neatly done too." Hal looked around. "Has she gone?"

"Yes."

"So why are you hanging about out here?"

"I'm making sure she doesn't come back."

"While your corporal makes sure the beer is up to standard?"

Hal had been advancing while she spoke. She was now mere centimeters away. Ellen felt her heart start to pound, but this time she was ready to deal with the woman. Ellen folded her arms as a barrier and planted her feet squarely on the cobbles. She would take Chris's advice, play Hal along, and enjoy the game, but she would take care that she did not drop her guard—not until she was certain Hal was on the level.

"Corporal Rasheed is ensuring that the situation in the tavern is under control."

"Really? Is that what she told you? And do you believe her?" Hal's tone was flippant. She made a show of looking around the square. Her arm brushed against Ellen's. "Well, it all seems under control outside, so what are you going to do for the next ten minutes?"

"I'll stand here and keep watch."

"Like you've been told to?"

"Yes."

"And don't you ever get tired of doing what you're told?"

"No. Else I'd be a pretty poor officer of the law."

Hal tilted her head to one side. "You don't ever get a kick from breaking the rules? From thinking you've got one over on the ass kissers who make them up?"

"No."

"And you don't get pissed off, standing around in the dark, while somebody getting twice your salary helps herself to free beer?"

"That's not your concern."

"Which I guess means yes." Hal laughed. "You know, you really should try your hand at a bit of misconduct sometime. You might find it fun."

Hal raised her index finger and traced a line across Ellen's forearm and up to her bicep. The thick black material of the Militia shirt did nothing to shield Ellen from the sensation. The contact burned like fire, melting her resolve. She took a half step back, hands dropping to her side.

"I'm not supposed to." Even to Ellen's own ears, the words

sounded ridiculously defensive. They were unlikely to have been any more authoritative for Hal.

"To do what?" Hal laughed softly. "Your corporal doesn't worry much about what she's not supposed to do. Tell me, what's the worse infraction of the rules, drinking while on duty, or having a quick kiss with a law-abiding citizen who would otherwise be enduring a rather dull evening?"

Ellen licked her lips, but could not speak. She felt the rough contact of bricks rasping on her shirtsleeve and realized she had been backing away. Hal had her cornered. There was no easy escape—not that Ellen could work out whether she wanted one.

Hal moved in closer. Her thighs brushed against Ellen's and her hands rested lightly on Ellen's hips. She leaned forward. At the last moment, Ellen gave in and closed her eyes. Hal's lips fastened onto hers in soft domination. Moving on their own accord, Ellen's arms curved around Hal's back. Hal pressed in harder, forcing Ellen against the wall.

Hal's mouth felt good, molded on hers. Hal's body was firm—not so robustly athletic as Ellen's, but wiry and strong. The muscles in her back flowed hard under Ellen's hands. Ellen lost herself in the kiss, sucking Hal's tongue into her mouth. She heard the rough hiss of Hal's breath, short and fast, matching her own. Ellen's body could not get enough of the contact and ached for more. When Hal forced a leg between hers, it was not nearly enough. Ellen moaned. She was aware of nothing but Hal.

Abruptly Hal peeled herself away. The sudden absence of the weight against her made Ellen gasp. But then, like being doused in cold water, the world flowed back, reminding her of where she was and what she should, and should not, be doing. Ellen shook her head, shocked at how completely all self-discipline had deserted her.

Hal backed off another step, smiling. Her teeth were white in the moonlight, her cheeks sunken dark hollows. "Well, there you go. That's one rule broken. It wasn't so hard, was it?"

In a flash of anger, Ellen straightened herself, pushing away from the wall. "That wasn't—" She stopped. Even in her own head she did not know how to finish the sentence. Fair? Funny? Right? All would sound childish.

"I'll leave you to keep watch. I abandoned Jo inside, keeping an eye on my drink. She's been with the family for years, and is as reliable as they come, but it doesn't pay to put too much temptation in the way of employees. The beer is first rate here. I'm not surprised your corporal was happy to sample it." Hal's tone was light, teasing, as if it were all a big joke. She turned away but then glanced back. "Remind me, just when are you going to have an evening off duty?"

"Why?"

"Do you seriously need me to answer that question?"

Ellen clenched her teeth, but forced herself to relax. Hal had outplayed her. Sulking like a fool would not make things any better, and it was not as if kissing her had been unpleasant. Ellen's lips still tingled and her heart was pounding. "When we've finished the farm checks. The way the schedule is going, I ought to be free on the sixth of August, unless something crops up."

"The sixth?" Hal's smiled broadened. "Good night, Officer." She flicked her forefinger off her forehead in an informal salute, then turned and sauntered back into the Three Barrels Tavern.

Ellen was left alone in the empty square, rubbing her face and wondering just what was happening to her.

❖

Ellen slipped in through the open door of the Roadsend temple and peered around while her eyes adjusted to the gloom. To her relief, it looked as if the main hall was empty. She tiptoed down the side aisle, past the multicolored statues of various Elder-Ones, until she reached her destination, the small military shrine.

Roadsend had a minor temple, possessing no inner sanctum or Guards' barracks. The half dozen Sisters and similar number of Guards lived in a house to the rear. Women wishing a child had to travel to Eastford, the nearest temple where Imprinters performed their divinely sanctified work. The Sisters based in Roadsend had no role other than to protect and guide the souls of Celaeno's daughters—as long as the daughters gave them the chance.

Ellen caught her lip in her teeth. She knew she had been decidedly lax in her devotions recently, but she had her reasons for staying away.

Unfortunately, they were reasons she might have some difficulty explaining to the Sisters.

Today, she had to put in an appearance—August 3, her eighteenth birthday. Ellen knelt before the military shrine with its trio of Elder-Ones, and lit a candle. The statues looked down on her with blank carved eyes, the patrons of the Militia, the Rangers, and the Guards. Ellen dropped the small bag of coins into the offering bowl, a gift for the Elder-One David Croft, patron of the Militia, in recognition and thanks that she was now a full adult.

At the age of twelve, a girl was no longer counted as a child. She could hold money and land in her own name. She was responsible for her own debts. She could sign a contract, the commonest contract being for employment. Most would leave school and start work, unless their parents were wealthy enough to fund their further education.

At fourteen, a young woman became legally responsible for her actions, and liable to all the penalties of law, except execution. She could buy alcohol and weapons. On her sixteenth birthday, she could join the military or the Sisterhood—Ellen had signed up on the first of the month immediately following hers. At eighteen, she was a full adult. She could vote for the Town Mayor and other elected officials. She could become a mother.

To celebrate this occasion, a gift to the temple and a few suitable prayers were expected, and although nobody would check to see that Ellen carried out this act of piety, her mothers would be outraged if she did not. Ellen just hoped she would be able to do the necessary bits and get away without being spotted. However, she had barely started on the litany when she heard footsteps behind her. Ellen bent her head and closed her eyes. The footsteps stopped and stayed. Whoever it was clearly wanted to talk. With luck, it would just be Sister Ripatti, planning on castigating her for her absence over the past two months.

Ellen finished her prayers, stood up, and turned around. Mandy Colman smiled up at her. Ellen felt her heart sink into her boots.

"Happy birthday, Ellen."

"Um...thanks."

"I was wondering if I'd see you here."

"Well, it's, like you say, my birthday."

Mandy worked as a general assistant in the temple, cleaning, repairing, and tending to the Sisters' belongings. As a lay employee, she was not bound by the same rules of celibacy as the Sister and initiates. With hindsight, Ellen felt this was a regrettable oversight.

"I haven't seen you around much."

"I've been busy."

"I heard about what happened to your sergeant. How are you?"

"I'm fine and um...she's getting better and I need to..." Ellen tried to sidle away.

Mandy moved closer, blocking her in. Her eyes glittered in the candlelight. "I've missed you."

Ellen shrugged awkwardly. What could she say?

Mandy touched her finger to Ellen's forearm and traced a line along it, the same gesture as Hal, a few days before, but so very different in style and effect, supplicant rather than teasing. "We were so good together. Everyone said it. What went wrong?"

You were as interesting to talk to as a dead sheep. "You'll find someone else."

"I haven't got you a birthday present. But if there's something that you'd like." Mandy pushed her breasts forward. Subtlety had not been her strong point either.

"I'm sorry. I've got to—"

"I'd do anything you want."

Except act like you were enjoying it. Mandy had always made it clear that sex was something she granted purely as a favor, and expected Ellen to feel suitably indebted. "It's not—"

"We're going to be at the Silver Flagon tonight. Me, Jed, Trudy, and the rest. We could buy you a drink for your birthday." Mandy put her head on the side and rolled her eyes up at Ellen, acting as if she were a toddler. Ellen was sure she had never found the pose attractive, even in the early besotted stages of dating, although Mandy had clearly thought she should.

"I'm working tonight."

"Oh, that's not fair, on your birthday. When are you next off duty?"

"In a few days."

"I could see you then."

"I might be seeing someone el—" Too late, Ellen cut back her words.

Mandy backed away, her eyes filling with tears. They came so easily to her, as if she could turn them on and off at will, yet they never failed to make Ellen feel as if she had been a complete bitch.

Mandy's next words summed up everything that had not worked between them, although not for the reasons she might think. "Is she prettier than me?"

"It's not that." *But I suspect she won't cry as much.*

❖

Ellen let go of the pump handle but made no attempt to pick up the bucket. Instead she gazed absentmindedly at the reflected image of blue sky in the water. Her thoughts drifted like the stray wisps of clouds, but not for long. The same lure that had been snaring her head for the last six days coalesced. Hal and the memory of the touch of her lips, the muscles in her back, the pressure of her thigh. Tomorrow night, Ellen would be off duty. Would Hal remember? Would they meet? Ellen closed her eyes and swallowed, trying to still the turmoil rippling in her stomach. If it kept up much longer, she would get indigestion. After another deep breath, she opened her eyes and lifted the bucket.

Her family's cottage shared a washroom and latrine with seven others. The water pump stood in the middle of the rutted yard that the cottages backed onto. Ellen carried the bucket the dozen meters to their home and filled the water butt by the stove. After another three trips, the container was full.

Ellen hung the bucket back on its hook by the door. "There you go, Mom."

Mama Becky put down her sewing and smiled. "Thanks. Are you off now?"

Ellen looked at the sun, judging its position. She and Terrie Rasheed had visited the last of their farms that morning, concluding the pointless waste of time, but they still had one more evening patrol to go.

"I've got an hour before I need to be at the station. I thought I'd visit the baths." Ellen shrugged, aware of the layer of dust and sweat from the morning ride coating her skin. "I don't feel like I've been properly clean for a month."

"Okay, dear."

Ellen turned away.

"Oh, I'm such a pudding-head. I've just remembered." Mama Becky called her back.

"What?"

"A message came for you." She pulled a scrap of paper from a pocket.

"Who's it from?"

"I don't know. Jill Simamora's youngest brought it over."

"You didn't ask who gave it to her?"

"You know I don't like to meddle in what you're up to."

This was not strictly true, but Ellen chose not to challenge it.

Mama Becky passed over the paper, clearly trying not to appear eager. "I thought it might be from Mandy. You know that she's still fond of you? She's such a sweet girl."

Ellen said nothing and took the letter. Her name was scrawled on the outside, and already Ellen knew it was not from her ex-girlfriend. The handwriting was far too untidy. But might it be Hal? Did she know where Ellen lived? Was passing notes her style? Did Hal want to arrange a meeting for tomorrow?

Ellen was worried by how much the thought excited her. Chris had said to string Hal along to see if she was on the level, and to get information if she was not. But Chris had also said to be careful, and to keep her emotions under control. However, Ellen's emotions were showing no sign of doing what she told them to and were wildly galloping away with her.

Ellen opened the letter and read.

Officer Mittal,

Please don't try to find me out, or I will be dead. You know what happened to Husmann and Sanchez.

I've heard that the gang from Eastford who stole all the sheep will be picking up supplies from the Diaz warehouse on Upper Dockside at 17 o'clock tonight. They have threatened Diaz that they will hurt her family if she does not give them what they want. She has caved in, but somebody has to stop them, or they will bleed us all dry.

I did not know who best to send this to. I would have written to Sanchez, but I've heard that she is still sick. Your lieutenant is useless. You stood up to them before. Please, can you do something now?

The letter was not signed. This was hardly a surprise.

"Is it from Mandy?"

"No." Ellen looked up. "Are you sure you've no idea who sent it?"

"None. You could go and ask young Pat if you want."

Ellen shook her head. Pat Simamora was four years old—a well-behaved and helpful child, but not a particularly bright one. Tracking her down was unlikely to produce any answer other than "a lady" and Ellen knew she did not have time to waste.

"Is it something important?" Mama Becky was starting to sound worried.

"No, but er...I've got to rush." Ellen took two steps backward. "I'll be back later." She turned and ran.

She crossed Newbridge road into the more prosperous parts of town. The streets were busy, yet nobody got in her way. Citizens stepped aside, seeing a running woman in the black Militia uniform. Ellen pelted past. Every back route and shortcut in town was familiar to her. She raced across a small square and turned into a deserted alleyway, but then doubts caught up with her. The pace left her feet and she coasted to an indecisive halt. Ellen stood with her hand braced against a wall, eyes closed, gasping for breath and thinking.

Where was she going?

The rules said that, on receiving important information about a crime, a rookie should report directly to her commanding officer. Yet Ellen knew Cohen would reject the letter outright. Most likely, she would declare it a hoax and set the Militia on the task of uncovering the source, which was the very last thing they should do. If any harm came to the letter writer, it would put anyone else off informing on the Butcher.

In her mind, Ellen had been on her way to Chris Sanchez's home—but what was the point in that? She already knew what Chris would say. There was only one sensible course of action. The words Chris had spoken in the garden echoed in Ellen's head. *The Rangers are your best bet. If you find out something they need to know, then tell them.*

Despite what the rule book might say, Ellen knew she had to bypass Cohen and hand the letter directly to the Rangers. And the sooner the better. Talking it over with Chris would be reassuring, but time was pressing and the Ranger Barracks were near at hand. Why race across town and back?

Ellen glanced up at the sun. She could easily get to the Ranger barracks, hand the letter over to Captain Aitkin, explain as much as she knew, and still be at the Militia station in time to start the evening patrol. With luck, Lieutenant Cohen would never learn about her role in the matter.

Ellen took a deep breath and stepped away from the wall. Chris had said that initiative would be called for. Now was not a bad time to start. Ellen turned around and ran back the way she had come.

Chapter Five—The Warehouse Pick-up

The Ranger barracks were on the northern side of town, backing on to the eastern branch of the River Tamer. A high brick wall surrounded the site, although it was mainly for show, underlining the military nature of the compound. As ever, the gates were open and unguarded. Ellen jogged through, past bunkhouses and stables, until she reached the central parade ground. The administration building was on the far side. This was the most likely place to find Captain Aitkin, and even if she was not there, the staff orderlies would know where she was.

Two Rangers were in the outer room when Ellen entered. They looked up from their paperwork. Ellen wondered if she imagined the instant disdain in their eyes at the sight of her black uniform.

"What do you want?"

"I'd like to speak to Captain Aitkin. Is she around?"

"She's busy."

"It's important."

The Rangers exchanged glances, but then one stood and walked to an inner door. "Who shall I say it is?"

"I'm Rookie Ellen Mittal. That won't interest her much, but say I have news about the Butcher's gang."

The supplemental information evidently did interest Aitkin, even if the name did not, and Ellen was immediately shown in to the captain's office. Aitkin sat at her desk. She looked up when Ellen entered. The captain of the 12th Squadron was in her early forties, with weathered skin, pinched cheeks, and an unwavering gaze.

Captain Aitkin's expression was guarded, but did not quite manage to conceal her curiosity or surprise. She waited until the door had closed before speaking. "Don't tell me Lieutenant Cohen has sent you to ask my help with the gang."

"No, ma'am. She doesn't know I've come to see you."

Aitkin let the silence drag out, while Ellen tried not to wilt under her stare. At last the captain asked, "So why are you here?"

Ellen pulled the note from her pocket. "This was handed to me a short while ago. I thought you'd make better use of it than Lieutenant Cohen."

Up until now, Aitkin's manner had been dry and dismissive. She still tried to appear aloof, but the sharpening of her interest was unmistakable as she opened the sheet of paper. After a few seconds her eyes darted back to Ellen. Now there was no attempt to disguise her attentiveness. For the first time, Captain Aitkin regarded Ellen as if she was someone worth taking seriously.

"Where did you get this?"

"It was passed on by one of the young kids who lives on the same street as me." Ellen did not want to drag her mother into the affair.

"You don't think it's a game on this kid's part?"

"She's too young. She can't write."

"Somebody might be using her."

"If it's a hoaxer's idea of a joke, making us look like fools by running after nothing, she'd want to share the laugh with her friends. But nobody will be around that late at night. And she'd have to know we suspected the Eastford gang."

"If it's not a joke then it might be a trap."

"It might. But in that case, it's a trap set for the Militia. They won't be expecting the Rangers."

Captain Aitkin leaned back in the chair and considered Ellen. "Is that why you brought the letter here, rather than giving it to your commanding officer?"

The question was an awkward one that Ellen did not want to answer in too much detail. She felt her cheeks start to burn, but forced herself to speak. "In part, ma'am. But mainly, like I said, I thought you'd be the best people to deal with it. Lieutenant Cohen might not want to..." Ellen swallowed, unwilling to finish the sentence.

A flicker of a smile crossed the captain's face. "No. You're right. She probably wouldn't." In a fluid move, Aitkin swung off her chair, stepped around her desk, and opened the door. "Get Lieutenant Green and the sergeants. I want them here on the double."

At the sharp command, the two orderlies literally dropped the papers in their hands and sped off. Aitkin turned to Ellen, stepping back, but still holding the door open. "Wait outside until I call for you."

"I'm due at the Militia station soon, ma'am."

Aitkin shook her head sharply. "I won't be keeping you long, but I think we might need more of your assistance. If it gets sticky with Lieutenant Cohen, you can blame me for commandeering you. But only once the whole affair is over. I don't want you saying anything until then."

So much for hopes of keeping her part hidden from Cohen. Ellen found a stool in a corner of the main office and sat down, anxiously. Would Aitkin really be able to protect her from any repercussions? Cohen was certain to be furious. Ellen chewed her lip, trying to take comfort in the thought that she had done the only sensible thing, and it was not as if she had so much to lose. Cohen had never expressed any approval of her hard work or dedication. Thinking about it, Ellen could not remember a single word of praise. She sighed and stared at the ceiling, trying to convince herself that, no matter how it turned out, things were not going to get any worse.

Ellen's brooding was interrupted by the arrival of the five summoned Rangers—four sergeants and a lieutenant. In quick succession, they hurried into the office. None of them spared more than a disinterested glance at Ellen. The door shut after the last one. Ellen sat, shoulders slumped, wondering if maybe she should have first talked it over with Chris Sanchez after all.

The two staff orderlies returned and went back to their work. They made a show of ignoring Ellen, although a couple of times she caught expressions of frank curiosity directed her way. For a while there was only the rumble of voices from the captain's office, and then the door opened again.

"Militiawoman Mittal."

Ellen felt hideously self-conscious as she returned to the captain's office, and not merely for the way her black uniform stood out in a room full of green. Everyone outranked her. The faces studying her displayed varying combinations of mistrust and bemusement.

Aitkin was the only one to smile. "Mittal. I want to thank you for bringing this to our attention. For what it's worth, I think you've done the right thing, and I suspect a lot of other people will too. We're going to have a number of Rangers on hand tonight, ready to seize the gang members, if that's who they turn out to be. But we want some more help from you." She beckoned Ellen forward and pointed to a street map of Roadsend laid out on her desk. "The warehouse mentioned. It's here, correct?"

"Yes, ma'am."

"I want you to be the one who initially challenges the gang. But don't worry. We'll be there. You'll have plenty of support to back you up if it turns violent."

"Um..." Ellen felt her insides cramp. "Why me, ma'am?"

"Because we don't want to alert the gang and scare them off. They aren't going to run from one lone Militiawoman on patrol. If they see a Ranger they'll know something funny is going on. And equally, we don't want to pounce on some innocent traders if it's a hoax—and that's if anyone turns up at all. You're local. You know all the people in town. You'll spot if they're strangers, or local women acting out of character. I'm sure it will only take you a few seconds to work out whether they're thieves or honest traders making a late night pick-up. We'll get into position early and make sure we don't get seen. You should also try to keep out of sight until the wagon or whatever arrives. Then go and challenge them. If they're on the level you can just walk away."

"And if they're not?" Ellen tried not to sound panicked.

"Wave your hands, shout for help, do something. We don't need to worry with fancy signals. We'll be watching and we'll be able to tell what you mean."

"I'm supposed to be on duty tonight, patrolling the town."

"Perfect. You can patrol by Upper Dockside."

"I'm only a rookie. Corporal Rasheed will pick our route."

"A pity. Then you're going to have to slip away from her and get to the rendezvous on your own. I don't want anyone else told about this. And certainly not Corporal Rasheed. I've dealt with her before. She can be a..." Aitkin's tone implied that *complete pain in the ass* was how she wanted to end the sentence.

"But—"

Aitkin straightened up and fixed a stern glare on Ellen. Her tone also hardened. "It's not a suggestion. It's an order. Be at Diaz warehouse by seventeen o'clock. And don't worry about any disciplinary charges. I'll clear it with your Lieutenant Cohen tomorrow."

Ellen pulled herself rigidly to attention. "Yes, ma'am."

Strictly speaking, Aitkin was exceeding her authority. The Rangers and the Militia did not have the same chain of command and Aitkin was not entitled to issue direct orders to any Militiawoman. However she was a captain, and all the branches of the military were supposed to work together. Ellen could refuse to obey, but then she would have to refer the issue to Lieutenant Cohen. No matter how it worked out, that option could only land her in a lot more trouble. At least this way she would have Aitkin on her side and taking a share of the responsibility.

Aitkin nodded. "And don't breathe a word to anyone."

❖

Ellen charged through the door of the Militia station and stumbled to a halt, gasping for breath. Terrie Rasheed was standing by the table, mug in hand. She twisted around, scowling. "What sort of time do you call this? You're late."

"Sorry, ma'am."

"What happened?"

"I just, um..." Ellen shrugged apologetically.

"Well? What?"

"I lost track of time. I...er..."

"Is that the best frigging excuse you can come up with?"

"I went home and put my feet up. I didn't mean it, but I must have drifted off to sleep."

"You fell asleep?"

"Yes, ma'am."

Terrie snorted but then turned away, drained her tea, then dumped the empty mug on the table. "Damned rookies, sauntering in whenever they feel like it."

Ellen concentrated on catching her breath and controlling her expression. This was the first time she had ever been late, and it was only by a bare quarter hour. Terrie was the one with the reputation for slack timekeeping. It would be a rare occurrence if she had been on time today. Ellen was prepared to bet money that Terrie had only been waiting for a few minutes—just long enough to make and drink a cup of tea.

Terrie pushed past her to the door. "Well, come on. Don't stand there gawking. You've wasted enough time as it is."

Ellen followed on. Suddenly her anger drained away, overwhelmed by the thought that she was now committed to her course of action. More even than by not handing the letter over to her commanding officer—that was a breach of protocol. She had just lied to a senior officer.

❖

The Twisted Crook had the reputation of being the rowdiest tavern in Roadsend. From two streets away, Ellen could hear the racket being raised in its taproom. It got louder with each step closer. She and Terrie emerged from the alleyway onto the dockside. Overhead, small Laurel was just starting to sink and the other moon, Hardie, was rising, nearly full. To the west lay open country, cut by the silver river winding off into the darkness. The sheep docks were deserted, the empty pens a maze of railings and gates. Two barges were moored alongside, but the crews were nowhere in sight. Most likely they were in the Twisted Crook.

The Militiawomen skirted the pens, approaching the tavern door. Shouting came from inside, but there was no anger in the voices, the speakers were merely trying to be heard over the clamor of singing and laughter.

Terrie stamped to a halt and gestured to Ellen. "I'm going to check that everything is okay in here. You scout along the dock and give the barges the once-over."

"Yes, ma'am."

Ellen turned away sharply to conceal her expression. Looking at the outside of the barges was a pointless exercise. It was insulting if Terrie seriously thought she was incapable of seeing through the ploy. However, Ellen's main reaction was of elation. She had been worried about how to get away, but Terrie's timing of an illicit beer could not have been better. From the moons' position, it was nearly a quarter to 17 o'clock. The Diaz warehouse was midway between the Ranger Barracks and East Bridge, on the other side of town, but a quarter hour was easily long enough to get there.

Ellen marched to the nearer barge—the *Susie-Louise*, according to the name painted on its side. A quick glance over her shoulder was just in time to catch the tavern door swing shut after Terrie. Smiling,

Ellen left the docks, jogging through the dark streets of Roadsend. Her route crossed the Clemswood Road, taking her into the genteel district, north of the main square, where the best houses were found. However, the wealth faded rapidly and by the time she passed the square where the not so genteel Three Barrels stood, the roads were lined with shops and the homes of tradeswomen. The area was no longer so fashionable, although still far above the Northside slums where Ellen's family lived.

Ellen emerged onto Main Drove. To her right, the wide street went to South Bridge, on the way crossing the main square where the town hall, infirmary, and Militia station were situated. Was Lieutenant Cohen currently there, oblivious to events in progress? How would she respond when she found out? The thought made Ellen's footsteps falter for a second, but this was not the time to engage in doubts.

A short way to Ellen's left, Main Drove terminated in a T-junction with Upper Dockside. The Diaz warehouse was less than a hundred meters away. However, rather than go directly there, Ellen crossed the road and ducked into an alleyway that ran parallel to Upper Dockside. After a short distance she turned down a side passage, tiptoeing silently through the shadows. She finally stopped at the end of the passage, with a clear view across Upper Dockside to the door of Diaz's warehouse.

No wagon was in sight. Was the letter a hoax? The closely packed buildings blocked her view of either moon, but Ellen was sure that 17 o'clock was not far away. She took a deep breath, trying to settle any nerves. The night felt heavy, closing around her. All Ellen could hear were the distant cries of a baby, the creak of a hinge swinging in the breeze, the scuffing of some vermin burrowing through a nearby pile of rubbish, and the thud of her own heartbeat. Then, faintly, came the unmistakable hollow sound of hooves and wooden wheels, clattering over cobblestones.

The sound got louder and louder, until it seemed deafening in Ellen's ears. At last the wagon rumbled into view. It was a standard two-horse cart, a style that could be seen all around the region, with boarded sides and large, eight-spoked wheels. Every farm had at least one. It could be used for transporting sheep or, as now, getting supplies from town. Two figures sat on the seat at the front. The driver pulled on the reins, bringing the horses to a standstill at the door of the Diaz warehouse. The woman sitting beside her jumped down.

"The door ought to be left unlocked," the driver said.

"Right."

"The stuff will be piled inside."

"Yeah, yeah. I know. I heard the instructions too."

"You surprise me."

"Why?"

"Because I didn't know if you were listening. You never pay any fucking attention when I tell you things."

"That's 'cause you talk a load of crap."

Despite the words, the tone was light-hearted—friendly banter, rather than an argument—and although it was clearly said in jest, the exchange was enough for Ellen to know that this was not a normal pick-up. Whoever heard of an owner leaving the door to her warehouse open? Or not being present to count out the goods and sign the receipt? Yet it was not at all surprising if the instructions had come from the gang, to prevent the Knives from being seen by anyone who might then be able to identify them.

Ellen felt her heart racing as she stepped from the passageway. Captain Aitkin had promised that the Rangers would be on hand. Ellen had seen no sign of them, which was according to plan, but supposing something had gone wrong? Supposing they were in the wrong place? Ellen offered up a prayer to the Goddess that nothing unforeseen had gotten in their way, and they were ready to jump on her signal.

Both suspects were now hidden from view on the other side of the horses. The warehouse door creaked open. Ellen rounded the back of the cart, trying to make her footsteps ring loud on the cobbles. In the hope of keeping things as calm and controlled as possible, she did not want to surprise them too much. Yet even with the current critical situation, Ellen could not stop herself from checking the cart as she passed. She remembered Jo, the farm hand, fitting the new planks. To her relief, all the boarding was well weathered. Wherever the cart came from, it was not Broken Hills Ranch.

"What's that? Did you hear something?" one of the women whispered from just inside the warehouse door.

Ellen raised her voice. "Good evening. What's going on here?"

"Shit." The word was hissed so softly that it would have been missed, were Ellen's senses not on high alert.

After a moment of shuffling, one of the figures appeared around the warehouse door, into the narrow gap between it and the side of the cart. The sight of Ellen's uniform produced an instant reaction and the woman backed away. Her gaze swept up and down Ellen once more and then fastened on her face.

"Shit," she repeated.

The feeling was mutual. Ellen recognized Trish Eriksen, Ade's younger sister.

"What is it?" The voice from inside the warehouse was louder, clearly anxious.

"Fucking Blackshirts."

"They shouldn't be—" The words cut off as the second woman sprung into view, diving for the cart.

Ellen took a step forward, thinking that the two were about to flee. Instead the woman spun back, this time holding a cudgel in her hand. Ellen barely managed to avoid the vicious swipe, aimed at her head. She stumbled away, ducking a second blow that smashed into the side of the wagon. The woman came after her, again swinging her club. Ellen kept retreating frantically, until an uneven cobblestone caught her heel. Her footing slipped and she ended up flat on her back.

"It's them. They're here."

Ellen was scarcely aware of what she shouted. Her entire attention was fixed on the advancing figure, looming over her. The cudgel was hoisted high, blocking out the stars. Ellen braced her hands on the ground, ready to shunt either left or right on the downswing. A sudden clamor from across the street made her flinch, but her eyes never left the weapon, lofted over her head. All else was irrelevant. Her assailant though, reacted instantly. The cudgel clattered on the ground, cast aside as the Knife whirled away and raced for the cart.

It took a moment for Ellen to realize she was no longer in danger. She pushed herself up off the ground. On the other side of the street, a door had opened and a half dozen Rangers were spilling out. The two Knives had scrambled aboard the cart, but neither was yet sitting in place. One clung to the side. The other was sprawled face down across the seat, scrabbling for the reins.

The Rangers were closing in. With no time left, the woman on the seat yelped to the horses, frantically snapping the reins like a whip.

The horses surged forward, but before they had picked up speed, more Rangers emerged from an alleyway ahead. The driver was now kneeling, still struggling to get properly seated. She shouted, urging the horses on, but the animals were not so eager to plow into the advancing women.

One horse reared up, pawing the air. The other was wrenched around by the momentum of the vehicle. Its back hooves skittered across the cobbles and only the harness kept it from falling. The cart slewed violently sideways, slamming into a wall. Something snapped with an explosive crack. A scream from the woman on the sideboard, caught between cart and wall, was cut short. The chassis teetered and then tipped over.

More footsteps sounded behind Ellen. Rangers were arriving on all sides, running. But before they reached the cart, a figure pulled herself clear of the wreckage, ducked past the bucking horses and set off at full pelt. One of the advancing Rangers stood in her way.

Moonlight glinted on something in the Knife's hand. The memory of the blade sinking into Chris's back flashed over Ellen. In panic, she opened her mouth to shout a warning, but she was not in time. Two figures collided in the moonlight, but it was the Knife who stumbled away, hands gripped to her stomach. Her knees buckled and she dropped. The other figure, the Ranger, was still upright, frozen in the "on guard" position, her sword outstretched. When had she drawn it? Ellen had not seen the motion.

The wounded woman was on her knees, curling forward. First her head then her shoulders hit the ground. Convulsive spasms ran through her, heaving her onto her back. Fingers clawed the air. Her knee pulled up, heel raking across the cobbles and then stopped. The Knife's leg flopped to the side and she lay motionless.

Ellen pulled her feet under her and stood. Her legs were trembling with the effects of adrenaline. Her head spun and ripples of nausea unsettled her gut. She looked around. At least twenty Rangers were gathered in the street. The familiar figure of Captain Aitkin was by the cart, but then she turned and came over to Ellen.

"Good job."

Ellen stood with her arms wrapped around her waist, trying to stop the shaking. "Thank you, ma'am."

"Did you recognize either of them?"

"One. She's a local girl."

"Trouble?"

"She has been in the past."

The body of the Knife lay only a few meters away. Ellen stumbled across and stared down into Trish Eriksen's open eyes. A Ranger was kneeling beside Trish, feeling for a pulse in her neck. At Ellen and Captain Aitkin's approach she looked up and shook her head sharply, answering the unasked question.

Aitkin turned to those gathered around the wrecked cart and called, "How's the other one?"

"Badly wounded, ma'am. She got squished between the wagon and the wall."

"Can she still talk?" Aitkin was walking over as she spoke, her voice dropping.

"When she comes to, maybe. Her head took a bad knock."

Ellen looked away, blanking out the conversations around her. Trish Eriksen lay dead on the ground at her feet. Now Ellen recognized her voice. She had been the driver's assistant, the one who never listened. In that respect, she had not changed. Trish had never listened.

She was seventeen years old. A whole year younger than Ellen. The family used to live only a few streets away from Ellen's until Ade's behavior made them so unpopular with their neighbors that they had moved out of town, to an isolated cottage. Ellen searched for her first memory of Trish, and dug up an incident on the way home from school.

Ellen had been six or seven, walking with her friends Denny and Tess. They had come across two older children holding Trish down, rubbing her face in the mud. Ellen and her friends had run up and the bullies had fled. Trish had been crying, tears and snot streaking dirt across her face. Nobody had said anything, but they all knew what the trouble had been about. Trish, like Ellen and her friends, was from the wrong side of Newbridge Road. Anyone would have known it from Trish's grubby shirt, flapping slack around her neck, obviously inherited from an older sister. Some better-off children thought this made them good targets. Ellen and her friends had said comforting things and walked Trish home, holding the younger child's hand and feeling very grown-up. Ellen had heard that Ade went out that evening, looking for revenge, and had taken it on the first child she had found, wearing clothes marking her as not from Northside. What would Ade do now?

Trish had not, and never would have been a friend, even before Ellen joined the Militia. Trish had always been too willing to follow Ade's lead. A large girl who had outgrown the children around her, she had come to rely too much on her fists. Ellen took a deep breath, trying to calm the spasms in her stomach. That reliance was what had let Trish down. She had charged at the Ranger, confident she could outfight anyone, confident she would always win, confident she could pummel the world into doing what she wanted.

Trish had been in trouble most of her life, already arrested a dozen times. She had given Ellen a black eye in the course of one scuffle. Ellen swallowed the bile in her throat. She had not liked Trish, but seeing her dead was utterly final. So much about Trish had been wrong. Dead meant it could never be put right. All chances were gone.

Ellen's eyes stung, though no tears were there. She turned away, leaving Patricia Eriksen still staring up, unseeing, at the stars.

Chapter Six—The Captured Knife

After what I've said to you, how dare you deliberately ignore me?" The volume of Cohen's voice was enough to make Ellen flinch. "Running off like that? Leaving Corporal Rasheed without a word of explanation? Joining up with the Rangers for this... this shambles of an operation? What the hell did you think you were doing?"

"Captain Aitkin ordered me to, ma'am."

"She's not your commanding officer." Lieutenant Cohen leaned forward, glaring at Ellen. Her hands were balled in fists, white knuckles pressed on her desktop. "Why didn't you come and inform me?"

"She instructed me not to tell anyone."

Cohen pushed off her desk and turned away slightly. "She had no damned right to."

Ellen felt the tension in her guts ease a little, sensing that some of Cohen's anger was now targeted at Captain Aitkin.

Cohen paced across her room and then swung back to Ellen. "And Patricia Eriksen is dead. I've a good mind to go find the Ranger who did it and arrest her for murder."

Ellen said nothing. Saying as little as possible seemed the most sensible option. However, she recognized Cohen's words as empty blustering. Trish Eriksen was a known criminal who had died with a weapon in her hand, attacking a member of the military. Not only would no magistrate find the killer guilty, but she would be likely to issue a reprimand to the arresting officer for wasting the court's time.

"What about the other one? The prisoner they took away? Was that Adeola Eriksen?"

"I don't think so, ma'am."

"You don't think so? Don't evade the question." Cohen's voice raised yet another notch. Ellen's ears were ringing. "You know what she looks like, don't you?"

"It was dark and I only got a quick look at her during the engagement. Afterward she was badly injured. Her face was a mess, so..." Ellen finished with an awkward shrug.

"The whole damn thing was a mess." Cohen turned away, then glanced back. "But she was definitely still alive at the end?"

"Yes, ma'am."

"Then she belongs here in the station, not up at the Ranger Barracks." Cohen turned her head toward the door of her office and bellowed, "Rasheed!"

The door opened and Terrie's head appeared around it. Judging by her smug expression, she had heard all Cohen's side of the discussion—folk on the other side of town had probably caught some of it. "Ma'am?"

"I want the entire Militia, looking smart, assembled here for eight o'clock sharp. Let them know."

"Yes, ma'am." Terrie ducked back out of the room.

Cohen glared sourly at Ellen. "You can go too. But don't think this is the last you're going to hear about the matter. Be here with the others at eight."

"Yes, ma'am."

Ellen slipped out of the room, feeling surprised that it had gone so easily. She had been expecting a much harder time. For all the shouting, Cohen had made no mention of disciplinary action, not even as a vague threat.

Terrie was still in the briefing room. She looked as if she had been on the point of leaving, but at the sight of Ellen, she leaned her shoulder against the wall and sneered. "You had a fucking nerve. Ditching me like that. Do you know how long I spent looking for you? I thought you'd fallen in the river or something. Instead you'd run off to play with the Rangers."

"I'm sorry. I was under orders."

"Under orders." Terrie mimicked a whine. "That was from the fucking Rangers, wasn't it? Well, you don't take orders from the Rangers. You take them from Lieutenant Cohen or you take them from me. In the future, if you're out with me, you let me know what's going on, or I'll be puppy walking you on a leash. Get it?"

"Got it."

Ellen refrained from adding anything more, although various

thoughts shot through her head, not the least being that it was hard to keep officers informed if they were in the tavern, knocking back beer. Terrie had also missed that she had merely indicated she understood what had been said rather than agreeing to act in a different fashion in the future.

For her part, Terrie had not finished. “It’s what, less than a month till you finish your probation?”

“Yes.”

“And you’re counting on joining the Rangers.” Terrie said it as a statement of fact. “You think Aitkin will put in a good word for you. You think you’ll get to swan around in that fucking uniform. I tell you, the Rangers are a bunch of overrated, arrogant jerks.”

If you think that, why are you so upset at not being allowed to join them? Again Ellen did not voice her thought.

“They made a right foul-up last night, didn’t they?”

“In what way?”

Terrie looked taken aback. Clearly she had not expected Ellen to offer any sort of dissent. She floundered for a moment. “The...the…you know, Trish dead, and all.” She glared at Ellen, and returned to the attack. “You think they did a good job? Your head needs seeing to. You youngsters think the Rangers can walk on fucking water.”

“No. But they stopped a gang of thieves from getting supplies. They killed one. Took the other prisoner. They’ve confirmed it’s the big Eastford gang working out here. I don’t see why you think it’s a mess.”

For a moment, Terrie looked as if she was about to be sick, but then her usual surliness returned. “Stupid little brat. You’ll learn better—if you live that long.” She yanked the street door open. “Come on. You heard Cohen’s order. You find Thorensen and McCray and tell them. I’ll see you here at eight. Don’t be late.”

Terrie directed one last furious scowl at Ellen and then stepped out into the street.

❖

The small band of Militiawomen trooped through the gates of the Ranger Barracks. As they crossed the parade ground, they attracted a few curious stares. Ellen tagged on at the rear, thankful she would not be called on to play any significant role in the farce. Just what was Cohen hoping to achieve? Was it for show? Did she think the squadron of Rangers would be impressed by seven women in black uniforms? There was no practical need for so many. Even if the prisoner was too injured to walk, it would not require all of them to carry her.

Lieutenant Cohen stopped on the first of the short flight of steps leading up to the door of the administration block. From this slightly elevated position she looked down on her subordinates.

"Right. I'm going to talk to Captain Aitkin and get the prisoner handed over to us. Rasheed, come with me. The rest of you wait out here."

The two officers climbed the stairs and disappeared into the building.

Ellen glanced at the small lockup to the left of the admin block, presumably where the captured Knife was being held. Surely it was out of the question that the Rangers would relinquish their prisoner to anyone who had demonstrated Cohen's level of ineptitude.

The small knot of Militiawomen was attracting attention from the Rangers. Green and gray clad figures were gathering around the perimeter of the parade ground. Ellen did not need to see their faces to know they were vastly more amused than intimidated. Closer at hand, the four patrolwomen were directing their own suspicious looks at her. At last, Penny Rambaldi maneuvered around the edge of the group to Ellen's side.

"So, what's all this about?" Penny did not appear hostile.

"How much do you know already?"

"Diddly squat."

Ellen paused for a second, considering what she should say. Cohen, possibly by oversight, had not ordered her to keep the details secret from the rest of the Militia. Yet Ellen did not want to implicate herself more than she already had, in case word got back to Cohen. With luck, the lieutenant would never find out that she was the one who had passed on the letter from the informant.

"Last night, the Rangers got word that the gang who stole all the sheep would be picking up supplies in town. They staked out the warehouse and commandeered me to help them."

"Wow. So this prisoner, that's where they captured her?"

"Yes."

"Do we know her? Or anyone else in the gang?"

"I didn't recognize her, and there were only two bandits making the pick-up. But Trish Eriksen was the other one. She got killed."

"Right." Penny drew the word out into an exclamation of enlightenment. "I heard she'd died. So it was part of the same thing?"

"Yes."

"When I got the news, I'd assumed she'd finally come out worse in one of her brawls." Penny did not sound upset.

"She tried to escape. She had a knife and went for a Ranger standing in her way."

"She always was shit stupid. I guess we owe the Ranger a drink."

Ellen could not bring herself to say more. The image rose before her, of Trish's face, staring at the sky. The other three patrolwomen had been listening intently. They now exchanged muttered comments among themselves.

Della Murango was looking thoughtful. "Does this tie in with Chris getting stabbed, do you know?"

Ellen nodded. "It's the same lot. It's the Eastford Butcher and her gang, the ones who call themselves the Knives. They've spread out our way."

Jude McCray and Zar Thorensen were visibly shaken by the news, but nobody seemed completely astounded.

Penny kicked at the dry ground. She looked as if she was toying with a number of responses, evaluating their wisdom. "Yeah. You know, I'd wondered about that."

The door of the administration building opened and Cohen and Terrie emerged, looking unhappy. Ellen was not surprised. Had Jake Cohen seriously thought she stood a chance of achieving anything other than making the Militia look stupid? However, there was grimness in Terrie's expression that spoke of more than mere hurt pride.

"Are they going to hand over the prisoner, ma'am?" Jude was the one to ask the pointless question.

Cohen drew a deep breath and pursed her lips in an aggrieved expression. "They can't. Apparently she died of her injuries an hour ago."

❖

Chris Sanchez was looking far more like her old self. The color was back in her face and she moved with a trace of her former precision. However, the injured sergeant was still clearly not at full strength, although she refused help as she hobbled around her kitchen, making tea.

Outside, afternoon sunlight danced over the trees in the yard. Ellen sat at the table next to open window shutters. She was pleased for the chance to discuss the recent events with Chris. She had been worried that Lieutenant Cohen would dock her off-duty time, by way of punishment. However, on returning to the station, Cohen had ignored her. Terrie had been more of an ordeal, assigning her the most unpopular tasks and subjecting her to a string of verbal abuse. But eventually, Ellen had been released, and was now facing her first evening off since the night in the White Swan with Valerie.

Ellen's account ended just as the tea making was complete. Chris pushed the kettle to the back of the stove, picked up the two mugs, and then put them on the table.

"I thought Cohen would be harder on me, after the trouble I got in before. But she just shouted at me and didn't even threaten me with anything."

Chris laughed softly. "You're really surprised?"

"Yes."

"Jake Cohen has been staking everything on the hope that the problem will go away if she ignores it. She's lost the bet. She knows HQ has been informed about what's been going on here—or more like what's not been going on. She's in line to get her ass well and truly kicked. Her best chance is to take some of the credit for what you did, but she can't do that if she's in the process of bringing disciplinary charges against you for those very same actions."

"Oh." Ellen frowned. "Terrie was furious about me helping the Rangers."

"Terrie will never let common sense get in the way of spite. And it isn't her ass with the target on it."

Ellen stared at her mug while running the ideas around in her head. "Do you think Terrie put her up to that nonsense at the Barracks, trying to get the prisoner?"

"Maybe, but Jake would probably have done it anyway."

"Why? It was never going to work."

"It was a long shot, but she had nothing to lose. HQ will send somebody to take charge here. It'd be better for Cohen if she could pass over the information gotten from the prisoner, rather than let Aitkin take all the glory."

"What sort of information?"

"The location of the gang's hideout, for starters."

"I checked the cart. It wasn't from Broken Hills Ranch. That one has new side boards." Ellen dropped her eyes, aware she had been a little too eager.

"The gang could be using a farm as a front or they could have a hideout, somewhere in the Wildlands. It's a shame the prisoner died."

"Do you think she's really dead? Some of the patrolwomen were wondering about it on the way back to the station."

"Probably. Aitkin has no need to lie."

Ellen drained the last of her tea. "It all gets a bit silly without you. Any idea when you'll be back?"

"Do you miss me?"

"Lots."

"I'm seeing Dr. Miller tomorrow. Hopefully she'll clear me for desk duty. But don't expect to see me pounding the beat before next month." Chris was silent for a while, but then continued, this time with a teasing undercurrent to her voice. "So have you heard any more from your flirting farmer?"

"Um...we've met once, briefly." Ellen felt her face burn. She would rather not confess to the kiss while on duty. "And a neighbor dropped off a note at the station this morning. Hal's going to be in the Three Barrels tonight and asked if I'd meet her there."

"Are you going?"

Ellen ducked her head self-consciously. Hal had clearly remembered when she was going to be off duty and had not wanted to waste a day. Hal was most definitely interested in her. However, it was her own eagerness worrying Ellen. Images of Hal kept slipping into her head, sending her pulse racing and sending ripples through her stomach. Events that evening might move too far and too fast. The Eastford gang were working in Roadsend and Hal was not in the clear—far from it. Meeting her might be unwise, but Ellen could not help herself where Hal was involved.

"Yes."

❖

Ellen's skin was still tingling from the visit to the town baths, her clothes were damp off the washing line, and her heart was pounding as she tried to look casual, strolling into the taproom of the Three Barrels Tavern. A few steps in, she stopped and looked around. The room was busy, but far from full. Outside, the sun was dropping. Weak bands of sunshine sliced through the windows, cutting the room into bands of light and dark, dazzling and cloaking by turns. Yet nerves rather than poor illumination were what gave Ellen the problem. She scanned the faces, and saw none of them.

Ellen took a breath, forcing her eyes to focus properly, when a voice at her shoulder said, "You decided to come, then? I was worried I'd scared you off."

Ellen jumped and spun around. Hal stood behind her, hands on hips, grinning.

"I, er..." Ellen's breath escaped in a sharp sigh. Her heart rate soared to a new high and her stomach bounced around like an overactive spring lamb, but she managed enough self-control to smile and string a few words together. "I don't scare quite that easily."

"Good." Hal tilted her head toward a table, without breaking eye contact with Ellen. "I was sitting over there, and just about to get another drink. Can I buy you one?"

Ellen scrabbled for the purse on her belt. "Why don't I get one for you?"

Hal laughed. "You can get the next round. I'll buy these."

Ellen slipped past her toward the table and sat, massaging her knees. On reflection, maybe it was not a bad idea for Hal to be the one standing at the bar. Ellen had the nasty suspicion that her own legs were about to give way. She clenched her teeth, trying to calm down.

The table was at the side of the room just to the right of the door, in an alcove formed by the high-backed seats. The position was good for spotting everyone who entered the tavern before they spotted you. That was why Hal had been able to sneak up behind her.

Hal returned from the bar, deposited the two tankards on the table, and then sat opposite. She took a sip of the beer and leaned back. Ellen was about to do likewise when she felt Hal's ankles clamping on either side of hers. She looked up. Hal was smiling at her, mischievously challenging.

Ellen put her tankard down. "I usually wait for a second date before playing footsie."

"Do you? So what happens on a first?"

"I was hoping for some small talk. To learn a bit about you."

"Really?" Hal's foot moved gently a few centimeters up and down Ellen's calf, but then stilled. "Okay. I do that as well. What would you like to know about?"

"How about your family? Sisters, mothers?"

Hal laughed. "Oh, believe me, you don't want to know about my family." At Ellen's determined look, Hal gave in and continued. "I've got two sisters. One younger. One older. My parents both work on Grandmas' farm, down near Monday Market."

"They're sheep farmers?"

"Cattle. It's the same general idea, but I'm having to pick up some new tricks." Hal tilted her head to one side. "How about you? Were either of your parents Militiawomen?"

"No. My gene mother was a shepherd but she had an accident."

"What sort of accident?"

"She was out riding alone and a mountain cat attacked her."

"Was it straight out of hibernation?"

"I think so—still too groggy to know it couldn't eat her. Mama Becky managed to kill it, but she got badly clawed and lost a lot of blood. She passed out. The other farm hands came and found her when her horse went back alone. She was in a coma for nine days. Mama Roz talks about never leaving her side."

"You said *was* a shepherd. She didn't make a full recovery?"

"She did from the cuts, but the dead cat had been lying on her. The healer reckons its blood must have seeped into Mom's wounds. It wasn't fatal, like if she'd eaten it, but the poison damaged all her muscles. Her heart as well. She can't ride—can barely walk."

"Shit." Hal looked shocked. "Was this before or after you were born?"

"Before."

"Do you have any sisters?"

"No. Mama Becky does what she can, but it's really just what

Mama Roz earns on the docks. It took them years to save up the imprinting fees. And once they had me to look after, they stood no chance of saving more money for the Temple. Of course, now there's my wage coming in. But they're too old to have another child."

"Which one did you get your good looks from?"

Ellen grinned at the compliment. "Mostly my gene mother."

"It would be such a shame if some thug were to flatten your nose. Why did you choose to become a Militiawoman?"

"It pays better than anything else I could do without a full apprenticeship."

"Do you like the job?"

"Mostly."

"I hear that you had a bit of trouble last night."

Ellen's head sunk as her mood dipped. "Yes."

"And you don't look as if you liked that bit of the job."

"Somebody I knew got killed."

"A friend?"

"No. I didn't like her. She was one of the local thugs, but..." Ellen shrugged, struggling with the emotions. "I knew her."

"How did she die?"

"She was raiding a warehouse with someone else. When we surrounded them, she attacked one of the Rangers. The Ranger came out best."

"What happened to the other woman?"

"She was taken prisoner by the Rangers. But she was badly wounded. She died this morning."

"In the infirmary?"

"At the Rangers' barracks."

Hal's expression dipped into something more somber and the grip on Ellen's ankles loosened before her grin returned. "Are you sure you want to do this small-talk thing? Wouldn't you rather come sit beside me and fool around?"

The suggestion was very tempting. "I, er..."

The opening of the tavern door interrupted Ellen's reply. Loud, excited voices drowned out all else as a score of Rangers stormed, or in some cases staggered across the room. Ellen recognized Valerie and her patrol comrades among them. The Rangers were in high spirits and this was clearly not the first tavern they had visited that evening.

Hal removed her feet from contact with Ellen's and sat up straighter. She looked irritated by the noisy intrusion, as did several other patrons around the room. At least five of the Rangers were simultaneously shouting at the woman behind the bar, demanding service.

Valerie was tagged on at the back of the mob, but on spotting Ellen she wandered over. "Hey. How you doing?"

"Okay."

Valerie looked expectantly at Hal.

Ellen took the hint. "Oh, this is Ahalya Drennen. She's the new forewoman at Broken Hills." Ellen indicated between them. "And this is Valerie Bergstrom, who used to be in the Militia here."

"Hi." Valerie smiled at Hal, who nodded in reply. She turned back to Ellen. "I hear you did well last night."

"I just did what I was told. How about you? I didn't see you there."

"My patrol were on horseback a few streets away. We were all set to chase them down if they escaped."

"Right." Ellen looked at the scrum by the bar, rowdy, even by the standards of Rangers. "Your gang seem happy. Is something up?"

"Oh yeah. We've got some real excitement lined up."

"What?"

"Can't say now. But you'll know all about it when it's over."

"You're onto the gang?"

Valerie held her hands up. "It's all secret. Wait just a bit longer." She smiled. "But don't worry. We'll sort all your problems out for you." A shout from the bar made her turn. Mel Ellis was holding up a full tankard, with a clear signal that it was for Valerie. "Catch you later." She returned to join her comrades.

"Arrogant bitches."

The tone as much as the words startled Ellen. She stared at Hal. "Don't you like the Rangers?"

Hal took a moment to reconsider. "Yeah, well. They do a good job. But don't you think that they're a bit too full of themselves? All that 'we'll sort out your problems' bullshit."

"If they sort out the problem, they can be as arrogant as they like, in my book." Ellen smiled to show that she did not want to seriously disagree with Hal. "What do you think is up with them?"

"I could make a guess."

"What?"

"They've learned something. Probably from the prisoner they took last night."

"She's dead."

"There's no saying how she died."

Ellen frowned. "What do you mean?"

"They had her for several hours. They'd have been trying to get her to spill what she knew. I'd guess they got their information, but somebody was a bit too vigorous in trying to thump the last few details out of her."

Ellen sat back, shocked. "You think she was beaten into talking?"

"It fits."

"She was badly injured before she was captured."

"So it wouldn't take much to overdo the interrogation."

At the bar, the Rangers were embarking on a traditional drinking song that was long, repetitive, and obscene. Ellen slumped against the backboard of the chair. The flirtatious mood between her and Hal had evaporated, killed by the arrival of the Rangers. She swallowed the last of her drink. "Do you want to move on to another tavern?"

"Nah. They look like they're on a pub crawl. They'll probably go in a while. If we move, they'll only catch us again." Hal also drained her tankard. "I'll buy you another."

Ellen scrambled for her purse. "It's my turn."

Hal was already on her feet. Something of her earlier grin returned. "It's okay. I'm hoping that if you end up feeling sufficiently indebted to me, I might be able to demand certain favors in repayment."

Ellen sank back in her seat, staring at the rafters in the ceiling and thinking about what Hal had said. Strict rules governed the treatment of prisoners. Surely the Rangers would not have broken them. But then Ellen remembered Aitkin's resolute manner. The Ranger captain would be ruthless, a dangerous woman to have as an adversary, far more so than Cohen, for all her bluster. Would Aitkin have allowed the beating of a prisoner—a badly injured woman? Would she condone torture? Ellen chewed her lip. Cohen might fail in her duty through incompetence, but she would never blatantly ignore the law. Aitkin was not so predictable.

Ellen turned her head, recalled from her musing by an awareness that Hal was taking a long time at the bar. Some of the Rangers were on to their second drink, monopolizing the barkeeper, which explained some of the delay. However, Hal had two full tankards in her hands, without showing any sign of leaving the counter. The Rangers were milling around, laughing, chatting, clowning. The song had, thankfully, come to an end.

Hal saw Ellen watching and returned to the table. She gave a one-shoulder shrug. "Okay. I confess. I was trying to hear what they were saying. I was curious."

"And?"

"They were pretty flattering about you, which was what caught my attention. Apparently, you're the one member of the Militia who's worth a fart in a barrel." Hal put the drinks down and grinned. "Do you reckon the fart is a good thing, or should you be insulted by anything less than a complete shit?"

Ellen laughed and took her drink. "As long as they include the barrel I don't mind. I wouldn't want to try picking either up otherwise."

Deliberately, Hal reached across the table and ran her forefinger over the knuckles of Ellen's empty hand, causing a rush of goose bumps to flare up Ellen's arm. She gently turned Ellen's hand over and pressed their palms together, while tracing small circles on the inside of her wrist.

"So, if you don't play footsie until a second date, how long is it normally until you fuck?"

Ellen half choked on her beer. She put down the tankard and wiped her mouth with the back of her free hand. "Um...I think I'd have to check back through my diary on that one."

Hal laughed, but before she could say anything Valerie again staggered over to their table. Hal released Ellen's hand and sat back.

Valerie crouched down at the end of the table, so her head was at the same height as Ellen's and leaned on her folded arms. She seemed oblivious to the idea that she might be interrupting. "What are you doing tomorrow night? Are you on duty?"

"I shouldn't be." Ellen tried to control her flash of irritation.

"My patrol is going to be at the White Swan. Come over. It'll be a good night. You'll get to hear all the details." The emphasis on the word "all" was unmistakable.

"I'm not sure if your Mel Ellis wants a Militiawoman as company."

"Ah, Mel's okay. She's a good Ranger. She can be a bit prickly, but Jay knows how to cure her when she gets the ass-ache. That's why they're friends. Jay's a laugh."

Ellen looked over Valerie's head at the assembled Rangers. The press at the bar had spread out. She spotted Jay Takeda off to the side, her arms wrapped around a civilian—a thin-faced woman with hair in a ponytail and the tar-stained clothes of barge crew. As Ellen watched, the two heads drew together in an ardent kiss. Everyone knew that many women were attracted to Rangers and would throw themselves at anyone in the green and gray uniform. Everyone also knew that a good percentage of Rangers were only too happy to catch them.

Valerie twisted, following the direction of Ellen's eyes. "Hey. It looks like Jay's scored."

"Do you think you Rangers will be staying in here for long?" Hal asked frostily.

Valerie was clearly taken aback at the unfriendly tone. She glanced quickly between Ellen and Hal, and then an expression of understanding spread over her face. She stood and backed away. Her smile returned and she gave a double thumbs-up gesture. "No. It's okay. I won't be, er...bothering you again this evening. Have fun." She winked at Ellen and turned back to the bar.

Ellen sighed and slumped in her seat. She looked apologetically at Hal, who leaned forward, about to speak when there was another loud outburst.

"The Butcher's gonna get the chop." Jay Takeda's voice was slurred. She had the barge crewwoman pinned in a corner. By the look of them, without the aid of the wall to lean on, they might have had trouble staying upright.

Mel Ellis was close by. She elbowed her friend in the ribs. "Quit the bragging and get back to making out. You know what you always tell me—play to your strengths."

A movement of the table made Ellen look back. Hal had slid out from behind it and stood up.

"Are we going?" Ellen was surprised.

"I am. I have to get back to the farm tonight. The sheep need me."

Hal was standing over Ellen. She twisted down, leaning with one hand on the table. Her lips brushed against Ellen's and then returned more forcefully, pushing Ellen back into the chair. Hal's lips were firm and soft in perfect proportion. Ellen felt herself melting in the heat. And she wanted more. She wanted all of Hal. She reached out and her hand found Hal's hip, but before she could take charge, pulling Hal down onto her lap, the contact was gone.

Ellen gasped and opened her eyes. Hal was grinning at her from mere centimeters away.

"I'm sorry," Hal said.

"What?"

"It's August."

Ellen shook her head, trying to clear her confusion. "What?"

"This is my month to play hard to get."

Without another word, Hal turned and left the Three Barrels.

Chapter Seven—Crossing the River

The Town Hall bell was chiming midday when Ellen pushed open the door of the Militia station and stepped inside, ready to start her shift. Zar Thorensen was sitting at the table, dealing out the cards for yet another game of patience. She looked up and smiled, tilting her head as if to catch the last peal of the bell.

"On time."

"Aren't I always?"

Zar scooped the cards up in a wad and rapped them on the table to form a neat deck. "I guess so."

"Anything exciting happen this morning?"

Zar pointed over her shoulder. "We've got one customer in the lockup."

"Who?"

"Fran Paparang."

Ellen took a step closer and dropped her voice. "Did Cohen order her brought in on spec?"

"No need. She's been playing her usual games." Zar rubbed her nose. "You'd think she'd be more careful, after what happened to Trish Eriksen. I guess some girls never learn."

"What's the charge?"

"Being an asshole."

Ellen kept on looking at Zar, waiting for a better answer.

"She was in the market, hanging around the stalls, obviously on the lookout for what she could nick. A couple of the stallholders told her to piss off. She started spoiling for a fight, and kicked some things over. Jude dragged her in here a couple of hours ago. I think she's been drinking."

"This early in the day?"

"Who knows? Maybe she really is cut up about her mate." Zar shrugged and stood. "Anyway. I'm off."

Before Zar could leave, Ellen pointed at the door of the captain's office and whispered, "Is she in?"

Zar shook her head. "Ain't seen our beloved leader all morning." The street door swung shut behind her.

Ellen stood indecisively by the table, drumming her fingers. Cohen's absence was a definite plus, although it might not last. There was no saying when the lieutenant might wander in. Regardless of whether she would want to repeat her thoughts about the warehouse skirmish, Ellen was happy to have as little contact with her as possible. This made a change from normal, when she would welcome just about anyone as company.

Station-minding duty was the most tedious of the routine assignments. Some days, nobody at all would call in. Those who did were invariably angry—if they did not feel that they were the victim of some wrong, they would not be making the report. All too many would vent their anger on the officer on duty and take as a sign of ineptitude that the Militiawoman did not immediately rush out to hunt down the girls who were knocking on doors and running away, or whatever the complaint was. No point in explaining that the rules said the station should be left unmanned only in urgent and serious cases.

Ellen slumped onto the bench and picked up the pack of cards, but made no attempt to deal them out. She stared at the top card, the jack of hearts, while trying to order her thoughts.

Hal was playing silly games—games such as rushing off the previous evening. It annoyed Ellen. But what annoyed her even more was that she was totally ensnared by the game playing. Previous girlfriends had always let Ellen take the lead. They had signaled their interest, and then waited for Ellen to make the moves. They might try to manipulate her, as with Mandy's tears, but never taunt and challenge her. Ellen had known exactly where she stood with them, and that was wherever she wanted to stand. She picked them up and she dropped them. With hindsight, it had all been so safe and predictable it was boring.

Hal was not predictable and she was the one calling the shots. Ellen was not in control. She wished to hell that she did not find it so exciting. Hal had a grip on her emotions beyond anything that Ellen had experienced before. She was surprised at how desperately she was looking forward to their next meeting, and the fact that she had no idea how this meeting would go only increased the anticipation. Hal had her. She was hooked and helpless, and loving it.

The faint sound of movement from the lockup caught Ellen's attention. Francesca Paparang was Valerie Bergstrom's younger sister. They both had a reckless self-confidence, but expressed it in very different ways. Valerie had been a hardworking member of the Militia, the first to put herself in the way of danger. Fran would need a dictionary to look up the meaning of work. As a young child she had the reputation of being a daredevil. Becoming friends with the Eriksen sisters had turned her into a hell-raiser.

Ellen blamed Tilly Paparang, Valerie's gene mother, who had raised both girls on her own after her partner deserted her. She had not raised them equally. Tilly Paparang had indulged Fran to the point of criminal culpability. Valerie, on the other hand, had never been coddled or shown much in the way of affection. Ellen suspected the blatant favoritism was, consciously or not, punishing Valerie for the way her birth mother had walked out. It was grossly unfair—not the least because Valerie had only been five years old at the time. But whatever the reason, Tilly Paparang had done Fran the greater injustice. Fran had been quite literally spoiled, and anything worthwhile she might have achieved in her life had been lost.

At sixteen, Fran was old enough to be responsible for her own fines, but there was no doubt that her mother would again be the one to do the paying. The thought crossed Ellen's mind that before long, Fran's behavior would earn her a flogging, or even a hanging. Would it come as a shock to Fran when her mother was not allowed to take her place?

Ellen pulled open the small barred hatch on the lockup door and peered in. Fran was sitting on the floor in the corner, resting her head in her hands.

"Fran."

She looked up blearily. "What?"

"How you feeling?"

"Like you care."

Ellen hesitated before replying. As a friend of Valerie's, she knew Fran on a personal level far better than she did either of the Eriksen sisters. Before Fran had come under Trish and Ade's influence, they had even met socially a few times at birthdays and the like. They had never been close, but they had shared affable conversations in the past.

The Eriksens had both joined the Eastford gang. Surely they would have tried to drag Fran along with them. Fran was not stupid—far from it. It was what made her such a dangerous accessory to the Eriksen sisters, adding her brains to Trish's brawn and Ade's malice. Perhaps Fran even had the sense to steer clear of the Butcher and her Knives, but she would have been told something, if only as a lure to get her to join. And Trish Eriksen would never have been able to withstand the temptation of bragging to a friend.

At the moment, Fran was their most likely source of information about the Butcher, but Ellen needed to play it right. "I wanted to say that I'm sorry about Trish."

"No, you're not."

"Honest. When I saw her lying dead, it..."

Fran scrambled unsteadily to her feet and lurched to the other side of the grill. There was no "maybe" about the drinking. Ellen could smell the alcohol on her.

"Which one of the bitches did it?"

"The name of the Ranger doesn't matter. In the end, Trish did it to herself. She was the one who attacked first. She should have known she'd stand no chance against a trained Ranger."

Fran spat, but at her own feet rather than Ellen—a good sign. "Trish never thought... She... It just wasn't—" Fran dashed the back of her hand across her eyes.

"She and Ade got mixed up with the big gang from Eastford, didn't they?"

"Yes."

"Did they try to get you to join?"

"I'm not that fucking stupid. I told them to stay clear. But Ade was..."

"She was what?" Ellen prompted gently.

"When she was in Eastford, she got to know some of them. And when the Butcher—" Fran broke off sharply and scowled at Ellen, suddenly a touch more sober. "Hey, no. You ain't going to get me to fucking run my mouth."

"You aren't one of the Knives. You said you weren't stupid enough to join."

"And I ain't stupid enough to sell them out either. I don't want to end up in an alley with a hole in my back and my head kicked in."

Several shouts rang out in the town square, the voices muted through the station walls, but loud enough to catch Ellen's attention. She glanced over her shoulder, frowning. However, it did not sound like a fight and nobody was screaming for help. She turned back to Fran, trying to ignore the disturbance.

"If you help us catch them they won't be a threat to you."

"You bunch of jerks stand no frigging chance of catching them."

"Believe me, we'll get them in the end."

"In your dreams. I'm keeping my ass out of it."

"It—"

The disturbance was becoming more riotous. Ellen turned around and stared at the street door, wondering if she should investigate. She had the time. Fran was not going anywhere until her mother had paid yet another fine.

The decision was made for her when sudden furious thumping shook the door on its hinges, sounding as if someone was trying to break in. Whatever the cause, the pounding was excessive and unnecessary. It was not as if the station was locked.

Ellen crossed the briefing room and yanked the door open. "What do you—"

From all directions, people were converging on the square, shouting, pointing. Others hung from windows, staring down. Her elevated position at the top of the steps meant Ellen had no trouble seeing over the heads to the center of the mob, where a farm cart was being led by two Rangers. They were clearly heading for the infirmary, but the crowd was blocking their path. A half dozen figures in green and gray lay in the back of the cart, blood-soaked and unmoving. Seven more Rangers, some of them also clearly wounded, staggered on at the rear, buffeted by the throng.

Ellen slipped her baton off her belt and swiped the alarm bell hanging by the station doorway as hard as she could. The discordant chime resounded deafeningly around the square, cutting above the uproar, and for an instant freezing everyone where they stood.

"Back off and give them space." Ellen bellowed at the top of her voice and then leapt down the steps.

Clearing a route for the cart was not easy. Ellen had to physically elbow the mob aside, jabbing with her baton where people were slow to move. However, the determination on her face had its effect and the crowd shuffled back, opening the way to cover the last few meters to the infirmary.

Mel Ellis was one of the Rangers at the front. Her uniform was also bloodstained, although from what Ellen could tell, none of it was hers. Ellen could not imagine what had happened, but the questions would wait. She did not need to check the injured women in the cart to know they needed medical care as soon as possible, and for some, even that would be too late.

Before the horses had come to a standstill, the door of the infirmary opened and Dr. Miller with her assistants spilled out. Ellen picked several fit-looking women from the crowd and propelled them toward the rear of the cart.

"Don't just gawk. Help carry the wounded in."

While the infirmary staff and co-opted porters did their work, Ellen paced around the cart, shoving back any onlookers who appeared likely to get in the way and threatening with her baton where necessary.

Valerie Bergstrom was one of the Rangers shuffling behind the cart. She appeared unhurt, although Ellen could see her trembling convulsively. Her face was red and swollen. As she stumbled through the infirmary door, fresh tears spilled down her cheeks. That sight, more than anything else, shocked Ellen. She had never seen Valerie cry before—never seen her show fear. What had gone so wrong?

Mel Ellis also stayed outside, working in unison with Ellen, keeping the morbidly curious crowd at bay. Only when all the others were inside the infirmary did Mel relax her guard. She had been by far the most focused and alert of the Rangers, the only one seeming fully in control of herself. Now she sagged against the wall, dazed. Ellen took her arm and coaxed her through the infirmary door, the last Ranger to go in.

The main room was in uproar. Wounded women lay on the floor. More medics were arriving by the minute as the word went out, and every woman gifted in the healer sense came to assist. Dr. Miller directed them like a field marshal while moving from body to body. Groans and the smell of blood filled the room.

Ellen guided Mel to a spot as much out of the way as was possible amid the frenzy. "What happened?"

The eyes Mel turned on her were focused on some distant horror. Her face was ashen, as if she was about to be sick. "We were ambushed."

"Where are all the rest?"
"Dead."

❖

Valerie Bergstrom was still shaking an hour later. Although uninjured, she was the most traumatized of the Rangers. Ellen sat by her, holding her hand, but not knowing what to say to calm her down.

"What's going to happen now?" Valerie had asked the same question a dozen times.

"Ranger command will sort it out."

"What will they do?"

"I don't know." Ellen squeezed Valerie's hand. "But I know they won't let them get away with this."

The scene of chaos in the infirmary had calmed. Most auxiliary medics had been dismissed. Lieutenant Cohen, Town Mayor Patel, and anyone else of enough importance to demand entry had come and gone. Ellen had been left to ensure that as few others as possible were allowed to intrude. All the injured were being cared for in the sickroom next door, with pallets on the floor being used once the beds were full. Two bodies had been taken away for burial and four Rangers had so far been discharged to return to their barracks. Yet the numbers did not begin to add up.

A full squadron was made up of thirty-four Rangers—a captain, a lieutenant, and four patrols, each of eight women, headed by a sergeant and a corporal. Nine Rangers had walked into town and a further four had been carried living from the cart. When added to the two who had not survived, that still left nineteen unaccounted for. Surely they could not all be dead.

"They were waiting for us. They knew we were coming. At the river. They had set it up...blocked the road. They started shooting. Captain Aitkin...she..."

"And you went to fucking pieces." A harsh voice cut in.

Ellen looked up. Mel was standing over them, sneering.

Valerie looked terrified. "It wasn't my fault."

"Someone else made you scream and cry like a baby?"

"I..."

Ellen glared at Mel. "You're not helping her."

"Help? What she needs is a good kick up the ass, not someone to hold her hand."

"You can't blame her. People react differently."

"Thank the Goddess everyone doesn't react like her. Else we'd all be dead. Jay didn't. She—" Abruptly, Mel's face contorted and her eyes filled. "Jay. She..."

Mel turned and all but ran from the room. Valerie meanwhile was gasping, hyperventilating. Her eyes rolled up, showing white. Ellen stood, about to get help, but it was already on the way. A healer arrived and placed her hand on Valerie's forehead. Within seconds the rising hysteria had calmed. Valerie's eyelids closed and her body slumped in her seat. The healer shook herself out of the light trance she had been in and looked at Ellen.

"Are you a relative of hers?"

"No, just a friend. But she does have relatives in town. Do you want me to fetch them?"

"No need today. Though I imagine they'd like to be informed. She needs rest. We'll keep her here tonight."

Ellen clamped her jaw and said nothing, wondering if Valerie's mother would be able to stop fretting about Fran in the lockup long enough to even think about her other daughter.

Another pallet was found for Valerie in the sickroom. Ellen helped carry her in and stayed to arrange the blanket. Even in sleep, Valerie looked weak and frightened. Ellen had seen Valerie tackle thugs, fires, and stampeding horses without turning a hair. She had admired her friend's courage, and tried to emulate it. What had happened?

Ellen looked around the sickroom. Most patients were unconscious, a state induced by the medics' use of their psychic healer sense. However, two were awake, talking quietly at the other side of the room, and another patient was sitting up on her bed. The right side of the Ranger's face was covered by bandages, yet Ellen was able to recognize Gill Adebeyo, Valerie's patrol corporal.

Ellen wandered over, hoping for some answers. "How are you doing? Is your face okay?"

"I'm not going to be any prettier than I was before. Just as well that I wasn't vain about my looks. But my leg is the main problem." Even through the blankets, the bandaging and splint were obvious.

"Is it badly damaged?"

"Don't know if I'll walk on it again." For a moment Gill's expression wavered. "Apart from that, I'm fine."

"Oh...I'm sorry."

The half of Gill's face that twisted in a grimace looked like a failed attempt at a smile. "To be honest, I'm lucky to be alive. Too many aren't."

Ellen moved closer to the bed. "What happened? Do you mind talking about it?"

"We walked into an ambush. Off to the southeast, on the road down to Jensdock. You know the place where the road fords a river? You come out of the forest and there's a cliff face on the opposite bank. Once you're across the ford, you have to go about fifty meters downstream, and then the road climbs up through a gully."

Ellen nodded, recognizing the description of the spot, about eight kilometers outside Roadsend. "It's the ford on Red Gorge Creek."

"Right. We crossed the river, rode into the gully, and found a cart had been upturned, blocking the path. And then archers on the top of the cliffs started shooting down at us." Gill looked sickened. "They picked their targets. Aitkin and Green were the first to drop. Sergeant Bertram called to retreat. At the time, it sounded like a good idea, but when we got back to the river, more of the gang were there. They'd used another wagon to block the road behind us on the other bank. More archers were hidden in the trees, and they started shooting as well."

"How many do you think there were?"

Gill pursed her lips, thoughtfully. "Over a dozen easily. Maybe as many as thirty all told. A couple of the sergeants started shouting conflicting orders, and we all milled around on the horses, getting shot, wondering which one to obey. Bertram got a bunch of her girls to charge the wagon, but only two got as far as reaching it. Some of the girls were riding up and down the riverbank, but with cliffs on one side and trees the other, there was nowhere for the horses to get out." Gill's expression changed to one of disgust. "I admit. I panicked. It was like a white light burning in my head and apart from that, my mind was empty. And that's when Mel stepped in."

"What did she do?"

"Started shouting orders, but differently to what had gone before. It was like she knew what was going on. She beat and bullied a group to dismount and take shelter behind some rocks on the riverbank. I was about to join her when an arrow got my horse. It went over and my leg was trapped under it." Gill indicated the bandage on her face. "Nasty sharp rocks there. One of them sliced my face open when I fell. I guess I'm lucky it didn't take my eye." She shrugged. "I managed to get out from under the horse, but my leg was a total mess. I couldn't walk so Mel picked me up and carried me to cover. She got about half the squadron there, but it was only a short-term solution. We were pinned down. We couldn't get out on horseback, and we couldn't hope to outrun them on foot—certainly not me in the state I was in. So Mel said to take to the river."

"The river?" Ellen searched her knowledge of area. Red Gorge Creek was fast flowing, but free of rapids and waterfalls. "You'd have been about two kilometers upriver of Kells hamlet."

"Yes. Not a tough swim with the current, although me and some of the others needed help. The only problem was, once we were in the water, we'd be sitting targets. If the archers came out of the woods, they'd be able to stand on the banks and pick us off as we floated by. So Jay said she'd stay behind. She was the best shot in the patrol. We left her with her bow and all the arrows and we dived in the water." Gill swallowed. "Actually, I didn't do much diving. Mel carried me again, and then went back for Sue and Raj. They were in an even worse state than me. The current took us to Kells, where we borrowed the cart."

"And Jay?"

"We heard her bowstring going as we swam off. We hoped that once we were away, she'd be able to jump in and follow us. We waited in Kells for her, but..."

"Shit." Ellen stared down at her hands.

"So. As I said, I'm just pleased to be alive. I wouldn't be if it weren't for Mel and Jay. And Jay is the..." Gill chewed on her lip, as if fighting back tears.

"Jay may be okay. Lieutenant Cohen is organizing a party, with carts and healers. We're going to pick up any wounded that are left there. We're setting off at twelve o'clock. They can't all be dead." Ellen forced a confident expression onto her face. "And for every Ranger who is, I promise, we'll make them pay."

❖

The overturned wagon was still in place, blocking the road. Ellen helped right it and push it aside, into the undergrowth. The volunteers in the rescue party now had an unrestricted view of the carnage.

For a long time nobody spoke, although Ellen heard the sound of someone behind her throwing up. On either side of the river was a broad expanse of sand and shingle, dotted with green-clad bodies. The nearest was only a couple of meters away. One arrow protruded from the Ranger's stomach and another from her shoulder. Both injuries looked serious, but neither was guaranteed to be fatal. However, the cut throat was. The wound gaped obscenely, deep enough to half sever her head, lined with raw red flesh.

Stunned, Ellen tottered down the road and waded the knee-high ford, to the far bank in the shadow of the cliff. This was where the greatest concentration of bodies lay, most bristling with arrows, all with their throats slit open. She went from face to face, matching them to her memories of the Three Barrels Tavern, when they had been laughing and singing. Others in the party spread out across the scene of the massacre with halting footsteps and whispered oaths.

"No." The first loud voice.

Ellen turned. Mel Ellis stood by a pile of boulders, looking down at the water's edge. Ellen hurried to her side, already knowing what she would see. The sand around the boulders was pockmarked with footprints. Presumably this was where Mel had gotten the Rangers to take cover, downriver of the shallow ford. It was also where Jay had made her stand, stopping the gang from leaving the cover of the woods opposite.

Jay Takeda lay curled on her side, as if in sleep, but her legs were in the water and the sand under her was pooled with red. Mel slithered down the bank, falling to her knees beside her friend. Gently she rolled Jay onto her back and cradled her head. No arrows were lodged in Jay's body, but the uniform over her stomach was sliced through and soaked with blood. She too had had her throat cut.

"We need to collect the bodies. There are nineteen women missing. We don't leave until we can account for every one." Lieutenant Cohen shouted the order. She glared around. "Well, don't just stare at me. Get to it. If someone managed to crawl away and hide we need to find her."

Across the riverbank, women began to move with a sense of purpose, taking refuge in the activity as a diversion from the horror around them. Everyone had to know that the chances of finding a survivor were too slim to reckon, but it gave them a reason to be doing rather than thinking. Ellen stared at Cohen in surprise. For the first time in months, the lieutenant had given the right order in the right way.

Soft sobbing made her look down. Mel was bent low over Jay's body, her shoulders shaking. Ellen scrambled down to her side and put her hand on Mel's shoulder. "We need to carry her to the cart."

"It should have been me."

"You did your bit. Gill told me. The group that got back. It was your lead that saved their lives."

"I should have been the one to stay behind."

"You couldn't do everything."

Mel lifted her face, tears streaming down it. "Do you know why I didn't?"

"Someone had to—"

"I couldn't stay because I'm a fucking awful shot. I'm the worst archer in the squadron. The assessment tests—the Goddess must have smiled on me that day, because it was pure luck I got over the minimum score. Never done it before or since."

"But you were the one who kept her head." Ellen shook Mel's shoulder gently, trying to rally her. "Come on. We need to take Jay back to town."

"I'm going to get the fucking shitheads who did this. I'll hunt them to the ends of the earth and beyond. I'll use their own guts to wrap around their necks and choke the air out of their fucking lungs." Mel's eyes again met Ellen's. "And the damned bitch who told them we were coming. Some treacherous fucking asshole betrayed us."

"It doesn't have to be a betrayal."

"Oh yes, it does." Mel swung her hand around wildly. "This road. It sees a fair bit of traffic. They couldn't have set up the roadblock the day before. Or even a few hours before. The risk of someone running into it and raising the alarm would have been too high. And they knew which route we were taking. Fuck! The bitches must have known as much as I did. The prisoner—before she died she told the captain where the bandits' hideout is. The captain and the sergeants had a full briefing yesterday afternoon. All they told the rest of us was that we were going to raid the Butcher's base. We were told when to assemble and what road out of town we were taking and that was it."

"Who else would have known?"

"Just the squadron."

"You think someone in the squadron is a traitor? Someone deliberately told your plans to the Butcher?"

Mel rubbed her hand over her face and looked around the scene blindly. "No. No. Not these girls. I'd trust every last one with my life. But last night in the tavern. You were there. You saw how some were. A bit too free with the drink." Mel's voice became more certain. "Somebody said more than she should and some fucking shithead overheard it."

Ellen's guts went cold, remembering Hal, standing by the bar, tankards in hand, eavesdropping on the Rangers. Every doubt Ellen had about the farmer returned in full force. Why had Hal been so anxious to hear? Had she been the one to pass on news about the Ranger's plans? Was that why she rushed away so abruptly? Ellen looked around the scene—the bodies, the blood. Nineteen lay here with another two dead already back at Roadsend awaiting burial.

Supposing Hal was involved. Supposing she was partly responsible for the slaughter. Ellen felt her skin prickle. Her stomach contracted so hard that it hurt. Would she be able to bear watching Hal tried, sentenced, and hanged? But surely, if Hal's guilt were proved, it would kill any emotions Ellen felt for her. She could not still be attracted to Hal, could she?

Mel had stopped crying. She sat back on her heels, her face set, breathing between clenched teeth. "I swear. I will get every last bitch responsible for this."

Ellen was working on controlling her own breath. This was not a string of thefts, or robbery with violence, or thugs in a fight pulling out knives when they looked to be losing. This was the casual, cold-blooded murder of wounded women, on a scale never seen since the day the blessed Himoti had first set foot on the new world. This was serious, like nothing had been before. And she was caught up in it.

Part Two

Lines of Inquiry

Chapter Eight—A New Badge

Broken Hill Ranch looked the same as the last time Ellen had been there, except for the addition of a new water trough in the yard. She slipped down from the saddle and caught hold of the reins. The horse was borrowed without permission from the Militia stables. She had to see Hal and talk to her, and the distance was too far to cover on foot. Asking Cohen would certainly have elicited a no as an answer, but Ellen knew the patrolwomen unofficially borrowed horses all the time.

Nobody was in sight, but Ellen heard barking. The noise got louder until a sheepdog appeared around the edge of the farmhouse. Ellen took a step back, certain that the animal would not remember her from before. The dog covered half the distance between them and then, to Ellen's relief, stopped with a renewed frenzy of barking—raising the alarm rather than attacking. A few seconds later Hal came into view. Despite all her doubts, Ellen felt her insides kick. With a sharp word of command, Hal called the dog back and sent it to sit by the barn.

The two women stared at each other in silence. For once, Hal seemed off balance. Did she also seem nervous and guilty? Ellen could not be sure. Then Hal's usual relaxed grin spread across her face and she strolled forward.

"Hi. I wasn't expecting to see you here."

"I wanted to talk to you."

"About?" Hal was now close enough to touch.

Ellen took a step back. "Did you hear about what happened to the 12th Squadron yesterday? The massacre?"

"I heard the Rangers had run into trouble."

"Twenty-one dead."

This time Ellen was more sure of the uneasy flicker of Hal's eyes, yet her voice stayed even as she said, "There can't be many left."

"That's all you have to say?"

"You mean, apart from wondering who's going to keep the mountain cats off my property next spring?" Hal shrugged. "Yeah. Okay. It's awful that so many are dead, and I'm worried more will die before it's over. In the meantime, I'm just looking out for me and my family."

"The wounded Rangers were killed in cold blood. The gang slit their throats. They killed defenseless, injured women."

"Slit their throats? So the bandits didn't beat the wounded to death, like the Rangers did with the prisoner they captured?"

"You don't know for certain they did that."

"And you don't know for certain they didn't."

Ellen took an angry step forward. "Whose side are you on?"

"The same side I've always been on. My own."

"And in the Three Barrels, when you were listening in on the Rangers, did you find out about their plans and pass the information on to the Butcher?"

"Ah." Hal smiled. "Is this what you came here to ask me?"

"Yes."

"Now, if I was part of the gang, would you honestly expect me to tell you the truth?"

Ellen stared into Hal's eyes, hoping to see past the taunting and the games. The exercise was pointless, as had been the rest of the visit to the farm. Without another word, Ellen got on her horse and rode away.

❖

Ellen sat outside her parents' cottage, staring at the sky and watching the first stars show. The days were getting noticeably shorter, although summer was far from over and the evening air was warm. More than an hour remained before Ellen would want to think about sleeping. She could go down into the town, locate some friends, and have a drink, but then she might possibly run into Hal. Or she could go and visit Valerie at the barracks and see how she was doing, in which case the chances of meeting Hal would be nonexistent. Running into Hal, or not? If only she could work out which of the two possibilities she most wanted not to happen, it would be much easier to decide what to do.

The visit to the ranch had been five days before and Ellen had not seen Hal since. Not an hour had passed without the conversation running through her head. Surely, if Hal were one of the Butcher's Knives, she would have acted more upset just to maintain her façade of being an honest farmer. Did this mean, then, that Hal was genuinely so self-centered and callous? Ellen leaned her head forward into her hands and winced. Her second big question was, had the last five days been this much of a torment for Hal as well? Ellen knew just how strongly she was attracted to Hal. Did Hal feel a fraction of the same emotions for her?

The sound of someone saying her name caught Ellen's ear. She looked up. At the corner of the road a Ranger was talking to young Pat Simamora. The child raised her arm, clearly pointing in Ellen's direction. Ellen's first thought was that Valerie had come to see her, but Valerie would not need directions.

The Ranger turned around, confirming that she was not Valerie Bergstrom. In fact, she was someone Ellen had never met before. Ellen stood up as the Ranger approached.

"Are you Militiawoman Ellen Mittal?"

"Yes."

"You're wanted at the barracks."

"The barracks?"

"Yes. Now." The Ranger's tone was uncompromising.

"What's it about?"

"You'll find out when you get there." She jerked her head, clearly intending to escort Ellen. "Come on."

"Er..." Ellen glanced through the open cottage door. "Do I need to bring anything?"

"No. Unless you want a jacket."

Ellen shook her head. The evening was not cold enough to warrant it. She set off beside the Ranger on the short walk across town.

The barracks seemed unnaturally quiet, as they had since the massacre. They had been designed to hold a full squadron. With just seven women released from the infirmary, the buildings had been less than a quarter occupied. Reinforcements had clearly now arrived—

more unfamiliar faces were around and horses were tethered by the stables—yet the air of subdued emptiness remained.

Three Rangers awaited Ellen in the inner office of the admin building. The oldest sat at the captain's desk. The others stood to one side. At the sight of them, Ellen came to a frozen halt, before creaking into a pose that was as close to attention as her tense muscles could manage. She recognized none of the faces, but the combined stars on their shoulder badges put the sky outside to shame. They were easily the most senior officers she had ever been within shouting distance of.

The seated Ranger said, "At ease."

Ellen tried to relax, with limited success.

"I'm Divisional Commander Belinski. You're Militia Rookie Mittal?"

"Yes, ma'am."

"I won't be staying in Roadsend long, but I wanted to see the state of affairs for myself and talk to everyone personally. I'll be leaving tomorrow and for the duration of this investigation Major Kallim here will be in charge."

One of the officers to the side nodded to acknowledge her name.

"We're co-opting your services. Until further notice, you'll be reporting directly to Major Kallim."

"Ma'am, Lieutenant Cohen has—"

"Lieutenant Cohen will not be a problem. She has already received due notification of this from the proper Militia authorities."

Ellen swallowed. "Yes, ma'am."

Belinski leaned forward over the desk. "I'm sure I don't need to tell you how seriously we take what happened to the 12th. We'll track down this so-called Mad Butcher and her Knives and make every last one pay for her crimes. Fort Krowe will be mustering every available Ranger for the job. However, that will take some time, and before we can act, we need more information. Not least, the location of the bandits' hideout. I don't suppose you have anything you can tell us about this."

"No, ma'am." Ellen frowned. "I thought the captured Knife had told Captain Aitkin."

"Yes. Apparently she did. Unfortunately, the only people Aitkin shared the information with were her lieutenant and her four sergeants, none of whom survived the massacre. And on that subject, the first task we have for you is to spread the story as widely as possible. We want news to get back to the Butcher that we don't know where she is. You can do that?"

"Yes, ma'am."

Ellen's bewilderment must have shown on her face. Belinski smiled at her grimly. "The reason is so she feels safe in her hideout and doesn't return to Eastford. Out here is where we'd prefer to tackle her. At the end of the day, it won't matter where she goes. We'll get her. But the Wildlands are our home ground. In order not to alarm her, we'll not make any great show of force in Roadsend. Only two temporary patrols are going to be stationed here. However, they'll be two of the best patrols we have. They're still going to need some help, though, which is where you come in. You have the local knowledge and the local contacts. A member of the Militia is going to attract less attention than a Ranger asking the same questions." Divisional Commander Belinski looked to the women at the side. "Major Kallim, you had some things you wanted to say."

The major nodded and looked straight at Ellen. "Yes. Have you heard that an informer leaked details of Captain Aitkin's plans to the gang?"

"Yes, ma'am."

"Before she set out, Aitkin sent a favorable report about you to divisional headquarters. You were the one who handed over the note that resulted in the prisoner being taken to start with. The rest of the Militia here have been ineffective to the extent that collusion with the gang cannot be ruled out. At the moment, you're the only one we trust. So, you will not discuss anything concerning this investigation with the other Militiawomen. If Lieutenant Cohen or anyone else tries to question you, or put obstructions in your way, you're to tell me immediately. Do you understand?"

"Yes, ma'am."

"You'll be receiving a full briefing tomorrow morning. But in short, other people will be pursuing other goals, which you needn't concern yourself with. What I want you to focus on is the source of the leak. It has to be someone in town, which is where you have the contacts. So, do you have any ideas to start with?"

"Um..."

Ellen opened her mouth and then closed it. She knew she ought to mention her doubts about Hal. Yet doubts were all they were. The three

Rangers looked stern, uncompromising. Hal claimed the Rangers had ill-treated their previous prisoner. What would they do to someone who was no more than a suspect?

"The only person I...I..." Ellen's jaw clenched as she tried to force herself to speak. She failed. She could not hand Hal over to them—not until she had something more than doubts.

"Well?" Major Kallim did not sound impatient, but she clearly wanted an intelligent reply.

"Er...no, ma'am. No suspects. But the...the only person I'd ask an exception to be made for, concerning talking to the rest of the Militia, is my sergeant, Sergeant Sanchez."

Judging by the instant response on the three faces, they were about to reject the appeal. Suddenly, Ellen was struck by the realization of just what she was in for, and how much she would need Chris's advice and help. Raising the request had been the first impulsive idea to come to mind when evading Kallim's question. However, the more she thought about it, the more Ellen knew that getting an exemption for Chris was essential. She went on quickly, before anyone else could speak.

"You say you trust me because I've proved I'm willing to oppose the Butcher's gang. So has Sergeant Sanchez. She's only just returned from sick leave, recovering from injuries she got in a fight with the gang. She nearly died. And you can be sure she's nothing to do with the leak, because she's still not able to get out and about. She's confined to desk duty at the moment."

"So she won't be any use in pursuing the investigation."

"She would be great for advice, ma'am. She's really the one with the local knowledge and experience. I'm just a rookie. She won't be doing any running around, but I know it'd be useful talking things over with her. With the letter, it was her advice I was acting on. She said to take any information on the gang straight to Captain Aitkin, rather than giving it to Lieutenant Cohen."

Major Kallim looked surprised. "Did she now?" She glanced at Belinski. "I tell you what. I'll review what we know about Sergeant Sanchez and give you an answer in the morning. You can go now. Be here for five o'clock tomorrow."

"Yes, ma'am."

Ellen slipped from the room. She guessed she ought to be feeling proud and excited, but the only emotions going through her were anxiety, confusion, and guilt. Why had she not been able to say Hal's name? Ellen thought of her oath to uphold the law to the utmost of her ability, without favor. Maybe she had not totally broken that oath, but she had withheld information—and for the sake of a woman she had only kissed twice.

❖

Chris herself answered the door. She was in uniform and obviously preparing to go to work. Seeing Ellen standing on the step, her initial smile turned to a worried frown. "Is something wrong?"

"No. Not exactly. But I want to talk to you."

"Here or at the station?"

"Here. I can't risk being overheard."

Chris stepped back. "Come in."

As Ellen passed, Chris reached out and caught hold of her arm to examine her shoulder badge. "Hey. Now that looks like good news. Except I thought it wasn't due until—"

"It's a few days early. It's part of what I want to talk to you about."

Rhonda was in the cluttered front room, feeding the baby. They exchanged smiles and a few words of greeting, and then Ellen followed Chris through to the kitchen at the rear.

Chris shut the door and then waved Ellen to a seat at the table. "Okay. So why the early promotion and the secrecy?"

Ellen shrugged self-consciously. The embroidered badges on her shoulders felt heavy. Surely the tiny amount of stitching, forming the single bar of a patrolwoman, could not weigh so much. News that her probation period was officially deemed over had greeted her at the Ranger barracks that morning, along with a new black shirt already bearing the badges.

"The Rangers have co-opted me to help them find the Butcher, but they don't want anyone else from the Militia involved. I had to get special permission even to talk to you."

"What do they want you to do?"

"Anything I feel like."

"Pardon?"

Ellen grimaced. The morning's briefing had basically amounted to telling her she could do what she wanted, when she wanted, and pursue whatever line of inquiry she thought best. It left her even more relieved than before that she had thought to ask permission for talking it over with Chris, and that the request had been granted.

"They want me to discover who leaked the information about the raid, and anything else useful I can find out. But they didn't seem to have any ideas about how I could do it, so they've left it all up to me."

"Nice of them."

"I'm not the only one on the hunt, but they wouldn't tell me who the others are, or what they're doing."

"At least they've promoted you to patrolwoman."

Ellen sighed and peered down at her shoulder badge, trying to catch sight of the embroidered bar. "Yeah, the promotion. Now I'm not a rookie, I can patrol on my own, without needing Terrie as a puppy walker. I guess that's why they did it."

"And it makes you harder to push around. Jake Cohen will know you have official approval, and she's likely to come out worse if she starts mucking about and getting in your way."

"If only I knew what I was doing."

"You've got a free hand. What do you think you should do?"

"That's what I came here to discuss with you."

Chris grinned. "It's your investigation, Patrolwoman Mittal. Why don't you tell me your ideas, and I'll tell you what I think of them?"

Ellen sighed, but she felt a smile tug at her lips. She was starting to like the sound of her new rank.

"Well...the leak. As Mel Ellis said, the gang knew the route and the timing. Since we don't know where the final destination was, maybe the route was obvious. It might be the only sensible way to get there, but the timing?" Ellen shook her head. "By coincidence, Jake Cohen finally got me doing something useful yesterday. I tracked down other people who'd passed the ford earlier that day. The road was clear an hour before the ambush. So the gang definitely had inside information, and it's not simply that someone saw the Rangers acting excited and drew conclusions."

"What ideas do you have about who might have passed on the details?"

"I can't believe any of the Rangers did it deliberately, but those in the Three Barrels were drinking heavily. One of them could easily have said more than she should. As for who might have overheard, the name that..." Ellen's voice died.

"The name?" Chris prompted, after a few seconds of silence.

"Hal. I caught her once, trying to eavesdrop on the Rangers. And then she dashed off very suddenly and left me."

"Did she give a reason?"

"She said she was playing hard to get."

"Is that in character?"

"Oh yes."

Chris threw back her head and laughed. "It sounds like you're in trouble there. If you're lucky it's just that she's a Knife."

"Don't I know it." Ellen ran her hand through her hair. "Admittedly, I wasn't paying too much attention, but apart from her, I didn't see anyone acting oddly, or recognize any known troublemakers."

"How about strangers?"

"There was one woman who looked like barge crew. She was making out with Jay Takeda."

"Ah."

Ellen nodded. "Yup. Jay was pretty drunk, and she was bragging about getting the Butcher. Maybe the stranger was a Knife, who latched onto Jay as a way to get information."

"It won't be a popular result, if you end up blaming her."

"I know. But..." Ellen sighed. "I'll talk to the innkeeper, ask her what she remembers of who was there. And talk to survivors. Only about half the squadron were in the Three Barrels. I need to find out where the rest were."

"Right. What else?"

Ellen frowned. "What sort of thing are you thinking of?"

"For ten months, Jake has had us doing absolutely nothing. Now you've got a free hand. What do you think we should have been doing?"

"Oh. The sheep."

"It's where it all started."

Ellen drew a deep breath. "Okay. What I don't understand is how they're getting past us. In order to sell that many sheep, they have to get them to Eastford or Landfall. They can't be loading them into barges downstream of Roadsend because of the marshland, and if they do it upstream, they still have to come through town. They must have found some way around the ear-stamp and paperwork."

"Forgery."

"Maybe. But it still means that somewhere the numbers won't add up. It might give us a lead. We've got the cloning records in the Temple. I want to tally up the figures from the docks and compare them."

"Sounds good."

"Another thing is to see what gossip I can pick up in town. I'll visit all the inns early in the day when it's quiet, and see if the innkeepers have noticed any suspicious new faces. It would also be interesting to have a little chat with some of our local troublemakers, and see if I can squeeze anything out of them. The Knives might have tried to recruit a few. I doubt we'll see anything of Ade Eriksen, though I'll ask after her. And Fran Paparang skipped town as soon as her mother paid her fine. She can't have been involved in the massacre, but she has to know something."

"Does Valerie know where she is?"

"No. I'll ask their mother, but I doubt she'd admit it, even if she does."

"Oh, I'm sure her mother does. Else she wouldn't know where to send money whenever her poor little Fran is broke."

Ellen grinned. "Of course."

"Well. You better get to it. Looks like you're going to be busy."

❖

Ellen decided to get the visit that was bound to be the more unpleasant of the two over with first. Not that either was going to be fun. She rode the short distance out of town, to the run-down cottage where the Eriksens and their relatives lived.

The black Militia uniform had its effect. Ellen had not reached the yard in front of the house when she saw three women line up belligerently before the door, and another sneaking off to an outbuilding at the rear. This figure held Ellen's attention briefly, but it was too tall to be Ade. Undoubtedly the woman was going to hide the evidence for some illegal activity. However, Ellen, on her own, was in no position to make a challenge, even if she were not concerned with more important things than illicit stills and petty theft.

Ellen reined in her horse. The oldest of the women advanced. Ellen recognized her as Sharon Bwatuti, Trish and Ade's gene mother.

"What the fuck do you want here?" Bwatuti's greeting was everything Ellen had expected.

"I'm looking for Adeola."

"So you can kill her too?"

"Believe it or not, I am sorry about Patricia. But she brought it on herself." Before Bwatuti could cut in, Ellen continued. "And you know very well why we want to find Adeola. If she hands herself in, she'll get a fair trial."

"Fuck that."

"Adeola has brought enough trouble to this family. If you know where she is, you'd be doing yourself a favor by telling us."

"You think I'd turn my own daughter over to you scum, just for an easy life?" Bwatuti's voice dripped scorn.

Another woman, Ade's cousin, now advanced to within a meter of Ellen's horse. She scowled at Ellen for the space of ten heartbeats. "Why don't you fuck off."

❖

Tilly Paparang was in her normal state of complete denial. "Fran's a sweet girl. She's too easygoing for her own good. She wants to please everyone. She always did, even when she was a baby. That's why she goes along with people when they suggest doing stupid things. She doesn't want to upset them."

Ellen opened her mouth, but was temporarily lost for words, stunned by the vision of Francesca Paparang as someone too amiably docile to say no when anyone suggested that she join in with a street robbery.

"That's why I tell Valerie to keep an eye on her. But Valerie can't be bothered. She's off, looking out for herself, like always."

Ellen could hardly believe what she was hearing. "Valerie's your daughter, and she could have been killed in the ambush."

For a moment Tilly faltered, before rallying to her customary refrain. "It's her own fault for joining the Rangers. I told her not to. She should be here, keeping an eye on Fran."

Ellen jumped on the cue. "And exactly where would Fran be now, if someone should want to keep an eye on her?"

"I don't know." Tilly's reply was noticeable by its atypical brevity. Not that Ellen needed any such confirmation she was lying.

"You don't know?"

"You Militia scared her off. Picking on her. It wasn't her fault about the sta—"

"The magistrate thought differently."

"They've always had it in for her. And why are you after her now? She hasn't done anything wrong."

"I just want to talk to her. We know the Eriksen sisters are tied up in the trouble here. I want to know if either of them said anything to her."

"I've told her to have nothing to do with the Eriksens."

"Then she's been ignoring you."

"You always believe the worst of her. Valerie should be here, sticking up for her sister. She—"

Ellen could take no more of it. "I won't take up any more of your time. Thanks for talking to me. If you should happen to find out where Fran is, you will let me know, won't you?"

"Yes. Of course." Another short, sharp answer. Another lie.

❖

The mail office was a small room at the rear of the Town Hall. For a fee, letters could be left there to be delivered anywhere across the Homelands. Post arrived whenever enough built up at the main office in Eastford to justify sending someone out to Roadsend with it in a sack. The delivery woman would then take away any outgoing mail. Eventually the letters would reach their destination.

News that mail had arrived would spread across Roadsend, and within hours, anyone expecting a letter would call by the office. Items left unclaimed after a few days would then be delivered by hand, again in return for a fee.

Ellen had never received a letter from outside Roadsend, but she knew the postmaster. Pol Jensen was her gene mother's cousin. She was also the Town Hall filing clerk and the recorder for the magistrates' court. Despite Pol holding down three jobs, in a small town like Roadsend, none of these were particularly arduous, so when Ellen opened the door of the mail office, she was not surprised to find Pol enjoying an after-dinner snooze.

Pol jerked awake. "Can I help you?" She then relaxed, recognizing Ellen. "Hi. What do you want?"

"A favor."

"What?"

"When the post comes in, if there are any letters for Tilly Paparang, can you put them aside and let me know?"

"I'm not sure if I—"

"This isn't just me talking. It's an official Militia request."

"I can notify Lieutenant Cohen."

"No."

"The rules—"

"You can tell me, or you can tell Major Kallim at the Ranger barracks, but no one else."

Pol's eyes widened. She stood up and sidled closer to Ellen, dropping her voice. "Is this to do with the killing at the ford? And the big gang?"

"I can't say."

"Right." Pol drew the word out, her eyes getting still wider. "What shall I tell Tilly?"

"She'll be able to have the letter after I've looked at it. When you take it to her, say it was late because it slipped behind the table, and you'd only just noticed it. Apologize for the delay and waive the delivery fee. She'll be happy with that. You can claim reimbursement from the barracks."

"Oh no. It will be fine. I'm ready to do my bit to help out. All those poor Rangers, dead." Pol was clearly thrilled to be involved in the drama. None of her three jobs involved much in the way of excitement.

❖

The innkeepers Ellen visited in the afternoon did not provide any new information, although a couple she suspected of saying less than they could. Even so, she kept her manner pleasant throughout and did not push. If they were left feeling well disposed to her, they were more likely to suffer a guilt attack afterward and send an anonymous note.

She also made a point of stopping her questioning in the midafternoon, to leave them free to prepare for the evening trade.

Ellen walked back to the north side of town. She intended to have a break, a meal, and then make a round of the taverns that night, in civilian clothes. Maybe she would pick up something. Her thoughts were interrupted when a loud, angry voice hailed her.

"Hey! What sort of stupid tricks have you been up to?" Terrie Rasheed stormed over.

"I've been working."

"Out on your own?"

Ellen turned her shoulder to show her new badge. "Didn't the lieutenant tell you?"

"Yeah. She mentioned it. But that doesn't mean you can swan around town doing what the frigging hell you like. So—what have you been doing?"

"I'm afraid I can't tell you."

"What the fuck!" Terrie looked ready to explode with rage. "That wasn't a request. You tell me what you've been doing, and you tell me right now."

"I'm not allowed to. You should go and talk to Lieutenant Cohen."

"You're reporting directly to her?"

"No."

"The fucking Rangers." Terrie had her face scant centimeters from Ellen. "Are you fucking stupid? How many times do you need to be told? You don't damned well report to them. You—"

"I do when I get orders direct from Militia HQ. Lieutenant Cohen has got it in writing."

Terrie took a step back, temporarily speechless, but it did not last. "You think you're so fucking clever. I always had you down as a brown-nosed little prat. How many asses did you have to kiss this time? It's the most fucking stupid—"

Ellen had listened to enough. "If you have a problem, why don't you write to central command and tell the majors and colonels about how they're being so fucking stupid? Because it wasn't my idea."

She turned away sharply and kept walking. Terrie did not pursue her and Ellen did not look back to see how her suggestion had been received.

By the time she reached her home, Ellen had gotten over being angry, and had reached the point of being surprised at herself. She had never spoken back like that before, and was just starting to worry she might have gone too far. Would she get into trouble for insubordination? Although, from what Belinski had said, central command were more likely to back her than Terrie.

As ever, Mama Becky was sewing by the door. She smiled. "You're home early."

"Yup." A surge of elation pushed away other emotions. Ellen grinned and turned her shoulder to her mother for inspection.

At first, nothing but confusion showed on Mama Becky's face, as her eyes tracked up and down Ellen's arm, trying to work out what she was supposed to be looking at. Then she spotted the new badge. "You've finished your probation? You're a patrolwoman?"

"Yes." Ellen felt her smile get wider.

"But I thought it wasn't due until..."

"The first of September. They've moved me up a few days early."

Mama Becky's expression collapsed into doubt. "Is it because of the trouble with the Rangers? Have they got you hunting down the gang on your own?"

"No, Mom. Of course not." Ellen paused, realizing she had just said an outright lie. But she could not tell the truth. Her parents would worry far too much, especially after what had happened to the 12th Squadron.

"So why..."

"Well, yes, in part it's because of the Butcher and her gang. And with Chris being out. We're shorthanded, with a lot do to. They need me to be more independent. But that's it. And my pay will go up."

The assurance did no good. Mama Becky's eyes were already filling with tears. "You will take care, won't you? If anything happened to you I'd...I'd..."

Ellen knelt beside her gene mother and hugged her. "It's all right, Mom. The Rangers will be taking care of it now. We Militia will just be in a support role. And I promise. I'll be very, very careful."

Chapter Nine—Boats on the River

Ellen stood in the shadows at the rear of the tavern, sipping her drink and observing. The Twisted Crook was not her favorite place for socializing. The beer was indifferent and the bar staff unfriendly, which was at least partly in reaction to the volatile clientele, made up of barge crew and itinerant farm hands and laborers. Anybody familiar with Roadsend would know where to find a better tavern. Thus it was a good place to start looking for strangers in town, and maybe overhear loose gossip.

However, Ellen did not intend to stay there all evening, and it was time to move on. She had noted the unfamiliar faces in the taproom, and the volume was now so loud that she stood little chance of hearing anything. She drained her tankard and dumped it on the bar.

Outside, the sun was sinking toward the horizon. Ellen took a deep breath of warm air—the smell of sheep dung was less objectionable than that of unwashed bodies and stale beer in the taproom—and started walking. The wide street called South Drove led toward the next tavern she wanted to check out, the Drovers Rest, by Old Docks. Ellen knew she would end up crawling if she tried visiting all the Roadsend taverns in one night, even if she limited herself to a small measure of beer in each, but she hoped to get around to those with the worst reputations.

Ellen was halfway along South Drove when she heard the sound of running feet coming from a side alley that joined the main street a short distance ahead. Seconds later, a figure cannoned into view, spun toward her, and froze. Ellen had been ready to take evasive action, were it needed, but she also came to an abrupt standstill, recognizing Hal.

Despite all the doubts in her head, Ellen's heart leapt at the sight of the woman who had been dominating her thoughts for days. Even so, she had not realized quite how desperately she wanted to see Hal again, and it was all she could do to keep a smile off her face. The bubbling feeling of excitement in her chest was stupid and misguided, but knowing this did not make it go away.

Hal was clearly out of breath, and uncharacteristically anxious, but still spoke first. "Hi. I was...I was looking for you."

"Me?"

"Your mother said you were visiting taverns. I've tried most others. It was going to be the Twisted Crook next."

"You've spoken to..." Ellen stopped herself. Why act like an idiot and ask what had already been answered? "How did you know where I live?"

A trace of Hal's normal smile returned. "I have my sources."

Ellen folded her arms. "So?"

"I wanted to say I'm sorry." Hal ran her hand through her hair and took a step nearer, closing the short distance between them. "When you came to the farm, I was in a shitty mood. Aunt Cassie had kept me up most of the night. Jo had just told me we've got to do more work on the jetty. And the sheep had been awkward buggers all morning. It'd taken me ages to get a bunch into the pen and then one jumped on my foot, and while I was hopping around in agony the rest escaped again. The dogs were having one of their funny turns and just watched them go. I was ready to kill something when you turned up."

"You sounded like you didn't care about the murdered Rangers."

"I cared all right."

"But you had more sympathy for the bandits?"

Hal leaned forward, shaking her head in denial. "Dead bandits are fine by me. Dead Rangers mean I'm in for more trouble next winter. I was pissed off at them for getting themselves killed."

"That's a bit illogical."

"You try being logical when you've just had a sheep dancing on your toes."

Ellen stared down at her own feet. Forget the sheep. Trying to be logical when Hal was standing so close was damned near impossible. But then she felt, rather than saw, Hal reach toward her. Summoning her willpower, Ellen backed away, out of range. If Hal touched her, Ellen knew any self-control would be lost.

"So why come looking for me now?"

"Because...because I've spent six days being miserable, hoping you'd call back. And I've realized you aren't going to. And I'm scared that if I don't shift my ass, some other slut is going to jump you."

"I haven't noticed a queue forming."

"Really? The women in this town must be blind."

Ellen ducked her head to hide her smile. Again she felt Hal get close. This time Ellen placed her hands on Hal's waist to hold her still and then stared into her eyes. The world stopped.

"So. I've not left it too late?" Hal asked.

"No."

"Are you going anywhere interesting?"

"Just making the rounds."

"You're not wearing your uniform. Are you on duty?"

"Sort of."

"Does that mean I can sort of tag along?"

"I'm afraid not." Ellen released Hal, letting her hands drop to her sides. If Hal was with her, there was no way she would be able to concentrate on her surroundings. As it was, the temptation to abandon the round of the taverns was overwhelming.

"You don't trust me." It was a statement rather than a question.

"I—"

"I don't blame you."

Ellen stared at her, unsure what to say.

"I'm a stranger in these parts. I arrived just when the thefts started. You've got no proof that I'm who I say I am. And I'm a disruptive pain in the ass. Of course you can't trust me."

"It's not that."

"Then it ought to be."

"It's not you. I'm not supposed to talk about what I'm doing with the other Militiawomen either."

"It's that secret?"

"Yes."

"Even so, I'd like to help."

"You can't."

"Maybe not tonight. It's all right; I'll kiss you, then go and leave you to get on. But if I can do anything to help you, I will."

"That's good of you but—"

"I have ulterior motives."

"What?"

Hal stepped close, slipping her arms around Ellen's waist and resting her forehead on Ellen's shoulder. "I want to get into your pants, and I don't think you're going to let me, until you know I'm in the clear."

❖

Ellen found Mel Ellis in the stables at the barracks, brushing down a horse. Straw on the ground muffled the sound of Ellen's feet and the Ranger seemed unaware of Ellen's presence until the horse raised its neck and nodded its head toward her. The animal's lips rolled back to reveal teeth, although its demeanor suggested that the gesture was an appeal for food, rather than threatening.

Mel broke off brushing and looked over her shoulder. "Do you want something?"

"To talk to you."

"About what?"

"I'm trying to track down whoever told the Butcher about your plans to raid her base."

"Good. I want to see the bitch swinging by her neck."

"I'll do my best. I'm starting off by trying to get some information."

"That's rare for the Militia."

Ellen chose to ignore the comment. "Do you have any ideas how the plans got leaked?"

"You were in the Three Barrels that night. You saw how excited some of the women were. Someone didn't watch her mouth like she should have. And somebody else was listening in."

"Is there anywhere else you could have been overheard? The Three Barrels wasn't the first tavern you visited that night, was it?"

Mel put down the brush and stepped away from the horse. "We'd started off in the White Swan. I don't think it was there. The girls weren't as high then, and the place was damn near empty. That was why we left. It was dead."

"How about the rest of the squadron? You weren't all in the Three Barrels. Do you know where the rest were?"

"Some stayed in the barracks all night. That's where the officers were, making plans. Some came to the White Swan with us but went back when we moved on. I don't think anyone was anywhere else."

"Okay. That's good. It means I can start narrowing down suspects. So, in the Three Barrels, did you hear anyone talking details? Such as when you were supposed to assemble?"

"No." Mel's answer was too short, sharp, and defensive.

Ellen tried to be conciliatory. "Look. I understand you don't want to name names. And I'm not aiming to pin the blame on anyone, but if I know which Rangers were talking the most, then I can work out who was close enough to listen in."

"I didn't hear anyone shooting her mouth off."

"Okay. How about afterward?"

"We all went back to the barracks. We weren't completely stupid. We knew we had a big day ahead."

"All of you?"

"Yes."

"How about Jay Takeda? It looked like she'd picked up someone."

"Jay was always picking up women."

Ellen noted that Mel had not answered her question. "The woman she picked up that night, do you know her?"

"Never saw her before."

"How about since?"

"No." Mel's tone was getting more surly.

"Did Jay spend the night with her?"

"What damned business is it of yours?"

"Jay was clearly drunk, and this stranger latched onto—"

Ellen got no further. Mel bounded across the space between them and grabbed two fistfuls of black shirt. "You've got a fucking nerve. Jay was a hundred times better woman than you could dream of being. She gave her life for us. And a little shithead like you dares wander in here, acting like you know the first fucking thing about—" Tears were in Mel's eyes, though they did nothing to weaken the fury in her expression. She shoved Ellen away violently. "If I ever hear you say one frigging word against Jay, I'll gut you. Do you hear me? Jay died... and...and it should have been me."

Mel picked up the discarded brush and hurled it at the wall with all her strength. The thunderous crash when it hit sent the horse skittering wildly in its stall, fighting the rope on its halter.

Ellen had regained her balance after nearly falling. She ducked in reflex at the thrown brush, although she was clearly not the target. Mel glared at her, fists clenching and unclenching in rage, then she turned and marched from the stable without another word.

❖

The Militia office on the sheep docks was tiny and functional. If three women were in the room at the same time they had to shuffle around to be able to open the door. A desk stood beneath the window, and a chest under it contained wads of receipts. A shelf to the side held a row of ledgers. The wall opposite had a couple of hooks to hang coats on. And that was it. After two days of standing at the desk, Ellen would have appreciated a chair.

She clasped her hands behind her head and stretched, trying with limited success to ease the cricks. The wind had picked up outside, enough to shake the flimsy walls, and the resulting draft on her back was not helping. Checking the shipping records was proving every bit as tedious as she had feared. The only thing to be said in its favor was that it was proceeding far quicker than the pointless tour of the farms. Ellen had already tallied up the previous eight months' worth of sheep through the docks, itemized by farm and barge. Another day should see the job completed.

Before any boatload of sheep was allowed to pass through Roadsend, the skipper had to hand over signed receipts from the sellers. Furthermore, the skippers were familiar with all the farmers, and would know if the sheep came from someone who had no right to sell them. The biggest farms would sometimes fill a barge. More often, the sheep would come from several sources. The Militia officer on duty was supposed to make sure the numbers agreed, and to check a sample of the ear tattoos. The barge skipper was then given a transport permit and allowed to go.

The system had served for years, keeping most of the farmers reasonably honest, but it was not foolproof, and it had not been designed with a view to a criminal working on the scale of the Butcher.

Intimidating a craftswoman into making an illegal ear stamp or two would be nothing to her. She could also have the entire crew of a barge in her pay and she would certainly know people who could make good forged sales receipts. All of the papers Ellen had checked looked authentic, but she knew there had to be some forgeries among them.

The cloning records held at the Temple would let Ellen know the maximum number of lambs each farm would have to sell. She was sure that when she made the final tally, the numbers would not crosscheck. When she knew which farms the gang were passing their stolen lambs off as coming from, she would recheck the receipts. She could even run them past the relevant farmers—after all, that was why the receipts were held in Roadsend, to be on hand in case of dispute. Surely the farmers would know the name of every barge that had legally carried their sheep. And, if all else failed, Ellen thought she ought to be able to work out the name of the barge that had taken exactly the number of lambs that year, to make the numbers balance.

The door opened, admitting gusts of wind. Ellen slapped her hands on the papers to stop them from blowing around. Jude McCray peered in, her face revealing a raw curiosity that Ellen was getting used to. Her colleagues were clearly desperately wondering about what she was doing, even when, as at the moment, it was all pretty obvious.

"Ah. I thought you'd be in here."

Ellen merely looked questioningly in reply.

"I've got a message for you. A note was dropped off at the station."

"Who's it from?"

"Don't know." Judging by Jude's expression, she was lying. Presumably she had read the note on the way down, which meant it was not sealed, which in turn, Ellen could only pray, meant it contained nothing too sensitive or secret.

Ellen sighed, laid her arm across the loose papers, and held her other hand out for the note. Sight of the handwriting on the outside made a pulse kick in Ellen's stomach. She was fairly sure it was from Hal.

Jude looked at the desk. "Do you want any help?"

Ellen shook her head, although she was very tempted to say yes, just to share the stiff back. "No. It was good of you to bring me the note."

"I was passing."

"Thanks anyway."

Jude continued to dither in the doorway. "I'll be going, then."

"Right."

At last, Jude appeared to give up on the hope that she might be invited to take part in some exciting covert activity, and left. Once the door had closed, Ellen was able to take her hands off the loose papers. She unfolded the single-page note.

Ellen,

I said I wanted to help, and I think I may have done it. I've got an idea. If you come up to Broken Hills tomorrow lunchtime, I'll tell you all about it. If you can't make tomorrow, I'll be in town the following night. Perhaps we could meet up in the Three Barrels.

Hal.

❖

Possibly Hal had been watching from an upstairs window, because she was waiting on the farmhouse steps when Ellen rode up. She stood, dusted down her trousers, and walked forward, carrying a bundle wrapped in cloth.

Ellen was about to dismount, but Hal forestalled her. "No. Stay where you are." She waved the object in her hand. "I'm bringing lunch. You can provide the transport. It's okay. We're not going far."

Hal lifted her arm to Ellen, clearly wanting a hand up onto the horse. Ellen laughed and obliged. Once Hal was in place behind her, she said, "You were confident I'd come?"

"Optimistic."

"So where do you want to go?"

"Down to the river. Near the jetty would be fine." Hal wrapped her arms around Ellen. The contact felt so good. Ellen felt a smile stretch across her face, wide enough to make her cheeks ache.

The wind of the previous day had died. Only faint wisps of cirrus marred the blue sky. Ellen guided the horse through the farmyard and down the hill to the river. About halfway there, she felt Hal's lips brush the back of her neck.

"That's a bit distracting."

"Don't complain. I'm keeping my hands still, aren't I?"

"No."

"Oh. I didn't think you'd notice."

Ellen caught Hal's hand, peeled it off her thigh, and returned it to her waist. "I noticed."

Hal directed Ellen to a spot a hundred meters downriver of the jetty, where the ground had not been churned to mud by sheeps' hooves. A small clump of trees and bushes obscured the farm buildings from view, creating a secluded feel. They set the horse to graze, and then sat side by side on the grass. Sunlight danced over the ripples on the river. Autumn was still a month or more away, and the day was warm enough that the breeze off the water was welcome. Hal untied the cloth to reveal bread, cheese, slices of cold mutton, and fruit. She also had a flagon of beer. She removed the cork, took a swig, and passed it to Ellen.

"Have you really got me out here just to have a picnic by the river?"

"No. But it's an added bonus." Hal broke the loaf of bread in half.

"So?"

"I've heard that you're checking the dock records."

"How do—"

"I have my sources."

Ellen shook her head in bemusement. "Okay. What about it?"

"I guess you're looking for numbers that don't add up." Hal placed the chunks of bread on the cloth, inviting Ellen to take her share.

"Maybe."

"Or forged documents."

"Again, maybe."

"I don't think you'll find any."

Ellen concentrated on the food. She knew she should not get drawn into discussing the investigation.

Hal was not put off by her silence. "The reason I think you're wasting your time is because I've thought of a way they can get the sheep past Roadsend without you noticing."

"How?" Surprise got the better of Ellen's caution.

Hal pointed at the river, waving the lump of cheese in her hand. "Small boats. You only check the barges. You don't pay any attention to the small stuff—two-woman rowboats and the like."

"That's because you could only fit a half dozen sheep on them, at most. And you couldn't transport them all the way to Eastford."

"But you could take them as far as the marshland."

Ellen frowned, trying to see where Hal was going. "True. But what would be the point?"

"Boats stick to the main channel through the marshes, but there are plenty of side branches deep enough for a barge to slip down, find a nice quiet spot surrounded by high reed beds, and drop anchor. Nobody would ever know it was there."

"With a kilometer of waist-deep mud before you got to solid ground."

"Which would keep curious eyes away."

"You couldn't get the sheep to it."

"Not from the land, but with enough willing hands, you could lift them up, one at a time, from a small boat."

"It'd take a dozen trips to move a barge load of sheep."

"Yup. Two trips a day. They'd be done inside a week. With the profit margin on stolen sheep, they can afford to waste the barge crew's time."

Ellen stared at the water, mulling it over. Hal was right. Dozens of small boats went up and down the river—shopkeepers transporting merchandise, farmers getting supplies, laborers moving building material. The river was the easiest way to transport goods. Generally, items were taken as close to their destination as possible by boat before transferring to horse-drawn cart.

Hal said nothing more until they had finished their lunch, and washed it down with a last mouthful of beer. "So. Do you want to know where I got this idea?"

"Innate deviousness?"

"Nope. By working on the jetty. I've been at it the last four days, and while I've been working, I've been seeing the same boat go up and down the river. Closer to Roadsend, it would get lost in the rest of the traffic, but it's more conspicuous out here. After the fifth time it went by I started to wonder who was wanting to move so much stuff."

"When was the last time?"

"I saw it go up river about two hours ago."

The news jolted Ellen. "You think the gang's barge is in the marsh right now?"

"It's a possibility."

"Why didn't you send an urgent message to the Rangers?"

"Because I'd rather have lunch with you than with a patrol of Rangers."

"That's—"

"And it may be completely aboveboard. Maybe somebody has a large load of goods to shift, and can't afford a bigger boat. But even if this boat I've seen is nothing to do with the gang, I still think it's a good idea and I wanted to share it with you."

"Thanks. But the Rangers need to be told."

Hal's voice became more serious. "That's your job. At the moment, I'm having a picnic with a woman I'd like to think of as my girlfriend, though it may be a little premature. If you spot something suspicious and take action, I can say it's nothing to do with me. If I call out the Rangers, from what I'm hearing in town, I'm looking to get my home torched and my head kicked in. And I don't want that."

Ellen felt her stomach tighten. "No. I wouldn't want you to get hurt."

"How about the girlfriend bit?"

All Ellen's common sense told her to pull back. The situation was deadly serious and this was not the time to take risks or lose her self-control. She dare not get involved. Yet she could not help herself. Reason and restraint stood no chance against the passion Hal stirred up in her.

"I think I'd like that."

Hal picked up the cloth with the remains of the food and moved it aside. She leaned forward, gently capturing Ellen's mouth with her own. Ellen closed her eyes. Her world became the texture of lips and teeth and tongue. The soft exploration was broken for a moment as Hal shunted closer, so their bodies were in contact from hips to shoulder. Even this brief interruption was a wrench, although the end effect was worth it. Ellen wrapped her arms around Hal and lay back on the grass, pulling Hal on top. Every square centimeter of Hal felt good, pressed against her.

For a while they lay entwined, kissing, and then Hal raised herself on an elbow. Ellen stared into the face hanging over her. Breathing became a difficult activity as she felt Hal's hand slide up her side and cup her breast through the thickness of her clothes. Moving in its own instinctive reflex, Ellen's body arched into the contact. She moaned. Hal's hand moved to the top button of her shirt.

Hal froze. "Shit."

The abrupt change in mood hit Ellen like a blow. "What is it?"

"Fucking awful timing. It's the boat I told you about."

Ellen wormed out from under Hal and sat up, shading her eyes against the sun. A rowboat was three hundred meters or so away, moving swiftly toward them with the current. "You're sure?"

"Yes. See the green canvas covering the rear of the boat? That's always there when they come downriver."

The boat was six meters long, manned by two women. The covered section was large enough to hold a half dozen sheep.

Ellen shook herself, shifting mental alignment, and stood up. "Stay here."

"What are you going to do?"

"I'm going to ask them to let me see what they've got in the boat. I'm in uniform. If they're on the level, they'll do what I say. And if they ignore me..." Ellen shrugged. "That will be our answer."

She left Hal by the trees and walked to the water's edge. Ripples lapped against the mud of the undercut bank. The boat got closer. Neither rower was instantly recognizable from the back, although this did not mean much. Ellen waited until they were within hailing distance.

"Hey. Can you come over here and stop a moment? I want to talk to you."

At the challenge, one woman glanced over her shoulder and then leaned forward to exchange a quick word with her companion. Initially, it seemed as if they would ignore Ellen and row on past, but just before they drew level with her, the one at the front dug an oar into the water as a brake, rotating the boat so it was heading for the bank.

Ellen paced along beside the river, keeping level with the boat. After another thirty meters downstream, the rowers shipped oars and the gunwales knocked against the bank. Ellen heard the sound of the hull grating on shingle. One woman reached out and grabbed a fistful of long grass to steady the craft. Ellen was close enough to look down into the stern. The green canvas was moving perceptibly. There was definitely something alive under it—and then Ellen saw a sheep hoof appear beneath the bottom.

The rowers clambered from the boat and faced her. A little too late, it occurred to Ellen that there was another way Knives might react to a challenge from a lone Militiawoman, other than simply ignoring her. Also, both were not complete strangers. One had a scarred chin and broken nose—the thug she had fought on the night Chris was stabbed.

After the massacre of the 12th Squadron, the stakes were higher, and deadly force was no longer the second resort. Without hesitation, both rowers drew their blades and advanced. Ellen backed away, step by step, retreating up the riverbank. Step by step, the two armed women followed her.

The sudden pounding of hoofbeats came without warning. A mounted rider charged through, between Ellen and her would-be assailants. Ellen had only an instant to identify Hal, wielding the pottery flagon like a bat, swinging it wildly. The Knife she was aiming at dived out of range of the flagon, tripped, stumbled, and went headfirst into the river. Water erupted like a fountain.

Ellen stood in surprise, watching Hal wheel the horse about, ready for another charge, but the remaining Knife did not hang about waiting for Hal's attack. She ran to the boat, leapt in, and pushed off from the bank, using her oar as a pole. The boat wobbled a few meters out into the river.

"Hey!" The woman in the water had surfaced, and was clearly anxious not to be left behind. She swam frantically toward the drifting boat. Her accomplice dropped the oar and moved to mid-ship, reaching out a hand to help.

Hal reined the horse to a stop beside Ellen and jumped down. "Are you all right?"

Ellen did not answer. The Knives were about to get away and she had to stop them.

The bank rose higher a few meters downstream, where a small hillock had been cut through by the meandering river. Ellen ran down to the high point. The drifting boat would be passing directly under the spot. She just had to get her timing right.

"Ellen. No," Hal shouted.

Ellen paid no attention. She took a running leap, launching herself off the top and landing in the open hull.

The boat rocked so violently that it was in danger of capsizing. Ellen staggered, almost pitching straight over the side. The woman in the boat was kneeling, leaning out to her comrade. She shouted, struggling to stop herself from tumbling overboard. For a moment it looked as if she would fail and end up in the river, but she managed to keep her grip on the gunnels. However, her weapon was lying beside her hand, and it slid over the edge, disappearing into the water with a soft plop.

Ellen was the first to recover her balance. She tore the baton off her belt and sprung forward. The Knife had been trying to stand. Now she fell back, avoiding the blow and landing on the green canvas that rippled and bucked beneath her. Ellen took another step forward, raising her baton.

A hand grabbed Ellen's ankle, making her stagger. She looked down. The second Knife had dragged herself half out of the water and reached into the boat. Ellen brought her baton down hard on the woman's wrist. The Knife yelped in pain and her grip loosened. A second swipe and she let go, slipping over the side. Ellen put her boot on the woman's forehead and shoved hard, speeding her departure.

The world turned inside out.

Some time later Ellen felt the crack. Her neck jarred sideways.

She was staring at the sky.

The Knife in the boat was standing over her, oar in hand, holding it like a spear. Ellen frowned. Where was she? The muscles in the woman's arms tensed, about to bring the end of the oar down into her face, and Ellen's head was throbbing too much to move.

"No," Hal screamed from the other end of a tunnel.

The woman with the oar froze, just for an instant, and looked up. An instant was all that was needed. The boat knocked into the bank and a shudder ran through the craft, unbalancing the Knife. Ellen tried to kick out, but her legs belonged to someone else.

Then Hal was in the boat, pushing the Knife, shouting at her and punching her. The bandit tripped, staggered, and plummeted overboard. The water that splashed on Ellen's face was a moment of clarity. She thought she might have a headache.

A horse whickered some distance away. Ellen rolled her head to the side, even though it felt heavy. The bank was a long way off. One Knife was sitting astride Ellen's horse. The other was staggering from the river, soaked and dripping. This woman levered herself onto the horse's rump while her accomplice grabbed her belt, hauling her clumsily up behind the saddle. Ellen realized they were taking her horse and, most annoyingly of all, they would not stay in focus while they did it.

"They've stolen my horse."

"Ellen. Ellen."

Somebody had been saying the name for a while. Ellen looked up. Hal was still there.

"They've stolen my horse."

"Ellen. How many fingers am I holding up?"

"Which hand?"

"Shit."

"They've stolen my horse."

"You're a fucking idiot. Do you know that?"

"Hal."

"What?"

"I'm going to be sick."

With Hal's help, she was able to get her head over the side of the boat first. Once Ellen was back, lying in the boat, Hal placed her hand on Ellen's forehead and closed her eyes. Ellen felt the fog in her head fade and the pounding headache receded. Clearly Hal had ability with the healer sense. A pit of darkness sucked Ellen in and then spat her out.

"What happened?"

Hal was sitting on the seat, rowing. "You've got a concussion. I've done a bit to help, but it isn't enough. Don't worry. I'm taking you into town as quick as I can. We'll find a proper healer."

"What happened?"

"You got hit on the head with an oar."

"They've stolen my horse."

"And we've got their boat."

The sky was a nice shade of blue. The oars made a rhythmical splashing.

"Hal."

"What?"

"I think I'm going to be sick again."

CHAPTER TEN—A LETTER HOME

The side of Ellen's head still felt tender, but the blinding headache had gone, her eyes had no trouble fixing on objects, and her stomach felt mercifully stable. In fact, she was well enough to feel like a fraud for lying in bed, and worse than that, bored with nothing to do. Ellen stared at the rafters of her home. Mama Roz had moved her mattress down to the main floor of the cottage, so that Mama Becky would be able to keep an eye on her during the day.

Ellen grimaced. Despite Dr. Miller's orders, if it were not for her gene mother's watchful presence, she would have been tempted to sneak off. The entertainment value of the new perspective on the cottage roof had long since worn thin.

"Hello. Have you come to see Ellen?" Mama Becky called from her normal spot outside the door.

The reply was too distant for Ellen to make out any details, but the prospect of a visitor was welcome. Even a chat with Lieutenant Cohen would be more fun than counting the rafters.

"She's due to see Dr. Miller again tomorrow." Mama Becky was either answering a question, or simply volunteering information.

"Will she be allowed back to work?"

Ellen's pulse leapt, recognizing Hal's voice, now much closer and clearer.

"She's hoping so." Mama Becky's voice dropped to a whisper that was still loud enough to hear inside the cottage, which Ellen suspected was her gene mother's intention. "She's not a good patient. Never has been. It always was a hard job to get her to do what she's told. See if you can't sort her out."

"I'll see what I can do." Ellen could hear the amusement in Hal's voice.

"You know we can't thank you enough for rowing her into town."

"I couldn't leave her to row herself."

"And you were able to heal her."

"Hardly. I've got a little of the sense, but I wasn't able to do much more than work out how badly she was hurt."

"I know you're just being modest. We didn't get to thank you properly at the infirmary, but if there's anything we can ever do for you."

"There's really no need."

"She means so much to us."

"I'm kind of fond of her too."

"Oh. I...I'm pleased. Go in and see her."

The light in the cottage dimmed briefly as Hal stepped through the open doorway.

"Hi. How are you doing?"

"A lot better for you being here."

Hal plunked herself down beside the mattress and then carefully took hold of Ellen's hand. "You'll have to come up with a more original line in sweet talk. I've heard that one before."

"Who from?"

"Never you mind." Hal smiled. "How's your head?"

"Still there. Who else has been flirting with you?"

"Nobody whose hand I'd still want to hold."

"An ex."

"I can see the blow hasn't harmed your ability to make those sort of lightning-quick deductions. You are an idiot, you know."

"I was just checking it was nobody current."

"I meant for jumping in the boat."

Ellen pouted, imitating a sullen infant. "That's not fair. You switched topic without warning. You have to go slow. I'm not well."

Hal kissed her quickly on the lips. "And you're lucky you're unwell, or else I'd tell you exactly what I think of your suicidal heroics. I'd managed to stop them from knifing you once, but that wasn't good enough. You wanted to give them a second go at it." Beneath Hal's smile was a serious edge. Not all of it was play-acting.

"I didn't want them to escape with the sheep."

"And you were going to stop them by getting your brains smashed to pulp?" Hal sat back, looking exasperated.

"I thought I could handle her, one on one."

"You mean you actually thought about it before jumping?"

"Not quite. I just knew they were criminals, they had some stolen sheep, and they were trying to escape."

"You could have been killed."

"It's my job."

"Nothing is worth dying for."

"Some things are."

"Half a dozen sheep?" Hal sounded incredulous.

"It's my duty to uphold the law."

"By risking your life?"

"If need be."

Hal lifted Ellen's hand to her lips and sighed. "Whoever thought I'd fall for someone as pigheadedly virtuous as you?"

"You said that like it's a bad thing."

Hal pressed Ellen's hand against the side of her face and closed her eyes. "I think maybe it is for me." Her tone might have been wistful, might have been sad. "So how much longer are you going to be lounging around here?"

"Not a second longer than I can help. I'm hoping Dr. Miller will give me the all clear to go back to work tomorrow."

Hal shook her head. "Pigheadedly virtuous and enthusiastic." But now her smile had returned, and she dropped their joined hands into her lap.

"I want to know how things are going—whether they've found any trace of the barge in the marshland."

"Has nobody been to see you?"

"Chris has."

"And?"

"The sheep in the boat weren't lambs. They were some of the breeding stock stolen last autumn, from South Hollow Ranch. They've been returned to the rightful owner."

"Is she pleased with you?"

"Have you met Jean Tulagi?"

"Does that mean no?"

"Apparently she's still moaning about the other thirty-two she's lost."

"You get your head cracked open, and she's not happy?"

"It's traditional for farmers to never be happy with anything the Militia does."

Hal nodded thoughtfully. "Well, I hate to break with tradition, but I'm hoping you're going to do some things to make me very happy."

"Are those the sort of things that will have to wait until I'm fully better?"

"Unfortunately, yes."

Ellen felt her body respond to the images Hal's words and tone aroused. Were it not for her mother's presence outside the door, she would have been more than willing to risk a relapse. "I'll try to get better quickly."

"Do that." Hal leaned forward and again kissed Ellen's lips, slower and more thoroughly than before, yet still holding back, clearly concerned for her health. Eventually she pulled away. "I have to go. I've got to pick up some things and get back to Broken Hills before nightfall. But I wanted to check on how you were."

"When will I see you next?"

"Whenever you're cleared to ride, come out to the farm and I'll throw a special welcoming party for you. Otherwise..." Hal pursed her lips while staring into space, presumably running through her job list. "I could make it into town again in four days' time."

"I'm sure I'll be fine by then."

"I do hope so."

Hal delivered one last quick kiss, then stood and left. The sound of her footsteps had barely faded away when Mama Becky bustled into the room.

"Are you okay, dear?"

"Yes, Mom."

"That woman, the one who saved you, do I know her?"

Ellen sighed, fully aware where her gene mother was heading. "I don't think so. Her name's Hal Drennen."

"Drennen...I know the name."

"Her great-aunt owns Broken Hills Ranch."

"Oh yes. And you two are...er..."

"Yes, Mom. She's my girlfriend."

"You've been keeping that quiet." Despite any criticism in the words, Mama Becky was blatantly delighted.

"We only just started, sort of."

"She seems very nice. Does she work for her aunt?"

Ellen closed her eyes, but there was no escape. She was in for the full inquisition, with extended cross-examination when Mama Roz got home. Both her parents would be delighted, pretty much regardless of what she said. In their eyes, any new girlfriend was a potential reason for her not to join the Rangers.

But how would they react if she told them her doubts—that Hal might be a member of the Butcher's gang? And did she still doubt Hal? Hal had helped her recover six stolen sheep. She had discovered how the gang were avoiding the Militia checks. She had also jumped into the boat, and fought the Knife. She had saved Ellen's life. Surely she was now in the clear.

❖

"Please, Officer."

Ellen looked down at the young urchin. Judging by her height, the girl was about ten years old, which meant she was either small for her age or a little too young to be out of school. However Ellen decided not to press the point. "Yes?"

"Got a message for you."

"From?"

"The post lady. In the office. She wants to see you."

"Thanks." Ellen pulled a small coin from her purse and flipped it in the air. The girl caught it one-handed and ran off, with a yelp of thanks.

Ellen marched swiftly through the town. This was her first day back at work. So far she was feeling fine, though she had strict instructions to go to the infirmary at the first sign of a headache or trouble with her vision.

Pol Jensen looked up from her desk when Ellen entered the post office. "You got the message?"

In Ellen's opinion, both the question and the clandestine whispering were unnecessary, but she nodded anyway.

"A letter's arrived for Tilly Paparang. I put it aside, like you said." Pol glanced melodramatically over her shoulder and then reached into a drawer. "Here you go."

The letter was folded in a knot but unsealed. Ellen teased it open.

Hi Mom,

I am okay and you do not need to worry about me, but I have to get my boots repaired and I am out of money. K says she will not lend it to me, even though I am working for her. She says she will pay me when the current batch are fired, if I stick the job out. I can tell that she does not trust me to do my share, but I am going to prove her wrong, and then I will be able to pay you back.

I hope you are well.

love

Fran

Ellen carefully refolded the letter and slipped it back into the knot. She returned it to Pol. "Thanks."

"Anything else I can do?"

"After she gets this, Tilly will come back to you with a letter in reply, although it will most likely not be for a few days. Can you make a note of the address it goes to?"

"Yes. Sure."

"And, I don't suppose you have any idea where this letter came from."

Pol nodded enthusiastically. "I thought you might ask. It was with the batch from Clemswood."

❖

In order for Fran's boots to need repairing, she would have had to exert herself in some way while wearing them. However, as anyone familiar with the young woman would know, this did not sound in the least bit likely. Ellen's own best guess was a drinking or gambling debt.

For all her protestations, Tilly Paparang would be as aware as anyone else that Fran's letter was not telling the undiluted truth, and that Fran was really hoping for far more than might reasonably be required to cover the cost of a new pair of heels. Tilly would scrape together as much money as she could, and this would take her several days, if not longer.

Feeling that she had already wasted too much time staring at the ceiling, Ellen was impatient to talk to Fran without delay. Fortunately, she knew of one potential shortcut, rather than wait until Tilly was ready to send the money. Ellen headed straight for the Ranger Barracks. She caught up with Valerie crossing the parade ground.

"Hey."

Valerie flinched perceptibly at the hail. She jerked around as if ready to ward off attack. At sight of Ellen, her anxious expression eased, but did not fade completely. "Oh. Hi."

"How are you doing?"

"Fine." The assertion was manifestly a lie. The emotional scars left by the massacre were showing no sign of healing. The few times Valerie had spoken to Ellen since leaving the infirmary, she had seemed frightened and withdrawn. Now she made an attempt to smile, but it lacked her former ease and warmth. "How's things? I hear you got in some trouble. Good to see you up and about."

"I had a bit of a run-in with some thugs." Ellen refrained from asking why Valerie had not visited her. "I'm okay now. But I've got a quick question for you. Do you have any relatives in Clemswood?"

"Clemswood? No."

"How about the villages around it?"

Valerie frowned in thought and then shrugged. "Just Aunt Karen. She owns a pottery in Shingleford, which is a dozen kilometers south of there."

"Thanks. That's great."

"Why do you want to know?"

Ellen glanced around, but nobody else was in earshot, and she had not been forbidden to discuss things with Rangers. "I think your sister is staying with her."

"Fran?"

"You don't have any other sisters, do you?" Ellen said, teasing, but the attempt at humor fell flat.

"She's a..." Valerie's shoulders twitched, irritably. "She makes me fucking mad. I'd wondered where she'd run off to. Mom refuses to say."

"Don't take it so personally. I know you feel the stupid stunts she pulls reflect on you, but they don't. You're not responsible. And you know she wasn't involved this time. She was in the station lockup when the..." Ellen broke off, seeing her friend's expression start to crumple. The whole topic was best avoided. "I only want to see if she overheard anything from the Eriksens. Or if she knows where Ade might be."

"She'll lie to you." Valerie's voice trembled.

"I'll try to scare the truth out of her."

"You don't have anyone else who can tell you about Ade?"

"Her family certainly weren't helpful."

"No. They wouldn't be." Valerie swallowed, visibly trying to muster her self-control. "Anyway, good luck with finding Fran. But I don't think you can trust a word the little shithead says."

Ellen patted Valerie's arm and turned away. Only then did she let the smile slip from her face. She could not imagine what the battle at the ford had been like, watching friends and comrades die around you, and then to live on afterward, knowing those you had left behind had been slaughtered like animals in cold blood. Valerie was clearly still going through hell, and Ellen had yet another score to settle with the Butcher and her gang—for the pain they had inflicted on her friend.

❖

The station briefing room was empty, apart from Chris sitting at the table with a pile of reports laid out before her. No sounds came from either the lieutenant's office or the lockup. Ellen paused just inside the door, considering checking them out first, but it would be easier to simply ask Chris.

Ellen slid onto the bench beside her. "Hi."

"Hi. How are you feeling?"

"Fine. How about you?"

"Fine." Chris grinned. "We're a right pair of old crocks, aren't we? Ready to be pensioned off." Chris's expression became more serious as she examined Ellen's face. "You sure you're okay? No headaches?"

"No."

"You're looking pained."

"I've been talking to Valerie Bergstrom. She's still in a real state."

"It's going to take a lot more than half a month to get her sorted and back on track."

"I know. I can't imagine what she's been through."

Chris shuffled the nearest reports into a neat pile. "Is there something you wanted to talk about?"

"Yes. I've got some news."

"What?"

Ellen glanced around the room and jerked her head toward Cohen's office. "Is anyone else in?"

"Nope. We're alone."

"I think I know where Fran Paparang is. She's at her aunt's in Shingleford. I want to go and talk to her."

Chris hesitated. "You will be careful?" Her tone made it a question.

"Of course. But it'll be safe. Fran's a pain in the ass, but she's not violent when she's on her own. She's not going to attack me. And there won't be anyone else in town I need to worry about."

"Does Dr. Miller say you're okay to travel?"

"She didn't say I wasn't."

"That's not a good answer."

"I'm not going to be galloping flat out. Shingleford is only two days away." Ellen paused, thinking that she would miss Hal's next visit to Roadsend. However, there was no reason why she could not go out to Broken Hills Ranch immediately on her return.

"Do you think talking to Fran is worth the journey?"

"Yes. She wasn't in with the gang but I'm sure she knows more about them than she let on. Maybe more than is good for her health. Trish and her were really close. And Trish never had the sense to know when to keep her mouth shut. I'm guessing Fran's hiding from the Knives as much as us."

Chris nodded. "Okay. But you know you don't need my permission to go."

"No. I'm going to discuss it with Major Kallim. But I'll feel happier, knowing you think my reasoning is good."

"Well, it's a damn sight more sensible than jumping into a boat full of armed thugs."

Ellen sighed and hung her head. "You too."

"Me too what?"

"Hal's already had a go at me about it."

"Then I agree with her." Chris paused. "And that reminds me, I've found out something."

"About Hal?"

"Maybe."

"What?"

"An address for Cassie Drennen's relatives. I've written to them."

"Asking if Hal is really Cassie's niece?"

"I wasn't quite that blunt. I phrased it as a routine request and said that since Ahalya is in charge of the farm, we need written instructions from Cassie's next of kin to amend the Town Hall registry—which has the added bonus of being true. If Cassie's incapable of being responsible for the ear stamp, someone should have notified us. If it's the first the family have heard about Hal running Broken Hills, they'll write back asking what the hell's going on, and if Hal's who she claims they'll apologize, and I'd then expect Hal to show up at the Town Hall in short order, with all the proper documentation."

"That would be a big relief."

"You like her?"

"Uh-huh. Lots."

❖

Fran hefted the axe menacingly, eyeing her target as if she was contemplating murder, but after a few more seconds of indecision she dumped the axe beside the block, released a tortured sigh, and started to collect the chopped logs. She moved with the speed generally associated with seventy-year-old crones, and for every two logs she picked up, she dropped one, but eventually her arms were full. She turned in the direction of the woodshed and promptly dropped everything, seeing Ellen leaning against the roof support, watching her.

Ellen laughed. "Goddess. I wish Valerie was here to see this. I don't think either of us have ever known you do five minutes work before. Are you finding it a strain? You look like you're suffering. Any blisters?"

Fran backed away, looking around and clearly thinking about running, but there was no point. Past experience had shown that Ellen easily possessed the speed to catch her, and Fran was neither dressed nor equipped for travel. She would have to return to her aunt's pottery before long, so Ellen could simply sit by the door and wait. The isolated village had nowhere for a fugitive to hide.

Fran's shoulders sagged, and she pouted sullenly at Ellen. "How did you know I was here?"

"Your aunt told me." Ellen scrunched her nose. "Actually, her words were 'the lazy little shit is out the back, pretending to work,' but I knew who she meant."

"No. Who told you I was in Shingleford?"

"Nobody told me."

"It's just luck that you wandered by here?"

Fran's skepticism was not unreasonable. Shingleford was a small village about eighty kilometers northeast of Roadsend, with a population of fewer than 200. The reason for the village's existence was the ford over the East Tamer River and the fine clay beds nearby. Pots and raw clay were transported downriver to Roadsend, Eastford, and beyond.

The nearest thing Shingleford had to a tavern was a space at the rear of the village store, where beer could be bought by the tankard. In the tightly knit community, strangers would be treated with suspicion, and since the village was too small to warrant a Militia station, the inhabitants might well take it on themselves to dispense justice to anyone causing them trouble. It was not somewhere Ellen could imagine Fran wanting to live, nor a place where the petty criminal was likely to be happy.

Ellen grinned. "You know, what I don't understand is how you've managed to run up a debt so quickly. I wouldn't have thought the storekeeper would let you drink on credit. I can't imagine you got an invite to the local card game so soon. But from what I can see, your boots look fine."

"You read my letter to Mom." Fran sounded outraged.

"Yes. She's put herself in a bit of a sticky spot, lying to the Militia about not knowing where you were."

"You leave my mom out of this."

"Don't tell me you've developed a guilty conscience about the trouble you cause your mother."

Fran jerked her shoulders in a gesture of irritation. "You've got no reason to ask her where I was in the first place. I ain't done anything wrong."

"That would be a first."

"So why are you here?"

"I want to ask you some questions."

"I don't know anything."

"You don't know what the questions are."

"I'm damned sure you haven't come all this way to ask me what my favorite color is." Fran had clearly gotten over the surprise of being found and was ready to go on the offensive.

Ellen pursed her lips pensively and tilted her head to the side. "Are you having fun here?"

"No, I'm not. That's what I want the money for. I want to go somewhere else."

"Is your cruel aunt making you work? That must be awful for you."

"Ha fucking ha. You don't—"

Ellen cut her off. "You see, this doesn't strike me as your sort of place. And the only reason I can think for you being here is because you're hiding from someone."

"I'm not hiding from you."

"So why didn't your mom say where you were?"

Fran scowled by way of an answer.

"But of course, you're not just hiding from us, are you? You're hiding from the Butcher's gang as well."

"I don't know anything about them."

"Your mates, Ade and Trish, were in the gang. I'm sure they told you something."

"They didn't."

Ellen had been advancing while she spoke. She was now within arm's reach, close enough to stare into the other woman's eyes. Fran shifted uncomfortably, but the chopping block hampered her retreat.

"I wonder if you realize how serious this is. Twenty-one murdered Rangers are buried back in Roadsend. It's not like any sort of trouble you've been in before, and you aren't going to get let off by pulling a sulk and waiting for mommy to sort it out for you."

"I'm not—"

Ellen carried on relentlessly. "Twenty-one women murdered. And it isn't going to end until everyone involved has paid for it in a hangman's noose. Us in the Militia—we're just trying to see justice done. The Rangers I've spoken to are out for revenge. If they think you and your mother are trying to shield the killers, you'll both be there as well, swinging by your necks."

Fran's head shot up. "I said, leave my mother out of it."

"You're the one who got her involved, when you ran off, and got her to lie about where you were."

"I don't know anything." But Fran was rattled, and a pleading edge entered her denial.

Ellen folded her arms, letting the seconds trickle by. "You can come back to Roadsend with me."

"No."

"It wasn't a suggestion. I'm taking you in for questioning. We'll give you a grilling in the Militia station, and when you've convinced us you're telling the truth, you can go and spend some time in the Ranger barracks and see if you can convince them. Maybe they'll have your mom in as well."

Fran's hands clenched in fists. "You can't do that."

"We can too."

"I don't—"

"Yes, I know. You don't know nothing." Ellen paused. "Why don't I ask you some questions, so we can find out the limits of your ignorance?"

Fran merely stared back, but Ellen could sense that something inside her had broken.

"When did Ade and Trish first get involved with the gang?"

"I don't..." Fran stopped and stared down at her feet.

Ellen waited for her to speak.

"Ade met up with the gang in Eastford. I don't know how or when. The first we knew was when she came back to Roadsend."

"And when was that?"

"The beginning of July."

"Did she try to talk you and Trish into joining?"

"Yes."

"Did you?"

"No."

"Trish did."

"I told her not to. At first she listened to me, but Ade was her sister." Fran's voice cracked. "Now she's dead."

"Why didn't you join?"

"Because I knew how it would end." Fran dashed a hand across her eyes. "When Ade told us about it, I knew it wasn't a game. It was way more serious than anything I'm going to touch."

"What did Ade tell you?"

"Nothing. Just things."

Ellen caught hold of Fran's arm. "Okay. We can finish this conversation in Roadsend."

"No."

Fran tried to pull away, but could not match Ellen's strength. Still she struggled until Ellen yanked her around and thrust her backward. They ended with Fran pressed against the wall of the woodshed, and Ellen's forearm across her throat.

"What had Ade been doing in Eastford? What was her role in the gang?"

Fran sagged against the wall. "You know what Ade can be like. She's got a nasty side. The Butcher had her threatening folk, keeping them in line."

"Threatening or beating the shit out of them?"

Fran shrugged as far as her pinned position allowed. "Depends if they took the threat seriously."

"And what's she been doing in Roadsend?"

"Same sort of stuff. The way she talked, she was going to end up as deputy to the Butcher."

"Do you know where the Butcher's hideout is?"

"Somewhere off in the Wildlands."

"Where?"

"I don't know. I never went there."

"How about Trish?"

"I think she went a couple of times, but she only joined the gang a few days before she...she..." Fran closed her eyes, but not before Ellen saw them filling with tears.

"You two were girlfriends?"

"Yes."

The answer was no great surprise. Ellen had suspected as much for a while. She relaxed the pressure on her forearm and when Fran made no attempt to escape, she let her arm drop and stepped back.

"And she still didn't tell you anything?"

"She knew I didn't like it."

"How far away was the gang's hideout?"

"I told you. I don't know."

"When Trish went there, how long did it take her?"

"She could go there and back in a day. It took her all day, but I don't know if she rushed, or how long she stayed. I think it was off to the southeast of town, in the canyons."

"Was the Butcher there in person, or just one of her henchwomen?"

"The Butcher was there. Trish said she'd met her."

"Is she still there?"

"How would I know?" Fran's denial sounded genuine. She was clearly now talking spontaneously and maybe ready to volunteer information rather than have it dragged out of her.

Ellen waited a few seconds "Okay. Now the really big question. Why are you hiding out here?"

"What?"

"I think you know something, and you're frightened the gang might want to make sure you can't tell anyone."

Fran slumped back, staring at her feet. When she spoke, her voice was a soft mumble. "I know where Ade is."

"Where?"

"It's to do with one of the gang. She's a bit flaky and the Butcher can't rely on her. But she does an important job, so they can't get rid of her. I overheard Ade telling Trish. Ade was saying she was going to be off for a couple of months, keeping an eye on this woman, making sure she stays in line. Ade was saying how it showed the Butcher trusted her, and she was on the way to becoming one of the Butcher's top women."

"Who was the woman? Do you know anything about her?"

"She's in Eastford somewhere. I just overheard a bit of it. Ade was bragging away and it was all getting boring. I wasn't paying much attention."

"Did you hear anything else about the woman?"

"Her name. Susan Lewis."

Chapter Eleven—The Red Dog Inn

"You will be very careful, won't you?"

"Yes, Mom. Bye. See you soon."

Ellen shouldered her pack and turned away, but before she had taken a step, Mama Roz grabbed her and wrapped her in another smothering hug.

"I mean it. We want you back here safe."

"I promise. I'll be watching out, every step of the way."

Ellen carefully peeled Mama Roz off her, ducked down to kiss Mama Becky's cheek, and made her escape. Only when she was safely out of earshot did Ellen give vent to her feelings in a deep sigh. It felt as if she had been escaping from people all morning. Already she had been in another argument with Terrie Rasheed, and had only narrowly avoided being cornered by a tearful Mandy Colman.

At the end of the road, Ellen stopped briefly to wave back at her mothers, who were still watching from the cottage door, and then marched on, through the twisting Northside dirt streets, until reaching the main Newbridge Road. With luck she would get to the docks without being waylaid again. Ellen did not want any more fuss. However, as she crossed the Clemswood Road another voice hailed her.

"Ellen. Wait."

Ellen looked back. Hal was jogging toward her.

"Hey. I didn't think to see you in town." Ellen could not stop the grin spreading across her face. Maybe there were some types of fuss she could handle.

Hal cannoned into her, grabbing her in a fierce embrace that was so very different from her mother's. "When did you get back?"

"Last night."

"And now you're leaving again?"

"I won't be gone long."

"You couldn't send me a message?" Hal sounded annoyed. "You

run off without a word. You don't tell me you're back. And now you're off again."

"I'm sorry. I thought you'd be out at Broken Hills."

"Sorry?"

"It's just the way it works out."

Hal pulled away and stared into Ellen's eyes. "What's that supposed to mean?"

"It's..." Ellen took a deep breath. "I don't have a choice. I mean, I really want to spend some time with you." The words were not mere mollifying sweet talk. Her whole groin was aching. Ellen wanted Hal with an intensity that surprised her. Absurdly, she found herself making pointless calculations about missing the barge and taking another, a day—a week later. Ellen knocked the thoughts aside.

"But?"

"But you know how important what I'm doing is. And that I can't talk about it. I've got to go away for a few days."

"How long is a few?"

"Eight or so."

"Where?"

"I can't say."

Hal growled and shook her. "That's no sort of answer."

"It's the best I can give. Anyway, what are you doing in town?"

"Worrying about you."

"How did you know—"

Hal looped an arm through Ellen's trying to drag her into a walk. "Let's go to a tavern and talk."

"I haven't got time."

"You can spare a half hour," Hal pleaded, her tone one of exasperation.

"The barge is going soon. I've got to be on it."

Hal disengaged her arm and stepped back. "You're going to Eastford."

"How..."

"Oh, come on! It's not complex arithmetic. Two days downstream with the current. A couple of days farting about on your secret business, whatever it is, and then four days upstream with the wind, if you're lucky. I can do the sums. There's nowhere else you could be going."

Ellen shrugged. "Okay, I'll—"

Hal again enveloped Ellen in a fierce hug, with an edge of desperation. Hal's hands clung to Ellen's back and her head burrowed into Ellen's neck. "Be careful. I want you to be so fucking careful."

"I will."

"It's not safe there." Hal shook Ellen without releasing her grip. Her words were muffled in the collar of Ellen's shirt. "I don't care what you're supposed to be doing in Eastford. Just find a nice inn, lock yourself in your room for a few days and then come back here and say you failed. No one will hold it against you."

"I can't do that."

"Why not?"

"Because it's my duty."

"So?"

"If I wasn't prepared to do the job then I wouldn't have the nerve to take the salary."

"You are just too fucking..." Hal released her grip and spun away to face a wall. She crossed her forearms on the brickwork at head height as a cushion for her forehead. Her hands made tight fists. The pose was tense, almost vulnerable, out of character with Hal's normal wry nonchalance.

"Too fucking what?"

"Too fucking upright to know when to duck."

Ellen slipped her arms around Hal from behind and gently kissed the back of her neck. "I'll be careful, I promise. And I'll be back in a few days."

Hal dropped her arms and leaned against Ellen. Her shoulders sagged. "That's what they all say."

❖

Eastford was huge. Ellen stood on the docks, daunted by the scale. The awe had set in on the barge, when the Tamer had joined with the Little Liffy River and Ellen had her first view of the town. They had drifted on, past building after building after building, taking ages to reach the final mooring at the central docks. Eastford was at least twenty times the size of Roadsend. The population must number in the tens of thousands. Ellen did not have the slightest idea where anything or anybody was, and although getting directions to the Militia station should be straightforward, Susan Lewis was sure to be a lot harder to find.

Ellen took a deep breath and hoisted her pack onto her shoulder. Then, amid the scramble of activity on the quay, she caught a glimpse of a familiar black shirt. She hurried after.

"Excuse me. I want to get to the Militia station."

The Eastford patrolwoman turned ponderously to face Ellen. She was a tall, square-faced woman in her mid-thirties, with a bellicose manner, but her officious scowl became marginally more receptive at the sight of Ellen's uniform.

"It's up by the temple." Her hand flicked in what was presumably the right direction, although the gesture looked more like someone flexing a cramped wrist.

"And the temple is...?"

"You not been to Eastford before?"

"No."

Judging by her reaction, the Militiawoman found this amusing. She pointed at the skyline. "That's the roof of the temple. It's the tallest building in Eastford, so you can't miss it. The station is on the left."

"Thanks."

The Eastford Militia station, when Ellen found it, also dwarfed the one in Roadsend. However, the sight of half-empty mugs of tea growing cold on the briefing room table, the sound of drunken snores from the lockup, and the smell of old boots was reassuringly the same. Her letter of introduction from Major Kallim quickly got Ellen a meeting with the senior officer in charge.

Captain Gomez sat behind her desk. She spent a minute reading the letter and then turned it over and spent nearly as long studying the back, even though it was blank. At last she put the sheet of paper down and looked up at Ellen.

"So. Some Rangers get hurt, and finally they're going to do something. But they still want the Militia to do all the running around. Who did you piss off to get landed with this?"

"Um..." It was not the first question Ellen had expected. "I'm not sure what it says in the letter, ma'am, but—"

"It says not a damned thing, except that I've got to help you as much as I can. But the address is the Roadsend Ranger barracks, and

I've been hearing the news on the grapevine, the same as everyone else has."

Ellen frantically tried to think of a suitable response, and failed.

"How old are you? Eighteen?"

"Yes, ma'am."

Captain Gomez sighed. "You look like a decent kid. So I tell you what, I'm going to do my best to help you make it to nineteen." She pointed to a chair. "Sit down."

"Thank you, ma'am."

"Nah—it's just that I don't want a crick in my neck from looking up at you, and this isn't going to be quick. I'm going to be helpful beyond your wildest dreams."

Ellen shunted the chair away from the wall. Gomez was clearly bitter and showing it far more than was appropriate between a senior officer and a newly promoted patrolwoman. Yet Ellen did not get the feeling that the captain was lax or unintelligent, or that she had reached her current state of cynicism without a fight.

Gomez waited until Ellen was seated before continuing. "You're here because of the Mad Butcher. Okay. I'll start with a history lesson. Eastford. It's a nice town. Enough action to stop us from getting bored, but nothing we couldn't handle. And if there was trouble, we always knew where to start looking—the Red Dog Inn. The innkeeper was a fence by the name of Svetlana Parker, and she allowed any sort of scum the free run of her place."

Ellen said nothing, although the casual acceptance surprised her. In Roadsend, any tavern permitting flagrant law breaking would have been closed down within days.

"About ten years ago, a new girl moved into town and started working for Parker. First off as a debt collector, then a bit more imaginatively collecting money off people who didn't actually owe it. Madeline Bucher was her name. I've dealt with plenty of thugs, but none who've come close to her for cold-blooded viciousness. When she started slicing people up, she got known as the Mad Butcher. It all got very nasty for a while at the Dog, and we were trying to work out what to do. Even thinking about shutting the Dog down. Then Parker had an accident. A very permanent sort of accident."

"Did the Butcher kill her?"

"She might have. She certainly took advantage of it. She became the new boss at the Red Dog. For a while it was quiet. Then we started finding bodies, dumped in the slums. But they were known villains, so we weren't overly bothered. The word we got was that a gang war was going on. The crooks fighting among themselves. And, like fools, we thought, 'Great. Let them wipe each other out.' We never stopped to think what would happen when there was a winner."

Gomez pursed her lips. "The winner was Madeline Bucher—the Mad Butcher. She was the one who started it, and she was the only one who understood where it was going. She had her tactics worked out. First kill enough people to get the right atmosphere of fear. Then dole out a few beatings. The victims were too scared to report the crime, in case they were given worse, and bingo—her target audience knew that her gang were above the law. Once she was secure, she built up her organization. And she's good at it. I'll give her that. If she was an honest businesswoman, she'd be a damned successful one. Her gang called themselves the Knives—the Butcher's Knives. Just so we'd know they've got a sense of humor."

"You could arrest her. Surely her organization would crumple."

"She's got us beat." Gomez looked sick. "It was a year after Parker died, when all the fuss seemed to be dying down, that the first Militiawoman was murdered. And then a second. And a third."

"We heard the rumors."

"And rumors were all you heard, right? Any official report would have claimed it was three coincidental deaths with no link between them."

Ellen nodded. "That's what our lieutenant told us, and she said it stood to reason that if a gang had murdered three Militiawomen, then something would have been done about it."

"Yeah, well, somebody was making damned certain that nothing happened. We were left on our own to fight the gang. We lost. And do you know the day I knew we'd lost?"

"When?" Ellen frowned, confused.

"The day one of my patrolwomen turned up for work with a face covered in cuts and bruises, and she claimed she'd had a run-in with an unknown drunk who got away."

"You think she'd really been attacked by the gang?"

"What do you think? Now folk know the Butcher's women can beat up the Militia and get away with it. Who'd dare testify against her even if we did bring her in?"

Ellen looked down at her hands, shocked. "But surely, if you know the Red Dog Inn is her base, you could mount a surprise raid and arrest everyone there. If you got the entire gang in the lockup, people wouldn't be afraid to come forward."

"The surprise is the tricky bit. I've got forty-two women in the Militia here. About a quarter of them I can depend on to do their duty to the letter. They're the ones I lie awake at night worrying about. The rest will look the other way if the Knives tell them to. And you can be sure the Butcher knows who's in which group. Then I've got one or two women who've gone over to the gang. They take bribes and pass on information. I don't know who they are, but I know they're there. They'd inform the Butcher if I tried to raid the Dog."

"You seriously..." Ellen was too stunned to finish.

"And of course, our other big problem is they know where we live. My youngest kid is now twelve, just left school. On the way to class, four years back, a rough-looking woman stopped her in the street and gave her a sealed letter to pass on to me."

"What did it say?"

"It was blank. There was no need to say anything." Gomez met Ellen's eyes. "Have you got family back in Roadsend?"

"My parents." Ellen felt ice crystallizing in her guts.

"You care about them?"

"Yes."

"Then you need to think very carefully about what you're going to do." Gomez leaned back in her chair. "So, what exactly do you want to do in Eastford?"

Ellen caught her lip in her teeth. She was not supposed to discuss details of the investigation with other members of the Militia, but there was not the slightest chance of achieving anything in Eastford without some help and local knowledge.

"I'm trying to find a woman. One of the Knives."

"Who?"

"Her name is Susan Lewis. She does an important job in the gang, but I don't know anything else about her."

"Susan Lewis?" Gomez's forehead knotted in concentration, but then she shook her head. "That's not a name I know. Why do you want to find her in particular, if you know so little about her?"

"It's not so much her, but I think another Knife will be with her, and that's the person I really want to catch. Her name is Adeola Eriksen—usually answers to Ade."

"Ah. Now that one I do recognize. She's not been in the gang for long, but she's already getting a reputation. Another vicious little brute. I imagine her and the Butcher get along like a house on fire."

"Have you seen her recently?"

"No. In fact, I'd heard a rumor that she was out of town." Gomez tilted her head to one side. "Did she show up in Roadsend?"

"Yes. It's where she's from originally. We've had a lot of dealings with her, and the rest of her family."

"Okay. So back to my first question, what are you going to do?"

"I guess I could check out this Red Dog Inn and see—"

Ellen broke off at the captain's pained expression. Gomez had closed her eyes and was shaking her head. "Have you listened to what I've said? If you're going to get yourself killed, you should at least try to do it in Roadsend so your parents won't have so far to go to visit your grave."

"I've got to do something."

"Why?"

"It's my..." Ellen frowned, unsure what to say.

"Do you want to know the one thought that's kept me going over the last few years?"

"What?"

"It was knowing that one day the Mad Butcher would go too far, and she'd run afoul of the Rangers. They're the people who should have been sent here, right back when the first of my women was murdered. They've got no family on hand to threaten, and they are way too tightly knit to crack apart and intimidate. Kill one and the rest will hunt you down, through this world and the next. The Rangers have to finish her, because nobody else can do it."

Ellen frowned. "You've got a temple here in Eastford. Couldn't the Guards have helped you?"

Gomez snorted in derision. "Oh, they're as incorruptible and fearless as you could wish. They're all so damn sure the Goddess is watching over them. But they're no damned use for anything other than standing around looking pretty. And the Butcher's been very careful not to interfere with them or the Sisterhood. She even gave some big donations to the temple funds. But my real problem is..." Gomez hesitated, clearly debating whether to continue. "Ah, what the fuck. I told you someone made sure the murder of my women was put down to a coincidence."

"Yes."

"I can't prove a thing, but I'm sure the Butcher has the town mayor in her pocket."

"The mayor?" Ellen was astounded at the seriousness of the accusation.

"Yeah. She changed the rules of operation so I can't do a frigging thing without her agreement. She refused to sign every request for more support from HQ. She was the one who insisted the murders weren't related. She tore up each report I wrote and sent off her own little make-believe versions instead."

"Is she allowed to do that?" It was certainly not the way things worked in Roadsend.

"If she wants." Gomez shrugged. "It's one of those obscure rules that most people don't know exists. The town council pay for the Militia, so Mayor Richards can insist on the last word on everything. But she doesn't pay for the Rangers, and they aren't going to have to ask her permission. The Butcher has either bought or scared Mayor Richards, but now it won't do her any good—not with twenty-nine Rangers lying in their graves."

"It was only twenty-one." Ellen hesitated. *Only* did not sound like the right word to use.

"Numbers always get bigger on the grapevine. But it's still a lot of dead women. The Butcher obviously reckoned the Rangers wouldn't be intimidated easily. Just killing two or three wouldn't be enough to scare the rest off. That's why she tried to wipe out a whole squadron. So the Rangers would be too frightened to dare stand up to her again." A humorless grin spread across Gomez's face. "She's going to be so surprised when she finds out it hasn't worked. And it hasn't, has it?"

Ellen shook her head. "No."

"Do you want my advice?"

"What?"

"My cousin owns an inn on the other side of the river. The Ace of Spades. It's a nice little establishment—quiet. The beer's all right. I'll give you directions and a note. Set yourself up in her taproom for a couple of days. Then go back to Roadsend and tell Major Whatever that you couldn't find Susan Lewis. The Rangers will get the Mad Butcher in the end. You can be sure of that. They don't need you to get yourself killed helping them."

❖

The borrowed trousers were a few centimeters too short, leaving a gap at Ellen's ankles, and the shirt could have done with a good wash, but the net effect left Ellen feeling nicely inconspicuous on the dirty, run-down street. She had not been surprised to learn that the Red Dog Inn was situated in the seedy part of town.

A mist of drizzle started to fall as Ellen got within sight of the Inn. Although true nightfall was still an hour away, a blanket of cloud hid the sun, and the light was fading. She hunched her shoulders against the cold and pushed open the door to the taproom.

Despite the gloom, no lanterns were yet lit inside. Three long tables filled most of the floor space, with a couple of smaller ones in an alcove at the rear. A door to one side clearly led to another room. A woman was leaning against the wall beside it, projecting an air of surly watchfulness, making it clear she was the doorkeeper and that any attempt to go through uninvited would not be permitted.

A dozen or so women were at the tables, drinking alone or with friends. A further small group of three were leaning against the counter, tankards before them. They stared at Ellen with manifest hostility, but said nothing and made no attempt to intercept her as she crossed the taproom to the bar.

An elderly barkeeper waddled over. "What will it be, pal?"

Despite the "pal" the barkeeper's manner was distant, as if she was half ignoring Ellen. Her eyes were on the counter, the ceiling, the wall, never once fully touching on Ellen. Maybe the woman was practiced at doing her job without seeing things.

"A half, please."

The drink arrived and Ellen paid the money. As she received her change, for the merest instant the barkeeper's eyes met hers, and

Ellen realized she had misjudged the woman. The barkeeper saw everything.

Although the urge to hide in the shadows at the edge of the room was overwhelming, Ellen took her drink to the middle table. Her best hope was to overhear loose gossip, and she could not do that by skulking in a corner. She needed to be in the midst of things.

As she sat down, the other customers glanced at her and then returned to their conversations, showing no reaction, either welcoming or hostile. Ellen took a mouthful of her beer. To her surprise it was not watered down, or off. But then, her fellow customers were not the sort of people any sensible barkeeper would want to upset. Ellen could easily believe that they were all thieves, thugs, and swindlers.

Ellen adopted a dejected posture, head slumped, staring morosely into her drink. She wanted to play the part of someone with a lot of time and little money, dragging out a half for the sake of somewhere warm and dry to sit. Surely a dozen women like that came through every week.

Yet, although her eyes were downcast, her ears were locked on the conversations around her, tuned to anything significant that might be said. Unfortunately, as time plodded on, it became clear that her fellow drinkers were all engaged in conversations of the utmost banality.

Apparently, Bernie had kicked out Steph, because she had been playing around. Dez had enjoyed her sister's birthday, even though her mother had suffered a minor yet predictable mishap with her knee. And Ren wanted a new job because she was tired of stinking of yeast, although everyone agreed it was not a bad smell.

At some point, the barkeeper lit two small lanterns. Ellen studied their wavering reflection in the surface of her beer. Was it all a waste of time? What had she been hoping for? Someone to say, "I've heard that Susan Lewis will be in the main square at half past two tomorrow"? The only thing of note that was likely to happen was for Ade Eriksen to walk in and spot her. While Ellen wanted to interview Ade, in the current setting she would be in no position to ask questions, and would not live long enough to report back with answers, anyway.

Ellen drained her tankard and stood up. She might as well go back to her lodgings at the Ace of Spades. Yet she still could not bring herself to follow Hal and Gomez's advice—to deliberately do nothing and report it as a failure. She would have to think of something else, just so she would know in her own heart that she had honestly tried her best.

"Cheers, pal." The barkeeper waved in Ellen's direction, still without appearing to look at her.

On impulse, Ellen switched direction.

The three women at the bar eyed her suspiciously. They were large women, with calloused hands and sour expressions. Their clothes were work-worn and much repaired. Their feet were encased in heavy boots. At least one had a bulge in her pocket that could have been a weapon.

Ellen leaned on the bar, as far from the thugs as she could. The barkeeper came and hovered nearby.

"What is it, pal?"

"I was just wondering. A friend of mine, I think she drinks in here from time to time. Her name is Susan Lewis. Do you know her?"

As she spoke, Ellen realized the stupidity of her question. For all she knew, the barkeeper might be Susan Lewis. However the woman merely shook her head.

"Afraid I don't know her. What does she look like?"

Ellen waved her hand dismissively. "It's okay. I can look her up elsewhere. Thanks." She turned and made her escape from the Red Dog.

Outside, dusk was falling and the rain had gotten harder. In this part of town, streetlights were nonexistent—not that there were any people walking around who might have benefited from them. Soon it would be too dark to see where she was going. Ellen turned up the collar of her borrowed shirt and set off at a quick march, hoping to get back to the Ace of Spades without getting either lost or completely soaked. She had covered no more than thirty meters when she heard the inn door open and close behind her.

Ellen looked back. The three thugs had also left the taproom and were standing outside the doorway. The light was not good enough to be sure, but Ellen had the nasty feeling that they were staring in her direction. She continued walking at an even sharper rate.

Then she heard footsteps and voices. They were following, at a pace that matched her own. The temptation to run almost took over, but Ellen managed to keep control. Running would only make herself conspicuous. Maybe her visit to the Red Dog had been foolhardy, but she had given the thugs no reason to follow and assault her. Most likely it was pure coincidence that they had left the inn so soon after she did. Once on the street, their only options were to turn either left or right, giving an even chance that they would head in the same direction as herself. They were walking quickly, but the weather did not lend itself to a casual amble.

Yet, despite all the logic, Ellen felt her heartbeat race. Her palms grew sticky.

At the next junction, Ellen turned right, onto a narrower road. This also was deserted. It was clearly not an area of town to stroll around after dark. She jogged a dozen meters to put a bit more space between her and the women from the Red Dog, but slowed again to a walk in time for when they would reach the junction. She did not want them to see her running.

Ellen walked on, but her head was turned over her shoulder, looking back. She saw the three women turn the corner without hesitation, following her. Ellen did not wait to see more. She fled. She had been the quickest of the Militiawomen in Roadsend. The thugs from the Red Dog did not have the look of sprinters. Ellen prayed the looks were not deceiving.

At the end of the road she turned another corner. A short way on, a narrow alley led off to the right. Without thinking, Ellen ducked into it. Yet even as she did so, she knew it was a bad move. She did not know the town. The alley might well be a dead end. She might have just trapped herself.

The alley bent left, then right. Around the next corner it broadened into a small courtyard. The light was so poor that Ellen knew this mainly by the change in echo. Unable to see where she was going, Ellen collided with a wall of wooded slats that shook under the impact. By touch, she realized empty crates were stacked in a corner of the yard. She dived behind them, squeezing herself between the boxes and the rough brick wall.

Ellen closed her eyes.

Silence—except for the thudding of her heart. The minutes trickled by.

Ellen leaned her head back against the wall. Cold rain fell on her face, into her eyes. She had been stupid all around. Stupid to go to the Red Dog. Stupid to ask the barkeeper about Susan Lewis. And stupid to think the thugs had been chasing her. Her nerves had made her into an even bigger fool than before. She wiped the rain from her face and slid out from behind the crates.

Before long, Ellen was out of the roughest area of town and onto a main thoroughfare. The buildings here were better repaired, the piles of refuse were gone, and the road was busier, with other pedestrians in sight. Ellen even thought she recognized where she was, although it was too dark to see the landmark temple roof. Again she set off at a brisk pace. The Ace of Spades was on the quieter north bank of the river. If she was right, the bridge over the Little Liffy was near at hand.

The wide street terminated on the river embankment. Ellen turned left, toward the bridge. The cloud was breaking up and the first glimmer of moonlight shimmered on the water. Another five minutes would see her safe in her lodgings.

Ellen's pulse had just returned to normal when, no more than twenty meters away, she saw them—the same three thugs. They were ambling toward her, talking among themselves. They looked up and spotted Ellen at the same moment. This time there was no doubt. One raised her arm and shouted and then all three charged forward.

Ellen turned and tore back along the embankment. Few people were about to watch her race by, and none made any move to intervene. Ellen doubted they would come to her aid, if she was overtaken. Her heart was pounding, but fear added speed to her legs, and from what she could hear, the thugs were not gaining on her. If anything, their voices and footsteps were fading behind, falling back.

Ellen rounded the corner of a large, featureless building. Ahead of her the path along the embankment abruptly widened out into a broad open expanse of flagstone—the docks. They were now deserted, the hectic daytime activity ceased. Moored barges were dark, silent hulks on the riverbank. Her pursuers were now too far back to hear, but Ellen kept running. Then she saw a light over a doorway and two women talking beneath it—two women in black uniforms.

At the sound of Ellen's racing footsteps, the women broke off and adopted a defensive stance. Only then did Ellen remember she was not in uniform. Not that it was a crucial point. Surely they would protect her anyway.

"What's up?" one challenged.

"I need...I...they..." Ellen staggered to a halt, bent double and gasping for air.

"What is it?"

A hand grabbed a fistful of the shirt on Ellen's shoulder, pulling her upright. "Hey. Don't I know you? You're the one who arrived here today."

The grip became less rough, guiding her around to lean against the wall while she caught her breath. In the light of the overhead lantern, Ellen recognized the square-faced Militiawoman from the morning.

"Is that the one the captain said we're supposed to keep an eye out for? From Roadsend?" the other asked.

"Yeah. That's her," the woman answered her colleague and then turned to Ellen. "So what's up?"

"The Butcher's Knives. Three of them. Chasing me."

The effect on the two women was immediate, as if every muscle in their bodies simultaneously tightened. One pushed open the door of the building behind her. "Get in here."

The room was clearly the Militia dockside office, larger than the one at Roadsend, but no more elaborately furnished. Ellen sank against the wall, feeling herself trembling, with shock, delayed fear, and now relief.

A Militiawoman lit the lantern on the desk. "So what happened?"

"I'm trying to find someone. I went to the Red Dog Inn."

"You went to the Dog?" Stunned surprise was evident in the woman's voice.

"Damned lucky to still be able to run," the other said.

"Who did you want to find?"

Ellen was too fraught to care about watching her tongue. "Ade Eriksen. I think she's in Eastford keeping an eye on Susan Lewis."

"Susan or Susie?"

"Does it matter?" Ellen shrugged. "I guess she might call herself Susie."

"It's not a her. The *Susie-Louise*. It's a barge on the Roadsend sheep run. I've seen Knives hanging around it."

"No. Lewis, not Louise. And it's not a barge that I'm..." Ellen stopped as all the words registered. She shook her head, confused. "The *Susie-Louise* isn't on the Roadsend sheep run."

"That's what the paperwork says. And I don't know where else the sheep come from, because they're onboard when the *Susie-Louise* gets here."

"Are you sure?"

"I don't hallucinate sheep." The woman sounded mildly irritated. "If you don't believe me, check the records. They're in the files."

Ellen turned around, bracing her hands on the desk, her mind racing.

"Do you want us to escort you somewhere safe? Where are you staying?" the other Militiawomen asked.

"The Ace of Spades, but...um... actually, I would like to check the records."

"You sure? Tell you what. We've got an hour left of our patrol. You can lock the door after we go, so you'll be safe here. We'll come back and collect you on our way home. I live out that way."

Ellen nodded slowly. "Thanks. That would be great."

❖

An hour later, Ellen put down the pen, folded the sheet of paper, and slipped it into her pocket. She would do a final crosscheck when she returned to Roadsend, but in her own mind it was unnecessary. She did not need more evidence.

Over the previous year, the *Susie-Louise* had unloaded five hundred sheep at the docks in Eastford, and had taken another three hundred through, bound for Landfall—half spring lambs and half older sheep. The barge had completed twelve round trips. Yet Ellen had never seen it during her stints as the officer on dock duty. What was the chance of that if the barge was conducting legitimate trade?

Even more conclusively, Ellen had not long finished her audit of the shipping log, and while not consigned to memory in its entirety, it was still fresh in her mind. She was certain she had never once seen the name *Susie-Louise* on a sales receipt.

The final check would be when she compared the record of the older sheep off the *Susie-Louise* against those stolen the previous autumn. Ellen was willing to stake anything that the ear tattoo numbers would match up.

The *Susie-Louise* had left the Eastford docks two days earlier, bound for Roadsend. Ellen shook her head at the thought she would have passed it on the river, going in the opposite direction. She had to take the very first barge she could, and hope she got to Roadsend in time to stop the *Susie-Louise* before it started its return journey.

If she was not in time, the Rangers back in Roadsend might get the chance to intercept the following load, but it could not be relied on. If what Captain Gomez suspected was true, then at least one member of the Eastford Militia was a spy. When the Butcher found out that the Susie-Louise had been identified, she would surely switch barges.

A knock on the door announced the return of her escort. Ellen left the docks in their company, but she would be back at first light, praying she could get quick transport upriver.

Chapter Twelve—The Barge Skipper

Even though everyone was clearly making an effort to include her, Ellen still felt out of place in the Rangers' mess hall. It was not just her uniform. Maggie LeCoup, at the end of the table, was also not dressed in the green and gray. However, in Maggie's case, it was because the Ranger sergeant was disguised as a civilian.

The sixteen Rangers eating dinner in the mess hall were the top-notch patrols that central command had assigned from Fort Krowe. The two days Ellen had spent living in the barracks with them had been an experience rarely granted to outsiders. She had been given an insight into an exclusive secret world that might be hers, if she chose to seek admission.

Ellen remembered Captain Gomez's words about the Rangers being too tightly knit to crack apart. Sitting in the middle of the patrol, Ellen could almost see the bonds holding the women together. The Rangers approved of her, but she was not one of them. Not yet. They would willingly work with her, but they would not die for her as they would for their own—as Jay Takeda had done.

The Ranger sitting opposite speared a chunk of meat on her fork and held it up, examining it critically from all sides. "I wonder how long it'd take before I got tired of well-cooked mutton?"

"A damn sight longer than it takes to get tired of the cats' piss they call beer in Macsfarm," another replied.

"Goddess, I hope we don't get sent there next."

More Rangers joined in. "It'd be better than a winter freezing our tits off with Northern Division."

"Or down by Coldmouth. The sand gets everywhere."

"Coldmouth would be warmer."

"Remember how the sand chafes? You don't want to know where I got blisters last time we were there."

"I know where you got blisters. You told us."

"Frequently."

"Offered to show us as well."

Ellen listened to the conversation, playing no part. There was no part she could play, but she hung on each word, feeling a bubbling excitement. The trip to Eastford was the farthest she had traveled—the farthest she might ever go in her life, if she stayed in the Militia. The places the Rangers spoke of were enticing names on a map. Ellen loved her parents, and Roadsend was her home, yet she wanted to see more of the world.

Maggie LeCoup said, "Don't overdo it on the mutton, because I think you're going to be eating it for a while to come, even after we sort out the Butcher and her Knives."

"You reckon we'll be assigned to Eastern Division for winter?"

"And beyond. What I've heard is they're still trying to work out what to do about the 12th, work around what's left or disband the squadron and build a new one from scratch. Either way, they aren't going to sort it overnight. Eastern is going to be down a squadron. On top of that, there's going to be some reorganization. HQ thinks this all got out of hand because the sheep thefts were treated as a paperwork problem for the Militia, and we weren't called in soon enough. In the future the Militia are going to be responsible only for what happens in town. Everything else will go straight to us. Eastern Division is going to have more work and fewer Rangers. I reckon HQ will want us to fill in until they can build up the numbers."

"Where are they going to get the recruits? Do you think they'll let women who narrowly failed retake the test?"

"They may have to, but it will be last resort." Maggie frowned. "I think they'll start with trying to get more Militiawomen to apply."

The Ranger opposite Ellen nodded at her. "How about you? When this is all over, have you thought about joining the Rangers?"

The question was one Ellen had been asked repeatedly over the previous two days. "I'm not sure."

"I think you'd do well."

Ellen smiled. "Thank you."

"The Militia are—" The speaker broke off abruptly, her head turning to the window.

Throughout the mess hall, the silence spread, leaping from Ranger to Ranger. The only sound in the resulting void was of pounding hooves, growing louder by the second.

"Outside." Maggie snapped the order.

The Rangers abandoned their meal, filing from the mess hall quicker, and with less fuss, than Ellen would have thought possible. She was carried along with the flow.

The sky was pale washed blue, with a few ragged bands of cloud drifting over. The evening breeze was stiffening into chill gusts and the shadows were lengthening across the central parade ground. Sunset was under an hour away. Ellen shielded her eyes against the low sun. As she expected, the figure jumping down from horseback was Mel Ellis.

The remnants of the 12th Squadron were still on official leave of absence, yet Mel had pleaded for the chance to be involved in the capture of the *Susie-Louise*. Ellen suspected the refusal to let Mel play an active role was due to fears that her desire for revenge might prejudice the taking of live prisoners, rather than any doubts about her fitness. Giving her the lookout duty had been a compromise.

With another member of the 12th, Mel had been camped in a patch of woodland, upriver of Roadsend. The spot was on the bank, close enough to the water to read the names on passing barges, yet with enough cover for the Rangers to stay hidden from the crews. It was also at a suitable distance so that, on a fast horse, the lookouts could get news to the barracks in time for the two Patrols to be in position and waiting for the *Susie-Louise* at the docks. This was why Ellen had been living with the Rangers. When word came, it would not be possible to summon her from elsewhere. The timing would be down to seconds.

Mel's arrival had brought Major Kallim from the admin block. She called from the top of the steps, "You've spotted it?"

"Yes, ma'am. I reckon the *Susie-Louise* will be at the docks in a quarter hour."

Mel's voice was sharp and controlled, although her body was knotted with tension. Ellen wondered if she imagined a sound like sparks of leaping static.

Kallim faced the gathered Rangers. "Okay. You know the plan."

A wagon was ready waiting, and horses were harnessed. Ellen clambered onto the driver's seat beside Maggie LeCoup. The frame shook as the rest of the Rangers piled in behind. Even before the activity had ceased, Maggie shook the reins, urging the horses into a steady trot.

Ellen twisted around and leaned back, assisting in pulling up the canvas that would hide the uniformed Rangers from view.

The wagon rounded the corner of a building, leaving the parade ground. Ellen gave a last tug at the canvas and then glanced up. Kallim and another officer were saddling horses by the steps of the admin block, ready to follow discreetly. Mel stood hunched, a lonely figure in the middle of the expanse of trampled dirt, staring fixedly at the departing wagon. Even at a distance, the expression on her face made Ellen recoil. Mel wielded her grief and anger like an assassin with a poisoned blade.

The barrack gateway and then the familiar streets of Roadsend slipped by to the steady clop of hooves. Ellen listened with half an ear to the whispered comments from under the canvas, hoping to distract her thoughts. It did not work. She was unsure whether her main emotion was apprehension or relief. The waiting was over, along with all the preparation and planning.

At the Eastford docks, Ellen had been lucky to catch a ride on a private ferry, rather than a slower cargo barge, and had reached Roadsend mere hours after the *Susie-Louise* had left, heading upriver. The fact the barge had gone through Roadsend was taken to mean that Ellen's interception of the rowboat had forced the gang to change tactics. Ellen regarded this as a minor victory. Maybe jumping into the boat had been poorly thought out, but it had achieved something worthwhile.

Now the *Susie-Louise* was returning, presumably with a load of stolen sheep as cargo, and some sort of forged documentation to get past the Militia inspection. Ellen chewed on her lip, wondering if she had missed something obvious and was about to end up looking stupid. Had Fran really misheard the name *Susie-Louise* and innocently assumed it referred to a person? The barge was certainly fulfilling a vital role in the gang's operation. Maybe the loyalty of the crew was in question from the Butcher's point of view. So was Ade Eriksen on board, acting as a minder? Things might turn very nasty. Ade would never let herself be captured without a fight.

The journey to the sheep docks was soon over and the quayside appeared before them at the end of the road. Ellen needed to get off the wagon before it emerged into the open. The sight of a Militiawoman hitching a ride was not unusual enough to attract attention in town.

However, it would jeopardize the plan if the crew associated Ellen with the wagon. After a last word of encouragement from Maggie, Ellen jumped down. The cobbles felt unusually solid beneath her feet. The wagon rolled on.

Ellen jogged down a side alley that led her onto the sheep docks. No barges were moored on the quay and the pens were deserted, except for a couple of farmers talking animatedly, with their dogs lying at their feet. The nearby doors of the Twisted Crook Tavern were propped open.

Off to Ellen's right, the Rangers' wagon had just trundled onto the docks and was moving into position. Meanwhile, upriver, a distant barge, sails and mast down, was negotiating the arches under South Bridge. Was this the *Susie-Louise*? The thought added extra impetus as Ellen marched toward the Militia office. She rounded the corner.

Terrie Rasheed was standing by the doorway, also watching the barge. The sound of feet made her turn. "What's the... What do you want?" Terrie's tone became appreciably more hostile when she recognized Ellen.

"There's a barge coming."

"Yeah? Do you think I can't see it?"

"It's called the *Susie-Louise*."

"And what—"

Ellen cut her off. She did not have time to play at question-and-answer. "When it gets here, I want you to tell it to moor down there. I'm going to inspect it." Ellen pointed along the dockside, to a point close by where Maggie had just stopped the wagon.

"I don't have to do what you tell me to."

"It's not me who's telling you to do it."

"You just did."

"And you know who I'm speaking on behalf of."

"Supposing I decide to say no?"

Ellen sighed. Terrie's petty-minded belligerence was getting tedious. "Then you'll be out of a job tomorrow, without a pension."

"I—"

"Look. Just let it go and stop acting like an idiot."

Terrie literally took a step back. "I'm the one on duty here. You think you're so great, kissing the major's ass. All the fucking Rangers are—"

"Okay. Just shove off. Get off the dock altogether and leave it to me."

Ellen glanced around briefly. Maggie LeCoup had jumped down from the driver's seat and tied the horses' reins to a rail. The Rangers had said they wanted Ellen on hand when the boat moored, since she was the only one who would recognize Adeola Eriksen's face, but there was no reason why she could not direct the barge to move down the dock and then follow on foot. The disguised Ranger sergeant was definitely astute enough to catch on and adapt to the minor change in plan.

Terrie's face held an expression like thunder, but then she ducked her head and spat on the ground. "Fuck it. I don't give a shit. You go and play your stupid-assed games with the Rangers." She stormed into the Militia office, slamming the door behind her.

The barge was now less than fifty meters upstream, heading to the dock. Despite the failing light, it was close enough for Ellen to read the letters *ise* painted on the prow where it curved around, the ending of the barge's name. Three women were visible on deck, the skipper at the tiller at the rear and two others, balanced at the front. Normally, barges had a crew of four. Where was the other one? Ellen took a deep breath. Was the barge shorthanded? Or was the missing person Ade Eriksen, who was keeping out of sight for fear of being recognized in her hometown?

Ellen marched down the quay. Maggie was watering the horses, acting like an ordinary warehouse owner, taking a late delivery. Ellen stopped a few meters away—close enough so the concealed Rangers could jump down beside her in an instant, yet not so close as to link herself with the wagon.

At the other end of the dock, the *Susie-Louise* drifted slowly closer. One of the crew had a coiled rope in hand, ready to moor the vessel. The other had a barge pole planted in the riverbed, putting her weight into guiding the *Susie-Louise* through the last couple of meters.

Terrie reappeared from the office and stomped to the waterside. Her posture, fists on hips, made it clear that her temper had not improved. Just before the barge knocked against the dock wall, Terrie held up her hands, in a gesture that could only mean "stop."

The skipper called out indistinctly. Terrie did not reply, but instead, in one long step, boarded the barge. She sidled along the gunwales to the rear. The two crewmembers watched her talk with the skipper, while exchanging their own comments, too low to be overheard. The one with the rope tossed it halfheartedly around a bollard, but made no attempt to pull it tight and moor the barge securely, clearly waiting for instructions.

Ellen clenched her jaw. Of course, she had not told Terrie to keep off the barge and the pig-headed corporal was going to be as awkward as she could, without stepping over the line of disobeying orders. Ellen's frustration moved up yet another notch when Terrie and the skipper disappeared below deck. There was nothing she could do. Boarding the barge herself was dangerous and unnecessary. Ellen wanted the Rangers at hand for any confrontation with Ade Eriksen, and sooner or later, Terrie would have to stop mucking around.

After an increasingly tense minute, the skipper's head appeared through the hatchway. She waved at her crew. "Take it down. By where the other Blackshirt is. We're mooring there."

The skipper again ducked out of sight. The crewwomen moved to follow instructions. One slipped the rope free while the other leaned on her pole, easing the *Susie-Louise* along the dockside.

The barge bobbed closer to Ellen. Oblique sunlight was smeared across the river with an oily golden sheen. The creak of wood and the slop of water against the hull overlay the distant bleating of sheep and the first stanza of song from the Twisted Crook taproom.

Ellen took a step to the side, waving the barge on and pointing to a convenient bollard. The woman with the rope nodded. If she was a Knife, she was also a good actress. Her expression was bland and untroubled, showing no trace of guilt. Her colleague looked less content, but only what might be expected from someone who had been given extra work to do. Ellen fought to keep her own face and manner relaxed. Answers would be forthcoming, just as soon as the barge was securely tied up.

Without warning, shouts erupted below deck, changing to a scream and then dying. A second cry ended in an agonized moan.

Maggie LeCoup was the first to react, barking an order. Ellen's eyes remained fixed on the *Susie-Louise*, but she did not need to look back to sense the Rangers surging into action. She heard the sound of canvas being kicked aside and then boots hitting the cobbles. Green-clad figures fanned out on either side.

The crew had flinched at the first cry, but made no move to either flee or investigate. Now both were frozen in indecision. The barge was less than a meter from the dock. Ellen was about to jump aboard when a figure burst through the hatchway, onto the deck. Even in the fading light, Ellen instantly recognized Ade Eriksen. An instant was all she got. Ade's eyes raked along the dock, taking in the welcoming party, and then she turned and dived into the river. A second later, another splash announced that someone else had joined her in the water.

"No, you don't."

The sharp voice snared Ellen's attention. Her head jerked toward the sound. Two Rangers had already boarded the *Susie-Louise* and grabbed the remaining crewmember—the one who had held the rope. The woman struggled fruitlessly until a third Ranger arrived with cord to bind her hands.

All along the dockside was tightly controlled chaos. Maggie and the other sergeant were shouting orders. More Rangers had boarded the barge and dropped down through the open hatch. Others were moving downriver, hunting the fugitives who had dived in. The prisoner was bundled off the barge, reaching the wagon just as Major Kallim and the other officer arrived on horseback. The plan had been for them to watch from a position, nearby, yet out of sight.

A Ranger by the hatch was relaying information from the others who had gone below deck.

"Front hold clear—nothing but sheep. Main cabin—one dead, one wounded."

Ellen jumped onto the barge. Her instructions for after the *Susie-Louise* was captured had been vague. Certainly she had not been ordered to stay on the dock. And much as she disliked Terrie Rasheed, that did not mean she wished the woman dead. Who had screamed?

The light below decks was dim, and moving dark figures further blocked Ellen's view, but she had been in enough barges to know the layout. The front of the barge was the main hold, where the sheep were kept. The rear of the barge held their fodder. Midship was the crew quarters, with the skipper's cabin and the bunkroom. Indirect lamplight glinted from this region and someone was moaning.

Ellen stopped at the doorway of the skipper's cabin—a cramped space three meters square, containing a bunk, a table, a tall cupboard, and two chairs. The lantern hung from the ceiling. Two Rangers were standing in there, sending huge shadows leaping around the room as they moved, and Terrie Rasheed was sitting on the floor, her back propped against the wall. The hilt of a knife protruded from her shoulder. Her lips were white, but twitching in gasps.

Another woman, the skipper, lay on her back, twisted awkwardly between table and wall. The front of the skipper's shirt was soaked red. More blood trickled across the floorboards beneath her.

"What's the score here?"

Ellen stepped back at Major Kallim's voice. "The skipper's dead, ma'am. Corporal Rasheed is injured."

"What the hell was she playing at? Going below deck?"

"I don't know, ma'am. I didn't..." Ellen stopped. Judging by the major's expression, this was not the time for debate and excuses.

Kallim stood at the doorway studying the interior. "Is the Militia corporal okay to move?"

"Yes, ma'am. I'd have said so," one of the Rangers answered.

"Then get her up on deck and out of the way. And get the two sergeants to meet me down here immediately."

Ignoring Terrie's whimper of complaint, the two Rangers hoisted her off the floor. Ellen moved to assist, but Kallim held her back. "I want you to have a look at the skipper. See if you recognize her. Or can spot anything in her cabin out of place. You know how it ought to be."

Once the room was empty, Ellen slipped in, trying to avoid treading in blood. It was not easy. She crouched beside the dead skipper. The woman was a little below average height, with a pinched face, long nose, and hair tied back in a ponytail.

"Do you know her?"

Ellen chewed her lip as a memory stirred. "I...I think maybe."

Footsteps interrupted, as Maggie and the other sergeant arrived. "Ma'am?"

"The two who got away. Any news?"

"Archers got one. We're fishing her out at the moment. We think the other's got away."

Kallim nodded. "Right. Get back up there and tell your girls if they spot her to make sure their aim isn't too good."

"You want her to get away?"

"For now. We'll have a briefing in twenty minutes, on the docks. Who are your two best trackers?"

The sergeants exchanged a glance. Maggie spoke for them. "That would be Corporal O'Neil from my patrol and Leading Ranger Chan from 10B."

"I want them at the briefing as well." Kallim looked at Ellen. "You too. You've got twenty minutes to see if you can find out anything of use."

The Rangers departed, leaving Ellen alone with the dead skipper.

❖

By the time Ellen trotted down the gangplank of the now securely moored barge, the sun had touched the horizon and light was fading fast. News had spread and a collection of inquisitive townsfolk were being kept at bay by a cordon of Rangers. Drinkers from the Twisted Crook had come out, tankards in hand, to watch.

Terrie had been put in the back of the wagon and one of Dr. Miller's healers was on hand, tending to her. Both sergeants hovered nearby, with two other Rangers. Even before Ellen stopped by the tailgate of the wagon, she could hear Terrie complaining. Some things never changed.

Kallim marched up. "Okay. First thing." She looked at the healer. "Can the corporal speak?"

The healer's expression made it clear that shutting Terrie up was a bigger challenge. "Yes. I want to get her to the infirmary. But there's no rush."

Terrie scowled, but did not argue.

Kallim folded her arms. "So? What happened? Why did you go below deck?"

Terrie gestured at Ellen with her good arm. "She didn't warn me not to."

"I'll bet she didn't tell you not to hit yourself over the head with a baseball bat either. Some things you ought to be able to leave to common sense. You could have worked out there was trouble with the barge." Kallim was clearly not about to put up with the surly excuses.

Terrie modified her tone. "The skipper called me on. She said she wanted to show me something below deck."

"You didn't think that was suspicious?"

"Like you said. There was obviously something up with the boat, but I didn't know what. I thought the skipper might have information you'd need."

"So what did she say?"

"She reckoned she'd picked up the sheep from Jan's Creek and Three Dollars, but some of the ear tattoos didn't match up. She wanted to show me the sales receipts. I went down to her cabin. We talked a bit. I was in the corner. She was by the door. Then Ade Eriksen rushed in." Terrie pouted. "You hadn't been careful enough and she seen something. She knew it was a trap. For some reason, she blamed the skipper. She said, 'The Boss was right to have me watch you.' Then she pulled a knife. Before I could move, she'd stabbed the skipper twice. She went to run off. I tried to grab her and she stabbed me as well. And that's all I know."

A covered shape also lay on the floor of the wagon. Kallim pulled back the blanket to reveal a face. "Is this Ade Eriksen?"

"No."

Kallim nodded at the medic. "Okay. You can take her."

The wagon rumbled away. Kallim turned to the Rangers. "This might just work out very well. Ade Eriksen is the one who's got away. She's well known in town, so won't hang around here." Kallim glanced at Ellen for a nod of confirmation. "Without the barge, her only option is to steal a horse and hightail it to the gang's hideout. You've been recommended as trackers. You saw what she was wearing, so you'll recognize her?"

Both Rangers nodded.

"All we know about the hideout's location is that it's less than half a day's travel, southeast of town. I want you to get some good horses and lie in wait. One of you by the ford where the ambush was, since that's on the way. The other closer to town, just in case she goes by some other route. She might evade one of you, but hopefully not both. Don't stop her. Don't even let her know you're there. Just follow her. When you find the location of the hideout come straight back here and report. Clear?"

"Yes, ma'am." The two designated trackers departed.

Lastly, Kallim turned to Ellen. "Did you find anything?"

Ellen held out two bloodstained sheets of paper. "Sales receipts. They must be forgeries. I found them in the skipper's breast pocket. The knife went straight through them, and they're soaked in blood.

They won't be easy to read, but maybe we can learn something from them."

"Right. And the skipper? You thought you recognized her. Is she known locally?"

"No. I've only ever seen her once—that's if it's the same person. But I think she might have been in the Three Barrels Tavern, the night before the massacre, when the 12th Squadron were there."

Kallim looked thoughtful. "You think she might have overheard something? Be the source of the leaked information?"

"Yes, ma'am."

"But you're not sure it's her?"

"No. She was on the other side of the taproom. And I wasn't paying a lot of attention. I didn't look at her much." Ellen did not add that identification was further hampered by the fact that the woman had been in a lip-lock with Jay Takeda for most of the time. "Maybe if I get some of the survivors from the 12th to look at her. They might be more certain."

Kallim nodded. "Do it."

❖

A small room at the back of the infirmary served as a morgue. The dead barge skipper lay there, stretched out on a table. Thanks to information from the captured crewmember, Ellen now knew her name was Yuan Beaumont. When she was buried that afternoon, it would not be in an unmarked grave—but would anyone ever come to pay their respects? Who would mourn Yuan Beaumont?

Ellen stared at the flaccid features. Already death was distorting them, as the cheeks sank down, bulging into heavy jowls. Memories of the evening in the Three Barrels skittered around in Ellen's head, refusing to drop into focus. Was it the same woman who had been swaying drunkenly and laughing while she kissed Jay Takeda?

The door of the morgue opened.

"I don't know what you think this is frigging going to prove." Mel's voice preceded her, sounding every bit as combative as Ellen had expected.

Chris answered. "We just want you to see if you recognize her."

"Your young kid was there. Don't she know how to use her eyes?"

"Patrolwoman Mittal was on the other side of the room and did not get a good look at the woman."

"She's as fucking useless as the rest of you."

Mel stamped into the room. Seeing Ellen there, she scowled, her expression showing no trace of apology, even though she had to know her remarks had been overheard. Chris slipped into the room behind her, also looking annoyed. When the written request for Mel to view the body had been ignored, Chris had been forced to go in person and escort her over from the barracks. Clearly it had not been a pleasant task.

For her part, Ellen was very grateful that Chris was now fully recovered and the Rangers were allowing her to take an active part in the investigation. Tackling Mel Ellis was not something Ellen had felt up to handling on her own.

Chris took a position beside the door. "Is that the woman who hooked up with Jay Takeda in the tavern?"

"No."

Mel had not even glanced at Yuan Beaumont's body. She turned around, but before she got to the door, Chris reached across and slammed it shut, keeping her fist on the handle. Her eyes narrowed in anger.

"Okay. You can wait here. I'll go and get Kallim. And then we'll see if you can do this properly."

Ellen watched the two women glare at each other in confrontation. It was clear that Chris meant what she said, and it required no guesswork to know how Major Kallim would feel if she was dragged in to resolve the issue. Even so, Ellen was surprised when Mel backed down. The Ranger went back to the table. For the space of three heartbeats, she stared at the skipper's face and then she turned away again.

"It's not her." Her tone was provocative, as if challenging Chris to accuse her of lying.

Chris pursed her lips, but then let her hand fall and stepped away. She did not move again until the sound of Mel's footsteps had faded.

Ellen sighed. "That was a complete waste of time."

"Not really." Chris's expression changed to a lopsided grimace. "Mel Ellis is a lousy liar. She definitely thinks it's the same woman. I could see it in her eyes."

"That's not going to count as proof."

"We'll report it at the meeting this afternoon. See how Kallim wants to play it, but I wouldn't be surprised if she's happy to leave the matter unproved. Pushing things further isn't going to do any good." Chris nodded at the body. "The woman who got the information and passed it on is dead. Jay Takeda more than paid for her lapse. She died a hero. There's no way it was a deliberate betrayal on her part. I can't see Kallim wanting to formally lay the blame on her."

"That will make Mel Ellis happy."

Chris scrunched her nose. "Mel happy or unhappy—will anyone be able to spot the difference?"

Ellen grinned and wandered toward the door.

Chris also made to leave the room, but then stopped. "While I remember. I've got one bit of definite proof that ought to make you very happy."

"What?"

"While you were in Eastford, Hal Drennen turned up at the Town Hall, rather sheepishly so I've been told, and apologized for not informing them about her great-aunt's condition beforehand. She had all the right documentation with her. She's definitely Cassie's niece and lawfully authorized to run the farm on her aunt's behalf."

Ellen felt her heart pound. Her legs trembled. It was a childish overreaction, but she could not help it. She glanced back at the body on the table, while a grin stretched her lips so wide it hurt. Hal had not been the one who passed on information to the Butcher and her gang, and she really was who she said she was. And that evening, once the meeting was over, Ellen was definitely due some off-duty time.

CHAPTER THIRTEEN—A NEW MAP

"We haven't been able to find anyone who's willing to swear to the identification, but we're fairly sure it's the same woman." Chris paused in her report.

Standing at one side of the room, Ellen nodded, noting the careful choice of words.

Chris went on. "And we know from the log that on the night in question, the *Susie-Louise* was moored in town. What we suspect happened was that Yuan Beaumont chanced to be in the Three Barrels. She overheard enough to be suspicious and latched onto Jay Takeda, as someone who was obviously under the influence of alcohol. During the course of the time they spent together, she managed to extract more information, which she passed on to her associates."

Major Kallim sank back in her chair. Her eyes fixed pensively on the office ceiling. "Leading Ranger Jay Takeda. She was the one who volunteered to stay behind, providing cover so her comrades could escape, wasn't she?"

"Yes, ma'am."

Kallim turned to one of the attending orderlies. "Does she leave any family?"

"Her parents. They live in Eastford. And two younger sisters."

"Her mothers can be proud of the way their daughter died." Kallim's eyes returned to Chris. "Your identification is not certain?"

"No, ma'am."

"And your suspicions are just guesswork?"

"Yes, ma'am."

Kallim tapped her fingertips thoughtfully on the table, and then nodded, clearly having reached a decision. "I fear we'll never know for sure how the gang learned of the 12th's planned raid. We don't have enough evidence to work with, but fortunately, we don't need the information to trace any gang members. In my opinion, it's not worth pursuing the matter any further. I'll forward a report to Fort Krowe to this effect." She sat up, looking more purposeful. "What else?"

This was Ellen's cue. "Ma'am, I've examined the receipts I found in Skipper Beaumont's pocket. It looks like they're good forgeries. Because of the state they're in, it's hard to be sure about much, but the way the ink ran suggests they'd been altered at some point. The receipts were for Jan's Creek Ranch and Three Dollars Ranch, which match about two-thirds of the sheep on the barge. We suspect the crew arranged for these sheep to be in the easier-to-get-to spots, so they'd most likely be the ones checked by the Militiawoman on duty."

"Only suspect?"

"The fuss from the search of the barge mixed them up."

"It was a bit of a chance the skipper was taking."

"That was probably why they waited until the end of the day, when the light was poor."

"And the Militiawoman was eager to get home," Kallim added dryly.

Ellen said nothing, but Terrie would certainly not have exerted herself checking the tattoos at any time of day.

"The owners of these farms, have you spoken to them?" Kallim asked.

"Yes, ma'am. They deny all knowledge of their animals being on the *Susie-Louise*. The sheep were mature ewes, matching breeding stock reported stolen last autumn."

"Okay. What have we found out from the prisoner?"

One of the other Rangers present answered. "Not a lot, I'm afraid, ma'am. She claims to be a casual dockhand from Eastford, hired on a trip-by-trip basis. She says this is the first time she's worked on the *Susie-Louise*. Denies all knowledge of the Butcher."

"Do you believe her?"

The Ranger pursed her lips. "She might be telling the truth. She's either a good actress or extremely dim-witted."

"Mindless muscle?"

"Not even much in the way of muscle, which explains why no skipper wants her as permanent crew. We're going to take her up the river tomorrow, to see if she can spot where the sheep were loaded, but

I'm not holding out much hope. She's not the sort to notice things and remember."

"Right." Kallim turned to the last contributor. "Corporal O'Neil, what have you to tell us?"

This was the big one. Ellen felt a tingle of excitement. The other reports, her own included, had been routine. However, Ellen had witnessed the Ranger's return to Roadsend, less than an hour before, and while nothing official had yet been said, the word on the barracks' grapevine was that the mission had been successful.

Ash O'Neil was a hard-eyed woman in her early twenties, with a no-nonsense manner, quieter than most Rangers and less quick to laugh. Yet despite her dour appearance, she was one of the Rangers who had made the most effort to be friendly to Ellen. She had a reputation for bushcraft skills that impressed even the other Rangers. Ellen had heard several stories during her time in the barracks and had not been surprised when Maggie LeCoup recommended her as a tracker.

Ash spoke evenly, without any trace of self-importance. "I was stationed at the ford on Red Gorge Creek. Eriksen came through there just after dawn. I reckon she'd holed up outside town until first light and stolen a horse. She hadn't managed a saddle and was riding bareback. I tailed her for the next three hours until she reached a homestead out in the Wildlands."

Kallim pushed a map across the table. "Can you pinpoint where it was?"

O'Neil went to the desk and stared down, frowning. "We came over there and across. There was a river running..." Her frown deepened. "I don't think this map has the spot marked, but I'd say it was about... there." She placed her finger on a blank area of the map.

"I haven't ridden out that way since I was a lieutenant with the 8th. It was a long time ago." Kallim sighed and looked up. "Sanchez, Mittal. It's your region. Do you know where this base is?"

Ellen joined the other two women at the table. O'Neil's description of detail on the journey was precise and comprehensive, recounting the features she had passed. They added together the clues, but it was not easy. Off to the southeast were hundreds of canyons. They had never been mapped—nowhere out there had been, and most landmarks were without a name. Yet despite the difficulty, Ellen had to work to keep a smile off her face. Her last crumb of doubt had been that Ash would track Adeola Eriksen back to Broken Hills Ranch.

"That sounds like it's the other side of Flinttop," Chris said.

Ellen tried to picture the region, but a Militiawomen's duties rarely took her so far into the Wildlands. "The river has to be one of the tributaries of the Yallack."

"True, but there's enough of them," Chris agreed, staring at the map and clearly digging through her memories. "You said it was about two kilometers from a small lake shaped like a boot?"

Ash nodded. "Yes."

"Then I think—"

"Do you know where the hideout is?" Kallim interrupted.

Chris caught her lip in her teeth and then looked at Ash. "When you were facing the homestead across the river, was there another canyon breaking off behind it, heading toward a mountain with a crest like this..." Chris illustrated the shape with her hands.

Ash nodded. "Yes."

Chris stood up straighter. "Then I know the spot. I was out that way eight or so years ago. There were no buildings back then."

"They didn't look like they'd been around for long."

"This region is unmapped?" Major Kallim asked.

Chris smiled. "At the moment. But I could draw you one of how to get there."

"Good enough to find it, coming from north, south, and east?"

"Yes, ma'am."

"I want it by this evening."

"Yes, ma'am."

"Then I think we've covered all we need to. I want three copies of the map before sunset. I've got eight squadrons ready to hunt down this scum. We'll all rendezvous at the Butcher's base in fourteen days' time." Kallim smiled without humor. "And then we'll put an end to the matter."

❖

The yard in front of the farmhouse was deserted when Ellen arrived at Broken Hills Ranch in the early evening. She sat in the saddle for a moment, patting the horse's neck, while trying to work out if she was surprised at how nervous she felt. Even in her first fumbling encounter, aged fourteen, with Tina Scott in Tina's family hay barn, Ellen did not remember being so unconfident and off balance.

No sign of activity issued from the farmhouse. Was all her anxiety for nothing? Was Hal elsewhere? It would be too ironic, and disappointing. Ellen slipped her foot free of the stirrup, swung her leg over the horse's rump, and jumped down. She stroked the horse's nose, more to soothe herself than the horse, before turning back to the door. A jolt ran through her, rippling out from her stomach.

Hal stood at the top of the steps, arms folded, grinning down at her. "You're back."

"No. You're imagining things."

Hal laughed, hopping down the steps. "Okay. I asked for that."

"You did."

Ellen advanced until she and Hal were mere centimeters apart, yet still not touching.

"When did you get into Roadsend?"

"A couple of days ago."

"You couldn't let me know before?"

"I'm sorry. I wasn't able to get away."

"And now? Are you on duty or off?"

"Off."

"You're staying here tonight."

"I'd like to."

"That last one wasn't a question."

Hal raised her hand to Ellen's face. Ellen leaned into the touch, closing her eyes. She felt Hal's fingers slide to the base of her neck, urging her forward. Their lips met.

Ellen wrapped her arms around Hal, partly for support. The muscles in Hal's shoulders were hard and firm. Ellen slid her hands lower, tracing the line of Hal's spine to its end. Her world consisted only of Hal's mouth working against hers and the softness of Hal's backside, twin mounds filling her hands. Ellen tightened the grip of her fingers, pressing their thighs still more firmly together.

The bang of the farmhouse door came as a shock, jerking Ellen back to the farmyard. She pulled away, feeling dazed. However, Hal did not release her own hold and they remained locked together from the waist down. Ellen turned her head. The farm hand, Jo, now stood at the top of the steps, grinning with amusement.

Hal planted a last quick, pecked kiss, let go of Ellen, and trotted over to her employee. They exchanged a few brief comments, too low to be overheard. Ellen felt a blush rise on her face. Even without knowing the details of what was said, from the way Jo's grin got still wider, she could make a fair guess at the gist of it. Jo lightly punched Hal's arm and then ambled toward Ellen's horse.

Hal beckoned. "It's okay. Jo's going to sort it out in the stable."

From the entrance hall immediately inside the farmhouse door stairs led to the upper floor. Ellen eyed them—presumably the bedrooms were up there. However, Hal had turned right, into the kitchen. Ellen followed. A pot bubbling on the iron stove filled the room with the rich smell of lamb cooking. Nobody else was present, although through the open back door, Ellen could see Cassie Drennen's knees. The old woman was ensconced in her usual spot.

Hal pointed to the table. "Sit."

Ellen obeyed, slipping onto the bench. A flagon of beer and two pewter tankards were already on the table.

Hal went to the stove and stirred the contents of the pot. "Just about done. Help yourself to beer." She grinned back over her shoulder. "I'm going to fuck you, but first I'm going to feed you."

From the way Ellen's stomach was jumping around, she was not sure if food was a good idea. "I don't know if I want..."

"It'd better be dinner you're expressing doubts about."

"Uh...yeah."

Hal deposited a bowl of stew on the table before Ellen. "Eat. You're going to need your strength. And besides, if you knew how cute you look, sitting there squirming, you'd understand why I intend to make you wait."

Ellen ducked her head.

Hal sat down opposite. "There's no point hiding your face. I can see from your ears that you've gone red."

Despite feeling her cheeks burn hotter still, Ellen laughed and picked up a spoon and a chunk of bread. She noted that only two bowls were on the table. "Is Jo not..."

"She's going to visit some friends on the next farm over. It is her dinner you're eating, but she told me to tell you that she doesn't mind. She won't be coming back until tomorrow morning. She wants a decent night's sleep, and she thought it might get a little noisy here."

Ellen concentrated on eating. Her stomach was still bouncing all over the place, but the food was not affecting it one way or the other. She could only pray that she did not get indigestion later.

"Is the stew okay?" Hal asked.

"Yup."

Without raising her head, Ellen glanced up. Hal was sitting back, chewing slowly and watching her. Ellen swallowed, knowing her own performance was somewhere below infantile. It was not as if she had anything to fear, or that she did not like looking at Hal. Ellen forced her back to straighten and her death-grip on the spoon to loosen.

She met Hal's eyes. "The food's fine. Thank you."

"You're welcome. But I expect to be repaid in kind."

"I'll do my best."

The smile on Hal's face was teasingly assured. Was she really as relaxed as she looked? Hal was, at most, seven years the elder. Was it those few years that made the difference? Every one of Ellen's previous girlfriends had been aged within a year or two of herself, and had passively waited for her to make all the moves. Ellen was quite sure that Hal had an alternate plan mapped out.

The sharp cut of Hal's face matched her personality, emphasizing her rakish grin. Her body was well formed, lean, and straight. She was undeniably good-looking. But Ellen knew it was the self-assured, devil-may-care glint in Hal's eye that she found as sexy as hell. For the first time in her life, Ellen understood what it was to have her insides turn to mush.

Hal tore off a strip of bread to mop up the last of her stew and then pushed the empty bowl away. "I'm going to see to Aunt Cassie. The washroom and latrine are out the back, which you might want to avail yourself of."

"Do you need help with your aunt?"

"No. She ate earlier. She gets stomach cramps if she has dinner too late. Not that she eats much anymore. I just need to see her settled in her room for the night." Hal stood up and went to collect her aunt.

Cassie shuffled through the kitchen, leaning on Hal's arm, while picking at something invisible on her shirt. "I need to...it's all, what's it...you know." They left the kitchen and Ellen heard a ground floor door on the other side of the entrance hall open and close. The elderly woman was clearly too infirm to manage the stairs.

Ellen had visited the Roadsend bathhouse before leaving town, but the latrine was a good idea. She was back in the kitchen just in time to catch Hal wish Cassie good night and then the sound of a key turning. Hal reappeared in the kitchen.

"You lock your aunt in her room?"

"Have to. If she wakes in the night she can get confused and wander off. She did it last winter. If the door slamming hadn't woken Jo and me, she'd have frozen to death. She didn't have coat or boots and the snow was knee high."

Ellen had splashed cold water on her face in the washroom, and now felt marginally calmer and more controlled. She stepped closer to Hal, intending for them to kiss again, but was stopped before she got halfway.

Hal pointed to the bench. "Sit. Wait."

"You say that like I'm a sheepdog."

"And I'm going to make you howl." Hal went out the back door.

Ellen sat and waited. In a few minutes, Hal returned. Wordlessly, she took Ellen's hand and towed her from the room and up the stairs.

Hal's bedroom occupied the area directly above the kitchen, although it was somewhat smaller than the room below, due to being built into the eaves of the house. Light from the sinking sun streamed in through a casement window at the front, dusting the room with gold. The floorboards were bare, polished only by the passage of feet over decades. Furniture was sparse—a chest and a bed.

Hal went to the window and pulled the shutters closed, making the light soften into a warm gloom. She turned and rested her shoulders against the wall behind her, arms folded, legs crossed at the ankle. Her gaze traveled deliberately, slowly, challengingly up and down Ellen's body. Ellen again walked toward her and again was stopped.

Hal pressed one forefinger into Ellen's shoulder, keeping her at bay. "Stand still."

"I—"

"And don't talk."

The command delivered a jolt like lightning through Ellen's core. Breathing suddenly became a struggle. Her legs were shaking. Ellen locked her knees to stop herself from falling.

Hal returned her arms to the folded position. "Take your shirt off."

Ellen's fingers were clumsy, but she was amazed they obeyed her at all, slipping each button free. She tossed the shirt aside. A draft of air tickled the exposed skin on Ellen's back, but it was not this that made her body tingle with gooseflesh.

Hal pushed away from the wall. She reached out, cupping both Ellen's breasts. Ellen's head fell back, eyes closed. Hal's palms were warm and rough, calloused from farm work. Her thumbs pressed on Ellen's nipples, rubbing them and rolling them. Ellen did not know how she managed to stay upright. Her breath came in gasps. The muscles in her thighs were twitching. The pulse beat so hard in her stomach that her whole body shook.

Hal's hands slipped to Ellen's waist. Deftly, she loosened the belt, and then eased the band over Ellen's hips. The remainder of Ellen's clothes landed around her ankles. Hal now stepped closer, enfolding Ellen in a firm embrace. The harsh texture of Hal's work gear rubbed on Ellen's skin, inflaming her, as did the touch of Hal's hands, gently prising open the cleft of her backside and running her fingers inside.

Ellen rested her forehead on Hal's shoulder. "Please."

"What?"

"I don't think I can stand up any longer."

"You don't?" Hal laughed, making no attempt to stop her actions. Her fingers probed further, finding even more sensitive spots.

Ellen could stay unmoving no longer. She clung to Hal, gasping. "Please."

Hal turned her head. Her lips brushed Ellen's neck, followed by the light touch of teeth. Ellen's left knee buckled. Only Hal's support saved her from ending up on the floor.

"Okay. You can go and lie down." Hal stepped back, releasing her.

Leaning down to loosen her boots would take more balance than Ellen could muster. Instead she dropped to her knees and then flopped back. Getting her ankles free of her clothes took an inordinate amount of effort, as if the material was fighting her. The few steps to the bed and pulling back the covers were a challenge, but then Ellen was able to roll onto the bed. She lay on her back, grateful that demands were no longer being made of her legs, and turned her head.

Hal was completing the removal of her own boots. She sauntered across the room and mounted the bed.

"What about your clothes?"

"I'll take them off when I'm ready. There's no rush."

Hal prised Ellen's legs apart, forced a knee between, and then sat astride her thigh. Ellen started to lever herself up, reaching out, intending to strip off Hal's shirt, but her actions were clumsy with desire and easily outmaneuvered. Hal captured her wrists and pushed her back, pinning her to the bed.

Ellen looked up at Hal, hanging over her. The light was dim, but not enough to hide the hunger in Hal's expression, overlaying her normal smile. It was the hunger that turned Ellen's bones to rubber. Even had she wanted to, Ellen could not have stopped Hal's knee from pushing higher until it made hard contact with the apex of her legs.

Hal's farm clothes were thick, rough cloth. Every coarse fiber traced its own trail of dry friction. Ellen's body arched out of her control. Every surge of her pulse magnified the effect of Hal's knee, moving mere millimeters, and driving a storm through Ellen.

The pressure inside Ellen was building to a climax, but then Hal's knee was gone and her wrists were free. Ellen opened her eyes. She could not remember closing them. Hal knelt between her legs, staring at her. Ellen had never felt so utterly naked in her life as she did under Hal's prolonged examination. The awareness honed the edge of her desire, sharpening it unbearably. Each second made the ache grow.

"Please, Hal, can't you—"

"You want me to touch you?" The teasing tone had not left Hal's voice. She reached out and placed one forefinger on the hood over Ellen's clitoris. "Like this?"

The air left Ellen's lungs in a grunt.

Hal's finger traced a long, slow loop down between Ellen's legs and back. "Or like this?" The finger again drifted down, but this time slowly slid into Ellen.

Ellen could not have answered. A groan was torn from the back of her throat. In reflex, her head pressed back hard into the bed, lifting her shoulders.

"Or like this?" The finger withdrew but then returned, forcefully, with company. Ellen cried out, in both surprise and passion, as Hal filled her.

Hal's fingers felt so good, entering her, stretching her, taking her. Each thrust of Hal's hand went deeper than before. Ellen's existence was distilled into the sensation of Hal inside her. Hal's other hand pressed down on Ellen's mound, holding her steady. Then Hal's thumb brushed over Ellen's clitoris. Ellen was beyond ready. On the third touch, her orgasm erupted.

Ellen heard herself give voice, a shout high and long, ending in a long gasped hiss. *I'm going to make you howl.* Memory of the promise lurched through Ellen's head. She had not regained her breath when Hal picked up the rhythm again.

The waves of orgasm pounded over her, until her body was too weak to respond and she no longer had the breath to do more than whimper. And then the movement of Hal's hand stopped. Slowly, gently, Hal pulled out of her. The feeling of emptiness was a shock in itself. Ellen gasped and opened her eyes. Hal still sat, fully clothed, watching her.

The corner of Hal's lips twitched. "You know, Jo was right. She wouldn't be getting much sleep."

"I...er...it..." Ellen felt so good, she could not think of any words to string into a sentence.

"Save your breath. You're going to need it."

While Ellen watched, Hal loosened her top button and pulled her shirt off over her head. Her trousers followed in short order. Hal's body looked the way it felt, sharply defined and well proportioned. Her breasts were small and tight, exactly the right shape to fit into the hollow of Ellen's palms. Her hands ached to touch them. She tried to sit, but although her heartbeat was slowing, her body was too relaxed to be anything other than sluggish.

"Stay where you are." Hal's tone was not as autocratic as before, but no less insistent, making it clear that she expected to be the one in control.

Hal crawled up the bed, until she was beside Ellen's head. In a quick movement, she straddled Ellen's face. Her toes pressed against Ellen's forearms. "Can you guess what I want you to do now?" She lowered herself onto Ellen.

Ellen looked up, past the misting of hair, the beading of sweat on Hal's flat stomach, the firm breasts, and met Hal's eyes. Ellen opened her mouth and sucked Hal in.

Her tongue dug deep, tasting Hal, slipping through folds of hot flesh, exploring the opening that clenched around her, and returning over and over to the hard knot of nerve endings. Ellen's cheeks grew slick, coated in Hal's wetness as she watched Hal's body jerk in response to the dance of her tongue.

Hal climaxed, her body rigid. A high keening broke from her, pulsing in time with the shudders racking her body, and then she sagged forward. For a moment, Hal was still and then she started to twist to the side, but Ellen was not ready to let her go. She curled her arms up, clamping then over Hal's thighs and holding her in place. Again, Ellen set her tongue to work.

In triumph, Ellen saw that Hal now had to lean on the wall to keep her balance, resting her head on her forearm. Hal was moaning, helpless. Hal was hers. She took Hal over the edge again and then a third time. When she finally released her grip, Hal fell to the bed, gasping. Ellen rolled over and hugged her.

Eventually, Hal's breathing eased, and her arms in turn tightened around Ellen. Without opening her eyes, a lazy grin spread across her face. "Good counterattack."

"I didn't want you to have it all your own way." Ellen felt Hal shake with weak laughter.

"Ugh. My mouth's dry."

"As you said, Jo wouldn't be getting much sleep."

"Your legs are probably working better than mine at the moment. I think there's some beer left in the flagon. Why don't you go down and get it?"

Ellen planted a quick kiss on Hal's lips and then swung off the bed. She flexed her legs experimentally. They were not completely steady, but she thought they would be good to get her downstairs and back. "Okay."

As she reached the bedroom door, Hal spoke again. "And in the left-hand drawer of the dresser, there's a large candle. You could bring that up as well."

Ellen nodded. Sunset was close and darkness in the room was thickening. "Should I light it off the stove, or do you have a flint up here?"

Hal laughed. "Who said anything about lighting it? I haven't finished with you yet."

❖

Ellen awoke on her back. She opened her eyes and lay staring at the ceiling. Her body felt heavy and relaxed. The twinge of a pulled muscle in her thigh produced nothing but a sense of contentment. The world was a wonderful place. The muted stinging across her back only made her smile broaden. It added sensation to the memory of exactly what she had been doing when Hal scratched her.

Ellen rolled her head to the side. She studied Hal's face on the pillow beside her. Even in sleep, Hal looked roguish. The laughter lines at either side of her mouth were too deeply etched to go away. Ellen took a long time, taking each feature in turn before she continued her inspection downward.

The tendons in Hal's neck stood out, crisply intersected by the sharp line of her collarbone. Ellen felt completely juvenile pleasure in spotting the marks she had left there. Below that, the bedclothes were suitably disheveled. The bits of Hal's body on view were as she remembered, wiry with cleanly defined bone and muscle.

Ellen rolled out of bed, went to the window, and pushed the shutters open. The sun was rising behind the house so no direct beams entered, but the sudden increase in light drew a groan from behind her. Ellen took a few seconds longer, considering the view over the farmyard to the paddocks beyond, and then sauntered back toward the bed.

The flagon was on the chest. Ellen scooped it up in passing and took a sip. Unsurprisingly, the beer was now stale and flat, but the liquid was welcome, clearing her throat. She flexed the muscles in her neck and then swallowed another mouthful.

"Don't tell me you're one of those people who are disgustingly bouncy first thing in the morning." Hal spoke without opening her eyes.

Ellen laughed. "You mean you're the sort who likes to imitate the walking dead for the first hour each day?"

"Don't mock. It's not funny." Hal groaned and lifted her arm. "What's the beer like?"

"Awful."

"I'll take it."

Ellen made sure Hal was sitting upright and had both hands securely wrapped around the flagon before relinquishing her own hold. She rolled back onto the bed, stretching out beside Hal, with her head on the pillow.

The vertebrae of Hal's spine were perfectly defined between bands of muscle, as were her ribs and shoulder blades. Ellen noted that she had not inflicted similar scratches to those she had received—not that she had intended to. Then Ellen noted something else. A series of fine white scars were scored across Hal's back, either twenty or thirty at a guess, knowing the magistrate's love of round numbers. The lines were mostly parallel to each other, although some crossed in places. They were scars that Ellen recognized far better than she liked.

The flogging of criminals was the part of being a Militiawoman Ellen enjoyed the least. Fortunately, both Roadsend magistrates preferred fines to the whip as a means of judicial punishment. Even so, Ellen had been required to assist on numerous occasions. When she was a rookie, she could not be called on to do more than assist. Now that she was a patrolwoman, she was not looking forward to the day when it would be her duty to wield the whip.

Ellen ran her finger over the scars. "Er..."

Hal looked back, her face showing instant comprehension. "Yes. They're a present from your colleagues in Monday Market."

"Oh. I..."

"It's okay. It hurt like fuck, but I deserved it."

"What did you do?"

"I made some very stupid friends. But of course we all thought we were being really clever. Making easy money. And then we got caught." Hal shrugged. "I still reckon the magistrate was being a bitch, seeing as it was a first offense and all. But it was probably the best thing that could have happened for me."

"Why?"

"Because I learned my lesson. My friends didn't, so I made some new ones. Maybe if I'd got off lightly that first time, I'd have stayed around until I was too caught up in the lifestyle to get out."

"You still like breaking rules."

"True. But the lesson I learned was never to assume I'm going to get away with it. I make sure I know the consequences of being caught, and that I can deal with them. My friends who didn't learn—last thing I heard, two of them had been hanged. And that's the sort of consequence I never want to deal with." Hal grimaced. "Which is all far too serious a topic for a morning like this. Though I'd point out the consequences for getting a Militiawoman to have a quick kiss while on duty have been no problem so far."

Hal leaned over the side of the bed to put the flagon on the floor, then rolled back to face Ellen. They lay side by side. Hal ran her fingernails lightly down Ellen's ribs. "When do you have to be back in Roadsend?"

"Not until midday."

"Really? Well, Aunt Cassie isn't likely to stir for another hour, and when she does she'll just want taking to the latrine and then putting in her chair with some leftover stew. Jo said she'd take the dogs and go down to the north paddock when she gets here. I could go and help her. But I'm sure she can cope on her own, and she knows I'd do the same for her. So..."

Slightly clumsily, Hal hoisted herself forward, until she was lying on top of Ellen, staring down into her face. "You know, it's not everyone I'd stir myself for, this early in the morning." Hal ducked her head, kissing Ellen quickly on the lips. "But I'd have to say"—she kissed Ellen again—"that on evidence of last night"—another kiss—"you're worth it."

Ellen stared into Hal's eyes, mere centimeters away. *I think I'm falling in love with you.* The words shot through Ellen's head, threatening to find their way to her lips. But then Hal pressed her knee down, between Ellen's legs, and the contact drove all words away.

Part Three

Split Verdict

Chapter Fourteen—Trust and Doubt

The sound of movement from the floor of the cottage woke Ellen. She rolled over as the door was pulled open. Pre-dawn light ghosted gray on the rafters. Below, Mama Roz stood silhouetted in the doorway, yawning and stretching her arms over her head. A light rain was falling outside, heard rather than seen, to the accompaniment of gusts of wind. At an estimate, under half an hour remained before sunrise, when Mama Roz was due to start work at the Old Docks.

Ellen grabbed her discarded clothes and pulled them on, except for her boots, which were down by the hearth, next to Mama Roz's. She did up the last button and vaulted down the ladder.

Mama Roz turned around. "Good morning."

Ellen gave her birth mother a quick hug of greeting. "Morning."

"You on duty today?"

"Up till fourteen o'clock."

"Any chance I'll get to see you this evening?"

Just the faintest hint of reproach underlay Mama Roz's tone. They had not exchanged more than a few words since Ellen had left to track down Fran Paparung in Shingleford.

"Uh...no. I was planning on spending the night—"

"Are you going to see Hal?" Mama Becky interrupted eagerly, while shuffling out from the curtained off bed area.

"Yes, Mom."

Mama Roz laughed and gave Ellen a squeeze before releasing her. "I'm sure you'll have more fun with her than discussing the weather here with me."

"Hal seems very nice," Mama Becky said.

Ellen was not sure if *nice* was the right word for Hal, but chose to agree anyway. "Yes, she is."

"And it's good the way she looks after her aunt."

"Yes."

"I suppose eventually the farm will be hers?"

"I don't know. I haven't asked her. When Cassie dies, I guess it will go to her family, so Hal might end up with it."

"When your time with the Militia is over, you could go and work on the farm with her."

"Mom!" Ellen felt exasperated. Already her mother was planning her life out for her.

"Oh, I know I'm being silly, but you must invite Hal over to meet us properly. She's welcome to stay here overnight. We'd love to get to know her better."

"She's got the farm to run. And a busy time of year is coming up." Ellen made the excuse.

"What about once the cloning is over and the sheep are back on the hills?" Mama Becky's zeal was unmistakable.

"Maybe. I'll mention it to her."

Ellen made the vague commitment, hoping to end the debate. Her reticence was not because she objected to her parents meeting Hal, and of course they both knew that she and a new girlfriend would not be spending the evening playing tic-tac-toe. Ellen glanced up at her open sleeping platform. But there was a difference between knowing and hearing every sound. This evening would be only her and Hal's third time, and restraint was not likely to be much in evidence. Perhaps, in another month or two, they would be able to spend a night together without running the risk of finishing to a round of applause from the surrounding houses.

At the thought, Ellen felt a grin split her face. A month or two with Hal sounded good. A year or two sounded better. Maybe even the rest of her life. She had dismissed Mama Becky's ideas about her future on reflex, but to be fair, they did not seem too bad. The thought of her and Hal, living on the farm together, was definitely one she could get to like.

Mama Roz sat by the hearth and pulled her boots toward her. "You got anything interesting lined up work-wise today?"

"Just routine patrols." Ellen was grateful for the change in topic, and equally grateful that the patrols would be without Terrie. The corporal had been discharged from infirmary several days ago, and immediately requested a leave of absence. She had not been seen since.

"You won't be working with the Rangers?"

Ellen sighed. Straight from one tricky subject to another. "No, Mom."

"Do you know if the Rangers will be needing your help again?" Mama Roz was clearly making an effort to sound as if it was a casual question, but her tone gave her away.

"There's no plans for it."

Ellen knew her deployment with the Rangers frightened her parents. In part because of the danger, made all the more real by the massacre of the 12th, and in part because they were worried she might get a liking for the lifestyle.

Even without the curtailment of the normal probation period, her time as rookie was over. Ellen could now apply to join the Rangers, but there was no rush. Nothing in the regulations imposed a time limit on how long she had to submit her request. Surely it would be better to wait a month or more, to see how things worked out between her and Hal, and to put the whole affair with the Butcher and her gang into the past.

The meeting at the barracks had been nine days before. Now just five more were left to go. The squadrons of Rangers were currently converging on the Butcher's base, getting closer with each day, traveling through the Wildlands so that nobody would spot them. The first the Butcher would know was when her hideaway was surrounded. Five days, and the Butcher and her Knives would be either dead or prisoners, with just the headless scrag-end to wrap up in Eastford. When life had returned to normal, Ellen would have plenty of time to decide if normality was what she wanted from life.

"Those Rangers still haven't caught the gang. I don't know what they're up to." Mama Becky sounded as if she thought the Rangers were guilty of incompetence—even malicious stalling, in the hope of ensnaring her daughter.

"They will."

"They've been saying that for weeks."

"But now—" Ellen stopped. She was not supposed to say anything to anyone about the Rangers' plans, and although it was a ludicrous idea that her parents were involved with the gang, or even remotely likely to pass the news to anyone who was, they would be horrified to learn just how closely Ellen had been involved in the operation.

"I don't know what the world's coming to. It's awful." Mama Becky placed her hand on Ellen's arm. "You know we just want you safe."

"Yes, Mom. I know. I promise I'll be careful."

"That's what you said before you went and got your head cracked open."

"Oh, Mom. That was only..." Only something Ellen knew she was never going to hear the end of.

Mama Roz stood, stamping her boots into place. She took hold of Ellen's shoulders and turned her around, looking at her, eye to eye. "I know you think we worry too much. We're your mothers. It's our job. We know you're an adult now, and we can't look after you, but you have to understand it can be hard for us sometimes. When you have children of your own, you'll understand. But whatever happens, you know we love you, and we're proud of you."

Mama Roz pressed a quick kiss on Ellen's cheek and headed for the door.

❖

The next morning, Ellen was woken by movement beside her. She opened her eyes. Dawn was past and light crept through cracks in the closed shutters, along with the bleating of sheep from the paddocks. Judging by the strength of the sunshine, the sky outside was clear and the day promised to be better than the one before. Although, seeing as Ellen was scheduled for the late patrol in Roadsend, the evening was going to be much less fun.

Ellen stretched her arms up so they touched the wall above her head and then she rolled onto her side, a little surprised if Hal had woken before her—something that had not shown the slightest chance of happening on either of the two previous occasions. However, Hal had only been turning in her sleep. Ellen raised herself on an elbow and looked down at her sleeping lover.

Hal's face on the pillow was turned toward Ellen, eyes closed and mouth slightly open. Her skin was dark against the bleached cloth, her hair almost black, lying in spikes across her forehead. Beautiful was not the word that came to mind. For Ellen, such a description was for the studied contrivance of her previous girlfriends, who had worried about their haircuts and complexions and whether their clothes flattered their figure. Hal's looks were far too natural, too unique. Her face was totally Hal, and as Ellen lay studying it, she knew there was nothing under the Goddess's wide sky that she would rather look at.

A couple of times in the past, she thought she had been in love with her girlfriends. Now she knew that emotion had been no more than excitement and pleasure at a pretty face. What she felt for Hal was redefining everything she had thought she knew about herself. Her heart was Hal's.

Ellen brushed the hair back from Hal's cheek and kissed her gently on the lips. Hal groaned and grimaced. She twisted her neck as if trying to bury her face in the pillow.

"Good morning."

"Is it?" Hal mumbled.

"It's morning."

"What's so good about it?"

Ellen lay down on her side and placed her free arm around Hal's shoulders. After a few seconds, Hal opened her eyes and stared back.

"What isn't good?"

Ellen raised her knee, so that it lay over Hal's thigh. With her fingers she traced the outline of Hal's biceps and then across her shoulder blades. She pulled Hal close and pressed their lips together, at first a soft, sisterly kiss, but getting more ardent. Her tongue slipped between Hal's lips and then started to prise Hal's teeth apart.

Hal rolled away, chuckling softly. "You know I don't do this, first thing in the morning."

The protest was not to be taken seriously. Ellen had felt Hal respond. "Then lie still, while I do it."

Ellen rolled on, to lie half over Hal, pinning her down, while still leaving most of her body free to explore. Ellen cupped Hal's breast, pinching gently at the nipple. Hal sighed and opened her eyes again. In them there was manifest hunger, and humor and also tenderness. This last emotion struck at Ellen. She had not seen it so clearly before in Hal's expression, and had not expected to, at least not so soon in their relationship. Hal's arms crept around Ellen's back, weak and uncoordinated, as Hal was when she first woke, but clear in their intent. Feeling totally happy, Ellen lowered her head and continued kissing Hal.

The sound of horses arriving in the farmyard interrupted.

"Hey. Hal." A voice rang out.

"Fuck." Hal pushed Ellen away and sat up.

"What is it?"

"I...hopefully nothing." Hal half fell out of bed and then stood, swaying groggily, before lurching to the window.

"What is—" Ellen scrambled from the bed.

"No. Stay where you are." Hal pulled open the shutters, peered out, waved, and then closed them again.

"What's..."

"It's one of my neighbors. Must be some problem with the sheep." Hal drew a deep breath, and then shook her head sharply, as if hoping to dislodge her torpor. "It's okay. I'll go to see what she wants. You stay where you are." She pointed, emphasizing her words. "Stay just where you are. Don't move a centimeter. I'll be back."

Hal grabbed the nearest set of clothes and left the room, still pulling the shirt over her head. Her bare footsteps slapped unsteadily on the stairs and then the front door opened.

Ellen lay, listening to the voices in the yard. Someone sounded angry, although Ellen was unable to make out any words. A number of horses seemed to be milling around. A couple of times, Ellen picked out Hal's voice, but again, not clearly enough for words. Hal did not sound happy, but neither did she sound hostile, so presumably, whatever the cause of the other speaker's anger, it was not directed at Hal.

"Okay. Ten minutes," somebody other than Hal shouted—the first words Ellen could decipher since the initial hail. The discussion was clearly drawing to a close and the horses moving away.

But what was going to happen in ten minutes? Ellen's curiosity could be held in check no longer. She bounced out of bed and opened the window shutters. Sudden glaring sunlight made her wince and by the time her eyes had adjusted, it was too late. She caught only the rump of the last horse, disappearing around the side of the farmhouse.

The front door closed and Hal's feet sounded again on the stairs. Ellen closed the shutters and was sitting on the side of the bed when Hal returned.

"What was it?"

"Like I thought, trouble with the sheep."

"What sort of trouble?"

"Nothing that need concern the Militia. Just sheep being their usual, damned awkward, pain in the fucking ass selves." Hal sighed. "And I'm afraid I'm going to have to go and sort it out immediately."

"Will it take long?"

"Most of the day, I expect. Unless the sheep have a funny turn and cooperate with me. You never know. They might decide to do it for once, just for a laugh." Hal pouted. "If you get yourself dressed, I'll go and saddle your horse while you grab breakfast in the kitchen."

Ellen slumped on the bed, feeling deflated. "Are you sure? What will you do about breakfast?"

"I'll head off as soon as you're gone and eat something on the way."

"When will I see you next?"

The question clearly caught Hal by surprise. She froze, her expression pained. "Er...whenever you're next off duty. I...I'll be here." She looked down sharply, and then pulled up the bottom of her shirt for inspection. "That's lucky. I didn't grab your clothes. I'll get your horse ready. See you in the kitchen in a minute." Without meeting Ellen's eyes, Hal grabbed her boots and hurried from the room.

Once she was dressed, Ellen followed on more slowly. The house was silent and the kitchen was empty. Nobody could be seen through the front or rear windows. Where was Jo? She was supposed to be around that morning. Had she already gone off with the neighbor? And which neighbor was it? Ellen had not recognized what little she had heard of the voice. The "ten minutes" had to be the time for a rendezvous. But what could be so urgent? Something decidedly strange was going on. Ellen frowned, trying to make sense of it all.

Food was kept on a slate slab in the pantry. Ellen cut off a chunk of yesterday's bread, and a slice of salted mutton, but her appetite was poor, and she put the food aside, half eaten. If she wrapped it in an oilcloth from her saddlebag, maybe she would feel more like breakfast later on. The ride into Roadsend would take her over an hour.

Ellen dithered around, trying to think of something useful to do. If Hal was in such a hurry to be off, would it be helpful to get Cassie out and into her chair? However, Ellen did not know where the room key was. She was about to go to the stable and see if she could lend a hand with the horses, when the front door opened and Hal returned.

"Your horse is ready and in the yard."

"Is there nothing I can do to help?"

"No. We just need to go off and track the buggers down."

"What about your aunt?"

"Er..." Hal looked distracted, as if her thoughts were elsewhere. "We'll see to her once you've gone."

"Who was it?"

"Who..."

"Who was the neighbor?"

"Oh. Fay Wisniewski from Three Firs."

"Who was with her?" Seeing Hal's frown, Ellen added. "I could hear there was more than one horse."

"She had a couple of her shepherds along." Hal had been holding the front door open while she spoke; now she backed out, clearly wanting Ellen to go as quickly as possible.

Ellen picked up the uneaten remains of breakfast in one hand and followed Hal onto the top of the steps. Her horse was ready, waiting at the foot, its reins tied to a post. Ellen stashed the food in a bag and tied her jacket behind the saddle. Yesterday she had needed it, but her shirt should be adequate now that the rain was gone. She looked up at Hal, feeling both confused and rejected.

Hal's expression was blank, her mood impossible to deduce. She was clearly trying to hide something that might have been regret, might have been anger, might even have been fear. Ellen trotted up the steps and slipped her arms around Hal's waist.

"What's wrong?"

"Nothing's wrong. Except the sheep have been little shits and done me out of a few hours in bed with you. I will personally and individually kick their asses for it when I catch them." Some of Hal's normal humor had returned. She enfolded Ellen's shoulders in a hug and claimed her mouth in a long, forceful kiss.

Ellen responded. She could feel Hal soften against her, as the tension and irritation ebbed away. Their mouths were joined in mutual desire. Hal's body fitted into her arms, filling Ellen with a sense of completeness. For a moment, all her doubts were gone. Ellen knew she had been created for no purpose other than to hold Hal close. Nothing was wrong. What could be wrong?

And then Hal broke away and pushed her gently down the steps. "Go on. I'll see you again in a few days."

Now smiling, Ellen loosened the horse's reins and hopped into the saddle. As she rode away, she glanced back over her shoulder repeatedly. Hal remained on the top of the steps, watching her go. The sight made Ellen's smile broaden, until confusion returned. Where had all Hal's urgency gone? Up until then, Hal had been acting as if there was not a second to waste. Now she had time to stand around, waving good-bye—except she was not waving. Hal stood uncharacteristically motionless.

Ellen's doubts returned, growing with each thud of her horse's hooves. Fifty meters from the farmhouse, she reined her horse to a stop and stared at the ground, trying to define the contours of the barbed knot in her mind. What was going on? Why was she so worried? And which aspect worried her the most?

The road to the farmyard was trampled earth, still damp from yesterday's rain. The hoof prints from her own horse, arriving the previous evening, could be seen soft and partially washed away. Overlying them were half a dozen or more fresh tracks going to the house. So at least six horses had arrived that morning, which was certainly the way it had sounded. Had Hal lied when she claimed only three riders had arrived? Or was it possible that each rider had brought a spare horse in tow?

On the other side of the dry stone wall, the sheep in the paddock were peacefully grazing. One shuffled closer, until it was in Ellen's shadow. She stared at it, while the questions surged around in her head. The sheep's fleece was already showing signs of thickening, ready for winter. A few straggly tuffs trailed away from its rump. More clung over its shoulders. Suddenly Ellen's focus hardened, recognizing what she saw. The sheep had not been shorn in the spring, instead its fleece had been allowed to brush away on passing vegetation.

This happened occasionally, when a farmer failed to round up all her sheep from the hills, but not often. Wool was too valuable to waste. Yet, now that Ellen looked, over half the sheep in the paddock were showing similar signs. Ellen slipped from her horse and leaned over the wall, peering closer. The sheep turned away, flicking its ears, but not before Ellen had caught the numerals 73 at the end of its tattoo. Whatever the full number was, the sheep did not belong to Broken Hills Ranch.

Ellen looked back at the farmhouse. Hal still stood unmoving on the steps, watching her. Ellen's head spun as half thoughts and conjectures collided with each other. In any other farm, Ellen knew she would have gotten on her horse quickly and rode away to report to the Rangers what she had seen. But if she leveled accusations at Hal, it would put one hell of a damper on their relationship, even if the suspicions turned out to be unfounded. And surely there had to be some innocent explanation. Perhaps Fay Wisniewski had deposited the sheep there for safekeeping, having found it straying as part of the undisclosed crisis. Perhaps there was a good reason for the waste of wool.

Ellen had to give Hal the chance to explain first. She owed her that much. She walked slowly back to the farmyard, leading her horse behind her, while she tried to work out what she was going to say. At the foot of the steps, she stopped and looked up. Hal's face was impassive, unreadable.

"Hal. There's a sheep in your paddock that doesn't belong to you. Do you know what it's doing there?"

For a second, Hal's expression wavered. She looked down quickly, concealing her face. Ellen was about to mount the steps when she heard movement in the house. A woman appeared in the doorway behind Hal.

The woman was not Fay Wisniewski, or anyone Ellen had seen before. She was in her early thirties, four or five centimeters shorter than Hal, and more sturdily built, with heavy shoulders and jowls. Yet something in her mouth, nose, and cheekbones suggested a family bond between them.

"You want to know what it's doing there?" The woman shifted forward and stood beside Hal. She looked down at Ellen, her similar lips forming a humorless, taunting parody of Hal's grin. "Simple. We stole it."

Ellen backed away, but the sound of more activity made her glance to her right. Three other strangers had appeared around the corner of the farmhouse, two holding bows, with arrows nocked on the strings. They made no attempt to draw the bows, but it was obvious that they would shoot if she tried to run. Ellen froze. A further pair of women emerged from the farmhouse, squeezed past Hal, and advanced to take up position on either side of Ellen. They grasped her arms, twisting them into a firm lock.

The woman who had spoken now sauntered down the steps until she was face to face with Ellen. "You're Patrolwoman Ellen Mittal. I've heard all about you from my cousin Hal." She indicated by jerking her thumb back over her shoulder. As if Ellen might have any doubt as to who Hal was. "And I know you've heard all about me. My name's Madeline Bucher—Maddy to my friends and family, although most people know me as the Butcher." Suddenly her hand formed a fist that slammed into Ellen's gut. "But you can call me ma'am."

Ellen fought to breathe, but her lungs refused to work. Bright lights wavered before her eyes and her knees folded, although the women holding her would not let her fall. Even before the spasm eased and she could again suck in air, Ellen's hands had been pulled out in front of her and she felt cord bound tightly around her wrists.

Through the distortion of ringing in her ears, Ellen heard the Butcher shouting commands. "Okay. Bring over the horses. Let's get out of here."

"What we going to do about the old woman, Boss?"

"Leave her. Someone will come looking for our little Blackshirt here. They'll find Aunt Cassie. And if they don't, it's no great loss."

Ellen's head cleared and she was able to put weight on her legs although sparks still drifted at the edge of her vision when she looked up. On the other side of the yard, Jo and another woman were coming from the stables, both leading a string of horses.

Hal was still stationary at the top of the farmhouse steps, staring at her feet. She had not moved a step since the moment Ellen first rode away. Ellen kept her eyes fixed on Hal, willing her to look up. Ellen had to know what expression was on Hal's face. How deeply was Hal involved with the gang? How much had she lied? How did she feel now?

The warm brown flank of a horse stopped directly in front of Ellen, blocking her view. She raised her eyes. The Butcher, now mounted, reached down and caught the trailing end of the cord around Ellen's wrists. The two minders let go of Ellen and moved away.

"Damned Blackshirts. You're all a fucking waste of time. And my cousin certainly wasted her time in fucking you, though she probably enjoyed it. Hal always was a fool for a pretty face. I've told her she should think with what she puts under her hat, not what she puts in her pants. But the kid never listens. Anyway, I'm going to have my turn with you. I'm sure you'll be more useful than Terrie fucking Rasheed has been."

"Terrie?"

"Yeah. Your shit for brains corporal. She's the one we came all this way to talk to."

Ellen looked around, confused. "Where is she?"

"Now that's a good question. The stupid bitch has run off."

"Why?"

"'Cause she's a fucking coward. If she'd just sat tight, she'd have been fine. Nobody suspected her. But now your mates will work out she's been up to something. And if they track her down, she'll blab everything she knows."

"Terrie's one of your Knives?" Ellen was struggling to follow.

The Butcher snorted in contempt. "Do me credit. I paid her—complete fucking waste of money. But I wouldn't trust a turd like her. She doesn't know much, but she knows about Hal and this farm. Which is why we're going to have to pull out. Even though Hal does keep her brain between her legs, I still wouldn't let any of the family get caught by you Blackshirts."

The Butcher yanked hard on the cord and wrapped it around the saddle horn. Ellen looked left and right. All the Knives were now mounted, Hal and Jo among them. Both were on the far side of the farmyard, chatting with the rest of the gang, looking relaxed and happy. Neither spared a glance in Ellen's direction.

Another tug on the cord reclaimed Ellen's attention. Her hands were up at head height, and securely attached to the Butcher's saddle horn, with just a short length of loose cord.

"Rasheed was supposed to be passing information to us. She was useless. And Hal was no better at getting anything out of you. So now we're going to my homestead in the hills, and we're going to have a little chat. We'll see if my way of asking questions works any better with you. Rasheed doesn't have the first idea where my homestead is, so even if your friends catch her, there's no risk of us being disturbed." The Butcher leered down at Ellen. "What are you like at running, Blackshirt?"

Without waiting for an answer, the Butcher urged her horse into a canter.

❖

The journey to the Butcher's base took over two hours. Ellen was allowed to ride for the second half of it, once her exhausted stumbling put too much drag on the Butcher's horse, and threats, kicks, and blows could not extract any further effort from her. For the final ten kilometers the route passed along a rough track through the wilderness, presumably made by the gang for bringing in supplies and stolen sheep.

When they got to it, the base was a collection of rough-built timber buildings, set on the floor of a steep-sided canyon. In construction, the Butcher's hideaway looked much like a poor homestead, made from simple split logs, but its scale matched that of the largest ranch. The three biggest buildings were laid out to define a yard, with a corral on the remaining side. Twenty or more horses were currently there. Other buildings, looking like stables, barn, and stores were scattered behind.

The west wall of the canyon was a vertical cliff face, a hundred meters or more in height. The gradient on the eastern flank was less sheer, rising in broken tiers that allowed bands of bushes, and even the occasional tree, to take root. A boulder-strewn river ran along the bottom. Most of the flat canyon floor was densely wooded, but the area around the buildings had been largely cleared of trees, although a few still dotted the site.

The nearby opening to a second narrower canyon split the sheer cliff face, with a waist-high wickerwork fence across the entrance. The ground beyond the fence also was deforested, and given over to pasture where sheep were grazing.

Despite the appearance of being a farm, none of the dozen women in sight seemed to be doing anything that might count as work. The largest group were sitting in the shade of an isolated tree, close by the corral, passing around a flagon. They waved and cheered at the sight of the approaching riders.

"Hey. Welcome home, Boss."

One held out the flagon. "Wash the dust away, Boss."

Laughing, the Butcher swung down beside them and took the offered drink. "That's what I call a welcome."

Someone immediately took the reins of the Butcher's horse and led it into the corral. The other riders dismounted. Ellen's bound hands made it awkward, but she was about to do likewise when a violent shove sent her flying backward over the horse's rump, to land hard, sprawled in the dust. Several women laughed.

The sound attracted the Butcher's attention. "Put the Blackshirt in the cave for now. I'll talk to her later, after I've had time to relax a bit."

Ellen was kicked when she did not get up quickly enough and then hauled toward the bottom of the cliff face. A section of wooden boarding, about five meters wide, filled in at one spot. As they approached, a gang member opened the door in the middle and Ellen was booted through.

Inside was a natural cave, the rear stacked with crates, sacks, and barrels. Ellen could not tell how deep it went, since light from the open door did not penetrate the full depth. The gang were clearly making use of the cold underground for food storage.

Two Knives entered the cave after Ellen. They dragged her another few meters, to where a two-meter length of chain and manacle had been bolted to the solid rock wall. Obviously, she was not the Butcher's first unwilling guest. One woman snapped the manacle around Ellen's ankle and gave a tug on the chain as if wanting to prove that it was firmly attached. The other stood back, studying Ellen with an unsettling intensity. The Knives then left. After the door closed came the sound of a bolt sliding into place and then that of the two women laughing as they walked away.

Slowly, Ellen's eyes adjusted to the darkness. She sat with her back leaning against the cold rock wall and tried to rest. Her legs were rubbery although they had partly recovered from being forced to run for kilometers. Her arms felt as if they had been wrenched from their sockets. The stinging on her feet could only be from broken blisters, and she had already acquired a selection of bruises. Yet things were likely to soon get a lot worse.

One thing alone gave her hope. The Butcher's base was exactly where Chris and Ash O'Neil had worked out. At that very moment, eight squadrons of Rangers were on their way, and Ellen was sure they would arrive precisely when they were due, without mistakes. In another four days, they would have surrounded the base.

Ellen just had to pray she would be able to stay alive for four more days.

Chapter Fifteen—Love and Hate

The door opened, allowing afternoon sunshine to flood in. Ellen felt her guts clench, even as her eyes watered at the light. She had no illusions that what was about to happen would be pleasant. The Butcher had said she wanted to have a chat, using her own way of asking questions. The sort of techniques that the Butcher's way would involve were not in much doubt.

Hal's attempts to get information had failed. The bitterness of that thought was enough to drive away Ellen's fear. While she had been falling in love, Hal had been playing her for a fool. The water in Ellen's eyes was no longer just a reaction to the sunlight. Had she really meant nothing to Hal? Just how gullible a fool had she been?

Ellen ducked her head, blinking rapidly to clear the tears. She did not want the Butcher to think she was already crying with fright. However, when she looked up, she saw that it was two Knives who had entered the cave. They used a pronged spike to remove the manacle from her ankle and then hoisted her to her feet.

Outside, over twenty women were gathered by the corral, forming a loose horseshoe around the tree that the group with the flagon had been sitting under earlier. Was this everyone at the base, or were there more? The poses were casual, some even perched on the corral fence, Hal among them, laughing with the woman who sat beside her. The mood among the crowd was expectant and lighthearted, as if they were awaiting some entertainment. Panic rose in Ellen's throat as she realized that this was indeed the case, and the entertainment was to be her.

Ellen's escort stopped beneath the tree. One tied a new length of rope to the binding at her wrists and then tossed the end over a thick branch, a meter or so above their heads. Together, the pair hauled on the rope until Ellen's arms were stretched so high that her heels were barely in contact with the ground. Ellen clenched her teeth at the pain flaring in her already strained shoulder joints. After tying the rope off on a protruding root, the two Knives then went to join their friends.

"She's ready for you, Boss."

The Butcher waved her hand to acknowledge the call from her subordinates, but was clearly in no hurry. She was in the same group as Hal, standing in front of her, joining in with the happy banter.

Ellen studied the assembled faces. Most looked her way from time to time with expressions ranging from contempt to amusement. Others were staring at her with undisguised eagerness. The only one who never once glanced in her direction was Hal.

Eventually, the Butcher turned and slowly strolled toward Ellen. Around the circle, the buzz of conversation faded as the gang leader stopped a meter away from Ellen, hands on hips. And at last, over the Butcher's shoulder, Ellen saw Hal's face turn her way. Yet still Hal did not meet her eyes. Hal's gaze drifted through her, as if she were not there, caught briefly on her bound hands over her head, and then rose higher into the branches of the tree. Why would Hal not look at her?

Pain exploded in Ellen's left knee. The resultant jerk fired fresh darts into her shoulders. The Butcher had kicked her. When Ellen had recovered enough to open her eyes, the Butcher treated her to a broad, cheery smile.

"I know you enjoy looking at my cousin. But for just now, I'd like some of your attention."

Ellen knew that if she tried to speak, she would only whimper.

"We paid Terrie Rasheed far more than she was worth to let us know what was going on in town, as well as her doing a few other favors for us. Unfortunately, she didn't know much. Partly because she's shit stupid and partly because the Rangers only let you in on their plans, and you wouldn't tell her anything. But you're going to tell me, aren't you?"

"I don't know—"

"Don't be stupid. You know lots. We know that you do." The Butcher walked to the tree trunk and picked up a wooden rod that had been leaning against it, over a meter long and two centimeters in diameter. She came back to Ellen, swinging the rod back and forth so it hissed through the air. She grinned again. "Let me give your memory a prod."

The Butcher stepped back and then whipped the rod across, harder and faster than before. It struck Ellen's stomach in a searing line, cutting her with white-hot agony. The material of her shirt was no protection. Ellen screamed. Whoops and cheers came from the onlookers.

The Butcher walked around her, striking repeatedly. Ellen spun and twisted on the rope, but shielding herself would be impossible, even were her hands free. The Butcher showed no sign of picking any particular target, and let the rod land where it would, like a housekeeper, beating the dust from a carpet. One blow struck the back of Ellen's thighs. Another hit at head height, cutting her cheek. Had her arms not taken the main force of the strike, it would have split her face wide open. No part of Ellen escaped.

When the barrage eventually stopped, Ellen was crying, high-pitched squeals issuing from the back of her throat. Her body was on fire. Blood was trickling down her face and under her clothes. Her heartbeat pounded in her ears, but not enough to drown out the excited comments from the Knives.

"Hey, Boss. If your arm gets tired, I'll take over." Ellen recognized Ade Eriksen's voice.

The Butcher laughed and shouted back. "Thanks, but I'm doing fine so far. I can do with the exercise." She grabbed a fistful of the black Militia shirt and swung Ellen around to face her. "Now you know I'm not playing. So let's be hearing some answers. What are the Rangers' plans?"

Summoning all her will power, Ellen clamped her jaw shut.

"Oh well, if that's what you want. Like I said to Ade, my arm isn't even beginning to get tired." The rod fell again on Ellen's side and then above her knees. A dozen more blows followed.

"No...I'll tell you...I'll..." Ellen screamed between sobs. She could take no more.

The beating ceased. "Okay. Talk."

The Butcher's face was no more than twenty centimeters away. Ellen could see the wrinkling of fine lines around her eyes that ought to have denoted humor, but the coldness in the Butcher's eyes spoke of nothing but malice.

"The Rangers, they've gathered a force to come and get you."

"How many?"

"Eight squadrons."

The lines around the Butcher's eyes deepened. "Do you think I'm stupid? How'd they know where to find me, huh? They wouldn't drag that many women out here on the off chance. And I'd know about it if they did. Eight squadrons is way too many women to hide. You think you can scare me, making up big numbers? There's no way they've put that big a force together." The Butcher stepped away and drew back her arm.

"Only four squadrons." Ellen was swamped in panic. She saw the rod raised. "Just two." The air hissed as the rod sliced through.

By the time that the blows again stopped, Ellen's world contained nothing but pain and the Butcher's face, filled with confidence and cruelty.

"Right. We'll try again. What are the Rangers' plans?"

Ellen kept her eyes locked on the Butcher's. What did the gang leader want to hear? What would she accept as true? The cynical words of the Eastford Militia captain surfaced in Ellen's mind. *That's why she tried to wipe out a whole squadron. So the Rangers would be too frightened to dare stand up to her again. She's going to be so surprised when she finds out it hasn't worked.*

"The Rangers, they're frightened of you."

The lines around the Butcher's eyes softened. "And?"

"They won't attack you again out here. They can't afford to lose more women."

"Go on. What are they going to do?"

"They're waiting for you to go back to Eastford."

The lines deepened momentarily and then eased. "What about the Rangers stationed in Roadsend?"

"That's just two patrols. Their job is to try to make things awkward for you, like stopping the *Susie-Louise*, but they aren't supposed to take risks. They want you to go back to Eastford."

"And when I go back? How are they going to catch me in Eastford? I own the town. Will the Rangers follow me in?"

"The Militia." The lines hardened immediately, but fear was driving Ellen's mind at double speed. Before the Butcher could say anything, she went on. "They wanted them to do the dirty work, but the Militia are even more scared of you than the Rangers are. They're going to use the Temple Guard."

"The Guards?" The Butcher looked surprised, but the wrinkling at the eyes had again faded. "Are you sure?"

"HQ reckon you can't bribe the Guards and they're so sure their souls are going straight to Celaeno, they ain't afraid of dying."

"Everyone went along with this?"

"I'm just a Militia patrolwoman; they didn't include me in the briefings."

"Go on, make a guess."

The Butcher swung the rod so it hissed. Even though it did not land, Ellen flinched. She scoured her memory, searching for something that would make the Butcher believe her. The Eastford Militia captain claimed that the town mayor was working for the Butcher. Was it true?

"I think, somebody…the town mayor"—Ellen fought with her memory—"Mayor Richards. She tried to keep the Guards out of it. But she got overruled. Twenty-one Rangers dead. That was enough to swing the decision, and the mayor didn't have any jurisdiction over the Rangers or the Guards. I'm not sure, but from what I heard, maybe there was something like that going on."

The Butcher's expression changed to a scowl, but the lines did not return. "And maybe, I should have thought of that."

Unlike all her previous words, which had been delivered loudly enough for the audience to hear, the last line was spoken in an undertone. The Butcher's gaze traveled slowly over Ellen, from head to foot, and then her self-satisfied smile reappeared. She tossed the rod aside and reached to the sheath on her belt for a long knife.

The memory of the Rangers at the ford, with their throats slit, tried to force its way into Ellen's head, but she hurt too much to care. However, instead of her throat, the Butcher sawed through the rope above the tree root. Ellen fell to the ground hard, causing all her injuries to explode in renewed fury.

The Butcher turned away, again raising her voice. "Take her back to the cave. I might have more questions for her tomorrow. And I think she's pissed herself. Dunk her in the river for a good rinse off first." She strolled away, still talking loudly. "You see, Hal? I told you my way worked better."

"Yeah. But mine was more fun." Laughter greeted Hal's words.

Ade again piped up. "Hey. Why don't you give us a demonstration of your way so we can make a comparison?"

"I'd love to. But I'm not sure I'd get the necessary cooperation."

Ellen's face was pressed into the ground. Sobs racked her, filling her mouth with dirt to add to the sour tastes of blood and bile. Surely the pain ought to leave her immune to the sound of Hal's voice. She hurt everywhere. She hurt so much she wanted to die. Ellen knew it was pathetically stupid for Hal's words to matter to her, but they did.

❖

Ellen was so hungry that the breakfast of stale bread and lukewarm porridge was more than welcome, and apart from filling her stomach, it gave hope that the Butcher was intending to keep her alive for a while longer. Sunlight was falling directly on the outside of the cave, and glowing through cracks in the wooden wall. The time must be an hour after sunrise. She had survived a whole day in the Butcher's hands. In just three more, the Rangers would be there.

Unsurprisingly, she had not slept well. Even through her clothes, the rod had drawn blood and the nighttime chill had stiffened her injuries. Now, her whole body was drained and sore. However, she was alive, and had sustained no damage that would not heal—except for the scars on her soul.

The sound of the bolt being drawn back made Ellen recoil. Of course, those three days might be an unbearably long time. Had the Butcher thought of more questions? Or was it merely someone come to collect the empty porridge bowl?

Two women entered, which was one more than necessary for the bowl. The removal of the manacle from her ankle confirmed Ellen's fears, but she resisted the urge to fight as she was taken from the cave. It would achieve nothing, other than to let them know how scared she was.

No audience was gathered around the tree. Ellen's initial surge of relief was immediately swamped by the realization this could only mean she was being taken to another venue, with unknown potential for inflicting pain. The one thing she could be sure of was that nothing good would happen to her there.

Ellen's escort led her into the largest of the buildings, the one facing the corral. This was obviously the Butcher's residence, and despite the rough construction, the large room was filled with surprising luxury for the wilderness. Sheepskin rugs covered most of the earthen floor and the furnishings were clearly expensive. Books, a guitar, and a flute were displayed haphazardly on an ornate dresser, but judging by the smell of stale beer, drinking was the primary form of entertainment.

The Butcher was waiting, sitting on a bench, with her arms draped along the edge of a table that was serving her as a backrest. Three other women were present, Hal and Ade among them. Ellen tried not to look at Hal—tried not to think about her.

Ellen was brought to a stop in front of the Butcher, and then a kick on her calf sent her crashing to her knees.

The Butcher smiled at her. "Good morning."

Ellen said nothing. The Butcher nodded to one of the escort and a hefty blow landed on the side of Ellen's head.

The Butcher waited until Ellen had regained her balance. "When I say 'good morning' to you, you say 'good morning, ma'am' back. Shall we try again? Good morning."

Three days. The words pounded in Ellen's head. "Good morning, ma'am."

"Much better." The Butcher's smile broadened. "You know, I don't like Militiawomen. While you were getting naked with my cousin, you must have seen the little reminders your pals left on her back. I've got a matching collection. In fact, I've got a much bigger collection, because I was a lot more unlucky than her. I can't begin to tell you how much I enjoyed paying some of them back yesterday. I'm tempted to do it all over again today, just for the fun of it." She sighed, mimicking deep thought. "Alternately, I wonder if this place would be brightened up by a hunting trophy. Your head, mounted up there over the fireplace. What do you think?"

Three days. "I don't know, ma'am."

"You do learn quick. I'll say that for you. But just how amenable are you?" The Butcher laughed. "Oh look. There's a dirty patch, there on the toe of my right boot. Lick it clean for me."

Ellen closed her eyes. *Three days. Three days. Three days.*

Ignoring complaints from her injuries, Ellen shuffled forward on her knees, then braced her bound hands on the ground and lowered her head. No patch on the Butcher's boots was any dirtier than another. It was a game, a test to see how far she could be pushed. Laughter rolled around the room. Ellen squeezed her eyes so tightly shut they hurt—to hold back the tears of shame, and because she could not shut her ears. She did not want to pick Hal's laughter out from the rest.

She extended her tongue until it made contact with shoe leather. The texture of grit and the taste of filth made Ellen's stomach twist no worse than did the whoops and ironic cheers from the watchers. She fought back a sob. How enthusiastic an effort would the Butcher want to see? But then, before Ellen could react, the Butcher's foot jerked sharply, back and then up, kicking her in the face. The laughter intensified. Ellen sat back, tasting blood from a split lip. *Three days.* Was it worth it? She stared at the ground.

The Butcher spoke. "So, Hal. What should we do with her? Does she have any uses?"

"She's a good fuck. But like I said yesterday, I doubt she'd be very cooperative right now."

"I don't know. Just look at how nice and clean my boot is."

More laughter.

The Butcher continued. "But I'm thinking, a nice ornament above the mantelpiece there, or even by the door, so I could hang my hat on it when I come in. Come on, Hal, what do you think? Should I cut her head off?"

"It's up to you, Maddy." Hal's tone was relaxed, but Ellen sensed the undercurrents. Some sort of contest was taking place between the cousins. Ellen did not miss that Hal was the first person she had heard address the Butcher by name, rather than the deferential "Boss."

"She was very informative yesterday, and you never know, I might think of some more questions for her. I was right, wasn't I, that we should bring her along for a chat. Lucky for us she didn't shoot off when you gave her the chance."

"Yeah. You were right. I was wrong."

"I'm pleased to hear you say that." The Butcher's tone eased. The concession was clearly what she had wanted. She clapped her hands together. "I know what. Mac was telling me the latrine needs digging out, and she hasn't been able to get anyone to volunteer." She reached out with her boot and tapped Ellen. "Hey, Blackshirt. You'd like to volunteer to dig out the latrine, wouldn't you?"

Ellen looked up. *Three days.* "Yes, ma'am."

"We'll have someone keeping an eye on you, but I know you're not going to get any silly ideas about running off. Because, your parents, it must be so hard when one is an invalid. It would be awful if anything happened to your birth mother, when she was walking home alone from the Docks. You do understand me, don't you?"

"Yes, ma'am."

The Butcher raised both hands in a dual-fisted gesture of triumph. "Great. Tell Mac we've got a volunteer for her."

❖

The cave was in utter darkness. From the homestead came the sound of shouting and laughter. The gang were clearly spending another drunken evening. On the basis of yesterday's experience, it would continue well into the night. Further away were the intermittent bleating of sheep and the cry of a hunting bird.

Ellen shifted around, in a pointless attempt to get comfortable. Not only was her body aching and sore, both from the beating and the day's hard labor, but the ground was hard, lumpy, and cold, and she had not even a blanket for warmth. Her hands had been untied while she worked, but were now bound again. She had been allowed to wash thoroughly at the end of the day—a request Ellen suspected had been granted solely because she was being held in the food store rather than for any concern over her welfare. However, her clothes were still damp and the temperature was dropping.

Ellen curled herself into a ball. The position was no more excruciating than any other, and it might conserve her body heat. If she could just get through the night, she would have made it to the halfway point. Two more days and the Rangers would arrive.

The soft rasp of metal on metal cut beneath the distant ruckus. Someone was drawing back the bolt on the door. Ellen turned her head at the sound. Lamplight danced through cracks in the wood and then the door opened. The beams struck Ellen full in the face, dazzling after the darkness, so she could see nothing. She raised her hands to shield her eyes, desperate to know who had come, and why. The door shut with a dull rattle. Squinting against the light, Ellen was able to make out the outline of a single person, standing over her. The figure hung the lantern from a hook on the roof, illuminating both the cave and herself.

Hal adjusted the wick, and turned to face Ellen. "I couldn't get to see you earlier. Maddy's been keeping an eye on me. So—how you doing?"

Ellen struggled into a sitting position. "Guess."

"You should have run when I gave you the chance."

"Easy with hindsight."

"That goes for everything in life. I wish I…" Hal's face looked as if she was trying for a carefree grin, and failing. She shrugged. "Wishing is also pretty pointless." Her voice had softened to an undertone.

"Tell me about it."

Hal knelt beside Ellen and softly ran her thumb over the cut on Ellen's cheek. "It'll mend."

Ellen pulled her face away and hunched her head down, but she could not stop her thoughts seething in turmoil. Although there had been tenderness in Hal's voice, how could she put any trust in it? Yet Ellen's heart tempted her to pretend the previous two days had not happened, to put her head on Hal's shoulder and take what comfort she could. Ellen was appalled at her own weakness. Tears burned her eyes. *I'm not going to cry. I'm not.*

Hal was not put off. She stroked the hair back off Ellen's face. "It's your own fault. You should never have trusted me."

Ellen scrunched her eyes shut, fighting to stay in control of herself, but it was so hard. She remembered the "nice and nasty" game the Militia played with prisoners they were questioning. One officer would be stridently aggressive, threatening violence. Another would play the part of the prisoner's friend, restraining her colleague.

Ellen had always been surprised at how the prisoners fell for it. Surely they had to know it was all a game. But now she understood. The desperate need to have someone on your side overwhelmed all common sense. Alone, vulnerable, powerless, and frightened, how could anyone turn down an offer of friendship, even when knowing it was a sham?

Ellen summoned her anger as a defense. She looked up, meeting Hal's eyes. "Damn right I shouldn't have trusted you. But you had your tricks all worked out. How did you manage to get the documents showing that you were Cassie Drennen's niece? What's your true name?"

"You were behind the Town Hall summons? I did wonder."

"Who are you?"

"I really am Ahalya Drennen. And Cassie Drennen really is my great-aunt. She was the...I don't know about white, but maybe the dingy cream sheep of the family. She didn't hold with the thieving and fighting the rest of us got up to, so she ran out on us and went off to become an honest farmer."

"Your whole family are thieves?"

"Only the clever ones. The rest just get drunk and hit people."

"And the Butcher is your cousin?"

"My gene mother and her birth mother are sisters."

"Cassie Drennen's been at Broken Hills for decades."

"Yes. She was gone years before I was born." Hal sat back, looking wistful. "I think she's the first of us who's tried to go straight in seven generations. And look where it's got her."

"Old age catches everyone."

"True, but Cassie brought it partly on herself." At Ellen's questioning look, Hal went on. "We knew the name of her farm, because she wrote to Grandma once or twice, but there's been no other contact. Then Ade joined us in Eastford. She was the one with the plan for stealing sheep, and Maddy had been thinking about getting an out-of-town hideaway. Then we remembered Aunt Cassie's farm, and the ideas sort of came together. It seemed perfect. We went to see her, offered her a fair cut—I mean, she ran out on us, but she's still family. She said no." Hal shrugged. "So Maddy kicked her around a bit. And she hasn't been the same since."

"The state she's in, it's due to a head injury you gave her?"

"It wasn't intended."

"You didn't think of taking her to a healer?"

"Be sensible. What could we say? We've just hit our aunt over the head. Can you sort her out? It wasn't as if she'd been all there to start with."

"You're proud of yourself? Beating up old women?"

"I've done worse. I'll do whatever I have to, for the sake of the family. Back in Monday Market, if your name's Drennen, you don't get a chance. Nobody would give any of us an honest job, even if we wanted one. If we tried playing by their rules, we'd starve. So we play by our rules."

"Your aunt went straight."

"How do you think she got the money to buy the farm in the first place?" Hal paused. "But no, I'm not proud of all the things I've done, but I'm not apologizing for them either. I'll never disown my family." Hal's voice was softly serious. "Like I said, you shouldn't have trusted me."

"Because you've been playing with me. That's all it's been from the start, isn't it? An act, trying to get information out of me."

"No. Not at the very start."

"What was it, then?"

"It was all due to Terrie Rasheed. The woman's nothing but a damned liability."

"What did—" Ellen broke off, ducking her head. Did she really want to know the answers? What chance was there that they would make her feel any better? "Forget it."

However, Hal was clearly in the mood to talk. "The day you first came to Broken Hills. Rasheed had warned us you were both coming, so we had all the paperwork in order and sorted. She was supposed to get you adding up the numbers. But the stupid bitch said she'd check the receipts, and told you to go outside and look around. She didn't trust our papers." Hal grimaced. "They were fine but we had fifty stolen sheep out the back. As soon as you were out of the room, I told Rasheed just what I thought of her and dashed after you. I sent Jo off with the dogs to round up the sheep we didn't want you to see, while I tried to distract you as much as I could. Flirting was an easy call."

Bitterness washed over Ellen. She looked up angrily. "You were so sure I'd fall for you?"

"It didn't matter, either way. There aren't many things as distracting as being hit on by someone you don't want, who won't believe you mean it when you tell her to piss off." Hal met Ellen's eyes, her expression softer. "But I must admit, I was pleased when you didn't tell me to piss off. Believe it or not, I honestly find you very attractive. It may have started as an act, but it didn't stay that way. I really have come to…" Hal turned her face away, clearly struggling with an emotion that Ellen did not want to recognize.

Ellen dropped her head and closed her eyes, trying to shut everything out. *She's lying. Don't trust her. It's a trick. She's lying.* The words pounded through Ellen's head, but without force. Regardless of whether they were true, she did not want to believe them.

After several seconds, Hal spoke again, sounding more focused. "And if I carry on like this, it will just lead me to another set of pointless wishes. So…the reason I'm here."

The palm of Hal's hand pressed against Ellen's forehead, raising her face. Ellen kept her eyes shut, refusing to meet Hal's gaze, but then she felt a change run though her. The pain from her injuries eased. The cold and bone-deep aching left her muscles. Not a complete cure, but still a real improvement in her condition. In surprise, Ellen opened her eyes, but Hal's eyelids were closed. She was clearly in the light trance of someone using the healer sense.

Despite all resolve, Ellen could not stop herself from studying Hal's face, recalling other times, watching Hal sleep. Ellen's breath shortened and her heart began to hammer. She was confused, bewildered, repulsed. How could Hal still affect her like this? When at last Hal opened her eyes, Ellen could not bring herself to look away. The seconds drew out as their eye contact intensified.

At first, Hal looked a little surprised, but then she smiled. Her hand slid over Ellen's head, to the back of her neck. Gently Hal pulled Ellen forward and placed a kiss on her lips, softly, slowly, yet with a force to turn Ellen's stomach upside down. Ellen tried not to respond, but Hal's kiss felt so good. The caress of Hal's lips was soft and firm and necessary for Ellen's existence. Her mouth opened involuntarily, molding against Hal's, doing what it was supposed to. Her tongue slid against Hal's in an intimate dance as a wave of desire swallowed her. Ellen closed her eyes, savoring the contact, the taste and texture of Hal.

Abruptly, awareness returned to Ellen, where she was, who Hal was, and all the reasons why she should not be doing what she was. She thrust out her bound hands, punching Hal in the chest and knocking her away.

"No."

Hal landed back awkwardly on an elbow. The lamplight fell on her face, showing her expression, first of confusion and then of hurt, quickly covered, but the brief glimpse was enough. Ellen felt her anger vanish.

"Hal. I'm sorry."

Hal gave a wry smile. "You don't have to apologize. Most people would say you were quite justified in wanting to kill me."

"I don't want t…" Ellen shook her head, trying to clear her thoughts.

Hal shifted around, getting back onto her knees beside Ellen. "So what do you want?"

"I…I'm an officer of the law. It's my duty." Ellen tried to hang on to the thought, but the emotions churning inside her washed away any meaning.

"I didn't ask about your job." Hal's hand cupped the side of Ellen's face and then her lips returned, brushing Ellen's forehead, in a soft, sisterly kiss. "I asked about you."

Ellen knew she should say something, but she could not command her voice. She ought to pull away and rebuff Hal's advance, but was it so bad to simply sit still? For now, she was not hurting, was not frightened, was not alone. How could she forego the comfort Hal offered? Why should she?

Hal's mouth traveled down Ellen's cheek, burrowing into her neck. Hal's tongue traced the rim of Ellen's ear. Teeth scraped lightly on Ellen's earlobe. Then Ellen felt Hal's hand at the top button of her shirt, slipping it free. The next three buttons followed. Ellen's eyes closed—in either desire or denial; she could not tell. Her shirt fell open.

Hal's breath caught. A half gasp in a moment of silence. "Oh, she has made a right mess of you."

Hal placed her forefinger on the end of a long cut and very lightly traced its length. Ellen clenched her teeth to hold back the groan. Her body was melting under Hal's touch, the same way that it always did, as if nothing else mattered. As if her oath to uphold the law did not matter. As if every lie Hal had spoken did not matter. As if tomorrow and the world waiting outside the cave did not matter. Yet it did matter. Ellen's conscience called to her, but softly and from far away.

"Hal, don't." However, Ellen lacked any will to back up her words.

Hal's hands slid around her waist.

"Please."

"You always say that word so beautifully."

Hal's lips returned to Ellen's neck, sucking softly.

"Please, Hal. Stop." But Ellen could hear her own voice was weak, without force.

The mouth and hands went. Ellen opened her eyes. Hal was sat back, watching her.

"You want me to stop?"

It took five seconds for Ellen to find the strength of will to say "Yes."

"I tell you what. You ask me to stop one more time and I promise I will."

Without taking her eyes off Ellen, Hal reached out and fanned her fingers out over Ellen's stomach.

Ellen closed her eyes. She would allow herself this one last brief moment, to savor in her memory and strengthen her for the days ahead. Just a few seconds to say good-bye to the dreams of a future with Hal. *I'm going to count to three and tell her to stop. One. Two...*

Hal's hand slipped beneath Ellen's open shirt and skimmed up her right side, a feather-light touch that seemed to ignite her skin.

I'm going to count to three and tell her to stop. One...

Hal's hand moved on, tacking a grip behind Ellen's back, then Hal's lips touched her collarbone. Her tongue drew patterns on Ellen's skin.

I'm going to count to five and tell her to stop.

Hal's mouth traveled slowly down until reaching her breast.

I'm going to count...

All thought was lost. Ellen's soul was gripped by the rapture of Hal making love to her, touching her so tenderly that the cuts and bruises existed only as areas of heightened sensitivity. After so much pain, Ellen had forgotten how good her body could feel. After all the fear, she needed Hal to make her feel safe and cared for. Hal's touch made everything all right.

Ellen was aware of Hal's hands at her waist, tugging at the material. She braced her feet on the floor to raise her hips, so that Hal could ease her trousers down.

"Untie my hands. I won't fight you."

"You're fine as you are."

The manacle prevented Ellen's trousers from being removed, but once they were low enough, Hal pressed her knees apart, and then stroked the inside of her legs. Ellen's back arched, heedless of damaged muscles and torn skin. The passion consuming her could no longer tell pain from pleasure. There was no difference.

"Do you want me inside you?"

"Yes."

Hal entered Ellen, claiming her more softly, yet more completely than ever before. The slow rhythm carried Ellen over the edge. She climaxed in a maelstrom of ecstasy, pulsing around the fullness of Hal's hand. The world turned around, and then fell back into place.

Ellen opened her eyes and stared at the lantern, while reality again took over her life. She was sitting on the floor of a cave, chained to the wall, with her trousers around her ankles and the fingers of a self-confessed thief and thug inside her. And she had wanted it. She had given herself to someone who had only ever used, deceived, and betrayed her. She had renounced all self-respect for the sake of a quick fuck and it was now far too late to say stop.

Ellen curled forward, as far as her bound hands allowed. She felt her face twist in a grimace. Tears flooded her eyes as the first sob hit her.

"Ellen?"

Hal's fingers withdrew, and then Ellen was enfolded in Hal's arms.

"Ellen, are you okay?"

Ellen could not speak. The sobs wracked her. She was a fool—a thrice damned fool. Words did not exist to express the depth of the contempt she held herself in.

"Ellen, I'm so..." Hal's voice broke off and her arms fell away.

Ellen pressed her hands to her eyes, not in any hope of stemming the tears but to hide her face from the world. She felt Hal make an attempt to pull up her trousers, but Ellen did not to care enough to assist, and they got no higher than her knees. Hal moved away. Ellen heard her rummaging among the goods stored at the rear of the cave, and then a succession of items was placed beside her. Ellen neither knew nor cared what they were.

And then Hal and the lamplight were gone.

❖

Ellen lay awake. The storm of crying had left her exhausted, but she could not sleep. Her thoughts would not let her. The revelry at the homestead had ended long ago; even the sheep were quiet. Soon it would be dawn. Ellen remembered waking up, two days before, in Hal's bed. She remembered being happy. Why could her life not have ended then?

She hated Hal, but not as much as she hated herself for not hating Hal enough to wipe out all other emotions. The logic made an impossible, hopeless loop.

Hal had left her with a three-quarters-empty sack of grain as a pillow and two cloaks to use as blankets. Even with her bound hands, she had been able to sort out her clothing. Physically, she was better provided for than she had been before, but her head and heart were in hell.

In two more days, the Rangers would arrive. A battle would ensue. Some of the Knives would be killed. The rest would be taken as prisoners back to Roadsend, tried, and then hanged. No other outcome was possible.

One way or another, within a few days, Hal would be dead. Ellen could only hope that she was as well, so she did not have to work her way through the hate and the anger and the pain.

And the love.

Ellen did not know what she wanted to happen. The only thing she knew was what she wanted now. More than anything, Ellen wished that Hal was there, lying beside her.

Chapter Sixteen—Anger and Remorse

Ellen swung the axe one last time and heard a satisfactory crack from the sapling. After a good shoulder thump, the young tree keeled over and fell. Ellen worked her way down it, lopping off branches. More strokes cut the trunk into meter lengths, each with a pointed end.

The work was far more pleasant than yesterday's digging out of the latrine, and Ellen's body did not feel so stiff. The touch of Hal's hands had bestowed some lasting good, either through the healer sense or from her lovemaking. Ellen clenched her jaw, willing herself not to toy with the memory and rerun each moment through her head. Bad enough that she had let herself be so easily seduced at the time. Nothing good could come of continuing to stir up the emotions. All it could lead to was more misery and pain.

Ellen picked up the stakes. She walked the dozen meters back to the fence and tossed them over, to join the pile on the other side. The longer, springy branches followed. Ellen considered the patches in the fence that needed reinforcement, and then the amount of material she had assembled for the task. It looked about right.

The gang used the smaller offshoot canyon as a large sheep paddock. Ellen guessed the floor had been cleared by burning, to allow grass to grow, and then the canyon sealed at two points, about a kilometer apart. Where Ellen stood, outside the upper wickerwork fence, the original covering of vegetation remained, a dense lacework of spindly saplings, taller, mature trees, and matted undergrowth. On the other side, the rich green of the grass was broken only by a shallow river running through, and a fair number of sheep. The upper fence had been constructed at a point where the canyon narrowed to fifty meters or so. At the Butcher's suggestion, Ellen had volunteered to repair it.

Ellen went to collect the axe, then came back and threw it over by the pile of prepared wood. Negotiating the fence herself was a touch more tricky. The wickerwork was not strong enough to safely take her weight for climbing, and even with the improvement in her condition, she still felt too stiff to be capable of jumping it. Instead, Ellen leaned over the fence, grabbed a firm branch near the bottom and then flipped her legs over. She landed in an ungraceful heap, wincing as pain flared from her cuts and bruises.

A snort of laughter came from the two Knives who were keeping an eye on her. They sat on a rocky protrusion from the canyon wall, three meters high, with a good view of where Ellen was working. One had a strung bow, with an arrow nocked on the string. The other was Ade Eriksen.

Ade jumped down and walked to within ten meters of Ellen. "Throw the axe over here. I don't want you getting any funny ideas about it."

Ellen did as she was told, moving slowly and deliberately. She did not want to give the archer a reason to shoot, or Ade an excuse to demonstrate her fondness for violence. The metal head thudded onto the ground a meter from Ade's feet. The wooden handle bounced once and then fell flat.

Ade in turn tossed the axe toward where her companion was sitting, but rather than return to her perch, Ade wandered closer to Ellen, and stood, arms folded. For a while she watched in silence as Ellen used a flat stone to hammer the stakes into the ground.

"You were there when they killed Trish, weren't you?"

Ellen glanced around. Denying it would be pointless. "Yes."

"Which one of the bitches was it?"

"I'm not sure."

Ade got closer still, and her voice dropped. "You better try and remember. The Boss likes me. I'm sure, as a favor, she'll let me have another go at you with her little stick."

Ellen stopped hammering and closed her eyes, trying to recall the scene. "It was one of the corporals. I think her name was Wade, Waheed, something like that."

"Wadden?"

"Yes."

"That's what the other bitch said."

"Who?"

"The Ranger. Just before I slit her throat."

"You took part in the massacre?"

"Massacre? It was a battle and we won."

"And cutting their throats afterward? What was that?"

"That was teaching the Rangers a lesson. If you're not careful, you'll be learning a lesson or two as well."

Ellen returned to hammering the stakes.

Ade had not finished. "I so wanted to make the bitch who killed Trish pay for it, but she was already dead when I got to her. But I got a good laugh from some of the others. Have you ever heard a Ranger wail and cry like a baby? A bit like you the other day, when the Boss was working you over. I did enjoy the look in their eyes when I pulled the knife across their throats and they realized they were finished."

The gloating in Ade's voice made Ellen feel sick. "Did you enjoy killing the barge skipper as well?"

"Nah. That was just a job."

"Why did you do it?"

"Because Yuan was a spineless sap. That's why I was on the barge to start with. The Boss was worried she was going to jump ship. If the Rangers had captured her, she'd have spilled her guts to them in an instant."

"Was that why you tried to kill Terrie Rasheed as well?"

"I wasn't trying to kill her. I mean, I wish I had now, but I was just adding a bit of authenticity to her story. Admit it, you fell for the knife in the shoulder bit, didn't you?"

"You planned it between you?"

Ade sniggered. "Not quite. I planned it and told her why afterward. I mean, I was doing it as favor. But I knew a coward like her wouldn't have seen the sense in it." Ade sighed. "I wish I knew where she was now, because I'd love to go and finish the job."

"You'd kill her just for the fun of it?"

"Not just fun. Terrie's another spineless jerk who'll spill her guts at the first push. She don't know much, but she'll tell all if your friends catch her. I thought about killing her on the barge, but I reckoned if I stabbed her you'd go easy on the questions, and I knew you didn't suspect her, else you wouldn't have given her the chance to warn us you were waiting." Ade laughed. "Goddess! Outplayed by Terrie shit-for-brains Rasheed. How stupid can you get?"

Ellen said nothing as she bent to pick up another stake. To be fair, for once she was in complete agreement with Ade.

"Terrie came on board and told us we had trouble. She hadn't worked out what was going on, but if you were interested in the *Susie-Louise*, then the Rangers would be too, so they had to be around somewhere. Terrie was mainly concerned with covering her own ass, so she'd brought a selection of old receipts from the office with her. She wanted to make it look like Yuan had some forgeries to hand over. We picked a couple of receipts that best matched what we had on board and changed the date and things. I told Yuan to put them in her breast pocket, and then I stabbed her through it. She looked so surprised. I hadn't explained that bit of my plan to her—her blood masking the changes."

"Does the Butcher appreciate you making plans like that for her workers?"

"You know, I think she does." Ade grinned. "For sure when it comes to jerks like Yuan and Terrie. The Boss knows she can trust me, and I can think on my feet. I worked it all out in seconds. I told Terrie what she had to say to you as I left the cabin. Then I dived into the river, swam under the barge, and came up in the gap between the boat and the wall where I couldn't be seen. I stayed there until it was dark. It was fucking freezing, but I wasn't going to let the Rangers use me for target practice, like they did with Kelly. I saw them fish the poor jerk out."

"Was she a Knife as well?"

"Nah. Both the crew were dock trash we picked up at Eastford. They'd worked for us a few times, but mainly they were a pair of mules who knew not to ask questions. I don't know why Kelly jumped in, but then, the dumb jerk always was trying to copy me."

The stakes were all in place for the first section of the fence in need of repair. Ellen knelt down and started on the thin branches, weaving them between the supports. Despite her attempt to appear calm, her thoughts seethed, running through what Ade had said. Outplayed by Terrie Rasheed. *Stupid* was far too mild a word to describe it.

"The barge skipper didn't start with any forged documents?" Ellen asked.

"Not one."

"So it wasn't just luck that Terrie was the Militiawoman on duty? The plan had been for her to let you by without any paperwork at all."

"Yup. The same as it always had been."

"Always? You'd done it before?"

"You were totally suckered by Hal's game with the rowboat, weren't you?"

Ellen dropped the branch she was holding and pressed her hands over her eyes. *Stupid* was positively flattering.

Ade continued. "We always moved the sheep the same way. We took them from here down to Broken Hills Ranch. The *Susie-Louise* moored at Roadsend, until the day before Rasheed was due to be on late shift at the docks, then it would go to the Broken Hills jetty, pick up the sheep, and come back when Terrie was there to wave it through. It was all my plan. I sold it to the Boss."

"You knew Terrie would go along with it?"

"She's been taking bribes from my family for years."

Ellen picked up the dropped branch and kept weaving.

Ade watched her for a while. "The thing with the rowboat was Hal's idea. You were sniffing around, and you weren't telling her nothing. She came up with the plan, thinking it would do two things at once. It'd send you off on the wrong track so you'd waste your time down in the marches. And if you thought she'd helped you, maybe you'd trust her and let her in on your plans. It didn't go right, though. You were supposed to see the sheep and then the boat was to get away. Instead you jumped in. Sasha brained you, and she'd have put the end of the oar through your face if Hal hadn't stopped her. I heard all about it."

Ellen tried to concentrate on her work. Thinking about how gullible she had been could be left until later.

"Hal's plan failed all the way. You found out about the *Susie-Louise*, and you still didn't tell her things. Though you did let her fuck you, so maybe it wasn't a complete loss from her point of view." Ade gave a mock sigh of contemplation. "You know, I think sometimes Hal's devotion to work is a bit suspect. I mean, we all like getting laid, but it wasn't the most important thing. Someone should have told her that when people talk about fucking Blackshirts, she didn't need to take it literally. Or maybe she just enjoyed showing you up as a jerk. We had a bit of fun with it as well. Did you know we were running a sweepstake here on how long it'd take her to get into your pants? I didn't win, assuming it really was the first time you let her have you, the night after the *Susie-Louise*—"

"How do you...?" Ellen bit her lip, fighting to control her expression. "Jo?" It would hurt so much more if Hal was the one who had made the game report.

"Yeah, her. Pat and Mac as well. They'd gone to give Hal the news about the *Susie-Louise* being captured. They were in the farmhouse when you rode up. So Hal kept you busy in the yard while they slipped out the back." Ade yelped with laughter. "Though they did stop for a moment to watch her delaying technique. They told us about it. We tried to get them to give a dramatic re-enactment, but they said no. Jo tidied up any sign of Pat and Mac being there, then gave the all clear. She came back here with them to get the full story, while Hal gave you the full works. And you didn't spot a thing, did you?"

The branch in Ellen's hands was fighting her and her vision was getting blurred.

Ade shifted around and leaned against the fence so that she was in a position to see Ellen's face. "Goddess, she had you totally suckered. That's not tears I can see, are they? Are you upset now you know she never truly loved you? You fell for her, didn't you? I can see the scene now. You lying back with your legs wide open"—Ade's voice changed to a high-pitched parody—"Oh Hal! Deeper. Harder. Hal, Hal my darling." She paused. "Or was it the other way? Was Hal the one doing the squealing? I mean, I've never seen her as a squealer, but people can be hard to predict. Don't you find that?"

Ellen dashed her hand across her eyes and took a firmer grip on the branch.

"Though, you know, I think Hal's gone a bit soft recently. I don't think she enjoyed watching the Boss work you over with her little stick. I didn't see her laugh once. Of course, I didn't have my eye on her all the time, because it was much more fun watching you. Maybe Hal had a little snigger when I wasn't looking. But then again...you don't think it's possible that she's gone all mushy over you, do you?" Ade paused and then gave a loud laugh. "What a pair of jerks."

Ellen dug the end of the branch between the supports. She crawled along the fence, pulling the branch through. Ade kept pace with her, slowly shifting her weight from one foot to the other.

"You're not saying much." Ade's tone had lost even the veneer of humor.

"What do you want me to say?"

"Well, for instance…Hal reckoned you were a good fuck. How'd you rate her performance?"

Ellen said nothing. Ade's boot landed sharply on her thigh, knocking her off balance. She looked up.

"I asked you a question."

Ellen swallowed her first reply. "She was okay."

"Just okay?" Ade paused, and then her gaze ran over Ellen, catching at groin and breasts with clear intent. "Well, how would you like a really good fuck?"

"Not at the moment. I'm working."

The second kick from Ade sent Ellen sprawling on her back. "You need to watch your smart-ass mouth." She turned and stalked back to join her companion on the rock.

Ellen looked up at the sky. Afternoon was well advanced. Soon she would be taken back to the cave. She would sleep, and when she woke up there would be just one day left—for her, for Ade, and for Hal.

❖

The sound of the bolt being drawn back made Ellen's heart pound. She pressed the heels of her hands into her eyes, hating herself for wanting Hal to visit her again. However, when the lantern was hung from the hook on the cave roof, the person it revealed was Ade Eriksen. In her right hand, Ade held a long rod, identical to the one the Butcher had used, if not the very same. She tapped it on the cave wall as if she needed to get Ellen's attention.

Ellen scrambled to stand up. A kick knocked her back down.

"Stay where you are." Ade smiled at Ellen and then gestured with the rod, waving the tip in vague circles. "You remember this, don't you?"

Ellen's mouth was so dry she could only nod.

Ade turned around and propped the rod against the wall opposite where Ellen sat, moving with the thoughtful precision of an artist composing a sculpture. "There. I'm going to put it over here, like this, but I don't want you to forget about it." She turned back. "Because I won't. Just in case I don't get what I want."

"What do you want?"

Ade shook her head ruefully. "Have you forgotten my offer so quickly? I'm hurt. Really hurt. Here's a little reminder. You're not working now."

Ellen pressed herself against the cave wall in an instinctive, but pointless urge to back away. "I'm not..."

"Oh, but you are." Ade stood over Ellen. "Don't look so worried. Play along, and all you'll get is a good fucking."

Ellen stared down at her own bound hands. Just one more day. That was all she had to get through.

"Unbutton your shirt."

Ellen did not move. One more day. Surely she could survive even this.

"I said, unbutton your shirt. I want to see what's got Hal so worked up."

Still Ellen did not move, could not move.

Ade sighed, then turned and reached for the rod. "Oh dear. Right. Let's see if I can get some sort of response this way." Ade touched the end of the rod under Ellen's chin, lifting her head so their eyes met. "Unbutton your shirt."

Ellen's hands started to move of their own accord, but then stopped and fell back to her lap. She could not do it, not even to survive.

Ade drew a sharp breath and her face twisted in a snarl. "I'm going to make you scream. One way or another. It's your tough luck that I like both ways."

Ade's boot made contact with Ellen's shoulder, more shove than kick, knocking her flat on the floor. Ellen closed her eyes and clenched her teeth, bracing herself. The rod hissed through the air and landed across her shoulders. Ellen bit back her cry. The blow had been softer than those from the Butcher. A second strike hit her lower, sending pain flaring down her thigh. However, she heard Ade snort in something sounding like frustration, and the sound of Ade's feet as she moved position. Possibly the low cave ceiling restricted the swing and Ade was trying to find a better angle. Then Ellen heard the door open again.

"What the fuck do you think you're doing?" It was Hal's voice.

"I'm—" Ade's voice cut off, clearly surprised. After a few seconds of silence, Ade went on, "Just having a bit of fun."

Ellen squinted through half-open eyelids. She saw Hal storm across the cave, grab the rod in one hand and the front of Ade's shirt in the other and ram Ade back against the wall. "You keep your damned hands off her."

"You don't own her, or me," Ade said, her chin jutting out in defiance.

"Don't count on it."

"You're not that fucking big."

"Shall we go and ask Maddy just how big I am?"

Ade struggled free. "You're in for a surprise someday."

"Keep pushing your luck and you'll find out which of us has the delusions."

"I'm not scared of you."

Hal stood motionless, hands at her side, but her gaze raked up and down Ade's body in contemptuous appraisal. Her voice, when she spoke, was soft but resolute. "You should be. Lay one finger on her again and you're dead."

The two women stood, toe to toe, glaring at each other, but Ade's confidence was visibly slipping. She covered with a scowl of contempt and then barged past Hal. "Ah, keep your fucking slut. Just remember where her tongue's been."

The door slammed.

Hal threw the rod away angrily. She dropped to her knees by Ellen's side and helped her into a sitting position. Her hand ran softly over Ellen's head. "Are you okay? Did she hurt you? I swear, I'll kill her."

Ellen curled forward, into Hal's arms. At that moment nothing else mattered. She needed Hal, and the reassurance of Hal's physical presence. "I'm fine. She'd hardly touched me when you arrived."

"What was it all about?"

"She wanted me to have sex with her."

"I will kill her." Hal's tone suggested that she was not lightly using a figure of speech.

"Hal."

"What?"

"I promise I won't try to escape or anything, but could you untie my hands? I want to hold you."

Hal hesitated for just a second, and then untied the knots at Ellen's wrists. From the rear of the cave, Hal dragged forward a couple of sacks and another cloak, to construct a small nest, and then sat with her back against the wall. Ellen curled up in Hal's arms, her head resting on Hal's shoulder, her arms around Hal's waist. Against all reason, Ellen felt secure and content, her body insisting that it was where it was supposed to be.

Hal tilted her face and kissed Ellen, slowly and very thoroughly, then leaned her head against the wall behind her and sighed. "I'm sorry about Ade. I'm going to have to deal with her. It's time she made a permanent exit from the gang."

"Murdering her would be against the law. But I wouldn't knock myself out trying to stop you."

"Wouldn't you? Because I think something involving a heavy weight and water sounds good." Despite the return of humor to Hal's voice, a serious edge underlay it, and her arms around Ellen tightened.

"You'd kill her for attacking me?"

"Possibly, but it's not just that. She was doing it to get at me, and she's been playing that game for too long. I can't let her get away with it anymore."

"Why do you think she was getting at you?"

"Don't get me wrong. I should think anyone with eyes would want to get you in the sack. But has Ade ever shown an interest before?"

"No. Our relationship's been stuck in the stage of shouting abuse through the lockup door." Ellen nestled her head into the curve of Hal's neck. "Actually, she was talking about you first."

"When?"

"This afternoon, while I was working on the fence. She was trying to wind me up about you. And she said..."

"What?"

"She asked me to rate you in bed and offered to better it."

"Shit." Hal's grip tightened.

"I got the feeling she doesn't like you much."

"It's mutual. She's been trying to undermine me for months. Either hoping it'll make her look better, or because she thinks she can take my place."

The phrase "my place" stuck in Ellen's ears. Did she want to know what place Hal held in the Butcher's gang? Or what crimes she had committed to reach it? No chance that Hal was only peripherally involved, a virtual innocent, who might get off with a few harsh words and a fine from a magistrate. The mere fact that Ade was so eager to take over Hal's role was not a good sign.

"Could she?"

"She doesn't stand a hope in hell. She's not family and she's not smart enough. She's good at scaring people, which is useful, but it doesn't make her anything other than a cheap thug, and we've already got more of them than we need."

"You say *we.*" Ellen closed her eyes, trying not to grimace. "You're totally committed to the Knives?"

"I'm totally committed to my family."

"Your family and the Knives are the same thing?"

"No. Maddy's the one running the show. We follow her, in the gang or out of it."

"You don't have to."

"I do. We're family. When the shit starts coming, we stick together. Maddy taught me that. She's eight years older than me and she's always looked out for me, and the others."

"You're close?" Ellen found the idea impossible to reconcile with her own feelings.

Hal ran her fingers idly up and down Ellen's arm, tracing patterns. She looked to be debating with herself whether or not to speak, and how much to say. "Ten years back, when I was fifteen, Maddy and me were on a job one night, robbing a shop. The owner heard and came in, armed with a club, except she wasn't strong enough to do much with it. So we got the club off her, and thumped her with it a few times to show her how it ought to be done. She was screeching enough to wake the dead. We fled, but the noise set the Blackshirts onto us. Maddy held them off so I could escape. The shopkeeper was in a bad way, but she survived, which saved Maddy from the gallows. But it was the third time she'd been flogged. Did you spot when she reminded me of it?"

"You've been flogged as well."

"Not that time. The magistrate ordered two hundred lashes, and said it would be dropped to a hundred if Maddy would name the person with her. Maddy named the town Mayor, which they didn't believe. When I heard about it, I wanted to go and confess, to take my share. My parents wouldn't let me. They said my time would come to take one for the family—like Maddy was then. But you never let the bastards make you turn on one another. Afterward, Monday Market was too hot for Maddy, so she moved to Eastford. Once I'd got my own stripes, I joined her. We always stick together, and we never let anyone push us apart. It's going to come as such a surprise to Ade when she finally works it out."

"Ade thinks she's going to end up as your cousin's deputy."

"Ade has delusions, and she's worse since I've been away. When we first sorted our plans out, it was just going to be Jo at Broken Hills with Aunt Cassie. She used to be a shepherd, until some of her boss's sheep went missing. But with Cassie doing nothing except sitting and dribbling, once you started your checks, we needed a blood relative on hand."

"It's what you deserve for beating her head in."

"No point getting virtuous on me. I'm a bandit. It's what I do."

"And I'm a Blackshirt. I can't help it."

Hal laughed softly under her breath. "I know. But it's caused problems. Maddy has—" Hal stopped, chewing her lip. "Maddy's sharp. She's the one with plans and she knows how to manage folk. She always has. But she can lose contact with reality. It's the family's job to keep her grounded. She needs us, and we haven't been here for her."

"Where's the rest of your family?"

"A couple of my cousins are here, but it has to be someone she'll listen to. Not the dimbos, and much as I love my family, I'd have to admit we've got our share of them. My sister Wes and our aunt Ozzie could do it, but they're keeping an eye on things in Eastford. It was my job. I should have been here."

"She looks like she's been coping fine on her own."

Hal shook her head. "Ade's mad. She's been stirring Maddy up. That night I met you in the Three Barrels, it was obvious what the Rangers were planning. I dashed back here, to get Maddy to abandon the homestead, only to find Ade had talked her into the ambush. She'd convinced Maddy that if she hit the Rangers hard enough, she could frighten them off."

"You tried to talk her out of it?"

"Yes." Hal sighed. "But she was too...too excited. Sometimes Maddy gets carried away by the thought of blood. She knows it's a weakness, and normally puts a damper on it. But Ade just keeps stoking the fire, and I couldn't make Maddy see how dangerous it was."

"She pulled it off."

"Not dangerous in the fight itself. I could see we'd win that. I'm looking ahead. The Militia you can push around—" Hal held up her hand. "Sorry, but you know what I mean. The Rangers are a whole different game, and I still think we've brought more trouble down on our heads than we can handle."

"What did you do?"

Hal shrugged. "What could I do? It was a stupid idea, but at the end of the day, you stick with the family."

"You joined in the ambush?"

"Of course. But it made me realize Maddy was losing her grip. And afterward, her and Ade were spurring each other on. I've seen Maddy kill in cold blood before, but not like that."

"I saw. I helped pick up the bodies."

"Maddy's not normally so bad. I've been trying to talk her around. Hopefully, now that we've abandoned Broken Hills I'll have a chance."

"When your cousin was talking about cutting my head off, after I'd..." Ellen turned her face into Hal's shoulder, but there was no point pretending she had not done it. Hal had seen her. "After I'd licked her boot. I felt the tension. Was that part of the same thing?"

"Not really. That was your fault."

"Me?"

"Okay. If you want we can blame Terrie Rasheed."

Ellen pulled back and looked at Hal. "What had I done?"

"Been in the wrong place at the wrong time." Hal paused. "Actually, you were in my bed, which is the right place for you. But you were definitely there at the wrong time."

"At Broken Hills?"

"Yes. Terrie was supposed to contact me when she got out of the infirmary, but she didn't. I told Maddy, and she thought she'd take some of the girls into town to pay a nighttime visit—just rough Terrie up a little and get her into line. They found the asshole had legged it."

"She hadn't been in work that day either."

"Maddy guessed the Militia would be looking for her. Terrie's too stupid not to get caught, and she'd rat on me in an instant. So Maddy rode straight out to Broken Hills to warn me and Jo. When Maddy heard you were upstairs, she wanted to bring you back here. I said no. That's what we'd argued about. But it's a sign of how much she's changed that she wouldn't let it drop until I'd said she was right and I was wrong."

"Why did she agree to start with?"

"Because I made a stand. And she wasn't going to argue with me in front of the girls."

"I'm surprised she lets anyone argue with her."

"I'm family. I get some leeway."

"Will she hold it against you?"

"Not now. Especially since she got what she wanted in the end, even after giving me the ten minutes to get rid of you."

"I'm not so easy to get rid of."

"No." Hal's eyes scrunched closed. "I stood on the steps, praying to the Goddess that you'd keep going. Not that the Goddess would normally listen to someone like me, but I thought she might help, for your sake."

"The Goddess doesn't step in much to help the Militia either."

"So why bother being good?"

"That's not the point."

Hal buried her face in Ellen's shoulder. "I could have died when I saw you walking back and I knew what was going to happen. I've seen enough women get worked over by Maddy—even helped out a few times. It doesn't give me the same kick some of the others get, but it's never bothered me before, but seeing you—" Hal broke off breathing sharply. "If I could have swapped places with you, I would have."

Ellen lifted Hal's head and pulled her into a kiss. When eventually they separated, Ellen was surprised to see tears on Hal's face.

"It's okay. As you said, I'll mend. I don't blame you." The words were not completely true, but Ellen wanted them to be.

"At the start, I thought it was all such a big joke, and I was being so clever. And then—" Hal broke off. Ellen waited for her to continue. "After the fight by the ford, I suddenly thought, supposing you were there, one of the injured and..." Hal shrugged, swallowing back words. "When you came out to Broken Hills I tried to put you off."

"You didn't want me hurt?"

"No. Of course not. But more than that, I didn't want to lose my heart, and I knew I was going to, if I kept on seeing you. It hurt, but I thought I could cope. Then the Rangers took you on as their pet Blackshirt. Terrie came charging out to Broken Hills panicking that she couldn't get any information. It just happened Maddy was there at the time and she ordered me to get back with you." Hal took several deep breaths, clearly fighting to re-gather her composure. "It's just a fucking mess."

"Yup."

"I don't know if I'll be able to get Maddy to set you free."

"It's not..." *necessary*. Ellen's voice died as her thoughts ran on.

"Unless you want to work for us. How about it? Now that Terrie's gone we need someone inside the Roadsend Militia."

"You're joking, aren't you?"

"We pay well." Regardless of how serious she was being, Hal's voice had regained some of its normal strength and humor.

"No."

"Do you want to know the really sad thing?"

"What?"

"Part of the reason I'm so crazy about you is knowing that would be your answer." Hal released her breath in a sound that might have been amusement, might have been despair. "How did I fall for someone as absurdly honest as you?"

"How did I fall for a total villain like you?"

Hal's lips brushed Ellen's cheek. "There's no hope for us, is there?"

Tears filled Ellen's eyes. "None."

The Rangers were coming. In another day they would arrive. Their advance scouts were probably already monitoring the homestead, but if Hal left that night under cover of darkness, she might escape the net. They could never be together, yet life would be more bearable, knowing that Hal's smile was not gone from the world.

Yet, supposing Hal warned the rest? How many other murderers and thieves, the Butcher among them, would also escape, to bring more misery on the honest citizens Ellen had sworn to protect? Ellen had to get Hal to promise not to pass on what she was told, before she knew what she was promising. But how? The simple line "Hal, don't ask me why, just run" would not work. Ellen knew she would have to phrase her initial gambits exactly right.

She ran the words around in her head, but her head was not as clear as she would have liked. The past two nights with little sleep were making themselves felt. For the first time since arriving at the homestead, and even though she knew it was an illusion, Ellen felt safe. Hal's body was so solid in her arms. Hal's heartbeat was a steady comforting rhythm. Ellen put together a sentence in her head, only to have the words dissolve into a jumble as she sank into a sea of darkness.

When Ellen woke up, Hal was no longer there and her hands were again bound together.

Chapter Seventeen—Hope and Despair

Ellen deposited the last shovelful of horse dung on the pile. The corral and stable were finally clear. She straightened her back and wiped the sweat off her forehead, using the collar of her shirt as a towel. Presumably cleaning up after the horses was another of the jobs that had difficulty attracting volunteers. The mucking out had definitely been way overdue and if nothing else, the horses ought to be appreciative. Ellen flexed her shoulders to ease her aching muscles and gave a sigh, relieved that the job was complete.

One of Ellen's minders wandered over and examined her efforts. The woman rubbed her chin, parodying deep thought. "You know, now that I think about it, the shit pile would be better over there." She pointed to a spot, fifty meters away. "It's too close to the house here."

Her companion laughed. "Yeah. Well go on, Blackshirt. You heard what Jackie said. Get on with it."

Ellen kept her face impassive. She did not want to give her tormentors the satisfaction of seeing her react, and the more they thought it troubled her, the more likely that when she had moved the pile, she would be told to shift it again. She took a second to compose herself for more effort—just time for a deep breath and a quick glance around.

All day, the sun had shone from a cloudless blue sky, hot on Ellen's back while she worked. Now it was sinking, and the breeze was cooling. In two hours it would be dark, and then, regardless of where the pile was, she would be permitted to stop. Tomorrow, the gang would have other things to worry about than the location of a dung heap.

Around the homestead, a dozen or more Knives were lounging in the sunshine, talking, drinking, or sleeping. On the opposite side of the yard, the Butcher was sitting under the porch of the main house, chatting with three women. One of them was Hal. All the time while Ellen had been cleaning the stable, she had battled with herself not to look in Hal's direction, and every time she had lost the fight, tears had stung her eyes. It was too late for any warnings, too late to save Hal.

As Ellen watched, one of the Knives must have made a joke. The Butcher laughed and Hal smiled, etching deep lines around her mouth. The pulse kicked in Ellen's stomach. Hal's smile was unique. It summed up everything that Ellen loved about her, and soon it would be gone forever.

Ellen's vision blurred. She tore her eyes away, dug the wooden shovel into the pile, and lifted.

"Boss! Boss!"

The cry made everyone turn. A rider was pelting up the track on horseback. The animal's flanks were heaving and foam flecked its muzzle. Even before the horse had come to a stop, the rider had leapt down, stumbling in her haste.

The Butcher stood up, shading her eyes against the sun. "What is it?"

The woman pointed back the way she had come. "They got Sasha. I couldn't...they..." Her arm was shaking, due to either exertion or panic—and she was certainly panicking. There was no mistaking the agitation in her voice.

The Butcher grabbed the woman's shoulder and shook her. "What?"

"Rangers. Dozens of them. Whole squadrons."

"Where?"

"Three, four kilometers. Me and Sasha rode smack into them."

"That can't be—"

Ellen rested the tip of the shovel on the ground. Across the width of the yard, her eyes met Hal's. The rest of the scene vanished. *I'm sorry.* Ellen mimed the words although she doubted that Hal would see, or care. She heard uproar break out around her, but nothing mattered except for Hal. Already the surprise on Hal's face had faded, replaced by resignation and something that might even have been relief. Her eyes held Ellen's—twin still points amid the chaos.

The blow that knocked Ellen off her feet came without warning. Dazed, she looked at the Butcher, standing over her, holding the wooden shovel like a club. Ellen rolled to the right, half dodging the descending blow, so it struck her shoulder rather than her head.

"You fucking lied."

The shovel landed again, stronger and square on, hitting her stomach in an explosion of pain from previous injuries. More strikes followed.

"Maddy."

The battering stopped. Ellen's arms were over her head, in an attempt to shield herself. She parted them slightly, so she could see. Hal was there, wrestling the shovel from her cousin.

"She lied."

"So. What did you expect?"

The Butcher released her grip on the shovel, then reached down, grabbed the front of Ellen's shirt, and hauled her to her feet. "Now, tell me the truth."

Ellen had no reason to evade the question. Events were too well advanced for the answer to matter. "What I said first off. They've got eight full squadrons surrounding you."

The fury left the Butcher's face, to be replaced by a more frightening calm. "Then the first thing they'll see when they arrive will be your head on a post." She raised her voice. "Someone bring me a saw, and make sure it's a blunt one."

"Maddy. There's no point," Hal said.

"It'll make me feel better."

"She might still have a use."

"Such as?"

"I don't know. But if you think of it later, you can't fit her head back on." Hal's voice dropped. "We need to think. We need to plan. Pointless revenge is for when all other options are gone, and we're not finished yet."

The Butcher's expression softened. "You're right." She shoved Ellen away, then turned and shouted to the two minders. "Take this bitch back to the cave. Don't break anything or do any permanent damage. Anything else is up to you."

❖

Ellen lay in utter darkness. Nightfall was well past. She shifted around awkwardly, feeling the sting of newly inflicted damage. Her ribs had borne the worst, but thankfully, none of it was serious, and given the circumstances, the women who had taken her back to the cave had been very restrained, adding no more than a dozen bruises and a cut over her eye to her catalogue of injuries. The Knives had clearly been more anxious to get back to the main house and find out what was going on than to spend time venting their anger on her. Nobody else had visited since they left.

Would the Butcher, as a last act of spite, take her life? Would she see Hal again? The two questions circled in Ellen's head with equal importance. Would she see the sun set tomorrow? Would Hal? Tears trickled down Ellen's face. Would she be able to kiss Hal one last time? And even if she got the chance, would Hal want to kiss her?

The faint rasp of metal caught her ear. The bolt on the door was being eased back, but when she turned her head, Ellen could see no lamplight shining through the gaps in the wood.

"Ellen?"

"Hal."

Then Hal was beside her, holding her close.

"Hal. I'm sorry. I was going to warn you last night, while you still had a chance to get away, but I fell asleep."

"You knew the Rangers were coming, and when?"

"We had a briefing in Roadsend. Since the moment I got here, I've known I only had to last out four days. I wish I'd told you."

"You didn't tell Maddy, despite the beating."

"I tried to, but she didn't believe me, so I told her what she wanted to hear."

"Maddy's always been prone to overrate how well violence works." Hal gave a soft laugh. "To do her justice, it usually works very well. How did the Rangers know where we were?"

"After the barge was captured, the Rangers followed Ade. They put one of their top trackers on her."

"It's all Ade's fault. I'll enjoy telling her."

"I wanted you to run away last night. Now it's too late. I'm sorry."

Hal pulled back as if to look at her, although the faint moonlight was insufficient to reveal either of their faces. "I wouldn't have left Maddy."

"But—"

"And it doesn't matter now."

Ellen felt fumbling at her ankle. A metallic snap sounded and the manacle fell away.

"Are you okay to walk?" Hal asked.

"Yes."

Hal took Ellen's hands and pulled her to her feet.

"You're going to let me escape?"

"Yes."

"Supposing I say I won't leave you?"

"Then you'd be a fool. There's no point us both dying."

"But there's a point to you and your cousin dying together?"

"If you get to the Rangers, you'll be safe. My options are I can die here, with my family and friends, or I can try to run away, and get hunted down by the Rangers and die alone." Hal's arms wrapped around Ellen. "But I will die just that little bit easier, if I know you're safe."

"Come with me. I'll tell them you were just a bystander as well, taken prisoner by the gang at the farm."

"You'd lie for me? Break your oath about upholding the law, and all that?"

Ellen paused, weighing it all in her mind. She laid her head on Hal's shoulder. "Yes."

"I'm flattered." Hal's lips brushed her neck. "But it wouldn't work. Terrie Rasheed will get caught some time, and she knows who I am. And we left enough stuff at Broken Hills to hang me."

"I could speak for you. Tell them you saved my life. That might count for something."

"But not enough to cancel out what I've done."

"You can't have done—"

"Remember I said I took part in the ambush?"

"Yes."

Hal released Ellen from the embrace, then took her hand and led her to the entrance, where the moonlight was stronger, sufficient for untying her wrists. As Hal struggled with the knots, she kept talking.

"At the ambush, I was on the far side of the river where the trail climbs up, in charge of the group who blocked the road out. I had four Knives with me on the cliffs. We shot the first arrows. Took out the captain and the lieutenant. The rest of the Rangers panicked and ran. I left the others to take care of anyone who might try doubling back and went along to look down on the ford. I saw a group of Rangers were swimming away. But one archer had stayed behind. She was directly below where I was standing, hidden among the rocks and keeping Maddy and her girls back from the riverbank. She was a damned good shot. She'd hit three of us, but she didn't think to look behind her. I climbed down the cliff. Snuck up on her. She didn't know I was there until it was too late. I had my sword drawn. She tried to parry with her bow, but I sliced her open."

"Her name was Jay Takeda." The rope on Ellen's wrist came loose. Her hands dropped to her side.

"Right. I'm guessing she's a hero to the Rangers. The one who gave her life to cover her comrades' escape."

"Yes. She is."

"Then I'm the woman who killed Jay Takeda. Do you think they'd let me live?"

"They don't need to know."

"But you know now. Do you think I deserve to live?"

"I don't..." Ellen squeezed her eyes shut, trying to fight a way through her thoughts.

"You don't have to answer that. And even if I could escape hanging, I won't run out on my family."

"After the fight in the rowboat, when I got hit on the head, you told me nothing was worth dying for."

"I told you six sheep weren't worth dying for. Family is different." Hal's lips met Ellen's in a kiss, tender but brief.

"I won't leave you." Ellen had made up her mind. She did not care whether it made sense or not.

Hal wrapped Ellen in another hug, nestling her head into Ellen's neck. After a long pause she spoke again. "You have to go, and quickly. Maddy will be sending someone for you soon."

"Why?"

"I wasn't able to persuade her there was any other use for you."

"She's going to kill me?"

"Yes. Maddy is...She..." Hal was clearly searching for words. "She's changed. She wouldn't listen to me. Ade has been winding her up, trying to think of the most unpleasant way of killing you. Ade's got a nasty mind." Hal stepped back, took hold of Ellen's hand, and pulled her through the doorway. "The blunt saw would have been fun by comparison."

The sky was clear, mottled with stars. Only one moon lit the scene, Hardie in the third quarter, sinking to the west. The smaller orb of Laurel was not due to rise until just before dawn. Nothing was moving, but intermittent shouts came from the main house.

Hal closed and bolted the door, then urged Ellen off to the left, into the shadow of a barn. Together, they slipped between the patches of darkness, Hal leading the way, past the corral and down to the river, where a scattering of trees and bushes lined the bank. Hal pulled Ellen into the cover of a thicket and then glanced back through the branches. Still nobody was moving in the open and no alarm had been raised.

"Before it got dark, Maddy sent people out to do some scouting around. We know where the Rangers are." The moonlight was just strong enough to catch Hal's ironic smile. "Basically, they're everywhere. At least a squadron are in position about half a kilometer both ways along the main canyon. We're pretty sure more are on the other side of the sheep pasture. However, their main camp is up there." Hal indicated across the river, to the top of the canyon. "The river is easily fordable here. It's a tricky climb, but quite doable."

Ellen flexed her shoulders, feeling them ache. "Maybe in daylight, when you're fit but—"

"Believe me. It'll be safest for you. We've put lookouts, in case the Rangers try a surprise attack. If you go along the canyon floor, you might get spotted, and I can't come with you to distract any Knives. I need to get back before Maddy notices I'm gone."

"She'll still work out you were the one who helped me escape."

"Probably."

"How will she react?"

Hal shrugged. "She'll be pissed off with me again. But that's nothing unusual."

"You're sure your cousin won't harm you?"

"Of course." However, Hal's voice did not sound so confident.

Ellen stepped close and wrapped her arms around Hal. "You're not sure at all, are you?"

Hal returned the hug. "Maddy will want me at her side tomorrow. If somehow we're both alive and free at sunset, then she'll have time to worry about the pissed-off bit."

"There's not much chance of that, is there?"

"None. But"—Hal's arms tightened—"it might not be such a bad thing. I've underestimated Ade. Maddy always had a vicious streak, but she's had it in control. It's been a tool she's used. Now it's turned, so it's running her. It's all Ade's doing, winding Maddy up, and it will destroy the family. Like here, bringing the Rangers on us. I told you I thought the ambush was dangerous. If Maddy doesn't get stopped here, and she goes looking for revenge, she'll take the whole family down with her. And from the way she's talking, I think that's what she'll do. Wes and Ozzie are safe in Eastford. They'll be able to look after things, just as long as nobody stirs up more trouble than they can cope with. I...it's awful, but for the good of the family, Maddy has to go."

"You say that, yet still you want to die with her?"

"Yes. And it's why I can't leave her. I'm selling her out. So I have to stick by Maddy to the end, because I owe her one and it's the only way I can repay her. We're family."

"I don't want to leave you."

Hal released her hold on Ellen. "You have to, and now."

However, Ellen was not yet ready to let go. She placed her hand behind Hal's head and brought their lips together. For a moment Hal stood rigid, but then she softened against Ellen, returning the kiss with growing passion.

Ellen clung to Hal, trying to memorize every last detail of what it felt like to have Hal's body in her arms, to have Hal's mouth molded to hers, Hal's hands running the length of her back, the peace and the passion, the fulfillment and the longing. Hal overflowed her senses. Ellen knew with total certainty that this was what the Goddess had created her for, the reason she existed.

The kiss ended. Ellen dropped her head to Hal's shoulder, but did not relinquish her grip.

"Hal."

"Yes?"

"I love you."

Hal's body shook. Eventually she found her voice. "I love you. I've known it since I rowed you back into town, with you chucking your guts up every five minutes."

Ellen laughed—it was either that or scream. "I mean, how could I not love someone who says such romantic things?"

"I knew Sasha had given you a bad concussion. I could sense the fluid forming under your skull but I didn't have the talent to get rid of it. I was terrified you were going to die before I could get you to the infirmary—or end up like Aunt Cassie. And when I realized just how much I wanted you to be okay I knew..." Hal's hand stroked the back of Ellen's head, pressing Ellen's face into her neck. "I knew I loved you."

Hal raised Ellen's head and kissed her again, softly and slowly, but eventually she broke away and stepped back. "You really need to go now."

"I..." Ellen let her hands fall to her sides.

She stared at Hal, wondering what else to say, but she could not bring herself to form the word "good-bye," and no other phrase would fill the emptiness.

Ellen turned and stepped into the river. The water splashed around at calf height. She was midstream before she noticed how cold it was, and that her feet were wet. Taking her boots off before stepping in would have been a sensible idea, but wet feet were too trivial to worry about, and it was too late to do anything about it anyway—too late for everything.

The trees grew more densely on the far side of the river, where the gang had not cleared the canyon floor. Ellen pulled herself onto the bank and looked back. Hal had not moved, but now she raised her hand in a gesture of farewell, turned, and headed back toward the homestead. Ellen remained in place watching Hal walk past the corral, the yard, and reach the doorway.

This is what it feels like when your heart breaks.

Without looking back, Hal pushed open the door of the main house and disappeared from Ellen's view.

❖

Ellen grasped the protruding root and hauled herself up. Tired, bruised muscles screamed their complaint, but her foot found a toehold in a crack and her knee gained purchase on a hollow rock. One more effort, and she was over yet another step on the canyon wall. Ellen rolled clear of the edge, got to her knees and then her feet, and stood, shoulders sagging, regaining her breath.

Down below, the homestead lay so deceptively peaceful in the weak moonlight. Hal was there. No matter what the outcome of the following day's battle, Ellen would never hold her hand again, never kiss her again, never spend another night in her arms. Tears blurred the scene. Ellen could almost have given in to the temptation to stop climbing and return, but it was pointless. She turned her back on the homestead.

The top of the canyon wall was no more than twenty meters above her, forming a dark silhouette against the backdrop of stars. The gradient was easing, as the bedrock changed. The canyons were carved from layered red sandstone. Around Roadsend the tops were densely wooded, but here the upper plateaus were formed from harder stone, covered by only a thin, dry layer of topsoil, insufficient to support trees. Ahead of Ellen, the moonlight-dappled ground was covered by swaths of grass and dover fern, dotted with taller clumps of rock holly.

Hardie was sinking in the west. In an hour it would have dropped below the horizon, but for now, its light was strong enough to see by—if only Ellen could stop crying. She stumbled forward.

"Stop right there." The command rang out from a dark patch of undergrowth.

Ellen froze.

"Raise your hands."

Once she had obeyed, two sets of footsteps sounded behind her, and then her arms were grabbed and forced behind her back. She felt rope at her wrists. Two more Rangers emerged from cover, drawn swords in their hands. They joined their comrades, surrounding her. The green and gray of their uniforms were faded in the moonlight. Ellen knew her own black uniform would be hard to recognize, even were it not torn and covered in mud and filth.

The moonlight was just sufficient to pick out the three stripes of a sergeant on the badge of the woman standing directly in front. "Not thinking of running away, were you? Not when we've arranged such a fun party for you tomorrow."

Ellen shook her head. "I'm not a gang member."

"Just an innocent passer-by on a moonlight stroll up the hillside?" The sergeant laughed. "Oh, right then, we'd better let you be getting on your way." She took firm hold of Ellen's arm, tight enough to hurt. "Just how stupid do you think we are?"

"Is Major Kallim here? I need to talk to her."

"What about?"

"I'm Militia Patrolwoman Ellen Mittal. I was being held by the gang, but I've escaped. I was working for Major Kallim at Roadsend. She'll know who I am."

The sergeant nodded. "Well, by a mind-boggling coincidence, she was exactly the person we were going to take you to anyway. Come on."

With a Ranger holding her other arm, Ellen was marched up the hillside.

The sergeant's tone was still skeptical, but the grip on Ellen's arm had softened. "And don't take it personally, but we'll leave your hands tied until Kallim gives us the nod."

❖

"Patrolwoman Mittal."

Somebody shaking her shoulder woke Ellen. She opened her eyes. The face of the healer hung over her. Ellen was lying in the wagon from the infirmary—some means of transporting away the inevitable wounded was essential and the Knives' own track would have provided a passable route through the wilderness. In the background, the stars shone undimmed and small Laurel was still low on the horizon. Dawn was an hour away.

"What?"

"They're ready to start the briefing. Are you all right to join them?"

"Er...yeah."

"You feel strong enough?"

"Yes."

In fact, physically, Ellen felt better than she had for days. The Rangers had a competent healer in their retinue, whose paranormal skill had not only removed the pain from Ellen's injuries, but had already reversed some of the damage and sent her into the deep, dreamless sleep.

Ellen hoisted herself up onto her elbows. "Where are they?"

"You're sure you're up to it?"

"I'm fine." Ellen stripped back the blanket and kicked it aside. Beneath it she was wearing clothes borrowed from the Rangers, her own soiled and torn uniform discarded.

"You've been through a lot, and nobody expects—"

"Honest. I am perfectly okay for a meeting. Where do I have to go?" Ellen was already getting tired of the way she was being treated like an invalid. And they only saw the marks on her body. The ones that hurt the most were unseen and unacknowledged.

Ellen was directed to the center of the encampment, where twenty or more Rangers were gathered around a campfire, most with captain's or lieutenant's badges on their shoulders.

Major Kallim greeted Ellen's arrival. "Patrolwoman Mittal. I'm pleased you could join us. How are you?"

"I'm fine, thank you, ma'am." *Except that you're preparing to kill the woman I love.*

Kallim pointed to a spot on the ground. "Come and look here."

As Ellen moved around the campfire, the Rangers stepped out of her way. Two put a supportive hand under her arm as she passed, as if they thought she needed assistance. One patted her shoulder, in a clear gesture of approval.

When Ellen reached Major Kallim's side, she saw a patch of ground in the firelight had been cleared. Scratched in the earth was an outline map of the Butcher's homestead.

"We've drawn in as much as we can see from up here. What more can you tell us?"

"Um..." Ellen pointed. "Those are just barns and storerooms. That's the hay store. This is the stable." *Where I shoveled up every last dollop of horseshit.* "That's the bunk room. It's where most of the Knives sleep."

"I'll bet not many are sleeping at the moment," Kallim said with grim amusement.

"Judging by the noises I heard, most were in the main house when I left."

"Which one is that?"

Ellen pointed to the largest building. "There. It's where the Butcher lives." *Where I knelt and licked her boot.*

"That would be Madeline Bucher, the gang leader?"

"Yes."

"And she's definitely here at the moment?"

"Yes."

"Do you know how many of her bandits are present on the base?" Kallim asked.

"About twenty was the most I ever saw together at one time."

"How many others do you think there might be?"

"No more than one or two." *Who would have missed the fun of hearing me scream?*

"The main house. Do you think it's where they'll make their last stand?"

Ellen paused. "Maybe. But the Butcher's not stupid. She's someone who makes plans. She'll go for offense rather than defense. You might think she's cornered. She'll be looking for where to attack."

"Exactly right." Kallim nodded and glanced around the campfire. "If this was a common street thug we wouldn't all need to be gathered here." She returned to Ellen. "Is there anywhere else on the site they might retreat to? A defensive position?"

"Um...there's a cave here. They use it as a food store. It's where I was held captive most of the time." *Where Hal made love to me.* "They could retreat to it, but they'd be cornered, with no way out."

"What are their supplies like?"

"The cave looked well stocked. The river will give them water, and there's no shortage of mutton to eat."

"So we can't starve them out. Not that we'd intended to." Kallim looked around the fire. "Does anyone have any other questions?"

"Do they store weapons in this cave?" A sharp-eyed captain asked the question.

"Not that I saw. Mainly food." *And the cloaks Hal wrapped me in, the last time I slept in her arms.*

"These barricades here. What are they?" one of the lieutenants asked, pointing to the map.

"They're just fences. To keep the stolen sheep from straying." *I fixed the upper one, while Ade taunted me about loving Hal.*

"No defensive use?"

"Not unless you're a sheep."

The audience chuckled.

"Can the river be forded?" someone else asked.

"Certainly, in some spots." Ellen touched the map. "That's where

I crossed, earlier tonight." *And that's where I stood and kissed Hal for the last time.*

"So the gang might try to cross over and outflank us?"

"That bank is fairly densely overgrown." Ellen shrugged. "But I made my way through it"—*even though I was crying too hard to see*—"and the bushes would provide cover for archers."

"Yes. We need to watch out for that. Anything else?" When no one spoke, Kallim nodded to Ellen. "Thank you. You've been very helpful." She turned to the assembled Rangers. "All right. Dawn. The 14th are currently here." With a stick she pointed to the top of the sheep pasture. "I want the 27th squadron to go out and reinforce them. Take up position on the flanks of the canyon, wherever possible."

"Yes, ma'am."

"19th."

"Ma'am," another captain answered.

"The 2nd are here." Kallim's stick touched the map, upstream of the homestead. "I want you to cover this side of the river, around to here. Watch out for them trying to break out up the hill. In particular I want you to hold the points here and here. Get your best archers onto it and tell them to be on the lookout for bandits crossing the river."

"Yes, ma'am."

"That should hold them in. Everyone else. We're going to join with the 23rd in the main assault. I'll be leading you." She drew a line in the earth. "Up along here. This building that Patrolwoman Mittal identified as the hay store will be our first target. I doubt they'll be holding it in force, but it commands good lines of sight and once we've got control of it, if they put up any sort of defense in other buildings, we'll make a stack on the outside and burn them out. Captain Drewer."

"Ma'am."

"The only exception. I'd like half your squadron up here. Patrolwoman Mittal has demonstrated that scaling the canyon wall is quite possible. We don't want anyone sneaking away. Put your lieutenant in charge."

"Yes, ma'am."

Kallim nodded. "Any questions?"

There were none.

"Right. The assault starts at dawn. Dismissed."

The Rangers drifted away. Ellen stayed in place, staring at the map, trying to align the scratched marks in the earth with her memories. It was not a case of the conflict between imagination and reality. Reality was not always the truth. The world held depths that the mere facts could never reach.

"Patrolwoman Mittal?"

Ellen looked up. Major Kallim was staring at her with a concerned expression. "Ma'am?"

"How are you?"

"I'm...okay."

"I've had a report from the healer about your physical condition." Kallim stepped closer. Her voice dropped. "I know what they did to you, and I can make a good guess at why, at least for some of it. It's the healer's opinion that you were subjected to deliberate, sadistic torture. They wanted you to tell them about our plans, didn't they?"

"Yes. But..." Ellen closed her eyes as memories rushed into her head.

"It's all right; you don't have to say anything now. But clearly, you didn't tell them, and give them the chance to escape before we got here. When we eliminate the gang, it will be because of your courage. I'll be making a full report to that effect when I return to HQ."

Ellen opened her eyes. "No. I wasn't really...I mean I didn't... it..."

"Don't put yourself down." Kallim patted her arm. "Get back to the healer. You've more than done your share." She smiled. "But if you want, you ought to be able to get a good view of events tomorrow from the top of the hill." She gave a formal salute and walked away.

Ellen stared at the sky. The eastern horizon held the first shadowing of gray. Dawn was approaching—the last dawn that Hal would ever see.

And I can have a good view to watch her die.

Chapter Eighteen—Shades of Gray

The campfire was burning low. Red embers flared amid gray ash when the breeze stirred across the hilltop. The open tract of fern and grass ran for several kilometers, gently dropping away toward the west. Overhead, the sky was pale blue, speckled with just the faintest remnants of stars, except where banks of cloud were rolling in from the south. It might rain later that day. Ellen considered the clouds, trying to come to terms with the concept of the future in a world without Hal, and then turned her eyes back to the dying campfire.

The blackened wood still radiated a little heat, welcome in the dawn chill. Ellen adjusted the heavy leather jacket that someone had placed around her shoulders, although in truth, the cold bothered her no more than the prospect of rain. She sat, hugging her knees and staring at the fire, trying not to think, and most certainly not to remember.

Ellen was the only one still at the campsite. The Rangers had left immediately after the briefing to take up position. The healer had also gone, to be on hand when the fighting started, because it was a certainty that her skills would be needed. A few dozen horses were tethered in the middle of a nearby patch of grass. If Ellen turned around, she could pick out some of the Rangers who were guarding the route up the side of the canyon, although the majority had moved to spots over the rim, out of sight. Mostly she chose not to turn around.

And then, faintly in the still air, came the sound of distant shouting from the floor of the canyon. Ellen closed her eyes. It had started.

Nothing about the flow of events could be deduced from the shouts. This was fine by Ellen; she did not want to know. However, ignorance was no defense. Tears filled her eyes. Ellen pressed the heel of her hand into her mouth and bit, trying to stifle her sobs. Less than a kilometer from where she sat, a battle was going on. Hal would be fighting for her life and she would lose, might already have lost, might be lying dead.

The minutes rolled by and the shouting got louder. Ellen pressed her hands over her ears, trying to block it out. It did not work. The yells and screams seared their way into her soul. Her ears were playing games with her, taunting her. How could the sound of fighting be so close, so real?

Ellen dropped her hands and twisted around. Some way off, a thick plume of smoke climbed into the morning sky from the floor of the canyon. Were the Rangers burning the homestead this soon? Then Ellen noticed that the Rangers stationed on the hilltop had gone. Why had they moved? Was it just to get a better view?

More shouts and screams rang out, and now that Ellen had removed her hands from her ears, she knew it was not some trick of her nerves. The outcry was from just over the rim of the canyon. Ellen leapt to her feet. The added height gave her enough angle to see the tops of a few Rangers—archers, shooting at unseen targets below them on the hillside.

Ellen jogged forward a few meters so that more figures came into view. At first she saw Rangers, swords drawn and then Knives. Two of the gang were scrambling up the hill, until they were intercepted. The archers continued shooting down the hillside.

Ellen had not been keeping track of time, yet she was sure that a scant quarter hour had passed since the first shouts. The Butcher's gang could not have climbed the canyon wall so quickly. They must have set out before dawn, probably during the hours of complete darkness after Hardie had set, and hid themselves amid the bushes.

Of course the Butcher would not have sat and waited passively for the Rangers to attack. The hope must be to break through the thin line of Rangers and get to the horses, before the main body of troops could surround them. A bold plan, but it would not work. Ellen could see the Rangers were getting the better of the fighting. Already both visible Knives had fallen. The Rangers were fresh and had the advantage of the high ground, whereas the attackers needed to finish off the steep climb, just to stand level with them. Furthermore, even though the Rangers might be outnumbered, time was on their side. All they had to do was hold out for a few minutes and reinforcements would arrive from below, catching the gang front and rear, exposed on the steep hillside.

One of the horses whickered, shuffling its feet. Ellen glanced its way, momentarily distracted. As she turned back, her eyes glimpsed a figure, low to the ground, creeping silently through the dover ferns. Most of the woman was under cover, but what little could be seen was not encased in a green and gray uniform, which left only one alternative. Not that there was much doubt. A Ranger would not be skulking away from the fight.

While the rest of the Knives were occupying the Rangers, one of their number had succeeded in slipping through the net. For an instant, Ellen's heart leapt, but the figure was too stocky to be Hal. Ellen grabbed a half-burned log to use as a club and charged forward, shouting.

At Ellen's challenge, the woman sprung up and sprinted for the closest horse. However, Ellen was nearer and got there first, blocking the way. She skidded to a stop and turned to face the woman—the Butcher.

Outrage swept over Ellen. The so-called leader was a coward, using her followers and family as decoys to be killed while she saved her own skin. She was buying her life with Hal's. Ellen's hand tightened on the log.

The Butcher planted her feet on the ground, two meters from Ellen. Her eyes darted left and right as she clearly weighed up her options. Her expression was angry and frustrated, but then, unexpectedly, the tension left her in a visible wave. The Butcher's body relaxed and her face changed to show its normal, vindictive smile.

"Oh good. I was hoping to meet you." The Butcher drew a sword from the scabbard hanging by her side. "Or should I say, I was hoping to gut you? Can't even pass on a simple message, can you?"

Ellen slipped the jacket off her shoulders and grasped the collar in her left hand, letting the rest hang loose. "What message was that?"

"What Hal told you last night."

The Butcher sidestepped sharply to the right. Ellen countered, keeping between her and the horses. "Hal didn't tell me anything."

"Another shit-stupid Militiawoman. Were you too busy hoping she'd get your pants off for a quick fuck to listen to what she said?"

"How do you know what she said? How—"

The Butcher's sword flashed forward. Ellen swung the jacket across, catching the Butcher's arm and deflecting her thrust, and then struck out with the log, jabbing at the Butcher's face and forcing a retreat.

The Butcher took a long step back, regaining both her balance and her sneering belligerence. "I know what she said, because I told her to say it."

Ellen felt her arms drop slightly as confusion set in—but of course, that was exactly what the Butcher wanted. She clenched her jaw. *Ignore her.*

The Butcher went on. "Don't you remember? Hal told you we were going to break out through the sheep pasture. We were going to set fire to the fence so the smoke would conceal what we were doing. Then we were going to rush the squadron on the other side of the fence and escape through the woods."

"What did—"

The instant Ellen started to speak the Butcher leapt, slashing out with her sword. Again Ellen parried—just, but this time she was the one forced to step back.

"But you didn't pass the message on to the Rangers, did you?"

Don't talk to her.

"The Rangers ought to have gone charging into the pasture at the first sign of smoke, to try and catch us. But they didn't. They're all around by the homestead. They've spotted us on the hillside, and now they're picking off my girls, one by one, and it's all your stupid frigging fault."

She's trying to provoke you, to make you drop your guard. Ellen told herself. *Don't get drawn in.* Yet the temptation was too strong. "You knew Hal was going to let me escape?"

"Goddess, you're slow. Of course I fucking knew. It was my plan. Why did you think she did it?" The Butcher sniggered. "Talk about a gullible moron."

Ellen's heart had been hammering in her chest. Now it thundered to a new high, constricting her throat. Ellen's arms weakened as memories of Hal in the moonlight swept over her. *Don't listen to her. She's lying.*

The Butcher must have seen the taunts hit home. Her posture became even more cavalier, her expression derisive. "Did you honestly think"—The sword flicked up. Ellen flinched.—"that my cousin"—The blade sliced left and back, drawing Ellen's eyes.—"would fall for a damned Blackshirt"—The Butcher feigned a jab. Ellen brought the jacket across, but overreacted, leaving her side exposed.—"and a shit stupid one at that?" The sword darted in, coming straight for Ellen's heart.

Ellen leapt back. The last thrust had missed her by centimeters. Her lungs were refusing to work. "Hal is..."

"Hal is your darling?" The Butcher's sarcastic laugh turned Ellen's guts to ice. "You can't get enough of her, can you? You were even happy for her to fuck you when you were in the cave, chained to the wall. Or did that just add an extra thrill to it?"

"How do you know about..." *Don't talk to her. Don't get drawn in.*

"How do I know? Because Hal told me all about it. What did you think we were laughing about while we watched you shoveling horseshit? I tell you, I nearly pissed myself."

The blood pounded in Ellen's ears. White-hot fury erupted, sweeping over her, taking control of her hands, her legs. Ellen surged forward, swinging at the Butcher's head with the log. The Butcher ducked and then drove the sword point up for Ellen's throat.

The rage wiped all conscious thought from Ellen's head, yet still a cold, calm part of her mind watched the events in detachment, judging the solidity of the log in her hand, the speed of the sword, the ground under their feet, the drag of the jacket through the air, the shift in the Butcher's balance.

Acting of its own volition, Ellen's left arm shot out, snaring the Butcher's sword in the folds of the leather jacket. Her right hand swung in a smooth arc. The geometric precision of the motion was interrupted only as the log made contact with the Butcher's head. The wood cracked with the force of the impact. Ellen dropped the splintered remains, but continued her forward momentum. Her fist pounded into the Butcher's gut, sending the stunned woman crashing to the ground.

Ellen dropped on her fallen opponent, pinning the Butcher to the ground, and punched with all the force of her anger. The Butcher had dropped her sword as she fell, but now she fumbled at her waist, drawing a knife from its sheath. Ellen shifted position so she sat astride the Butcher's chest, her knees grinding into the Butcher's arms, trapping them. Again Ellen brought her fist down in a crushing backhand swing. The Butcher grunted and tried to squirm away, but the ascendancy was with Ellen.

By the fifth punch, the knife had slipped from the Butcher's limp fingers; by the tenth, she was no longer struggling, but Ellen did not stop. She remembered the Butcher with the rod in her hand, smiling at each scream wrung from her lips. She remembered the Butcher, holding out a boot to be licked. She remembered the Butcher, lying about Hal. Ellen's fists were going to knock down all the memories, until they no longer hurt.

The Butcher was whimpering at each punch. The sound spurred Ellen on, a savage balm for the rage in her heart, repayment for all the pain. At some point, she was aware of several footsteps running toward her but they halted a few meters away. Whoever it was did not try to intervene and Ellen dismissed them from her mind. Only when the Butcher had fallen silent, barely conscious, did Ellen stop her assault.

She looked up. Three Rangers stood a short way off, watching her. One made a small gesture, clearly indicating that they were happy to wait until Ellen had finished. At last, the fury started to fade. Ellen scrabbled unsteadily off the unresisting body and stood. She took a deep breath and stared down at the Butcher, helpless at her feet.

Somewhere in the rule book it said that prisoners should not be treated with more violence than was necessary to ensure their capture. Once they were restrained, they should not be subjected to any form of brutality. The Militia were the servants of the law, not the dispensers of it. Ellen considered the rules, then pulled back her leg and kicked the Butcher three times, using all the force she could muster. The shock of each kick reverberated up Ellen's leg.

At last, she stepped away and signaled to the waiting Rangers, half shrug, half nod. They moved in, hauling the Butcher to her feet. All were grinning. One winked at Ellen, then caught hold of the Butcher's hair and pulled her head up as if critically appraising the damage Ellen had inflicted to the Butcher's face.

She spoke in mocking tones. "You know, you shouldn't have resisted arrest like that. We saw you do it."

Another laughed. "But you know what they say about payback."

One of the Rangers collected the dropped sword, while the others tied the Butcher's arms behind her. The prisoner was barely semiconscious. Her legs were under her but incapable of taking her weight. The Rangers dragged her away.

For the first time, Ellen became aware that her knuckles were raw and her forearms ached. She held out the backs of her hands for inspection, but the focus of her eyes moved on. The patch of ground at Ellen's feet was splattered with flecks of the Butcher's blood. A glint of metal peeked from underneath a tussock of trampled grass. Ellen bent and picked up the Butcher's knife. Her last knife.

The rise in noise caught Ellen's attention. She looked around. Far more Rangers were at the campsite than the half squadron that had been positioned atop the canyon wall, and more were arriving by the second, coming up over the rim. They must have climbed from the homestead. Any Knives on the wall of the canyon would have been surrounded, killed, or captured.

The battle was over for everyone. Ellen put her face in her hands and cried.

❖

By midmorning, the cloud had crossed over and covered the sky, but no rain had yet fallen. Major Kallim had returned to the campsite, although many of the Rangers were still below, checking the homestead and making sure that none of the gang had escaped. The atmosphere was jubilant.

Ellen sat on her own, out of contact with the world. She stared at the torn skin on her knuckles. Breaking the rules had not made her feel better, but she did not regret one iota of it. Obeying them would have made her feel worse.

Major Kallim had been making the rounds. Now she stopped by Ellen, who started to get to her feet.

"No, stay as you are." Kallim dropped down and sat beside her, adopting a pose of deliberate casualness that Ellen tried not to see as condescending. "How are you doing?"

"All right, ma'am."

"Good work with the gang leader. I'd have hated for her to have escaped."

"Thank you, ma'am."

Kallim smiled. "It all turned out better than I expected. I was braced for losses when we took the homestead. The layout meant we were going to be exposed to crossfire some of the time. Catching them on the hillside was far less dangerous." Kallim paused and looked at Ellen. "I've been questioning the prisoners. You know they set fire to the farther away fence?"

"Yes, ma'am."

"They thought we'd go charging through to investigate. Do you know anything about that?"

"Um...I think I was supposed to pass the story on that it was part of a plan they had to escape."

"But you didn't."

"Their plans came unstuck somewhere. She never...I...we..." Ellen rubbed her forehead, struggling with her memories.

"It's all right. As I said, it worked out well." Kallim patted Ellen's shoulder. "If we'd swallowed the bait of the burning fence it might have gone differently, though. With the majority of us in the offshoot canyon, we might not have seen the bandits on the hillside when they made their move. They'd have been able to take their time on the final ascent. They had the advantage in numbers and some would quite likely have gotten to the horses and escaped. You were right about the gang leader, going for offense. You've got a good head on your shoulders, and you're no coward."

Ellen ducked her head, but could think of nothing appropriate to say.

"You've completed your probation with the Militia?"

"Yes, ma'am," Ellen confirmed, even though she knew the question was rhetorical. Kallim was the one who had ordered her early promotion.

"If you apply to the Rangers, I think I can guarantee you'll be accepted."

"Thank you, ma'am. But I haven't made my—"

"No rush. There are some interesting times ahead. This whole affair has shown that we need to sort out the way the three branches of the military work together, and the procedures for reporting back to HQ. What we had works for small-scale local trouble, but we don't want to get caught out if another organized gang go for the big time. You've got the experience and the talents we need. Think about it." Again, Kallim patted Ellen's shoulder and stood up. "The healer tells me you aren't fit to ride."

"I feel fine, ma'am."

"No. It's all right. Take it easy while you can. The wagon with the wounded is leaving for town in ten minutes. You've got a place on it."

"I'm not—"

"No arguing. Ten minutes. On the wagon." Kallim smiled broadly and walked away to join a small group of officers.

Ellen watched her go. Her eyes moved on. Thirty meters away, at the other side of the campsite, the prisoners were assembled, sitting on the ground in a line. There were nine in total, the Butcher and Ade Eriksen among them. They would all hang; that much was certain. A trial would be held, but the outcome was not in doubt. Ellen looked at each face in turn. Hal was not there. Ellen knew that already. Her gaze returned to the Butcher.

Some words from Chris Sanchez, spoken shortly after Ellen had first joined the Militia, rolled through her head. They had just broken up a fight in the street. Chris had said, "Angry women are hard to predict. When the rage takes over, women get stupid and they get dangerous. A lot of women just get stupid. The ones to be frightened of are the few who just get dangerous."

The Butcher had been trying to provoke her, taunting her about Hal, hoping she would become stupid and make a careless mistake. Ellen remembered the murderous calculating demon who had taken over her body. Whoever would have thought that she might become someone the Butcher should have been frightened of?

Now the demon had gone. Ellen's gaze hardened. The Butcher had deliberately been trying to anger her. Nothing said in the circumstances should be taken as truth—quite the opposite. The one thing Ellen could be sure of was that every word the Butcher had spoken was selected and twisted to cause the most hurt. Yet some facts could not be disputed.

Hal had lied. She had set Ellen free with the Butcher's knowledge. She had related the story of what had taken place in the cave. The Butcher had known that—betrayed, deceived, beaten, and humiliated—Ellen had been so besotted as to still willingly accept Hal as a lover.

When, why, and how Hal had passed on the details was uncertain. Maybe she had done it laughing and boasting as the Butcher claimed. Maybe she had been obliged to give an account when spied leaving the cave. Maybe she had spun a yarn, more fiction than fact, as part of some scheme. Ellen would never know the truth.

Yet Hal had not planted the false story of the planned escape through the sheep pasture. Ellen searched her memory. She knew no mention of it had been made, and it was inconceivable that Hal had simply forgotten.

So far, Ellen had come up with two scenarios. Over the years ahead, assuredly she would think of more.

Ellen's first scenario was that Hal had used the ploy of feeding false information to get the Butcher to agree to her escape. Hal had lied about the Butcher intending to kill Ellen only to ensure that she went. For the good of the whole family Hal had not wanted the Butcher to get away and was prepared to sacrifice her own life to ensure it. She had manipulated events to ruin the Butcher's plans, even by sending Ellen up the canyon wall to alert the Rangers to the risk. In this scenario, Hal had been telling the truth when she said, "I love you."

Or maybe Hal had double-crossed everyone. In the second scenario, Hal had strung both Ellen and the Butcher along. She had set up the Butcher and the rest of the gang as a lure. When the Rangers spotted the Knives, exposed on the hillside, they had been forced to change their attack plan. This was what Hal had counted on. She was hidden, waiting for a gap to appear as the Rangers adjusted to the unexpected. Even with her plans in ruins, the Butcher had been close to escape. If Hal's plan had been on track, might she have gone one step further and slipped through the net?

Across the campsite, Ellen stared at the Butcher. *Hal lied to us both, but who did she deceive?*

Ellen stood and turned to face another corner of the campsite, where a second group of bandits were being assembled by the Rangers. A pile of bodies. As Ellen watched, she saw one more limp form carried up. Other Rangers were at work, digging a mass grave at the side.

Was Hal lying over there? All Ellen's logic evaporated at the thought.

Hal was a liar, a thief, and a murderer. She had been a key member of the most vicious gang the world had seen. Ellen could not trust a word Hal had ever told her. Which scenario was the truth? In her final act, had Hal given her life for what she saw as the good of her family? Or was there truly nothing about her that Ellen could respect?

Ellen felt her eyes fill with tears. Despite everything, she loved Hal. She always would. But had Hal loved her? Had Hal been lying from beginning to end? Was everything she had said in the cave just part of a plot that had been interrupted by the arrival of the Rangers? Was she totally without regard for anyone else, even her own family? Had she tricked her cousin to save her own skin? Was Hal lying in the pile of bodies?

Ellen remembered waking up in Hal's bed, with Hal's body warm beside her; looking at Hal's sleeping face; Hal's smile and the dance of her eyes. Could she bear to look at Hal's body, cold, stiff, and broken? Or would it be better, thinking that maybe, somewhere, Hal was still walking the face of the earth, regardless of justice or the law?

Was Hal lying in the pile of bodies?

Ellen clamped her hand over her mouth. Supposing she discovered that Hal was not there. By her oath to uphold the law, she would be bound to report it, to tell Major Kallim that one dangerous criminal had escaped. But she did not have to look. Nobody had asked her to check for missing bandits. Tears trickled down Ellen's face and over her fingers. Would tomorrow be easier to get through, with just the merest hint of a possibility that one day she might see Hal again?

The Rangers carrying the body reached the pile and added the dead Knife to the rest. Ellen's hand fell to her side. If Hal was lying there, then she did not need to know.

Ellen turned and walked away down the hillside to the waiting wagon.

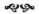

About the Author

Jane Fletcher is a GCLS award winning writer and has also been short-listed for the Gaylactic Spectrum and Lambda awards. She is author of two fantasy/romance series: the Lyremouth Chronicles—*The Exile and The Sorcerer*, *The Traitor and The Chalice*, and *The Empress and The Acolyte* and the Celaeno series—*The Walls of Westernfort*, *Rangers at Roadsend*, *The Temple at Landfall, Dynasty of Rogues*, and *Shadow of the Knife.*

Her love of fantasy began at the age of seven when she encountered Greek Mythology. This was compounded by a childhood spent clambering over every example of ancient masonry she could find (medieval castles, megalithic monuments, Roman villas). Her resolute ambition was to become an archaeologist when she grew up, so it was something of a surprise when she became a software engineer instead.

Born in Greenwich, London, in 1956, she now lives in southwest England, where she keeps herself busy writing both computer software and fiction, although generally not at the same time.

Books Available From Bold Strokes Books

Heartland by Julie Cannon. Political strategist Rachel Stanton and dude ranch owner Shivley McCoy collide on an empty country road and fate intervenes. (978-1-60282-009-8)

Shadow of the Knife by Jane Fletcher. Militia Rookie Ellen Mittal has no idea of just how complex and dangerous her life is about to become. A Celaeno series adventure romance. (978-1-60282-008-1)

To Protect and Serve by VK Powell. Lieutenant Alex Troy is caught in the paradox of her life—to hold steadfast to her professional oath or to protect the woman she loves. (978-1-60282-007-4)

Deeper by Ronica Black. Former homicide detective Erin McKenzie and her fiancée Elizabeth Adams couldn't be any happier—until the not so distant past comes knocking at the door. (978-1-60282-006-7)

The Lonely Hearts Club by Radclyffe. Take three friends, add two ex-lovers and several new ones, and the result is a recipe for explosive rivalries and incendiary romance. (978-1-60282-005-0)

Venus Besieged by Andrews & Austin. Teague Richfield heads for Sedona and the sensual arms of psychic astrologer Callie Rivers for a much needed romantic reunion. (978-1-60282-004-3)

Branded Ann by Merry Shannon. Pirate Branded Ann raids a merchant vessel to obtain a treasure map and gets more than she bargained for with the widow Violet. (978-1-60282-003-6)

American Goth by JD Glass. Trapped by an unsuspected inheritance and guided only by the guardian who holds the secret to her future, Samantha Cray fights to fulfill her destiny. (978-1-60282-002-9)

Learning Curve by Rachel Spangler. Ashton Clarke is perfectly content with her life until she meets the intriguing Professor Carrie Fletcher, who isn't looking for a relationship with anyone. (978-1-60282-001-2)

Place of Exile by Rose Beecham. Sheriff's detective Jude Devine struggles with ghosts of her past and an ex-lover who still haunts her dreams. (978-1-933110-98-1)

Fully Involved by Erin Dutton. A love that has smoldered for years ignites when two women and one little boy come together in the aftermath of tragedy. (978-1-933110-99-8)

Heart 2 Heart by Julie Cannon. Suffering from a devastating personal loss, Kyle Bain meets Lane Connor, and the chance for happiness suddenly seems possible. (978-1-60282-000-5)

Queens of Tristaine: Tristaine Book Four by Cate Culpepper. When a deadly plague stalks the Amazons of Tristaine, two warrior lovers must return to the place of their nightmares to find a cure. (978-1-933110-97-4)

The Crown of Valencia by Catherine Friend. Ex-lovers can really mess up your life…even, as Kate discovers, if they've traveled back to the 11th century! (978-1-933110-96-7)

Mine by Georgia Beers. What happens when you've already given your heart and love finds you again? Courtney McAllister is about to find out. (978-1-933110-95-0)

House of Clouds by KI Thompson. A sweeping saga of an impassioned romance between a Northern spy and a Southern sympathizer, set amidst the upheaval of a nation under siege. (978-1-933110-94-3)

Winds of Fortune by Radclyffe. Provincetown local Deo Camara agrees to rehab Dr. Nita Burgoyne's historic home, but she never said anything about mending her heart. (978-1-933110-93-6)

Focus of Desire by Kim Baldwin. Isabel Sterling is surprised when she wins a photography contest, but no more than photographer Natasha Kashnikova. Their promo tour becomes a ticket to romance. (978-1-933110-92-9)

Blind Leap by Diane and Jacob Anderson-Minshall. A Golden Gate Bridge suicide becomes suspect when a filmmaker's camera shows a different story. Yoshi Yakamota and the Blind Eye Detective Agency uncover evidence that could be worth killing for. (978-1-933110-91-2)

Wall of Silence, 2nd ed. by Gabrielle Goldsby. Life takes a dangerous turn when jaded police detective Foster Everett meets Riley Medeiros, a woman who isn't afraid to discover the truth no matter the cost. (978-1-933110-90-5)

Mistress of the Runes by Andrews & Austin. Passion ignites between two women with ties to ancient secrets, contemporary mysteries, and a shared quest for the meaning of life. (978-1-933110-89-9)

Sheridan's Fate by Gun Brooke. A dynamic, erotic romance between physical therapist Lark Mitchell and businesswoman Sheridan Ward set in the scorching hot days and humid, steamy nights of San Antonio. (978-1-933110-88-2)

Vulture's Kiss by Justine Saracen. Archeologist Valerie Foret, heir to a terrifying task, returns in a powerful desert adventure set in Egypt and Jerusalem. (978-1-933110-87-5)

Rising Storm by JLee Meyer. The sequel to *First Instinct* takes our heroines on a dangerous journey instead of the honeymoon they'd planned. (978-1-933110-86-8)

Not Single Enough by Grace Lennox. A funny, sexy modern romance about two lonely women who bond over the unexpected and fall in love along the way. (978-1-933110-85-1)

Second Season by Ali Vali. A romance set in New Orleans amidst betrayal, Hurricane Katrina, and the new beginnings hardship and heartbreak sometimes make possible. (978-1-933110-83-7)

Such a Pretty Face by Gabrielle Goldsby. A sexy, sometimes humorous, sometimes biting contemporary romance that gently exposes the damage to heart and soul when we fail to look beneath the surface for what truly matters. (978-1-933110-84-4)

Hearts Aflame by Ronica Black. A poignant, erotic romance between a hard-driving businesswoman and a solitary vet. Packed with adventure and set in the harsh beauty of the Arizona countryside. (978-1-933110-82-0)

Red Light by JD Glass. Tori forges her path as an EMT in the New York City 911 system while discovering what matters most to herself and the woman she loves. (978-1-933110-81-3)

Honor Under Siege by Radclyffe. Secret Service agent Cameron Roberts struggles to protect her lover while searching for a traitor who just may be another woman with a claim on her heart. (978-1-933110-80-6)

Dark Valentine by Jennifer Fulton. Danger and desire fuel a high stakes cat-and-mouse game when an attorney and an endangered witness team up to thwart a killer. (978-1-933110-79-0)

Sequestered Hearts by Erin Dutton. A popular artist suddenly goes into seclusion; a reluctant reporter wants to know why; and a heart locked away yearns to be set free. (978-1-933110-78-3)

Erotic Interludes 5: *Road Games* eds. Radclyffe and Stacia Seaman. Adventure, "sport," and sex on the road—hot stories of travel adventures and games of seduction. (978-1-933110-77-6)

The Spanish Pearl by Catherine Friend. On a trip to Spain, Kate Vincent is accidentally transported back in time...an epic saga spiced with humor, lust, and danger. (978-1-933110-76-9)

Lady Knight by L-J Baker. Loyalty and honour clash with love and ambition in a medieval world of magic when female knight Riannon meets Lady Eleanor. (978-1-933110-75-2)

Dark Dreamer by Jennifer Fulton. Best-selling horror author, Rowe Devlin falls under the spell of psychic Phoebe Temple. A Dark Vista romance. (978-1-933110-74-5)

Come and Get Me by Julie Cannon. Elliott Foster isn't used to pursuing women, but alluring attorney Lauren Collier makes her change her mind. (978-1-933110-73-8)

Blind Curves by Diane and Jacob Anderson-Minshall. Private eye Yoshi Yakamota comes to the aid of her ex-lover Velvet Erickson in the first Blind Eye mystery. (978-1-933110-72-1)

Dynasty of Rogues by Jane Fletcher. It's hate at first sight for Ranger Riki Sadiq and her new patrol corporal, Tanya Coppelli—except for their undeniable attraction. (978-1-933110-71-4)

Running With the Wind by Nell Stark. Sailing instructor Corrie Marsten has signed off on love until she meets Quinn Davies—one woman she can't ignore. (978-1-933110-70-7)

More than Paradise by Jennifer Fulton. Two women battle danger, risk all, and find in one another an unexpected ally and an unforgettable love. (978-1-933110-69-1)

Flight Risk by Kim Baldwin. For Blayne Keller, being in the wrong place at the wrong time just might turn out to be the best thing that ever happened to her. (978-1-933110-68-4)

Rebel's Quest, Supreme Constellations Book Two by Gun Brooke. On a world torn by war, two women discover a love that defies all boundaries. (978-1-933110-67-7)

Punk and Zen by JD Glass. Angst, sex, love, rock. Trace, Candace, Francesca...Samantha. Losing control—and finding the truth within. BSB Victory Editions. (1-933110-66-X)

Stellium in Scorpio by Andrews & Austin. The passionate reuniting of two powerful women on the glitzy Las Vegas Strip where everything is an illusion and love is a gamble. (1-933110-65-1)

When Dreams Tremble by Radclyffe. Two women whose lives turned out far differently than they'd once imagined discover that sometimes the shape of the future can only be found in the past. (1-933110-64-3)

The Devil Unleashed by Ali Vali. As the heat of violence rises, so does the passion. A Casey Family crime saga. (1-933110-61-9)

Burning Dreams by Susan Smith. The chronicle of the challenges faced by a young drag king and an older woman who share a love "outside the bounds." (1-933110-62-7)

Fresh Tracks by Georgia Beers. Seven women, seven days. A lot can happen when old friends, lovers, and a new girl in town get together in the mountains. (1-933110-63-5)

The Empress and the Acolyte by Jane Fletcher. Jemeryl and Tevi fight to protect the very fabric of their world: time. Lyremouth Chronicles Book Three. (1-933110-60-0)

First Instinct by JLee Meyer. When high-stakes security fraud leads to murder, one woman flees for her life while another risks her heart to protect her. (1-933110-59-7)

Erotic Interludes 4: Extreme Passions ed. by Radclyffe and Stacia Seaman. Thirty of today's hottest erotica writers set the pages aflame with love, lust, and steamy liaisons. (1-933110-58-9)

Storms of Change by Radclyffe. In the continuing saga of the Provincetown Tales, duty and love are at odds as Reese and Tory face their greatest challenge. (1-933110-57-0)

Unexpected Ties by Gina L. Dartt. With death before dessert, Kate Shannon and Nikki Harris are swept up in another tale of danger and romance. (1-933110-56-2)

Sleep of Reason by Rose Beecham. While Detective Jude Devine searches for a lost boy, her rocky relationship with Dr. Mercy Westmoreland gets a lot harder. (1-933110-53-8)

Passion's Bright Fury by Radclyffe. Passion strikes without warning when a trauma surgeon and a filmmaker become reluctant allies. (1-933110-54-6)

Broken Wings by L-J Baker. When Rye Woods meets beautiful dryad Flora Withe, her libido, as hidden as her wings, reawakens along with her heart. (1-933110-55-4)

Combust the Sun by Andrews & Austin. A Richfield and Rivers mystery set in L.A. Murder among the stars. (1-933110-52-X)

Of Drag Kings and the Wheel of Fate by Susan Smith. A blind date in a drag club leads to an unlikely romance. (1-933110-51-1)

Tristaine Rises by Cate Culpepper. Brenna, Jesstin, and the Amazons of Tristaine face their greatest challenge for survival. (1-933110-50-3)

Too Close to Touch by Georgia Beers. Kylie O'Brien believes in true love and is willing to wait for it, even though Gretchen, her new boss, is off-limits. (1-933110-47-3)

100th Generation by Justine Saracen. Ancient curses, modern-day villains, and an intriguing woman lead archeologist Valerie Foret on the adventure of her life. (1-933110-48-1)

Battle for Tristaine by Cate Culpepper. While Brenna struggles to find her place in the clan, Tristaine is threatened with destruction. Second in the Tristaine series. (1-933110-49-X)

The Traitor and the Chalice by Jane Fletcher. Tevi and Jemeryl risk all in the race to uncover a traitor. The Lyremouth Chronicles Book Two. (1-933110-43-0)

Promising Hearts by Radclyffe. Dr. Vance Phelps arrives in New Hope, Montana, with no hope of happiness—until she meets Mae. (1-933110-44-9)

Carly's Sound by Ali Vali. Poppy Valente and Julia Johnson form a bond of friendship that becomes something far more. A poignant romance about love and renewal. (1-933110-45-7)

Unexpected Sparks by Gina L. Dartt. Kate Shannon's attraction to much younger Nikki Harris is complication enough without a fatal fire that Kate can't ignore. (1-933110-46-5)

Whitewater Rendezvous by Kim Baldwin. Two women on a wilderness kayak adventure discover that true love may be nothing at all like they imagined. (1-933110-38-4)

Erotic Interludes 3: Lessons in Love ed. by Radclyffe and Stacia Seaman. Sign on for a class in love...the best lesbian erotica writers take us to "school." (1-9331100-39-2)

Punk Like Me by JD Glass. Twenty-one-year-old Nina has a way with the girls, and she doesn't always play by the rules. (1-933110-40-6)

Coffee Sonata by Gun Brooke. Four women whose lives unexpectedly intersect in a small town by the sea share one thing in common—they all have secrets. (1-933110-41-4)

The Clinic: Tristaine Book One by Cate Culpepper. Brenna, a prison medic, finds herself drawn to Jesstin, a warrior reputed to be descended from ancient Amazons. (1-933110-42-2)

Forever Found by JLee Meyer. Can time, tragedy, and shattered trust destroy a love that seemed destined? Chance reunites childhood friends separated by tragedy. (1-933110-37-6)

Sword of the Guardian by Merry Shannon. Princess Shasta's bold new bodyguard has a secret that could change both of their lives: *He* is actually a *she*. (1-933110-36-8)

Wild Abandon by Ronica Black. Dr. Chandler Brogan and Officer Sarah Monroe are drawn together by their common obsessions—sex, speed, and danger. (1-933110-35-X)

Turn Back Time by Radclyffe. Pearce Rifkin and Wynter Thompson have nothing in common but a shared passion for surgery—and unexpected attraction. (1-933110-34-1)

Chance by Grace Lennox. A sexy, funny, touching story of two women who, in finding themselves, also find one another. (1-933110-31-7)

The Exile and the Sorcerer by Jane Fletcher. First in the Lyremouth Chronicles. Tevi and a shy young sorcerer face monsters, magic, and the challenge of loving. (1-933110-32-5)

A Matter of Trust by Radclyffe. When what should be just business turns into much more, two women struggle to trust the unexpected. (1-933110-33-3)

Sweet Creek by Lee Lynch. A celebration of the enduring nature of love, friendship, and community in the heart-warming lesbian community of Waterfall Falls. (1-933110-29-5)

The Devil Inside by Ali Vali. The head of a New Orleans crime organization falls for a woman who turns her world upside down. (1-933110-30-9)

Grave Silence by Rose Beecham. Detective Jude Devine's investigation of ritual murders is complicated by her torrid affair with pathologist Dr. Mercy Westmoreland. (1-933110-25-2)

Honor Reclaimed by Radclyffe. Secret Service Agent Cameron Roberts and Blair Powell close ranks to find the would-be assassins who nearly claimed Blair's life. (1-933110-18-X)

Honor Bound by Radclyffe. Secret Service Agent Cameron Roberts and Blair Powell face political intrigue, a clandestine threat to Blair's safety, and the seemingly irreconcilable differences that force them ever farther apart. (1-933110-20-1)

Innocent Hearts by Radclyffe. In a wild and unforgiving land, two women learn about love, passion, and the wonders of the heart. (1-933110-21-X)

The Temple at Landfall by Jane Fletcher. An imprinter, one of Celaeno's most revered servants of the Goddess, is also a prisoner to the faith—until a Ranger frees her by claiming her heart. The Celaeno series. (1-933110-27-9)

Protector of the Realm, Supreme Constellations Book One by Gun Brooke. A space adventure filled with suspense and a daring intergalactic romance. (1-933110-26-0)

Force of Nature by Kim Baldwin. From tornados to forest fires, the forces of nature conspire to bring Gable McCoy and Erin Richards close to danger, and closer to each other. (1-933110-23-6)

In Too Deep by Ronica Black. Undercover homicide cop Erin McKenzie tracks a femme fatale who just might be a real killer…with love and danger hot on her heels. (1-933110-17-1)

Stolen Moments: Erotic Interludes 2 by Stacia Seaman and Radclyffe, eds. Love on the run, in the office, in the shadows…Fast, furious, and almost too hot to handle. (1-933110-16-3)

Course of Action by Gun Brooke. Actress Carolyn Black desperately wants the starring role in an upcoming film produced by Annelie Peterson. Just how far will she go for the dream part of a lifetime? (1-933110-22-8)

Rangers at Roadsend by Jane Fletcher. Sergeant Chip Coppelli has learned to spot trouble coming, and that is exactly what she sees in her new recruit, Katryn Nagata. The Celaeno series. (1-933110-28-7)

Justice Served by Radclyffe. Lieutenant Rebecca Frye and her lover, Dr. Catherine Rawlings, embark on a deadly game of hide-and-seek with an underworld kingpin who traffics in human souls. (1-933110-15-5)

Distant Shores, Silent Thunder by Radclyffe. Dr. Tory King—along with the women who love her—is forced to examine the boundaries of love, friendship, and the ties that transcend time. (1-933110-08-2)

Hunter's Pursuit by Kim Baldwin. A raging blizzard, a mountain hideaway, and a killer-for-hire set a scene for disaster—or desire—when Katarzyna Demetrious rescues a beautiful stranger. (1-933110-09-0)

The Walls of Westernfort by Jane Fletcher. All Temple Guard Natasha Ionadis wants is to serve the Goddess—until she falls in love with one of the rebels she is sworn to destroy. The Celaeno series. (1-933110-24-4)

Change Of Pace: *Erotic Interludes* by Radclyffe. Twenty-five hot-wired encounters guaranteed to spark more than just your imagination. Erotica as you've always dreamed of it. (1-933110-07-4)

Honor Guards by Radclyffe. In a wild flight for their lives, the president's daughter and those who are sworn to protect her wage a desperate struggle for survival. (1-933110-01-5)

Fated Love by Radclyffe. Amidst the chaos and drama of a busy emergency room, two women must contend not only with the fragile nature of life, but also with the irresistible forces of fate. (1-933110-05-8)

Justice in the Shadows by Radclyffe. In a shadow world of secrets and lies, Detective Sergeant Rebecca Frye and her lover, Dr. Catherine Rawlings, join forces in the elusive search for justice. (1-933110-03-1)

shadowland by Radclyffe. In a world on the far edge of desire, two women are drawn together by power, passion, and dark pleasures. An erotic romance. (1-933110-11-2)

Love's Masquerade by Radclyffe. Plunged into the indistinguishable realms of fiction, fantasy, and hidden desires, Auden Frost is forced to question all she believes about the nature of love. (1-933110-14-7)

Love & Honor by Radclyffe. The president's daughter and her lover are faced with difficult choices as they battle a tangled web of Washington intrigue for...love and honor. (1-933110-10-4)

Beyond the Breakwater by Radclyffe. One Provincetown summer, three women learn the true meaning of love, friendship, and family. (1-933110-06-6)

Tomorrow's Promise by Radclyffe. One timeless summer, two very different women discover the power of passion to heal and the promise of hope that only love can bestow. (1-933110-12-0)

Love's Tender Warriors by Radclyffe. Two women who have accepted loneliness as a way of life learn that love is worth fighting for and a battle they cannot afford to lose. (1-933110-02-3)

Love's Melody Lost by Radclyffe. A secretive artist with a haunted past and a young woman escaping a life that has proved to be a lie find their destinies entwined. (1-933110-00-7)

Safe Harbor by Radclyffe. A mysterious newcomer, a reclusive doctor, and a troubled gay teenager learn about love, friendship, and trust during one tumultuous summer in Provincetown. (1-933110-13-9)

Above All, Honor by Radclyffe. Secret Service Agent Cameron Roberts fights her desire for the one woman she can't have—Blair Powell, the daughter of the president of the United States. (1-933110-04-X)

BOLD
STROKES
BOOKS